Lyn Andrews was born and raised in Liverpool. The daughter of a policeman, she also married a policeman and, after becoming the mother of triplets, took some years off from her writing whilst she brought up her family. In 1983 Lyn was shortlisted for the Romantic Novelists' Association Award and has now written twelve hugely popular Liverpool novels. Lyn Andrews still lives in Merseyside.

D0057266

Also by Lyn Andrews

Maggie May
The Leaving of Liverpool
Liverpool Lou
The Sisters O'Donnell
The White Empress
Ellan Vannin
Mist over the Mersey
Mersey Blues
Liverpool Songbird
Liverpool Lamplight
Where the Mersey Flows

From This Day Forth

Lyn Andrews

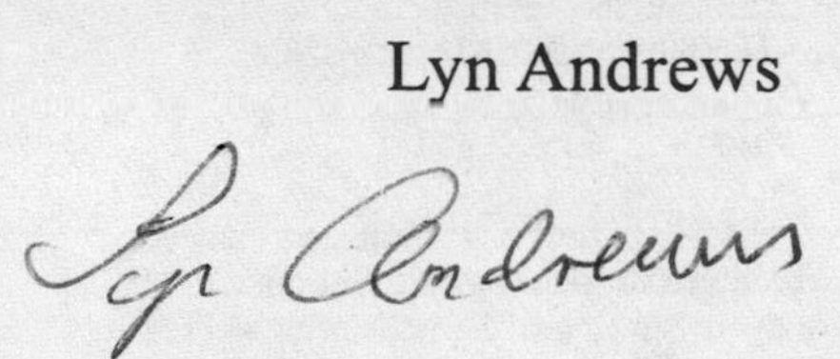

Copyright © 1997 Lyn Andrews

The right of Lyn Andrews to be identified as the Author of the Work has been asserted by her in accordance with the Copyright, Designs and Patents Act 1988.

First published in 1997
by HEADLINE BOOK PUBLISHING

First published in paperback in 1998
by HEADLINE BOOK PUBLISHING

10 9 8 7 6 5 4 3 2 1

All rights reserved. No part of this publication may be reproduced, stored in a retrieval system, or transmitted, in any form or by any means without the prior written permission of the publisher, nor be otherwise circulated in any form of binding or cover other than that in which it is published and without a similar condition being imposed on the subsequent purchaser.

All characters in this publication are fictitious and any resemblance to real persons, living or dead, is purely coincidental.

ISBN 0 7472 5177 0

Typeset by CBS, Felixstowe, Suffolk

Printed and bound in Great Britain by
Clays Ltd, St Ives PLC

HEADLINE BOOK PUBLISHING
A division of Hodder Headline PLC
338 Euston Road
London NW1 3BH

For all the men and women who worked for Cammell Laird Shipbuilders, Birkenhead, Merseyside. Particularly Charlie Campbell, Norman Roberts, John Haggerty and Arnie Locker.

'They can kill the yard but they can't kill our pride. We were shipbuilders and good ones, too.'

David Johnson, a former 'Laird's' man.

And also for my father, Frank (Pony) Moore, who served as Chief Petty Officer on the T-class submarine *Tally-Ho*, who told me of the tragedy of the Laird's-built submarine *Thetis*, and who has since answered my many questions with patience. Unfortunately, my father died in April and so never saw this dedication. I will sorely miss his advice and criticism.

My grateful thanks go to David Roberts, author of the excellent book, *Life at Lairds*, which gave me such a clear insight into the harsh working life and often atrocious conditions in which loyal and proud men built some of the best ships in the world. One was built every twenty days during the Second World War. *Life at Lairds* is a *must* for everyone, young or old, who has an interest in Merseyside and our history.

My thanks also go to my aunt, Mrs E. Sabell, for her verification of the circumstances and venue of her wedding.

Lyn Andrews, Southport, 1997.

PART ONE

1934

Chapter One

The October dusk was falling rapidly as Lizzie Slattery, Celia Milton and Alfie, the new delivery boy, stood watching Mr Henderson, Manager of Wm Costigan (Grocers) Ltd on Great Homer Street, lock and secure the shop door. This locking up was a daily ritual. A trifling and boring one, they all thought. As was standing outside the shop each morning at half-past eight, hail, rain or shine, until he arrived to open up. The shop didn't open for business until nine o'clock but there were always things to be done. Lizzie and Celia, called Cee by everyone except her father, always moaned that they would have nearly an extra half-hour in bed if it wasn't for all this palaver.

When George Henderson had finally dismissed them in his lugubrious tones the two girls turned and began to walk down the road in the direction of Scotland Road and town. They could walk together until they reached the junction of Great Homer Street and Rose Vale, when one or other of them would turn off up Rose Vale, go down Portland Place and into Roscommon Street where they both lived. The latter was the longer route and so they took it in turns.

When Mr Henderson and young Alfie were out of earshot Lizzie said, 'Me feet are killing me, and why he has to make us stand there like a pair of fools, God knows. I'm sure it's just out of spite or to make himself feel important. You'd think he was the manager of Coopers the way he says, "Good night and let us be prompt in the morning, ladies," as though we were late every day and about as old as me mam.'

Celia nodded her agreement. She was a tall, slim girl with short ash-blonde hair, blue eyes and a typical 'English rose' complexion. By nature she was quiet and unassuming. She worked efficiently and was polite to the customers but there were occasions when a gleam of mischief or determination could be detected in the depths of those cornflower-blue eyes. She turned up the collar of her navy-blue wool coat around her ears. The autumn dampness was creeping into the air and already the streetlights were coming on and people were hurrying towards the bus and tram stops.

Lizzie shivered and turned up her collar too, although her brown coat, bought second-hand two years ago, wasn't as smart or as warm.

'I hate this time of year. There's nothing to look forward to except Christmas and that usually ends in a row in our house. Me mam's worn out and bad-tempered and we're both too tired to go out on Christmas Eve. That's if she'd let me over the doorstep before Midnight Mass in case I broke me fast.'

To strangers they looked an oddly matched pair; in reality they were the best of friends. A fact that in itself was a minor miracle. Lizzie was much smaller than her friend and was exactly the opposite in character as well as looks. Her thick curly Titian hair that her mam said was like a furze bush, and her green eyes, betrayed her Irish ancestry, as did her temper. She was far more extrovert than Celia and laughed and joked with the customers when Mr Henderson wasn't looking. If she seemed a bit pushy it was because she'd always had to fight for her share of what little they had, including her mam's attention and affection. It was a bit different with her da. Lizzie knew she was *his* favourite.

'Well, at least we don't have to go and get crushed to death tomorrow over at Laird's for the launch of the *Clement*,' Celia replied. 'Could you see old Henderson's face if we asked for the morning off?'

'I wouldn't mind going. We could sort of "get lost" in the crowd and have a great time. We might even meet a couple of nice lads. I mean, look at the pair of us. Fifteen years of age and never been out with a lad, and we're not bad-looking.' Lizzie was indignant.

'And not likely to either, the way we're watched, and as for "getting lost", with them all following every move we make, we'd get belted all the way home. No thanks.'

Lizzie nodded glumly. 'You're right. Oh honestly, Cee, if we can be friends why can't they? Your da and your Billy, our Joe an' Fergal all work at Laird's so I don't see why my mam and yours 'ave to stick their noses in the air and cross to the other side of the street when they see each other, nor that Maudie Kemp either. Bossy old bag.'

'Neither do I but they do, and anyway it's not just Mam; you know what Da's like. He hates living in our house, in our street. You know how many times he's tried to find us another place. I don't think Mam really minds Roscommon Street, but if he gets somewhere else she'll have to go. We all will.'

Lizzie didn't reply but she understood. Her own da worked on the docks, when he could get work and was in a fit state to do it. His chest was weak and had been for years, and the soot- and fume-laden air of the city didn't help. Her oldest brother, Joe, who was seventeen, was a welder's mate at the shipyard on the other side of the Mersey but Celia's da was a foreman boilermaker. He even wore a 'blocker', a bowler hat which was like a badge of rank. Celia's brother Billy had started at fourteen as a marker boy at ten shillings a week, helping the plater and learning how to make templates. At the same time he'd gone to evening classes at the Mechanics Institute and had passed his exams first class, and now he was a journeyman plater. A skilled man, he was still too young to run a squad of apprentices, but he got a four-shilling-a-week docket on top of his wages. It had annoyed their Joe so much that he'd started going to the Mechanics Institute as well.

The Miltons were far better off than they were. There were only five of them in a three-bedroom house, to start with. Celia and Billy had good steady jobs and their da, Charlie Milton, Lizzie reckoned, must earn a fortune. It was no wonder he wanted them to move to a better neighbourhood. But housing in the 'better' areas was scarce and was snapped up very quickly. Lizzie thrust her hands deeper into her pockets. It was cold and the thought of the comforts of Celia's life depressed her.

There were eight Slatterys crammed into number twelve Roscommon Street and they managed to exist on Joe, Fergal and her wages. Joe had got Fergal the job of 'can lad' at Laird's – it was nearly always a matter of who you knew – but Fergal only earned coppers and he needed most of them for his fares.

Mam sometimes managed to get a few evenings' work cleaning offices, or joining the army of cleaners who descended on the Cunard Line's fast transatlantic liners, which needed to be turned around at the quickest possible speed. It was hard work and often Mam came home not only exhausted but fuming too. All ventilation shafts and systems were blocked off while bunkering – taking on fuel – was carried out. Inevitably the particles of dirt got through and everything had to be done again.

'It's about time the old *Maurie* was laid up for good. Me back's broke and I'm destroyed with all that bloody dust!' Brigid would mutter.

Lizzie knew her da felt terribly guilty about his inability to work and provide decently for his family, even though Father Minehan had had many reassuring and consoling conversations with him, and Mam didn't moan or complain too often. She had a sensitive side to her too . . . Sometimes, though, Lizzie was envious of Celia's clothes – not that she had a wardrobe full of them because Charlie Milton was tight-fisted. But at least the clothes Celia did get were new, and in winter she had gloves, a warm hat and scarf, and fleecy-lined boots, unlike herself who had to make do with the same pair of shoes winter and summer. And they were second-hand more often than not.

'Where will we go tomorrow afternoon then, seeing as it's half-day closing?' Celia asked, breaking into Lizzie's reverie.

'Dunno. All the rest of them won't be back until tea time. You know me mam, she'll make a day of it. She'll take butties for them and then she'll walk them all to New Brighton "for the sea air" and nothing else. No rides on the funfair, no ice creams. She's been saving ha'pennies and farthings for ages for the ferry fares.'

'Shall we go into town then, just to have a look around? No one will see us. Half the city will be over the water at Birkenhead and there'll be crowds down at the Pier Head, so the shops will be deserted. And then we could go to the Hippodrome in the evening?'

'Can I miss out town? I'll have to wash me hair and anyway for once I'll have the place all to myself. Mam said she thought Da would be up to going too and the kids have got a day off school.' Lizzie's eyes lit up. 'Oh, it'll be great. Peace and quiet for a couple of hours. I'm going to bank up the fire and do nothing, absolutely nothing all afternoon. But if we go to the Hippy it'll have to be the sixpenny seats, I can't afford more.'

Celia nodded. 'I've not got much left myself; I'm trying to save up for Mam's birthday present. I saw . . .' Her words died as she caught sight of Maude Kemp who lived in number eight Roscommon Street hurrying towards them.

'Oh damn! Quick! Nip into the shop doorway, it's Maudie Kemp,' she hissed at Lizzie. She herself quickened her pace, praying Maudie hadn't seen her talking to Lizzie.

Lizzie immediately darted into the furthest corner of the nearest shop doorway. She turned her back and peered intently into the window. Fortunately, it was a draper's shop and not a butcher's or a fishmonger's, otherwise, she thought; people would think she was cracked.

'Hello, Mrs Kemp. It's getting cold now, isn't it?' Celia hoped she sounded polite but casual.

Maudie's face was thin, pale and had a perpetually sour look. 'Oh, it's you, Celia. You haven't seen those two horrors of mine by any chance? I'll stiffen the pair of them. I left them doing their homework whilst I nipped down to the Maypole Dairy for milk but when I got back the birds had flown and not a sign of an exercise book or pencil – nothing! They've scarpered. I'll have Harold and Richie in any minute and you know how Mr Kemp feels about those two running wild.'

Celia breathed a sigh of relief. The disappearance of the Kemp twins, Frank and Eddie, was fully occupying their mam. She smiled to herself at the woman's words about her husband. Harry Kemp was the most hen-pecked man in the entire street, probably in the entire neighbourhood. He was only allowed out for a half-pint of beer on Saturday night with her da.

'No, sorry, I've not seen them,' she replied, and then walked away. There was a good chance that her brother Frederick, or Foxy as he was known to all the other kids, wouldn't be far away from the twins. The three of them were usually fighting, arguing and hurling abuse and sometimes stones. Once Foxy had had a catapult – every boy's dream – until he'd broken Mrs Walsh's window and Da had confiscated it. Lizzie's brother Emmet and his two mates were always the objects of these skirmishes. They were all the same age – nine – and were all hell-bent on following the example of their parents.

For Roscommon Street was one of the 'divided' streets. At the top end, which led on to Netherfield Road, the houses were occupied by Protestants, and at the other end, which led on to Great Homer Street, by Catholics. The Miltons had the greatest misfortune of all, according to Celia's mam and da, of being slap in the middle of Roscommon Street and having to live next door to the Slatterys, who took a similar view on the location of their own abode. Her father called them 'dirty bloody Papists' when he'd had a drink in the Wynnstay Arms on Saturdays with Harry Kemp. Lizzie had told her that Charlie Milton was referred to by her mam, Brigid, as 'That Stuck-up Orange Sod Next Door,' who'd called his son after King Billy, who hadn't even been a bloody Englishman anyway. William of Orange had been Dutch, which just went to show how 'educated' Charlie Milton really was. He had such airs he wouldn't even stand for nicknames. He called the lad William and the girl Celia and the young hooligan Frederick. Just trying to be 'posh' was how the tirade usually ended.

Occasionally, violent outbursts and confrontations occurred over the back yard wall or on the front steps between Celia's da and Brigid and Billy and Joe. On one memorable St Patrick's Day the whole street had been up, with the kids prancing around in delight, urging the protagonists on, as were many of their mothers, her own included. The police had been called to restore order and for weeks after you could feel the lingering animosity in the air. It was all this that made the friendship between the girls such a closely guarded secret.

They hadn't always been friends, but one summer, five years ago, Celia had come down the jigger that ran between the backs of the houses in Roscommon Street and Back Roscommon Street, in time to see her brother Billy and Richie Kemp run into the Kemps' back yard and slam the door shut. Then she'd noticed Lizzie sitting on the cobbles, huddled against the wall, crying her eyes out.

As she'd got nearer she had seen that Lizzie's arms and knees were grazed and bleeding and that there was blood on her forehead. She'd hesitated. She'd felt so sorry for Lizzie in her torn and grubby dress and yet she'd been scared to stop and speak to her.

At last she'd looked around at the houses cautiously. People would have to be in the back bedroom windows to see her, so she'd plucked up her courage and squatted down next to Lizzie.

'What's happened?' she'd asked.

Lizzie had raised a pale, grimy, tear-streaked face and an equally grubby hand to her bleeding forehead.

'They chased me an' I fell over and then . . . then they chucked stones at me an' called me names.' She'd struggled to put on a brave face. 'I don't care about the names, I'm used to them, and I can run faster than them two but . . .'

'But what?' Celia had asked, seeing the other girl's bottom lip begin to tremble.

'But I tripped up on something and now me head hurts. It's bleeding.'

Celia had gently examined the small cut on Lizzie's forehead, just above her eyebrow. An inch lower and poor Lizzie might have had a cut eye and who knew what that would have led to? Just wait until she got hold of their Billy, she'd thought grimly. A pair of cowards, that's what those two were.

'Come on, I'll help you up.'

Lizzie had looked at her with amazement.

'Oh God, if anyone sees us I'll be killed.'

'No one will see us, unless they're hanging out of their bedroom windows. There's no one else in the jigger.'

'What will I say to Mam?'

Celia had shrugged. 'Make something up. I'm going to threaten our Billy with telling Da about him and Richie Kemp throwing stones and seriously hurting people. And I'll say that your mam will be round and there'll be murder, and then our Billy will get a good hiding.'

Lizzie had looked at her curiously. 'Will you say that? Will you do that?'

'I will.'

'Then I'll just tell Mam I fell over and banged my head.'

Celia had gently drawn Lizzie to her feet, her arm around the thin shoulders.

'Get your mam to wash all the muck out of your knees and arms or they'll go septic,' she'd advised.

Lizzie had managed a smile. 'Ta. It's dead good of you,' and as Celia had helped her home they'd both felt a bond forming. Since then many and devious had been the ways in which they'd concealed their friendship.

It was Celia who had secretly got Lizzie the job in Costigan's, a job that, because it meant the two worked side by side, was considered a great misfortune by both the Slatterys and her own parents. Indeed her da had often told her she should find another, but she'd always managed to be evasive. As her mam shopped at Pegram's, which she considered far superior to Costigan's, and Mrs Slattery shopped mainly in the market, they'd dropped all pretence of indifference at work.

Lizzie caught up with Celia just before she reached the junction with Rose Place.

'Did she say anything to you?'

'No. She's out looking for the twins. She left them doing homework and they scarpered.'

Lizzie rolled her eyes heavenwards. 'Oh God, that means they'll all be half killing each other – again.'

'I know, and our Foxy is sure to be fighting with them. Da will go mad, he's told him not to go within arm's length of the riff-raff, as he calls them, from the other end of the street. He says they're beneath contempt but I don't think our Foxy understands the word "contempt" or if he does he ignores it.' It was Celia's turn to cast her eyes skywards. 'Mind you, by the time I get in he'll probably be back, all washed and changed and looking as if butter wouldn't melt in his mouth. They don't call him Foxy for nothing. I'll go the long way round tonight. You did it yesterday and besides, when Da does get in I'll have to put up with "The Launch" and I'm sick to death of hearing about it.'

Celia put on a stern voice. 'It's *important*, Celia. It's the one thousandth ship that's been built by Cammell Laird and I was privileged to hand Miss Caroline Vesty the wooden mallet to use for the ceremony of "Laying the Keel".' Celia pulled a face as she mimicked her father's tones, something she would only do in Lizzie's presence. Her father ruled them with a rod of iron, her mam included.

'Well, I'll see you in the morning then. And then outside the Hippy at seven, and don't be late. I hate hanging around – people think your feller's stood you up. Chance would be a fine thing, wouldn't it though?' Lizzie grinned and walked on ahead quickly. She'd be home soon and she'd be glad, for she was tired, cold and hungry.

She called a greeting to Maggie Walsh and Biddy Doyle who were standing on their doorsteps jangling as though it wasn't tea time. They had no husbands due in from work because there wasn't much of that commodity on offer to the unskilled in Liverpool these days. There were still a few kids playing in the street and a couple of them had a piece of rope tied around one of the arms of the streetlight and were swinging on it.

The houses were of the three-storeyed terrace type but without a cellar. Each had three steps leading up to the front door, which was set beneath an arch of brickwork. The windows of the front downstairs rooms were bays and most people had cotton lace curtains tacked across them. Some, though, were bare and some had missing panes replaced by cardboard or bits of wood.

It was a different picture at the top of the road. The windows all had pristine cotton lace *and* draw curtains. Celia said Maudie Kemp was fanatical about housework, you felt as though you shouldn't even breathe in their house. Maudie had half the kids in the street terrified even to set foot on the flagstones of the pavement outside her door, which she scrubbed and donkey-stoned each day along with her steps. Lizzie was thankful her mam wasn't like that.

'Mam, I'm home. Is me tea ready?' she called as she pushed open the front door and walked down the dim lobby to the kitchen.

'That's all any of youse lot think about, yer bellies!' Brigid Slattery stood with her hands on her hips and surveyed her daughter with mild irritation. She was a big woman with prematurely greying hair that had once been as black as a raven's wing. She wore the uniform of her age and class, a long black skirt, a cotton blouse and a rough unbleached calico apron.

'Oh, that's nice, Mam, I must say. All I said was "I'm home."'

Brigid smiled. She was by nature easy-going. 'Oh, I'm just heart scalded, luv, that's all. Yer da's took to his bed. Holy Mother of God! I hate the flaming winter. Yer poor da suffers something desperate with the damp an' he was lookin' forward to goin' over the water for the launch termorrer. Our Joe an' Fergal aren't in yet and them two little rossies, our Bernadette an' Josephine, are in with yer da, an' now I've gorra get a move on. The *Mauretania*'s in. I'll be all night getting shut of the bloody muck, but I suppose it'll be a few bob in me purse. You'll 'ave ter get the tea, like, an' I don't know where that little bowsie Emmet is.'

Lizzie took off her coat and threw it on the sofa, which was already half covered with clothes waiting to be ironed.

'Can I have a cup of tea first?' she pleaded.

Brigid poured a cup from the brown glazed teapot with the cracked spout. Above the Stanley range was suspended a clothes rack with yet more clothes draped over it. They were beyond the dripping stage, Lizzie noticed thankfully, but the odour of damp wool was heavy. The mantel shelf above the range was so cluttered that there wasn't an inch of space. The big table took up most of the room and was covered with newspaper and a collection of unwashed cups and dishes. A piece of greyish-looking curtain was tacked across the window.

Besides the sofa, the room contained an armchair, two long wooden benches (pushed under the table when not in use) and a dresser, the top of which was as crowded as the mantel shelf. On the wall beside the door, and covering a large patch of damp, was a picture of the Blessed Virgin and on the wall facing it another, of Pope Pius XI. The floor was covered with scuffed and dirty lino.

As well as the kitchen there was a scullery, a front parlour, two bedrooms and an attic room. Lizzie had the dubious luxury of having the attic room to herself. In winter it was freezing and in summer it was stifling. Her two younger sisters shared a bedroom, as did all her brothers, and Mam and Da had the front parlour. It was better for her da because it had a fireplace and there were no stairs to climb. In the yard were the privy and the ash can, and a collection of old and useless objects that Emmet insisted *were* of some use.

'Go on, Mam, get off or you'll miss your tram,' Lizzie urged, and her mother rummaged among the clothes on the sofa, found her heavy black shawl, wrapped it around her, slipped her worn purse into the pocket of her apron and made for the door.

When she'd gone Lizzie got up and went in to see her father. He didn't look at all well, she thought worriedly. If he had one of his 'little turns' now she knew there'd be no money for a doctor.

'Josie, get off that bed and get into the kitchen and fold up all those things on the sofa that need ironing. Bernie, clear the table and then boil some water for the dishes. I'm worn out and the lads will be in soon.'

Lizzie ignored the outburst of complaint, shoving them towards the door. When they'd gone, she sat on the edge of the bed recently vacated by her sister and smiled.

'How are you feeling, Da?'

Dessie Slattery's breathing was very laboured but he smiled back.

'Not too bad, girl. It's been worse. It's the damp an' I'm just sorry to miss the outing termorrer.'

'Well, I'm not going so I can keep you company after dinner.' There *were* times when it had indeed been worse, much worse, when the racking cough had exhausted him and kept everyone awake. When he literally fought for every breath, and Mam had kept a big pan of water constantly boiling on the fire. The steam seemed to be the only form of relief.

'Will I send our Josie in with a bit of scouse?'

He shook his head. 'No, just a cup of tea and a bit of bread an' dripping will do, luv.'

The guilt crept over him again as he looked at his eldest daughter. She was a good girl. She worked hard and was tired. He could see it in her face and in the sag of her shoulders. Now after a day on her feet she had to get a meal on the table and organise her siblings while poor Brigid had to hurry to the dock and get down on her knees and scrub floors and wash paintwork, probably twice, so the old *Maurie* would be ready to sail again in a day's time. That hurt him so much, and yet she seldom complained. She was still the buxom, fresh-faced, laughing girl from County Cork that he'd married. He ignored the encroaching grey in her dark hair and the lines of hardship etched in her face. Whenever he tried to apologise for his failings and his health she'd laugh.

'Ah, come on out of that now, Dessie. Didn't I take me wedding vows? Me promises to you before God in his holy church?'

He needed to be in a sanatorium or at least a place with pure fresh air, or so the only doctor he'd ever seen had told him. But sanatoriums and places with pure fresh air cost money and so were totally out of the question.

'Are you sure that's all? There's not much nourishment in bread an' dripping, Da.' Lizzie's forehead was creased in a worried frown.

'And there's not much in blind scouse either, luv.'

She nodded slowly and sadly before a commotion in the kitchen caused her to turn for the door. Now what? she thought angrily. Didn't she have enough to cope with?

Once in the kitchen she could see her sisters had made a bit of an effort, but the grimy, bloody face and torn jersey of Emmet caught her attention first. She looked up at Joe. The boys must all have arrived home together.

'In the name of God, what's up with him? she snapped irritably.

'Nothing that a good wash won't sort out,' Joe said grimly. 'Fergal and myself decided to come down the jigger, and wasn't there the mother and father of a fight going on with meladdo and his mates and Foxy Milton and the Kemp twins? They all scarpered quick, like, when we appeared.'

Lizzie shoved Emmet towards the scullery. 'Oh, get in there, you, and get a wash! As if I haven't enough to do. Poor Mam's had to go cleaning and Da's took bad and is in bed and won't be able to go on the outing tomorrow . . .'

Emmet, scowling beneath a shock of dark unruly hair at such unsympathetic treatment, disappeared into the scullery. Josie and Bernie carried on with their allotted tasks, while Lizzie stirred the huge pot of vegetables. The potatoes in it had broken down and made it thick and with some meat and red cabbage and thick slices of bread it would have been a great meal. Sadly, they had no cabbage and only half a loaf, and that had to do Da's tea and the lads' carry-out for the following day.

Joe sat on one end of the bench and bent to take off his boots. Both he and Fergal had brought home the usual bundle of cockwood, odd pieces that were of no use except for burning. Nearly every man and boy at Laird's took a bundle each night, shoving it under his jacket if it was raining.

He was bone weary. He'd been out since half-past five that morning to get to Central Station in time for the ten past six train to Rock Ferry. That arrived at Green Lane Station at five past seven, in plenty of time to clock on. Sometimes in summer he'd get the tram to the Pier Head and then the ferry across the river. It was cheaper.

Joe was like Lizzie in looks, except that his hair was more auburn than hers and he was much taller and broader. Ever since he'd left school, when other lads had had to go to the dole schools, he'd been fortunate enough in those terrible, depressed years to get a job in the shipyard. Father Minehan had had a word with a man he knew who worked there.

He'd taken over his da's responsibilities as best he could and things had got a bit better when first Lizzie and then Fergal got work. Now he went to evening classes twice a week, and that was hard after a long day and in all weathers on the bank, as the slipway was called. But every time he saw Billy Milton and Richie Kemp, who was an apprentice to a journeyman boilermaker, he became more determined to make something of his life. There just *had* to be something better than being a welder's mate and living in an overcrowded house in Roscommon Street.

'Are you tired?' Lizzie asked as she began to dish the scouse into bowls with the heavy metal ladle.

'Of course I'm flaming tired.'

'All right, there's no need to bite my head off. I just wondered if you were going to give night school a miss, what with the launch tomorrow?' Lizzie placed a steaming bowl in front of him.

'I'd like to. I really would like to, but I'd get behind. It's bad enough now. Half the time I really have to fight to stay awake and concentrate.'

Lizzie sighed and looked fondly at her brother.

'It'll be worth it in the end, Joe, really it will. You'll get more money and a better job and Mam will be really proud of you. You'll be like Billy Milton then, and Mam will be able to stick her nose in the air whenever she sees Maudie Kemp and won't it make *that* one green with envy?'

'I've got to pass my exams first, Lizzie,' Joe reminded her, but he was glad of her words of support and encouragement. The prospect of being on an equal footing with Billy Milton, and of Mam's pride, would keep him going – with a little help from his sister Lizzie. However much they might bicker, he and his eldest sister had always understood one another.

Chapter Two

As Celia turned her key in the lock she could hear her mother's voice. The usually quiet tone was raised in what for Annie Milton amounted to anger. Celia sighed as she walked down the lobby, the runner of carpet over the shining linoleum deadening her footsteps. She'd been right: Foxy had been out with the twins.

'Hello, Mam. Now what's he been up to?' she asked, annoyance in her own voice.

Annie Milton turned her gaze on her daughter as Celia hung up her coat on the hook behind the door, wishing her younger son were as well behaved as his sister and elder brother. It would certainly make life a lot easier for her. Charlie went mad at the antics of Frederick and then took it out on her and she *hated* rows and arguments. She'd go to any length to avoid one.

'Fighting again, after all your da said. Look at the state of him, and your da due in any minute.'

Celia gazed back with heartfelt sympathy. If everything wasn't spick and span, with the evening meal ready to be served straight away and piping hot, her father's mood would be grim to say the least.

Mam looked pale, but then she'd always been fair-skinned. Nor did the amount of work involved in running the house the way Da insisted it be done help in any way. Mam was working herself to death and never in her life had Celia heard her mam answer her da back.

Annie Milton was a small, fine-boned woman with clear grey

eyes. They were her most attractive feature, although these days they always had dark circles beneath them. Her hair, once light brown, was now pepper-and-salt coloured. She had a rigid schedule of work that seldom varied.

Monday was wash day. Tuesday was ironing day. On Wednesday the entire upstairs rooms were given a thorough clean. Thursday was the turn of the downstairs rooms, including the yard and the privy. The steps, front and back, were scrubbed and donkey-stoned every day. She baked on Friday and shopped on Saturday – and all that on top of the daily chores of washing up, tidying, and sewing and mending. She always changed into a decent dress at half-past four and over this she wore a clean wrapover pinafore of floral printed cotton.

'I'll just run up and change, then I'll set the table while you get him cleaned up.'

Annie cast Celia a grateful glance as she pushed young Frederick, the bane of her life, towards the scullery.

Celia hung her black shop dress on a hanger, then placed it in the wardrobe. She was a tidy girl, a habit instilled into her from a very early age. She changed into a dark-blue skirt and red-and-blue hand-knitted jumper, and then peered into the mirror of her small dressing table. She ran the brush through her hair, then returned it to its usual place between the blue-and-white china dressing-table set that was laid out neatly on crocheted mats. Mats that each week were washed, stiffened by dipping them in a solution of sugar and water and left to dry. Her bed was made each morning and covered with a pink and white cotton counterpane. The rag rug beside the bed was taken out into the yard each Wednesday, thrown over the washing line and beaten by her mam, along with all the other rugs. The windows always sparkled and the curtains were clean and crisp. Yes, Mam was working herself into the ground, as Maudie Kemp was always saying despite the fact that she herself set her own standards to match Mam's.

When Celia returned to the kitchen she immediately took the

tablecloth from the dresser drawer, along with the cutlery, and began to set the table quickly and neatly. Next the crockery, all of which matched, was taken down from the shelves of the dresser. From the mesh-fronted food press in the scullery she took the condiments.

'Why can't you just behave and leave those other lads alone?' she hissed at her brother, who was now sitting on a stool by the range.

His face and hands were clean and his hair combed and flattened into tidiness with water. His shirt had been replaced by a jumper knitted by his mother in the evenings when she didn't have mending to do. He was reading, or was supposed to be reading, Kipling's *The Jungle Book.* Da didn't approve of comics, which he called 'modern subversive trash'. The book, like most of the others belonging to Foxy, had been a Christmas or a birthday present, and also like the others it was often opened but never read. If he thought he could get away with it, Foxy even secreted a copy of *Boy's Own*, borrowed from one of his mates, inside the open pages.

He looked up at her sullenly. 'Don't you start on me, an' all! Mam's threatening to tell Da as it is. Anyway, they started it. THEY always start it.'

'Shut up! You're *all* as bad as each other, and one of these days Mam *will* tell Da and then it'll be the buckle end of his belt for you, meladdo.'

'They're Papists an' I'm sick of getting skitted at school for having to live next door to them.'

'Isn't there something in the Bible that says "Love thy neighbour as thy self"?'

'Well, if there is, that lot next door should know it, an' all. I hate that bloody Emmet.'

Celia threw at him the cloth she'd been using to burnish a knife. 'Here, even the floor cloth's too clean to wipe out your mouth! You let Mam hear you swearing and she won't wait for Da, she'll kill you herself.'

The conversation was abruptly terminated by the sound of voices in the lobby as Charlie Milton and Billy came into the kitchen.

Annie emerged from the scullery, a tea towel in her hand.

'Have you had a good day? There's time to wash your hands while I put the liver and onions out. Celia, drain and mash those potatoes for me, please, luv?'

There was always a note of anxiety in her mother's voice, Celia thought as she removed the pan from the range and took it into the scullery. It seemed as though Mam was unable to relax until she'd ascertained her husband's mood.

'Aye, everything is set for tomorrow. Let's hope the weather holds – the last thing we need is rain.'

Charlie added his coat to those on the back of the door and placed his bowler hat on the dresser, a habit that annoyed Annie intensely but on which she never commented. Later she'd give it its customary brush and place it on the hook above his overcoat. She would have liked a proper hallstand but the lobby was too narrow.

'It would be a shame if it was pouring down,' she agreed, following Charlie's gaze as it moved around the room taking note of everything. Then he slowly nodded his approval.

He addressed his younger son. 'Haven't you finished reading that yet, Frederick?'

Foxy looked up innocently. 'No, Da. It's . . . it's very interesting, like, but there's some very funny names in it and I have to remember that some are wolves, one is a bear, one is a tiger and—'

'"Funny"? I wouldn't describe Kipling's work as "funny",' Charlie interrupted. 'It's what Baden-Powell based his Scout Movement on. I really wish you'd join, Frederick.'

'Charlie, you know there isn't a Scout group anywhere around here or he would join,' Annie put in, trying to help the lad. Even if there had been one she knew she would have had a terrible job to persuade Frederick to join.

'I would, Da, and what I meant to say was strange . . . or unusual.'

Charlie nodded, irritated. Lads needed outlets for their energy otherwise they got up to all kinds of mischief. They needed to be taught useful things like self-discipline and self-sufficiency. He was very much in favour of Baden-Powell's movement. The lack of a Scout group was yet another reason for them to move from Roscommon Street.

'And I do have a lot of homework, Da,' Foxy added, ignoring the openly sceptical look Celia directed at him as she placed the bowl of mashed potato on the table.

'Have you got any plans for tonight, Billy?' she asked, to draw her da's attention away from her young brother. She could see her mam was biting her lip.

Billy Milton grinned at her. He was like his da, with pale, sandy-coloured hair and blue eyes. He knew she was sick of hearing about tomorrow's big event.

'I have, Cee. I thought I'd go into town with Richie. There's supposed to be a good film on at the Gaumont: *The Invisible Man* with Claude Rains.'

'He must be a new one. I've never heard of him before,' Celia replied, helping her mother to lay out the plates of liver and onions in their thick gravy.

'Well, you're not exactly a big fan of the pictures, Cee, are you?'

'There's nothing wrong in that. I can't understand why some people throw good money away on the rubbish they show these days,' her father cut in, having washed his hands and taken his place at the head of the table.

'It's better than propping up the bar of some pub, or gambling or chasing girls,' Annie quietly reminded him, then flushed deeply and looked down at her plate. Charlie liked a pint or two himself. She hated Saturday nights. He was always aggressive and argumentative after his visit to the Wynnstay and that's how most of the rows with the Slatterys started. Rows which terrified her, especially after the time Brigid Slattery had clouted Charlie so hard he'd literally staggered. It had been the beginning of a free-for-all which had ended with the police being called. She'd been shocked at Brigid Slattery but Maudie had said later, 'Well, what can you expect from a loud-mouthed, common slattern like that?'

But she'd always secretly admired her next-door neighbour because Charlie had called her all the names under the sun and the woman had no robust, healthy husband to answer back for her. And she had all those kids to cope with and not much money coming in. But these were thoughts Annie shared with no one, not even Celia.

Charlie signalled for silence and all heads were bowed as he said grace.

After the meal Celia helped her mam wash the dishes and prepare tomorrow's carry-out for her da, Billy and herself. Foxy had disappeared and Kipling's book had been returned to its place on the shelf. Her da was listening to a play on the wireless which sounded boring beyond belief. Mam had got out her darning and Billy was getting ready to depart to the cinema. She was bored. She'd read the newspaper, which seemed full of gloom and doom, and she'd glanced through her mother's *Woman's Weekly* magazine. It was Annie's only luxury in life and was approved of by Da because it gave recipes, knitting patterns, useful tips and articles for the housewife and some short stories, should any 'housewife' ever have time to read them.

Suddenly she noticed her mam jerking her head towards the stairs and looking worried. Celia was puzzled, her brow creasing in a frown. Then she realised her mother wanted to speak to her upstairs.

She got up. 'I'll just go and sponge my work dress and put a clean collar and cuffs on it,' she announced. The cream cotton collars and cuffs were detachable for frequent washing.

Annie set aside the basket of socks. 'I'll come up with you. Seeing I've got my sewing basket out I think that feather on the side of my hat might need an extra stitch or two. If it's windy I don't want to look a fool if it comes loose and blows away.' She forced herself to ignore the look her husband directed at her. If such a thing did happen he would consider it a major case of 'Showing Him Up' and she'd never hear the end of it.

Celia waited on the small landing for her mother.

'What's the matter?' she whispered.

'I've forgotten to get butter. We used the last of it on the sandwiches. There'll be none for his toast in the morning and that won't start the day off well. Will you nip down to Peggy Westhoff's for me?'

Glad of the opportunity to escape, but irritated that her mother was so afraid of her da that all this play-acting had to go on over half a pound of butter, Celia nodded eagerly. She might see someone and have a chat and by that time the play on the wireless would be finished and maybe something livelier and more interesting would be on instead.

Annie came down first, holding the hat she was to wear for the launch tomorrow, and Celia followed her.

'Where are you off to then, miss?' Charlie asked as she put on her coat.

'Only to Westhoff's, Da. Mam is getting low on thread, and I'll call and see if Mrs Kemp needs any messages too.' Peggy Westhoff in the corner shop sold almost everything.

'I've plenty for now, but I never like to get low on things,' Annie put in, casting a conspiratorial glance at her daughter while her husband nodded approvingly.

'If you see Frederick, tell him to get home here. It's ten past seven and I won't have him running the streets and mixing with riff-raff.'

'Right, Da,' Celia answered quickly as she left.

She did call on Maudie but it was Richie who opened the door to her, all done up in his good serge suit and a clean shirt.

'Celia Milton! Me dream's out!' He grinned smarmily.

'Well, you can cut that out for a start!' she snapped. She didn't particularly like Richie Kemp, who was the same age as Billy. There was too much of Maudie in him and virtually nothing at all of his da. Harry Kemp she *did* like and she felt sorry him, always being nagged to death by his sour-faced, bad-tempered, mischief-making wife, who now spared her any further conversation with Richie by appearing at the kitchen door to see who had called.

'What's up, Cee?' she asked, elbowing Richie to one side.

'Nothing, Mrs Kemp. I'm just on my way to Westhoff's for Mam. Is there anything you need?'

There were no thanks from Maudie for this offer.

'Nothing that I can think of, Cee, and it's not like yer mam to run out of anything.'

Celia bit her lip. Maudie would make a point of mentioning it tomorrow. She was jealous of Mam because of Da being a foreman and wearing a bowler for work. Harry didn't hold such an exalted position and he was never allowed to forget it.

'Well, we can't remember *everything* all the time, can we? She's not run out altogether, just getting a bit low and she's got so much on her plate, worrying about the big day tomorrow.'

Maudie's thin lips became even thinner. Annie Milton would have a much better position and more notice taken of her tomorrow than she herself would. Even though she'd spent more than she could afford on a new hat, she'd still be just a face in the crowd. The wives of all the blockermen would stand together with their husbands, not on the platform or anywhere near the bosses, but somewhere conspicuous, of that she was certain.

'I'd best get off then. I've got work in the morning, but I do hope it keeps fine for you,' Celia added, staring directly at Richie, who was fully aware that she was being sarcastic.

Damn her, he thought. Mam would nag even more now and go on about how all the Miltons thought they were a cut above everyone at their end of the street. Then he smiled to himself. He had high hopes of Celia Milton. When she was dressed up on Sundays she was a real stunner and she always obeyed her father. All he had to do was not blot his copybook in old Charlie Milton's eyes and go and ask the old fool's permission to court her.

Celia had bought the butter at the shop on the corner of Roscommon Street and Portland Place, and decided to make her way home slowly by going round the block, even though the air was damp and chilly. The light from the streetlamps shimmered through the fine drizzle and glistened softly on the wet pavement. As she turned into Back Roscommon Street and passed the Elephant pub, which was patronised by the Catholic element in the neighbourhood, she was suddenly confronted by the sight of her younger brother running hell for leather towards her, pursued by Lizzie's brother Emmet and two of his friends. As she stopped and looked on in astonishment, they caught up with Foxy and all four of them fell into a heaving heap on the ground, arms and legs flailing, all yelling and shouting.

Celia's temper flared. 'Get up, the lot of you! Get off him, you little hooligans, or I'll be round to see your priest about you!' she yelled, quickening her steps. Her words had no effect whatever and she could see she was going literally to have to drag them apart. There'd be hell to pay for this escapade.

Before she could attempt to part them, a large, apparently disembodied hand shot out, caught Emmet Slattery by the scruff of his neck and hauled him bodily out of the mêlée.

'You! Stay put there or I'll put your eye in a sling! And you get home. Three on to one's not fair, you bullies,' the voice behind her instructed and she recognised it as that of Joe Slattery. Acutely embarrassed she bent down and yanked Foxy to his feet.

'Look at the state of you! You little fright! That's twice today and this time Mam won't be able to cover up for you and I've no intention of doing it either!'

Foxy looked aggrieved. 'I never started it. I was going up for me mates, honest, an' they come beltin' up behind me.'

She turned to Joe Slattery, who held an unrelenting and glowering Emmet firmly by the collar of his jacket.

'Thanks. I – I . . . don't think I could have got them apart by myself.'

She looked up into his eyes. It was the first time she had ever been this close to him or even spoken to him properly. She was surprised to see mild amusement in his gaze and something else . . . admiration? She began to blush. He really wasn't a bad-looking lad and he was decently clothed in a tweed jacket, an open-necked shirt and dark trousers.

'That's all right. Meladdo here is in for a hiding too.'

She remembered that Lizzie had told her that Dessie Slattery wasn't a strong man. Presumably Joe would have to do the honours.

'So will he be. Da will go mad and then blame Mam and me. Have you been, I mean, were you going . . . somewhere?' She caught herself in time. She'd almost fallen into the trap of her own making. She wasn't supposed to know that he went to the Mechanics Institute.

'I'm on my way to evening classes at the place your Billy went to.'

They'd lived next door to each other for years. When he'd been Emmet's age he'd fought with Billy Milton and Richie Kemp for no other reason than religion. As he'd got older there'd been more serious altercations with her da. He saw her, in passing, half a dozen times a week and yet he'd never really *seen* her. Now as he looked at her, with the light from the streetlamp shining on her hair and her flushed cheeks, he realised that she was beautiful, really beautiful. You could abandon all reason and sense and lose yourself in those vivid blue pools that were her eyes. He pulled himself up quickly. That way of thinking was right out of the question.

Celia dropped her eyes, feeling the spark of emotion that flashed quickly between them.

'Well, thanks, anyway.'

'It was no trouble.'

Her cheeks were burning as she turned and frogmarched her brother down the street, knowing that Joe Slattery was still gazing after her.

Maudie had tried on the new hat with the coat she would wear tomorrow but she'd looked sourly at her reflection in the long mirror attached to the inside of the wardrobe door. She decided to go down and seek another opinion. Harry was useless but Richie was smarter.

'Well, how does it look?' she demanded as she entered the kitchen where Harry was reading a magazine about pigeons some colleague had lent him. Just the sight of it annoyed her. She was having no pigeon loft in her back yard. Horrible, dirty, smelly contraptions they were, and they encouraged vermin and there was enough of that already around here. Richie, who had been adjusting his tie, turned and looked at her appraisingly.

'Very nice, dear,' Harry ventured, lowering the magazine.

His wife ignored him.

'Pull the hat more over to one side, Mam.'

She complied and then peered into the mirror. 'It looks as if it's been knocked skewwhiff.'

'It doesn't, Mam. That's how it's supposed to be worn.'

'Oh, an expert on women's millinery now, are we?'

Richie shrugged. 'You asked and I answered. I don't know what all the flaming fuss is about. If it was that really big one they're building up at Clydebank, the *Queen Mary*, then it would be a *real* occasion. Queen Mary herself will probably launch it. Anyway Da and me will be in our work clothes tomorrow.'

Harry retreated behind the magazine. That had been the wrong thing to say entirely. Oh, it was all right for Richie, he was going out. It was himself who would now have to listen to her litany of complaints all night. If he could just rig up a small loft in the yard and get a couple of birds, it would be a great hobby and a retreat from the voice that whined on like a circular saw. He didn't ask or indeed get much pleasure out of life. He might use that as an argument for building a loft, at some later date.

'Oh, no you won't be in your work clothes! Not when Charlie Milton will be in a suit and a bowler.'

'Their Billy won't be in no suit. Anyway, how are we supposed to get washed and changed? There's no facilities for that. You know we all come home looking as though we'd been down a coal mine. There's no doors on the lavvies even . . .'

Maudie's sallow cheeks flushed at the mention of toilets. 'Don't be so . . . so disgusting. I don't want to know about things like that!'

'Well, it's a fact, Mam. So whether you like it or not, we'll be in our work clothes. I'm off now. I won't be late.'

Maudie stared after him with annoyance, then turned to her husband.

'I wish you'd say something to him, Harry, instead of just sitting there like a lump of lead.'

'Say what, luv? He's a grown lad, he's doing well at work.'

'Not as well as Billy Milton, but then *he's* got his da to push him forward, like.'

Harry knew from experience that this was one avenue not to go down. He sighed and put down the magazine.

'I'll make us a nice cup of tea, luv. You're getting all upset about tomorrow and there's no need. You'll look much smarter than Annie, poor soul. She's not got much taste,' he lied. 'It's a very smart hat, Maudie, and I know that Charlie is going to take you both into the parlour of the Royal Castle Hotel opposite the main gate for a drop of sherry afterwards, before he goes back to work.'

That didn't seem to have mollified her much, he thought as he went into the scullery to fill the kettle. Sometimes he wondered if it was worth opening his mouth at all. Everything he said she disagreed with. Every time he came home he was expected to give the twins a hiding for something, which half the time didn't seem fair, and as for Richie, well the lad *was* getting too big for his boots but he wasn't saying anything to him. He'd come a cropper soon enough.

He pushed the entire matter from his mind. To him tomorrow was just a working day, though he supposed it would be a *bit* special, like. It always made his heart beat a little faster when a ship he'd helped to create with his own two hands moved slowly, then ever more rapidly down the slipway towards the river to the cheers of the crowd. But Maudie had been going on and on about it for weeks now and he was heartily sick of it. He didn't ask much from life, which was just as well as he never got much, she saw to that. All he really wanted was a hobby – a few pigeons in a loft in the yard. Alfie Jones that he worked with could get him some biggish pieces of timber, he'd need a bit of wire mesh, which wouldn't break the bank, and Bert Scott had sort of promised him the pick of his young squabs. It was getting the loft built that was the problem. He wondered if he could build it somewhere else, in someone else's yard, then transport it here. It would be great then. He'd join one of the societies and go places, have trips with them. Whole days away from home.

'Harry Kemp, I'd like me tea before midnight if it's not too much trouble.' Maudie's high-pitched, sarcastic tone brought him down to earth and he sighed. If only he was like Charlie Milton, then Maudie wouldn't even have a say in the matter. But he wasn't like Charlie – that was part of the problem – and he knew he never would be.

Chapter Three

Lizzie had got up at her usual time but now, as she took her da his mug of tea, she heartily wished she'd got up earlier. Even on 'normal mornings' it was chaos as Mam shouted instructions and demands. Shoes and other articles of clothing went missing, which brought complaints and accusations from their owners and usually ended in tears, slaps and more shouting from Mam. Frequently, garments from the rack over the range were yanked down, felt and declared fit to wear as replacements for those which couldn't be tracked down.

Lizzie usually managed to ignore it all as she kept her work dresses and the small pile of other clothes she owned in a series of orange boxes in her attic bedroom. For her, the only fight was over the sink in the scullery, and Emmet always trying to avoid soap and water like the plague, but Mam, although harassed, always caught him.

It wasn't a bad morning, Lizzie thought. The sky was grey and overcast but not that lowering gunmetal grey which usually meant a heavy downpour sooner or later. It was more of a dove grey, which meant, with luck, it would clear a bit later on. There was no wind to speak of either, so at least the weather would cause no problems, she thought thankfully.

Dessie looked up and managed a smile as his oldest daughter entered the room. He'd been awake since Brigid had carefully got out of bed and crept around in the half-light, labouring under the delusion that she hadn't disturbed him. He'd not had a good night.

He'd sat up in bed for most of it and had stuffed a handful of the worn and faded quilt over his mouth to try to deaden the noise of the cough. He wished Brigid would let him swap with Lizzie, at least in summer. That way she'd get some sleep, but she wouldn't hear of it because of the stairs.

'You'd be destroyed with them stairs and we'd be having your wake within the month, so I'll hear no more about it,' had been the firm reply.

'You're awake, Da.' Lizzie was surprised as she put the mug down on the scratched, scored and stained bedside cabinet that held an assortment of objects pertinent to a sickroom.

'Aye, I've been awake ever since your mam got up. God luv 'er, she was creeping around so as not to disturb me.'

'I'm just sorry I didn't get up earlier – it's like Muldoon's picnic in the kitchen,' Lizzie said gloomily.

'I can hear it.' Dessie reached for the mug while Lizzie rushed to help him, beating the pillow, rolling up and shoving a couple of old coats behind it so he'd be able to sit in a more comfortable position.

'You know what Mam's like when she tries to organise things and the kids are that mad with excitement they're jumping up and down and running all over the place. Our Emmet started a fight with our Bernie, and Josie knocked the teapot over. I'm glad I'm going out to work, I can tell you.'

Dessie grinned. 'And maybe when they've finally gone I will get some peace and a bit of sleep.'

Lizzie kissed him on the cheek. 'I'll be in about a quarter past one, Da. You try and get some sleep. You must be worn out.' She made no reference to the fact that everyone except herself had been kept awake by his bouts of coughing.

He nodded, sipping the hot, weak liquid, and Lizzie closed the door reluctantly behind her.

The scene in the kitchen hadn't changed much since she'd left it.

Josie was on her hands and knees making a half-hearted attempt at mopping up the spilt tea with a piece of old rag that served as a floor cloth. Emmet was sitting on the sofa glowering and pulling faces at Bernie every time Brigid looked away. Bernie retaliated, safe in the knowledge that her mam couldn't see her as Brigid was standing behind her brushing out the tangle of curls that were so like Lizzie's.

'You've a head of hair on you that'd thatch a roof, so you have! Will you sit STILL, Bernie?' Brigid was flustered and losing her temper rapidly. Organisation wasn't one of her strong points.

'Mam, give me the brush, I'll do it. At least she'll sit still for me. Start and get yourself ready,' Lizzie said firmly, taking the situation in hand.

Brigid sighed. Only for the fact that they so seldom went on an outing as a family, she'd have gladly refused to traipse them all over to Birkenhead. 'Get ready, is it? Just what have I got to put on me back?'

'Oh, you know what I mean,' Lizzie replied, struggling with her sister's unruly mop and ignoring her occasional yells of pain. 'At this rate you'll be worn out by the time you go for the tram.'

'I will so with this lot. They have me heart scalded already. Emmet Slattery, I don't want you to move an inch off that sofa. Josephine Mary Slattery, you're making a right pig's ear of that. Get up off your knees and wring out that rag in the scullery instead of slopping it around. All you're doing is spreading the mess,' she instructed, as she started to saw away at the loaf of bread with a huge and dangerous-looking kitchen knife. She'd get the butties done first. She had a bit of margarine and a scraping of meat paste to go on them – sure signs that today was 'special', she mused. She just wished Dessie felt up to it. The air, the ferry ride, would have done him good.

Lizzie had finished her task and now turned her attention to her other sister. 'You look a mess!'

'And so would you if you'd been crawling around under that

table *and* it wasn't all my fault. Those two pushed me but Mam blamed me just the same,' Josie replied with some force.

Lizzie sighed. 'I know. But get a quick wash and run the brush through your hair and try and tidy up a bit for Mam. And for God's sake behave yourself. You're the eldest, so act your age and not your shoe size!'

'Lizzie, get off with you now or you'll be late. I'll be seeing you at about half-past four,' Brigid called.

'All right, Mam. I'll get me da something when I get back at dinner time, so don't worry and try and enjoy yourself,' she called back, before shrugging on her coat and letting herself out the back way.

She met Celia at the junction of Rose Vale and Portland Place.

'Thank God for some sanity at last. It's murder in our house.'

Celia grinned with understanding. 'It's been no picnic in ours either. Mam's terrified that Foxy will do something to disgrace her, or she won't look as well dressed or be as well spoken as all the other wives and that Da will think she is showing him up. Mind you, he is taking her and that Maudie Misery for a glass of port or sherry or something afterwards.'

'She'll look great, Cee. She's always so neat and tidy,' Lizzie replied, thinking that her own mam would look nice too if she had a good coat and a smart hat, instead of her heavy black shawl.

"I've been telling her that for weeks but Maudie Kemp has been to Frost's on County Road no less, and bought a new and, by the look of it, expensive hat.'

They'd reached the corner of Great Homer Street.

'So what?' Lizzie was derisive. 'She'll still look flaming miserable and I shouldn't wonder if the hat doesn't get ruined in the crush. She'll be in with the crowd, not separate like your mam, and I bet that narks her no end.'

Celia brightened perceptibly until Lizzie muttered sotto voce, 'Oh heck, here comes Misery Guts Henderson, but it's still better than being back in that lunatic asylum and it is only half a day.'

Somehow, by a series of minor miracles, Brigid had got them all down to the tram stop in plenty of time. They were going over the water by the ferry, which in itself was a treat for the kids. It cost tuppence each and most of the time that was all that remained in Brigid's purse on the day before Lizzie, Joe and Fergal got paid.

She cast an eye over her brood. They were fairly clean and tidy. There were no fancy hair ribbons for the girls or a smart Fair Isle pullover for Emmet but their frocks had been ironed and so had his Sunday shirt. That the dresses had been neatly mended and had let-down hems didn't matter. She was a very handy needlewoman, that was one of the good things the nuns had taught her at school back home. Emmet's jacket too had been repaired and she'd sewn patches on the elbows. His boots were clean, if not highly polished. His cap sat well on his head. Yes, she'd done her best, and there'd be lads there today who, despite the frantic efforts of their mams, would have neither jacket, cap nor boots.

It was very unfortunate that they arrived at the tram stop just ahead of Maudie Kemp and Annie Milton. Brigid glared at them both, feeling shabby and streelish as they were both wearing decent coats and smart, if plain, hats. All their kids were better turned out than her own too. She turned away, squaring her shoulders and mustering all the dignity she could until the tram arrived.

By this time there was a crowd waiting and as she pushed her brood aboard, there was an unseemly crush from behind.

''Old on there a mo! No pushin' an' shovin'. There's plenty of room on top but no standin' on me platform, it's against the Rules,' the conductor shouted bellicosely to the unruly crowd, composed mainly of women and kids.

'Well, if some people would shift themselves we *would* get a move on,' Maudie said loudly and acidly.

Brigid turned around. 'You just hold yer horses, missus. We were here first an' if yer think I'm going up them stairs to sit with all those fellers smoking like chimneys, you've got another think coming!' This last was to the conductor.

Annie flushed with embarrassment. 'Maudie, don't say anything more, please. We'll go upstairs.'

'No, we flaming well won't! I'm not having the likes of *her* telling me where to go!'

In all fairness it had been the conductor, not Brigid Slattery, who had issued that instruction, but Annie said nothing.

'I *will* be telling you where you can go in a minute, Maudie Kemp, yer sour-faced creature,' Brigid snapped.

Annie tugged at Maudie's arm. They were causing a scene which would eventually be relayed to Charlie: there were people in the restless queue who knew them. 'We'll go upstairs.'

'And sit all the way in all that mucky smoke up there?'

'Listen, missus, I don't care iffen yer cough yerself blue in the face or not, just gerron, there's other people waitin' an' you'll all miss the ferry at this rate!'

By this time Brigid had sat down on the long, slatted wooden seat that faced the aisle with Emmet and Bernie clutched half on, half off her knee and Josie hanging on to the metal bar by the platform.

Maudie, outwitted, stuck her nose in the air as she pushed the twins towards the spiral staircase and the upper deck, but couldn't resist having the last word.

'Some of us are going in style, on the train from James Street. You'd catch your death on the boat in this weather and end up looking like a dog's dinner into the bargain.'

'Sure, there's some who look like that already!' Brigid commented acidly, before the press of people crowding the platform pushed Maudie and Annie and their broods up the stairs.

'The carry-on out of the creature an' all because she's a new hat,' Brigid said as she paid the harassed conductor their fares. Finally he yanked on the bell strap, the signal for the driver to move off.

'Thank God they don't 'ave a launch every bloody day,' the man muttered.

'I'd be obliged if yer wouldn't take the Lord's name in vain in front of the kids,' Brigid said in a voice that brooked no smart-aleck reply, and the man raised his eyes to the ceiling, thankful his shift ended at dinner time and there would be no chance he'd get this lot on their way home.

At the shipyard there was still plenty of work to do: the finishing touches had to be made to the launch platform, the rubbish cleared away from the area around the ship, and a rope barrier erected. The greasing of the keel with the thick brown axle grease, which would ease her journey, was still in progress. And yards and yards of drag chains, which would slow the ship down as she descended the slipway, had to be positioned. Already the opposite bank of the river was thick with sightseers.

'Here, get this down yer, Joe. The blockerman said we could all have a mug now, on the hoof, like. There's no time to stop for anything and there'll be no time later either.' Fergal handed his brother a large metal can and an enamel cup. Joe poured out a measure of the hot dark liquid and gulped it down.

'God, look at the cut of yer! Me mam will go mad.'

'Then she'll have to go mad, won't she? You can't grease up and secure the drags and stay clean as the driven snow, can you?' Joe replied irritably.

'I wish Da could 'ave been here. Everyone else's da is.'

'Aye, but there's a cold wind getting up even now and it might rain later. He'd get pneumonia. Go on, get over to the others before the brew has gone cold,' Joe said firmly, but there was a regretful note in his tone and Fergal turned away as his brother resumed his work.

Joe *did* wish his da were here and it really didn't have anything to do with Harry Kemp or Charlie Milton. He'd show them one day. No, it was having someone who understood. Who worked with ships and understood the months of hard graft that had gone into building not just this particular ship but any ship. Mam would be here, of course, but she wouldn't really understand. All the women were the same. They came because it was a day's outing and they just might get a close glimpse of Lady Vesty in her finery as she launched the ship her husband's money had paid for.

He watched his brother go to another group, and then sullenly to Billy Milton and Richie Kemp who already felt the work assigned him was beneath his dignity as an apprentice welder. The fact that it was more degrading for Billy – a journeyman plater – he ignored.

As Joe watched he noted that Billy made no comment but that Richie said something that drew a heated retort from his brother. Joe's eyes narrowed. He'd show those two that he was as good, if not better, than them one day, when he too finished his evening classes and got results as good as Billy Milton's. That would mean a rise in wages and a better position. As he bent down again and began to heave and pull the heavy iron links of the chain, he wondered if he'd see Celia Milton today. Then he remembered she'd be at work like their Lizzie, and he felt strangely disappointed.

Just as Lady Vesty mounted the platform, watery sunlight broke through the clouds that were now being twisted into weird and intricate shapes by the rising wind coming in off the estuary. Everyone took it as a good omen. The dignitaries were all grouped together on the high platform. The old-fashioned supports for the staging of another ship in the process of being built reduced the standing space and made the crowd around the 5,000-ton ship look like an army of ants. From the *Clement*'s main mast flew the Union Jack, the Red Ensign and the house flag of the Booth Line – a red diagonal cross on a white background with the letter B in blue at the juncture of the red cross – followed by an array of pennants. Looming over it all were the gigantic cantilever cranes, idle now until after the ceremony.

People had been arriving since first thing but had been kept outside the yard gates until just a short while ago. To one side, in a group apart, stood all the foremen and their wives and families. Joe had no trouble spotting Charlie Milton, his mousy little wife and that young hooligan Foxy.

The families of the rest of the workers were crammed around the ship like sardines. It *was* a big event. Oh, you always felt proud to watch a ship successfully launched, but this was different. It was the one thousandth, and they had an order on the books from the Navy for the first purpose-built aircraft carrier, the *Ark Royal.*

Suddenly he noticed a ripple, then a parting in the crowd as Brigid, dragging the kids behind her, made her way towards him.

'Jesus, Mary and Joseph! Did you ever see such a crowd? You can't fit a feather between them. I was crafty, I said our Emmet was sickening for something.'

Joe laughed. Emmet looked far from sickening for anything, his face was flushed with excitement. It was the first time he'd ever been to a launch.

'I hope you tell that one in confession, Mam.'

'Don't I always?' Brigid replied with mock indignation.

'Here, Emmet, get up on our Fergal's shoulders and Mam, give us a hand with the girls or they'll see nothing.'

'You just mind you don't break your back with the weight of them,' said Brigid, ignoring her son's greasy clothes, 'and you two pull your frocks down; I won't be having people seeing your knickers.'

'You mean they've each got a pair on?' Joe joked.

Brigid didn't think it at all amusing. 'They have so and what's up with you, Joe Slattery, saying things like that in front of all these people?'

'Mam, Mam, it's great up 'ere,' Emmet yelled.

'If you don't keep still you'll have the pair of us on the floor!' Fergal yelled back, swaying and staggering under the burden of his young brother.

'I wish her ladyship would gerra move on, me feet are killin' me. I borrowed our Hannah's shoes,' a female voice announced from somewhere behind them.

The sentiment was being echoed silently by Annie, who stood next to Charlie, trying not to fidget or keep raising her hand to her hat with every gust of wind. She hated being 'on view' and she was cold.

If there had been any way at all to get out of coming, she'd have taken it. And that incident on the tram hadn't helped. Why couldn't Maudie keep her mouth shut for once? Mrs Slattery and her kids hadn't said a word at the tram stop. Why cause a scene?

It was quite a while before she realised that Foxy had disappeared from beside her. Her heart turned over. Charlie would be furious, really furious, if the lad did anything to disgrace them, and there were so many things that came under that category in Charlie's book.

She had picked out Maudie by the much-envied new hat, near the front of the crowd to their left. In fact Maudie would get a better view of the launch than she would. Foxy must have realised this and somehow slipped through the crowd to join the twins. How she'd ever find him later she just didn't know. She prayed silently that her husband wouldn't miss the lad, that he'd be too absorbed in his own thoughts. Oh dear God, what had possessed Foxy, today of all days? she thought, biting her lip, her eyes beginning to fill with tears.

After the first five minutes Foxy Milton had felt none of the excitement or elation of Emmet Slattery. He'd been bored just standing doing nothing except looking at the side of a ship, and if you peered up to the top deck you just got a crick in the neck. Anyway, what was it? Just a big lump of metal with a mast and a few flags. There wasn't even a funnel on it yet. He knew his mates were at the front with Maudie. No one would miss him. His da looked like a stuffed dummy from Hepworth's window. He was standing to attention almost, like a soldier in a bowler hat. His mam seemed lost in her own thoughts. He knew she hated these occasions and was terrified to move or speak in case she upset his da, so he slowly edged his way towards the end of the line and went to find his old sparring partners Frank and Eddie.

The first bit had been easy but now that he'd slid under the barrier he had to watch himself, first to make sure he wasn't noticed, and secondly stepping over great heaps of chains that someone had left carelessly lying around all over the place.

'Do you think there's ever going to be a chance that your one up there with the lampshade on her head and the bottle in her hand will get round to throwing the damned thing?' Brigid asked her eldest son. She too was cold and couldn't see what the hold-up was.

'Mam, it takes time. I told you that. She's got to shake hands and talk to people,' Joe answered mildly, then suddenly he swung his two startled sisters to the ground and his voice and expression changed.

'Holy Mother of God! He'll be killed!'

Brigid stared after him with astonishment as with shouts and curses he pushed his way to the front of the crowd.

At that moment Lady Vesty decided to speak. In clear, precise tones she uttered the time-honoured words, the bottle of champagne was smashed against the *Clement*'s hull, the main struts of the wooden cradle that had supported her on the keel blocks were demolished by sledgehammers and the ship began to move, very slowly at first, but gathering speed.

The cheers were deafening but Joe took no notice. Any minute now, at the speed she was going down the bank, young Foxy Milton would be cut in half by the drag chains as they uncoiled increasingly rapidly. Somehow the lad had managed to get entangled in them.

Just as Billy Milton, who had also spotted his brother's predicament, reached the front of the crowd, Joe caught Foxy by the collar of his jacket and yanked him clear. Like thick metallic serpents the drag chains uncoiled and crashed and clanked down the bank. The crowd hadn't noticed because at that precise moment the *Clement*'s stern hit the waters of the Mersey in a shower of spume and the crowds went wild. All the ships on the river blasted furiously on their steam whistles to add to the cacophony.

'You little fool! Didn't you see the bloody chains?' Joe yelled at the lad, who was white with shock now as understanding sunk in of how close he had come to death.

Billy had reached them, and people who had been at the front of the crowd whose attention had momentarily been diverted to witness the episode began to surge around them.

'What the hell was your old man thinking of letting him wander off?' Joe roared at an equally white-faced Billy.

'He probably doesn't know.' Embarrassed by the whole episode Billy belted his young brother hard. 'He'll bloody kill you for this, Foxy. You soft little get! You nearly got killed!'

Foxy had begun to cry, mainly with fright and shock.

The two older lads looked steadily at each other and the colour slowly stained Billy's cheeks. 'Thanks. Thanks from me and me mam anyway.' The words came with difficulty.

Joe shrugged. 'Anyone would have done the same. Take him back to your mam, she'll be worried. At least she didn't see the stupid little sod nearly cut in half.'

Billy began to drag Foxy away. 'Just you wait until Da hears about this, and he *will*. And now we have that bloody left-footer from next door to thank, too.'

Joe watched them for a few seconds, then turned and made his way back to his own family, acknowledging the praise of the small crowd just with curt nods of his head.

Chapter Four

All the way home on both train and tram Annie was silent and shocked. Maudie's voice droned on and on about how awful kids were these days and the antics they got up to with never a thought for their long-suffering parents. Never a thought for anyone but themselves. Oh no. Downright ungrateful and stupid they were.

The three young boys were also silent. Foxy's insides were churning with fear as he now remembered the feel of cold metal scraping his legs before Joe Slattery had yanked him clear. He hadn't known that big heavy chains like that could move so quickly. Now he did and that was only part of it. There was Da to face yet. Beside him, Frank and Eddie were gradually becoming aware of the awfulness of Foxy's position and were thankful they weren't in his shoes.

Charlie didn't as yet know, but Annie started to tremble when she thought of what he would be like when he finally arrived home. The offer of a glass of sherry, tempting though it had been, had been refused. She had no wish at all to be there when the incident was mentioned, and mentioned it would surely be. She'd said that they were all chilled to the marrow and would get back to their firesides and a cup of tea. They really weren't people who drank the likes of sherry in such places as the parlours of hotels.

She knew that had displeased her husband but it was a small price to pay for the brief respite. She also knew he would go over to the Royal Castle Hotel for a pint or two himself to celebrate and it would probably be in there that he'd hear every detail of his son's escapade. He'd be in dead on time for his tea tonight. She clenched her hands tightly in her lap as another bout of trembling began.

They'd all walked from the tram stop together but at the top of the road they'd met Celia, who had taken one look at her mother's face, had taken Annie's arm firmly and said abruptly she hoped they'd had a good day but Mam didn't look well so they were going straight in.

'Foxy, go on ahead. The door's open, put the kettle on. Now!' Celia's tone was sharp and she quickened her pace, leaving Maudie and the twins standing open-mouthed at the top of the street.

Something was wrong, terribly wrong, but she groaned inwardly as she saw Mrs Slattery and her brood heading towards them, having walked up from the Great Homer Street end of Roscommon Street. They were bound to arrive on their respective doorsteps simultaneously.

They did, and Brigid and Celia each opened their front doors and shoved the youngsters inside quickly. Then Brigid turned to Annie and for the first time in over ten years spoke without anger or scorn.

'I'm sorry for your trouble, Mrs Milton. Thank God it turned out well in the end. Get this girl here to give you a good strong cup of tea.'

Annie nodded and murmured her thanks while Celia's eyes widened with pure astonishment.

'Mam, what in heaven's name went on?' she demanded after she closed the front door, shepherding Annie down the lobby and into the kitchen. The kettle was already on the hob.

Annie, still with her hat, coat and gloves on, sank on to the chair by the range, still trembling. Foxy, too, stood clutching the back of the chair tightly. Haltingly Annie told the tale and as she did so her daughter's deep-blue eyes widened and the colour drained from her face.

'Da will kill him!' she said at last.

Annie nodded, then burst into tears. 'Oh, Cee, you know how I *hate* rows and fights and this . . .'

Celia put her arms around her. 'Oh, Mam, you take too much notice of him. We all do. You shouldn't be upset thinking about the row.'

'I know and I'm so shocked. Oh, Cee, he could have been killed before my very eyes.'

At this Foxy, too, broke down but his sister had little sympathy for him.

'Just you shut up, Frederick Milton! All you ever think about is yourself. Self! Self! Self! You just don't care about Mam. Well this time when Da's finished with you you won't be doing *anything* except your homework! Stop that flaming whingeing as well, it's upsetting Mam even more.'

Foxy's sobs became noisier and Celia lost her temper entirely, something she did very rarely. 'Oh, get up to your room! Go on. Get out of my sight!' she yelled.

She sat comforting Annie as best she could and wondering just how on earth she could get word to Lizzie that there was no way she'd be out tonight. But Lizzie too would hear the tale and might well put two and two together. Maybe she could pretend to go to the privy and shout over the wall, but no, that was no use. Da would hear her and there was always so much noise in the Slattery kitchen that she'd have to shout very loudly indeed to be heard. The thought occupied her for the rest of the afternoon, vying with her dread of her father's return and what would transpire then.

She'd made her mam take an aspirin and go for a lie-down. She'd promised to get Annie up at five and get the tea ready, and it was while she was peeling the potatoes that she thought of a note. She wouldn't sign it but Lizzie would know. She'd nip out and slip it under the door. She wiped her hands, found a piece of paper and a pen and wrote: 'Lizzie, in the yard tonight at ten.' Then she folded it and opened the front door quietly, praying that none of Lizzie's sisters or Emmet was playing either in the street or on their doorstep. She was in luck. She pushed the folded piece of paper under the door, darted back indoors again and carried on with her preparations.

The meal was ready to be put on the table. Annie had washed her face, changed her frock and wore a clean pinny. Foxy had also been washed and spruced up a bit but told to stay in his room.

As he entered the kitchen Charlie Milton's face was like thunder and both his wife and daughter cringed inwardly.

It had been Arnold Campbell, a foreman carpenter he'd had a few run-ins with in the past and heartily disliked, who'd told him in graphic detail the whole story. At least the man had taken him aside to do so, he'd grudgingly thought. He hadn't announced it to the entire crowd of foremen and skilled craftsmen in the saloon bar.

Frederick's behaviour was bad enough, as was Annie's negligence, as indeed was the knowledge that his young son could now be dead, but it was the fact that Joe Slattery had got to him in the nick of time, just ahead of Billy, that twisted the knife in his wounded pride. Joe Slattery. One of that tribe of common, dirty, scruffy, rowdy Catholics he was forced to live next door to that seemed to make it all far worse. To have to be beholden to the likes of *him* for something so important as his son's life, that's what really stuck in his craw.

Billy spoke first. 'Are you all right, Mam?'

Annie nodded.

'She was so upset I made her have a lie-down, what with the shock and all,' Celia said quietly, addressing her brother, her eyes full of fear.

Charlie exploded. 'SHOCK! BLOODY SHOCK!' he roared, his face turning puce. 'It's the DISGRACE, the BLOODY DISGRACE AND HUMILIATION! Are you that stupid, Annie, that you can't keep your eye on him for ten minutes? I'm the bloody laughing stock of the whole damned yard now! It had to be *my* son, didn't it? Me, the most meticulous, the most disciplined man in the bloody yard. Why the hell couldn't you have held on to him, in the name of God? You stupid bitch! And then to have him . . . that . . .' He could find no word bad enough to describe Joe Slattery and the tirade ended in furious spluttering.

The tears rolled silently down Annie's cheeks and she started to tremble again. Celia immediately went to her side. 'Don't get upset, Mam.'

'You mind your own business, girl! Upset! Upset! She has a right to be upset. I'll never live this down. I'll never command respect again—'

'Most of the fellers say all lads are holy terrors these days, Da,' Billy interrupted. He too thought it very unfair to blame Mam entirely.

Charlie ignored the attempted pacification. 'Where is he? Where is that young hooligan?'

'Upstairs, Da,' Celia answered, her arm around her still weeping mother's shoulders. She agreed her da had a right to be annoyed with Foxy and was right in some degree about respect, but to blame Mam entirely, to call her names and upset her to this extent, just wasn't fair. Nor was his rage against Joe Slattery. What did it matter *who* had rescued Foxy? But she dare not say anything else.

'Billy, get up there and bring the little sod down here.'

Billy did as he was bid. Charlie began to unbuckle the belt he wore. It wasn't as wide or as heavy as those worn by dockers, stevedores or even the men in the yard, but it would hurt just as much.

'Oh, Da! Please, not the buckle end, it'll cut his skin. Please. He's shocked too and he could have been killed,' Celia begged, the tears stinging her own eyes.

Billy had returned with the culprit and added his plea to that of his sister.

Charlie ignored both of them and spoke directly to his young, ashen-faced son. 'For the next two months you don't set foot over the doorstep except to go to school. And I don't want any whining or snivelling out of you. Turn around and bend over that chair. I'll teach you to damned well behave in future.'

His voice was so cold and quiet that Celia shuddered. Normally, he shouted the way he'd done only minutes ago, and this coldness really frightened her.

Annie closed her eyes and stuffed her hand in her mouth to stifle her cries as the loud crack of the leather belt resounded through the kitchen. She jumped nervously each time the belt raked her son's back, each blow accompanied by a term of abuse. As he went on and on in Charlie's mind his son became just an object he was beating. An object that took on the shape of that damned Joe Slattery from next door. His anger took hold of him completely and a red mist of hatred danced in front of his eyes.

In the end, it took Annie, Billy and Celia to restrain him. Both Annie and Celia were crying and Billy was white with fear, certain his father had lost control of his mind. Foxy, his back and buttocks a mass of red weals, crawled slowly up the stairs, sobbing. Annie moved to follow him.

'Stay where you are, woman. I'm the head of this household. His punishment was warranted and now I want my meal!'

His voice was calmer, he seemed more normal now, Billy thought thankfully.

Annie's hands shook so much that the plates and cups and saucers rattled. Celia helped her dish out the meal, knowing that neither herself nor her brother, let alone her poor mam, had any appetite.

Billy started to eat but then laid down his knife and fork and got up.

'Sit down and finish your meal,' his father snapped.

'No, Da, I'm going up to see him.'

Charlie thumped the handle of his fork hard on the table and the pepper pot fell on to its side. 'I said sit down. Do I have to use my belt again?'

Billy held his ground and Celia stood up.

'I'll go. *I* made the meal, if mine goes cold then I'll eat it like that.' And before anyone could utter a word she'd gone, taking the stairs two at a time.

Foxy was lying face down on his bed sobbing. Celia sat down beside him and laid her hand gently on his head.

'You asked for it. Now perhaps you'll behave. You'll think of the consequences before you go off on some mad scheme. I'm going to put some lotion on your back. It might sting for a bit but I can't help that. Then I'll bring you up a cup of tea and an aspirin.' The sobs subsided but Celia's hands shook as she gently examined the livid weals before going into her own room for cotton wool and a bottle of calamine lotion she kept in her drawer.

Celia cleared up, washed the dishes, did the sandwiches for Billy and her da's carry-out, helped by Annie and then Billy, who told his mother to get an early night as she looked awful. Urged on by them both Annie was relieved when Charlie didn't comment further. He was reading when she made her escape. She felt she'd got off lightly though she knew it would rankle with Charlie for a long, long time. But she couldn't put reins on the boy, he was nine years old.

Billy put on his jacket and cap.

'I'm going out for a walk for a bit of fresh air. Do you fancy coming, Cee?'

She thanked him but refused, saying she had a couple of collars and cuffs to iron and she was tired. Her gaze darted quickly to her father, wondering if he would remember that she'd had all afternoon to do them. His eyes never left the page and she breathed deeply.

She was therefore surprised when just before ten o'clock her da put on his jacket and announced he was off to the Wynnstay with Harry Kemp for the last half-hour. She nodded. It made her forthcoming tryst with Lizzie easier.

Ten minutes later, when she was sure he'd really gone, she pulled on a cardigan and crept out of the back door and down the yard. If she stood on the upturned dolly tub she could see into the Slatterys' yard. With as little noise as possible she climbed up and leaned over the top of the wall. A feeble light came from next door's kitchen window and she could just glimpse figures behind the curtain. It was dark, but as her eyes became accustomed to it she could make out a figure in the yard.

'Lizzie? Lizzie, is that you?' she whispered hoarsely.

'Oh, Mother of God, Cee, you scared me to death!'

'Why? You knew it would be me.'

'How could I know? I was going to the privy. Anyway, I heard what went on this morning and we all heard your da roaring an' beltin' your Foxy.'

'Oh, Lizzie, it was terrible. Our Billy and me and Mam had to drag the belt off him in the end. Mam was nearly fainting with fright.'

'Jesus, Mary and Joseph! Didn't he realise Foxy could have been killed but for our Joe?'

'He did but I don't think it helped,' Celia said grimly.

'No, it wouldn't have, and just how long has this been going on?'

Lizzie uttered a startled cry and Celia clapped her hand to her mouth, remembering now that Lizzie had said she had just been on her way to the privy.

Joe Slattery stood glaring at them both, Celia's note in his hand.

'I wondered what the hell this meant? It had blown up under the stairs by the time I got in. So, come on the pair of you, explain.'

It took Lizzie a moment to get over her shock. 'What's to explain?' she said defiantly. 'What's so terrible about it? Cee and me have been friends for five years now. She got me my job. So, we go to different churches but it's the one God, isn't it? It's the one Jesus Christ that died on the cross, isn't it? Anyway, don't come that with me, Joe Slattery. Did you stop and think what religion Foxy Milton was before you dragged him to safety? Did you suddenly think: Oh, I can't do nothin' to help *him*, he's a Proddydog? Like hell you did, so don't you go giving out to me!'

'She . . . she's right. You saved my brother's life today and I'm grateful *and* I'd do the same for your Emmet or Josie or Bernie.'

Joe's emotions were confused. He was angry with Lizzie for the deceit yet incredulous that they'd kept this friendship secret for five years. And he knew Lizzie was right: he'd not given the lad's religion a single thought and Celia had said she would have done the same. He looked up into the depths of the wide blue eyes and felt again that sensation, that feeling that passed like quicksilver between them. He was out of his depth here and he didn't like it.

'Get in then now. Mam will be wanting to know what's kept you out here so long.'

Lizzie glared at him then turned to Celia. 'See you in work in the morning.'

Celia nodded.

'You'd better get in too,' Joe said curtly.

'I will. I'm worn out, but . . . but thanks for saving Foxy. I mean that and I know Mam and our Billy do, too. Da . . . well . . .' she shrugged.

A smile hovered around the corners of Joe's mouth but he was glad she couldn't see it. 'Don't worry, I won't spoil your and our Lizzie's secret.'

'Promise?'

'Promise,' he replied.

Her head and shoulders vanished from sight and he heard the soft thud as she jumped down from whatever it was she'd been standing on.

After returning the dolly tub to its normal position, Celia went back into the house, shut the door and leaned against it. She felt drained. What a day it had been. They'd always remember the day the *Clement* was launched, that was for sure, but she was having trouble getting the handsome face of Joe Slattery out of her mind.

Chapter Five

In the depths of the following February, the money was scraped together by the Slatterys – with a small contribution from Celia, unbeknown to anyone except Lizzie – for a chest specialist to come to examine Dessie Slattery.

It had been a hard decision for Brigid to make but she knew she wanted the best for him. He'd always had a bit of a weakness in his chest, even when they were courting, but working on the docks in all weathers had turned his weakness into a crippling illness. Over the years she'd watched his failing health with growing concern. From the day he'd been unable to get down to the docks sacrifices had had to be made. She loved him dearly and she just couldn't go on like this, watching him fade away before her eyes. Especially if there was something, other than the fresh air and sanatorium the doctor had advised, that could be done for him.

She had made great economies. Anything that could be pawned or sold had been. The only bed in the house now was the one in the front room. Everyone else slept on 'donkeys' breakfasts', straw-stuffed mattresses laid on the floor or between two chairs.

The house was bare of all but the most basic and essential items. Small ornaments, brasses, statues and even the pictures of the Blessed Virgin and the Pope had gone. When she'd taken her wedding ring to the pawnshop Brigid knew that this time she'd never redeem it. It was gone for ever, that most cherished symbol of their life together. There were tears in her eyes that day as she walked home – there was no money now to spare for tram fares.

'It's freezing up in that attic but I've made Mam go up there at least for a few nights. She's worn to a shadow,' Lizzie confided to Celia as they left work, heads bent against the biting east wind in which there were flurries of snow, Celia with her thick hand-knitted woollen hat pulled down over her ears, Lizzie with an old headscarf knotted tightly under her chin. They both hated winter in the shop. The door was constantly being opened, letting in icy blasts, and they wore the same dresses as they did in summer.

'It's freezing in that shop. I wish he'd let us wear jackets or cardigans,' Celia complained.

'It's all right for him. He's probably got a woollen vest, then his shirt, a sleeveless pullover, a jacket and his heavy shop coat and trousers *and* I bet he wears long john underpants. I don't care, I'm going to see if I can fit an old flannel blouse under my dress tomorrow,' Lizzie said firmly.

'My feet are like two blocks of ice,' Celia added.

'Stop moaning, at least you've got thick stockings and a pair of fleecy-lined boots. I've only got stockings and shoes.'

'Is your da that bad?' Celia said, glancing anxiously at her friend.

'Aye. I'm going to sit up with him for a few nights.'

'But you'll be on your knees after a day at work.'

Lizzie shrugged. 'That doesn't matter. Our Josie's old enough to help. She can get a meal on the table and do the butties. I'll try and get a few hours after me tea. Mam will have enough on her plate, doing the shopping and washing the few bits we've got left. But she's got three evenings at some office in India Buildings and the *Berengaria*'s due in on Friday.'

They walked on in silence, each wrapped in her own thoughts.

Celia had heard her da complain about 'him next door' and the noise of the coughing and spitting but she'd said nothing. It distressed her that her father was so callous. They seemed to have every comfort, next door they had virtually nothing.

Things at home had eased a bit at Christmas when Foxy had served out the term of his punishment and had also, because of enforced reading and homework, come top of his class and had received a very good school report. She wondered gloomily how long it would last before he went off the rails again. It wasn't in his nature to be so docile. He had 'the divil's imp' in him according to Lizzie. And she'd noticed the strain seemed to be telling on her mam more and more. She seemed to be getting thinner and thinner and sometimes, in the evenings, as she sat under the light of the standard lamp mending or knitting, her face looked positively grey, her hair lank and lifeless.

Celia felt heartily sorry for Lizzie too. Lizzie loved her da so much, something she herself no longer did, if she had ever done so at all. She'd always been in awe of him, then she'd learned to fear and respect him. She didn't even respect him now, not after that awful day last October when he'd lost control of himself. Since then, whenever she looked at him she saw an overbearing, cruel, pompous bully.

It seemed as though Mr Slattery was really ill. Specialist doctors from Rodney Street cost a lot of money and it was causing hardship next door to find that money – she'd been happy to chip in.

It had been years since she'd seen Lizzie's da regularly. When she'd been younger, before her friendship with Lizzie began, he'd worked on the docks, not frequently, though, even then. She'd see him come slowly and wearily up the street, sometimes stopping and leaning against a wall or lamppost for a few minutes to get his breath, but he'd always looked a kind, quiet man and he'd never glared, made nasty comments or called her names like some of the other men from the other end of the street did. He didn't deserve what was happening to him – and neither did her friend.

Lizzie was so cold she couldn't feel either her hands or her feet, but that wasn't important. Tomorrow was important. The specialist was coming. At least the parlour would have to be clean and tidy, even if the rest of the house was its usual untidy, messy self, although since the mass removal of their belongings to the pawnbroker's there wasn't much to get it untidy with. In the morning she'd parcel the kids out early. They could wait at Biddy Doyle's house with Vinny and that tribe until it was time for school.

Mam would be out cleaning posh offices tonight, so Lizzie'd have to tidy and clean the parlour as best she could. She was very worried about her da. He was so thin and his skin looked stretched across his face and had no colour to speak of. In fact, it looked like tissue paper.

After school Emmet ran errands for the shopkeepers, carried heavy bags and parcels, anything he could get to earn a few pennies. Joe and Fergal were always late in these days. The order book at Laird's was healthy and they were both working on a destroyer for the Navy, Number 992 on the books, but it would be named HMS *Fearless*. Their extra money was badly needed. It helped keep a fire burning day and night in the front room now that Da never left his bed. It paid for the medicines from the dispensary, though they seemed to be of little use.

It was hard on Joe particularly because somehow he managed to drag himself along to the Mechanics Institute. His examination was in May and Lizzie knew how important it was to him. Both lads were now working in atrocious conditions, out on the bank where the wind off the river was raw and biting. Some mornings the staging and slipways were covered in ice and snow. When it rained or snowed, as it had done frequently in January, they'd been soaked to the skin. There were no facilities to store or change into dry clothes, so they had to keep on working and come home in those same saturated garments that had to be dried around the fire in the range, which effectively cut off the heat from the rest of the room, for the same clothes had to be used next day.

Celia and Lizzie were nearing the corner of Rose Vale but neither of them made any attempt to turn off – since it was pitch-dark and raining there were few people about to see them. They did however part company at the bottom of the street. Celia usually ran a few steps ahead in case anyone was looking out of their window.

As they walked together Celia's mind was also on Joe Slattery.

He'd been true to his word. He'd said nothing about herself and Lizzie. She'd seen him a few times coming home from work and passed him in the street once when the twins had had heavy chest colds and she'd been taking a jar of Vick Vapour Rub up to Maudie Kemp's. That night he'd looked exhausted but he'd nodded a greeting and she'd said how sorry she was his da was no better. He'd nodded again and then hunched his shoulders against the weather, his cap pulled down over his forehead. The collar of his jacket was turned up and he had a muffler around his neck, but he didn't even have an overcoat or a mackintosh, she'd thought sympathetically. She knew all his wages, apart from his fares, went into the housekeeping.

'Has Richie Kemp been at your house lately?' Lizzie asked, to take her mind off her worries.

'No. I can't *stand* the sight of him. He's such a . . . slimy creep! I told Da I wouldn't go out with him if he was the last feller on earth.'

'I bet that went down well,' Lizzie muttered.

Two bright spots of anger appeared on Celia's cheeks. 'The nerve of him, thinking that by coming creeping down to *ask* Da if he could *court* me, I would be like putty in his hands. That I'd do as Da told me, as if I was a kid like our Foxy. I ask you. Asking to "court" me in this day and age! It's a wonder he didn't say "walk out with me". *And* he only lives next door *and* I've known him since he was a snotty-nosed kid, and he was sly and sneaky then too. I *hate* him!'

'Well, I can't say I blame you. Anyone would have to be really hard up to go out with him!' Lizzie shuddered. 'It gives me goose bumps just thinking of him.'

Celia thought about that night, just after Christmas, when Richie Kemp, his hair plastered with brilliantine and in his good suit, had come to see Charlie Milton. Later, after Richie had gone, against all her da's persuasion, cajoling and finally demands bawled at her in a voice like that of a sergeant major, she'd refused point-blank and held her ground. Strangely enough it had been Billy, who was supposed to be Richie Kemp's mate, who had taken her side. In the end Da had given up. He deemed Richie to be decent enough but that was all. He wanted Celia to do better. She was still very young and in time she'd meet someone with far better prospects.

Maudie had taken great offence because she'd come round, on the bounce, and demanded to know from Mam just what was wrong with her son. Mam had been upset but Da just told her flatly that in his opinion his daughter was far too young to be courting anyone. But since then Maudie had never missed an opportunity to get a jibe or a snide remark in.

'I'd better run up now, Lizzie. I'll see you in the morning. Try and get some sleep,' she urged.

Lizzie nodded and slowed her pace so her friend got a good start.

Brigid was ready to leave as Lizzie entered the house.

'I've done the best I can, Lizzie, but the kids have the place destroyed.'

'I'll see to it all, Mam. Go on, get off now,' she said, not removing her coat, for the kitchen was far from warm.

'Right, where's our Emmet and Bernie?' she asked of Josie, who was trying with a small and almost bald brush and dustpan to sweep up the floor.

'Our Emmet's gone up to Mrs Westhoff's to run a few messages and our Bernie's in with me da.'

Lizzie nodded. 'Go and get her in here. Tell her she's to set the table and put the kettle on. What's for tea?'

'Herrings. Mam got some cheap from Herbert's. They're cooked an' in the oven ter keep warm. I've done some potatoes.'

Lizzie nodded. 'We'll have to keep our Joe and Fergal's warm.'

'It won't be very warm by the time they get in.'

'Our Joe won't notice, it's his school night. He'll be in and out in a flash.'

'Do yer think he'll pass, Lizzie?' Josie asked.

'Yes. And if he doesn't then it's all a fiddle because he's worked hard and he's cleverer than Billy Milton.'

'So then he'll get better money?' Josie persisted while sweeping up the old stained newspaper that covered the table and adding it to the fire.

'Yes. Josie, pull those clothes away from the fire, you'll have them scorched, and anyway it's almost as cold in here as it is in the street!'

Still with her coat on she went into the front room.

'Bernie, go and help our Josie. How are you, Da?' She bent to kiss the parchment-like cheek with its grizzled stubble.

Dessie's eyes seemed enormous in his shrunken face, but they lit up at the sight of his daughter.

'About the same, luv. Emmet's going ter call in at the dispensary for some more of that medicine. I don't know what's in it, they make it up themselves, but I do get a bit of relief from it.'

Lizzie smiled at him then she glanced around the room. She was already tired out but knew she'd have to start trying to get things to look decent in here and supervise the kids and then sit wrapped in an even older quilt than the one on the bed, and try to sleep in the old armchair.

She was so tired and anxious next day that she could hardly keep her eyes open. Three times Mr Henderson had told her off and twice she'd given the wrong change. At lunch time, when he shut himself up in his little office with his sandwiches and meat pie, his cup of tea and his copy of the *Daily Post*, without saying a word to Lizzie, Celia went and knocked on his door.

She was not well received for the intrusion but after she'd explained Lizzie's predicament his attitude softened a little and during the afternoon he'd told Lizzie to go and sort out the tins in the stockroom since the shop wasn't busy. The weather was terrible today, the rain falling as straight as stair rods; few people would be out.

She had wanted to run home in her dinner hour but Celia had stopped her. She shoved her back down on the straight-backed hard wooden chair.

'You're dead on your feet now, Lizzie. It's only a few more hours, you can stick it out. It won't help anyone if you go and collapse with exhaustion. Eat your dinner, I'll make us some tea.'

'I just want to *know*, Cee, that's all – and I couldn't eat a thing.' She looked without pleasure at the doorstep of bread with its scraping of dripping that Josie had made last night and wrapped up in a piece of much-used greaseproof paper.

'You'll *have* to eat something. Here, take mine.' Celia removed Lizzie's small parcel and handed her her own: two rounds of thinly cut white bread, buttered and filled with ham, wrapped in a clean neat parcel and with a red apple. Celia always gave her friend her apple or pear, it was the only fruit Lizzie got.

Worried though she was, Lizzie ate with relish. It was a long time since she'd had such nice soft white bread and tasty ham. After that she did feel better and somehow managed to get through the rest of the day.

In the late afternoon Celia did most of Lizzie's chores as well as her own, while young Alfie half-heartedly brushed the floor. Mr Henderson had even closed five minutes early, for they hadn't seen a single soul pass the shop window, let alone open the door, for the last hour and a half, and the torrential rain had eased but turned to sleet.

Celia opened her umbrella, slipped her arm through Lizzie's and together they hurried home.

Lizzie burst into the kitchen to find Brigid alone staring into the flames. There was no sign of any of the others and the place somehow seemed even more empty and devoid of comfort.

'Mam? Mam, did he come? What did he say?' Lizzie shook her mother gently by the shoulder.

Brigid turned towards her and Lizzie suddenly realised how

old and tired her mam looked, and how beaten down by hardship and anxiety.

'Sure, he came. A decent enough man for all the fine clothes and the posh voice and the dour face that he had on him.'

'What did he say?' Lizzie squatted down on her haunches and clutched her mam's arm.

'He examined your da thoroughly but he would have none of me staying in there with him while he did. Haven't we been man and wife nearly twenty-five years, I said, but it cut no ice with that feller. Then out he came into the lobby and, God forgive me, I kept him there. It's ashamed I was of the state of this poor bare kitchen.'

'Oh, never mind that, Mam, what did he *say*?'

Brigid sighed heavily. 'He asked your da and me a lot of questions and . . . it's the worst, Lizzie. I've been storming the gates of heaven with me prayers. It's a growth that's eating away your poor da's lungs. He used some fancy word. Car . . . car . . . something. I wasn't in my full mind to remember it.'

Lizzie was stricken. 'Isn't there anything he can do? Isn't there any medicine or even a stay in hospital or a sanatorium?'

'No, Lizzie, luv. Didn't I ask him those very things meself? He left some medicine and a note I've to take to the dispensary. They'll give us more and stronger stuff when we run out.'

'Did . . . did . . . he say how . . . long, Mam?' Lizzie felt cold. Icy cold.

Brigid shook her head. 'He hadn't an idea himself or so he said. It could be two months, it could be six or it could be tomorrow. All we can do, luv, is to keep him warm and comfortable.'

'Can I go and see him?' Her voice was cracked and hoarse with emotion.

'You can so, but he doesn't know, Lizzie. Himself, your man from Rodney Street, didn't think it wise to tell him.'

Before she went into the front room Lizzie leaned her head against the worn surface of the door. Everything seemed so unreal. The house was silent when normally you could hardly hear yourself speak. There was only her mam in the kitchen when usually it was crowded and this morning some strange, well-dressed and very learned man had come and cast the shadow of death over them all. She shuddered. She *had* to pull herself together. She *must not* break down and cry. She straightened her shoulders and went in.

Dessie was dozing and the firelight threw deep dark shadows into the corners of the unusually tidy room. She didn't want to switch on the light so she crept to his side and bent over him.

'Da. Da,' she said softly.

Dessie opened his eyes. 'Lizzie, is it that time already? It doesn't seem so long since that doctor was here.'

She sat down on the bed and took his hand and managed a weak smile.

'He said things were all right, didn't he, Da? He left you medicine.'

Dessie nodded. 'Rest and warmth and the right medicine. That's what I need. If he'd come sooner I'd have been on my feet now and maybe even back at work.'

'I know, Da,' she replied, fighting back the tears. 'We . . . we should have saved up sooner.' He had no idea that nearly all their possessions had been sold, he'd been confined to this room for so long.

'How were we to know that that's all it needed? Don't fret, girl. I said the same thing to yer mam.' He squeezed her hand tightly. 'Things will look up now, you see. I'll get back on my feet, our Joe will pass this exam and get promoted, and spring will be here soon. And do you know, Lizzie, in May it will be His Majesty's Silver Jubilee? Twenty-five years on the throne. There'll be something to celebrate then. I'll be back at work and we'll have a great do. Aye, I'm looking forward to spring, Lizzie.' His words ended in a bout of coughing and it was then that Lizzie's heart broke.

Only Joe and Fergal had been told; Brigid didn't consider the three young ones capable of either fully understanding or keeping their mouths shut. She'd wrapped herself in her heavy shawl and gone to work early. She'd call in and tell Father Minehan the news on her way.

When he'd stopped crying, Fergal had washed his face and gone over to collect Josie, Bernie and Emmet from Biddy Doyle's and Joe put on his jacket and cap. The house was oppressive, heavy with bleakness and suppressed sorrow. If he'd have had any spare money he'd have gone into one of the pubs for a drink, even though it was against the law, but he just didn't have any money. So he'd walk the streets in the wind and rain. Joe was used to that, at least.

As he closed the door behind him, a figure came hurrying towards him. Even with her head bent he knew it was Celia Milton.

She almost collided with him on the steps.

'Oh! It's . . . you!' She looked up into his face and even in the dim light saw the sorrow in his eyes. 'The specialist came then?'

He nodded.

'Lizzie told me he was coming. What . . . what did he say?'

Joe looked down at her. Wisps of silver-blonde hair had escaped from the scarf she wore over her head and in her eyes he saw true compassion.

'I can keep a secret, too. You never broke your promise to Lizzie and me, I won't break mine.'

He swallowed hard. 'Da . . . Da's dying. Some disease in his lungs . . .'

'Consumption?' Celia asked quietly, knowing that once that got out her father would make her give up her job and by hook or by crook he'd find them another house, for consumption carried with it a social stigma and that would be the last straw.

Joe shook his head. 'No. A growth that's spreading. There's nothing can be done. He doesn't know and neither do the kids.'

It was Celia's turn to shake her head. Oh poor Lizzie. Poor, poor Lizzie who idolised her da. It just wasn't fair at all. Without thinking she reached out and placed her hand on his arm. Then she felt him stiffen. She looked up again into his face.

'I'm sorry, I really am. Will you . . . will you tell Lizzie I said so? I know I'll see her in the morning, but things always seem worse at night.'

Joe was finding her words of comfort, spoken in that soft, sincere voice, hard to bear. His heart felt as though it were swelling in his chest with sorrow and she hadn't taken her hand from his arm. A crazy, overwhelming urge to draw her to him and hold her close and try to explain his despair surged through him but he fought it down. It was just the circumstances, shock, that's all.

'I'll tell her.' The words came out in a gruff voice which only added to his confusion. He hadn't meant to speak to her like that.

Before he'd had time to say anything more, she turned and pushed open the front door of their house and disappeared, leaving him with an even bigger void, a larger emptiness in his heart that he didn't understand at all.

Chapter Six

The build-up of excitement for the Silver Jubilee on 6 May had started at the beginning of March. It wasn't easy for most people to find extra money for anything, so events had to be planned for early.

There were two groups in Roscommon Street to organise the collection of money, no matter how small the amount, make out lists of the food, drink and street decorations, how much they would cost and what could be conjured up or improvised regarding decorating the street in a fit manner.

The group at the top end was inevitably headed by Maudie Kemp who, with her airs and graces and dictatorial manner, had managed to annoy everyone. At one stage there was so much arguing that it looked as if there would be no party at the top end of the street.

Annie Milton never liked to become involved in this sort of thing too much and she hated all the arguments. Organising and directing people was right up Maudie's street. Annie didn't mind helping in any other way, such as making cakes and sandwiches, lending out crockery and glasses, stitching red, white and blue pennants of material for bunting or painting pieces of cardboard in readiness for the slogans to be attached.

It was perhaps the one area of which Charlie actually approved and encouraged her involvement and activities. He certainly didn't want his wife to be seen to be running things or bossing people about. That might have lowered his standing and dignity, put him on the same level as Harry Kemp who'd given up trying to dominate and curb Maudie years ago. No, Annie would do her bit, pull her weight in her usual quiet, efficient way, he'd said to his neighbours and fellow drinkers in the Wynnstay.

The group at the other end of the street came under the auspices of Maggie Walsh, who had always wanted to be an organiser and fully intended to make the most of her chance. Normally, the task would have fallen to Brigid Slattery, she being more or less the most dominant character and the first occupant of the Catholic houses in the street, but Brigid, they all knew, had other things to worry about.

'Oh, aye, do yer remember, Biddy, how poor Brigid give Charlie Milton a great, thumping goalong on St Paddy's Day all them years ago?' Maggie reminded her neighbour and second in command in collecting the kitty. Biddy'd get blood out of a stone, Maggie always said. Biddy'd reply that with a husband as mean as hers, she'd had plenty of practice.

'Mind you, Charlie Milton was asking for it. Shockin', dead shockin' the names 'e called 'er, an' us, too, of course, but we've 'ad that for years, grown up with it, like. It was a wonder he wasn't struck down dead for calling the Pope all them terrible names: "The devil in skirts an' a bastard to boot," God help us all!' Both women crossed themselves and returned to the matter in hand.

'Poor Brigid has enough on her plate, Maggie, with Dessie and the kids. I don't know 'ow she copes.'

'The same as we all do, robbing Peter to pay Paul and going without. Many's the night we've both gone to bed hungry so the kids could eat, an' praying to God that we'd be able to scrape up the rent.'

'There's going without an' going without, Biddy. There's hardly a stick of furniture in that house now.'

Biddy nodded. 'That was to pay that posh doctor, and much good it seems to have done, an' all. With their Joe, Lizzie and Fergal's wages coming in an' the bit of cleaning she manages to get, I don't think there was any need to sell the whole damned lot.'

'Lizzie and Fergal don't earn a fortune, Biddy, and there's the rent and the gas and the lecky and coal. She's had to keep a fire going in that room all winter, an' the price of coal! Good coal mind, no slack. Slack's useless at giving out heat. And coke gives off fumes and he doesn't need any of that. The poor feller, he's not getting any better, not even with all the extra medicine. She said he sleeps a lot but then Mr High and Mighty from Rodney Street told her he needs plenty of rest. It doesn't look good for him at all.'

'Is she in the Burial Club?' Biddy asked, absent-mindedly drawing pound signs on the small piece of paper on which she was supposed to be making a list of food and drink.

'Of course she's in the flaming Burial Club, she runs it. 'Ave yer gone daft or something?'

'Oh, aye, I forgot. She gives it all to Father Minehan after the eleven o'clock Mass each week.'

'Aye, well in my opinion she's going to need her share soon.'

Biddy shook her head sadly. 'Ah, God luv 'im. A nicer feller yer couldn't meet in a month of Sundays.' Then she changed the subject. 'Now how much do you think they can afford each week? Sixpence? A shilling? One an' six?'

Maggie raised her eyes to the ceiling. 'Sometimes, Biddy Doyle, I think you need your bumps feeling. One and flaming six! Yer can feed the family for that! Don't forget there's the collection at Mass and the kids are always coming home asking for a ha'penny for the Mission or the Black Babies, and you want them to cough up most of the week's 'ousekeeping money. Tuppence or threepence, and try an' get a bit more out of the fellers.'

'I'll tell them it won't be much of a do if there's no ale, so they'd better start handing over the coppers now.'

Annie's head was spinning. Maudie had gone on and on about who was doing this, who was 'supposed' to be doing that but who hadn't and didn't seem in any hurry to do so either. She'd had more rows over this do than she'd had hot dinners. People just didn't seem to understand it was 'important'. Pride too was to be taken into account. They *had* to put on a better spread, have superior decorations than the residents further down the street but you just couldn't get people to 'commit' themselves these days.

What was also concerning was that there were some who had said that ninepence a week was on the high side. Hetty Robinson from number seven had said it was almost extortion and had asked were they going to throw in an outing in a charabanc too? The cheek of the woman, and her husband a First Class bedroom steward with Cunard. Good tips they got and she didn't even have him to feed very often either. They all had decent homes and the fellers were in work, most of the time. Of course there were men who didn't have good jobs like Harry and Richie. Charlie and Billy did, but when all was said and done they had to put on a good show.

'I can't see why there has to be two parties. Why can't we just have one? We're all celebrating the *King's* Jubilee after all, nothing else,' Celia stated calmly. She and Lizzie had discussed this often and had said they would try to get others to see reason. As it stood the whole situation was terribly fraught and could degenerate into chaos.

Maudie and Annie had looked at her totally dumbfounded, too taken aback to speak.

'Have I suddenly grown another head or something?' Celia asked.

'Cee, you can't mean sitting down and eating and drinking . . .' Annie's thin, wavering voice petered out.

'The thought! The very thought! And later on, singing and dancing with . . . with . . . THEM!' Maudie cried in horror.

The singing and dancing bit was what both Celia and Lizzie were more interested in. They'd hoped that after a few drinks and if things had gone well, there would be a chance for some intermingling that would go unnoticed, but obviously that wasn't going to happen.

She ducked her head. 'Sorry. It just seemed . . . easier somehow. I just thought we could all forget our differences just for a day. A couple of hours, really.'

She'd thought about Joe Slattery a lot lately and had been looking forward to the Jubilee party as a chance at least to hold a conversion with him. Lizzie had told her that he thought he'd done well in his exam and she hoped it was true. In her opinion he more than deserved it. He worked so hard at Laird's, and then there was all that travelling and when he got home he either went to night school or studied. How he managed to concentrate she didn't know for bedlam seemed to reign at all times, according to Lizzie, and by the thinness of the walls she knew her friend spoke the truth.

Lizzie had let the fire in the hearth die down and she'd even opened the window a little.

'It's much warmer out now, Da. A bit of fresh air in here might do you good,' she said cheerfully. Her optimism was false though. It broke her heart every time she looked at him. He'd become almost a skeleton and the skin, stretched tightly over the bones of his face, looked translucent. If only God spared him until the Jubilee, then he'd be happy, she thought. It was all he ever talked about, when he wasn't asleep.

'Aye, it'll soon be the sixth of May. How are all the arrangements for the do going?'

'Great, Da. Mrs Walsh and Mrs Doyle have worked wonders. Paddy McRory from the Elephant has promised to sell them a barrel of beer with a bit knocked off, providing the fellers call in for a quick one after the morning Mass.'

The day was to start with church services all over the city.

He managed a grin that was a death's-head grimace. 'Good man, McRory. Let's hope they make it back for the party then?'

'They better had or Mrs Walsh and Mrs Doyle will be round

there to crown Paddy McRory with his barrel of cheap ale!'

Dessie's expression changed and he looked anxiously up into her face. 'How's yer mam coping, Lizzie? I want the truth now.'

'Da, I've told you, she's great. She does have too much on her plate to be organising street parties, but she's determined to make our Josie and Bernie new frocks for the day. She got some gingham in the market that was going cheap because it was the end of a roll. And I'll have a new blouse, I've seen it in Blacklers. It doesn't cost a fortune and I've been managing to save. Mam's been great, she's let me keep some of my wages.' She didn't say that insisting on letting her keep a shilling a week meant when her mam went cleaning in town she walked all the way there and back and by the time she got home her face was grey from exhaustion.

'Oh, I'll be out there to see you all. I'll just have enough strength by then, please God, to sit in a chair and watch the goings-on.' Dessie's eyes were filled with a new light.

Lizzie's heart turned over. He knows, she thought. He knows! Oh, please God, don't take him before the Jubilee? she prayed as she looked down at him and smiled and managed to say chirpily, 'Of course you will, Da.'

The morning of 6 May dawned brightly. The rays of the rising sun streaked the pale-blue cloudless sky with fingers of gold and silver. As it edged higher in the sky the golden rays spread across the silent city. It splashed the grey waters of the Mersey with gold and clearly etched the silhouettes of the Liver Birds against the sky. It touched the yards of red, white and blue pennants that were strung across the streets, both narrow and broad, and the Union Jacks that were hung out of bedroom windows.

In the silent, peaceful morning air, at the top end of Roscommon Street the elaborate decorations looked magnificent. Maudie's nagging and bullying had produced great results.

Crepe paper flowers in wire baskets hung from the arms of the streetlamps. The lamps themselves were bound with strips of red, white and blue paper, making them look like Maypoles or huge sticks of seaside rock. Patriotic slogans, such as 'GOD SAVE THE KING' and 'GOD BLESS THEIR MAJESTIES' and even 'GEORGE V, DEFENDER OF THE FAITH' (the latter a sectarian dig at their neighbours), had been affixed to walls and windows, the letters made painstakingly in silver foil and glued to pieces of board painted black, which made the lettering stand out.

In an almost continuous line down the centre of the cobbled street – broken only by a gap of two feet in the middle – tables and trestles were laid out. As yet they were uncovered and bereft of food and coloured paper decorations. All that would come later on, after everyone had attended their various church services.

Annie had been up early, just after dawn in fact, as had Celia The sandwiches, fairy cakes and butterfly cakes, sprinkled on the top with icing sugar, and the big Victoria sponge with jam and butter cream in the middle had all spent the night in the cool, dark, mesh-fronted food press in the scullery, covered with damp tea towels. The cups, plates, glasses and cutlery were laid out in piles on the dresser in the kitchen. Two large spotlessly clean and crisp white sheets, which would act as tablecloths, were folded and placed on the top of the food press. Celia had laid the table for breakfast and they sat down with a cup of tea.

They'd both worked until after midnight so things would appear to be organised this morning. But there would be no deviation from their usual morning routine. Neither of them wanted Charlie to start the day off in a bad mood.

'That frock really suits you, Cee,' Annie smiled at her daughter who did indeed look very pretty in the cornflower-blue cotton dress that was edged with rows of white rickrack braid. The colour enhanced the blue of Celia's eyes.

'So do you, Mam. You'll knock the eyes out of her next door.'

Annie looked at her sharply and Celia realised that she'd unconsciously used a saying of Lizzie's, an 'Irishism', as Lizzie called them.

'That's an odd way of putting it, Cee.'

Celia appeared to be thinking about it. 'I suppose it is,' she mused. 'I must have heard someone use it in the shop. But anyway, she'll be green with envy.'

Annie smiled a little sadly. She wished she felt as well as she looked and besides, she really had not thought of Maudie when her nice pale pink grosgrain costume and cream crepe-de-Chine blouse had been bought. It had been Charlie who'd insisted on buying it. She thought it was just too grand. It was more suitable for a wedding, she thought. She looked again at her daughter and sighed. Celia was far too young to be contemplating marriage so the outfit would be well worn out by then. Hadn't she flatly refused to go out with Richie, and for that Annie was grateful although she'd said nothing. She disliked the lad. Marriage was no bed of roses either, as she could testify, unless you got a kind, considerate, even-tempered man like poor Mr Slattery next door. She'd heard that he wasn't getting any better and sometimes she wished she could stop her next-door neighbour in the street and enquire about him, offer sympathy or help as any normal person in any normal street would do. But this wasn't a 'normal' street. Maybe at some stage in the day she could have a surreptitious word with the woman, she determined with an unaccustomed flash of defiance.

Things next door were as chaotic as usual. Brigid, in a grey dress that had folds of grey crepe de Chine draped across the front and had been borrowed from Tessie Mulhinney, who was better off than most of them, still had curling papers in her hair as she scraped Bernie's mass of curls up with a length of pink ribbon, which matched the pink-and-white gingham dress of which she was rather proud. She'd had to do both dresses by hand as no-one had a sewing machine, often in poor light and always when she was tired. Lizzie, in the pale apple-green blouse with the embroidery on the collar and down the front, worn with a dark green skirt, looked very smart as she tried to cope with Josie's hair.

They looked like twins in those dresses, Brigid mused. She thought of Maudie Kemp's twins and she looked across at Emmet, sitting at the table, dressed in his best trousers, shirt and the dark grey waistcoat she'd made with a bit of a remnant of gaberdine she'd picked up in Paddy's market. He hated it and had said so and had earned himself a sharp dig in the ribs from Lizzie for his pains, plus the admonition not to be so ungrateful. Brigid had warned him severely that she would kill him with her own two hands if he misbehaved and spoiled the day that was in it, and Lizzie had grinned at the 'Irishism'. Mam's Cork accent hadn't changed in the thirty years she'd lived in Liverpool.

'Mam, I think it's about time you took all those things out of your hair,' Joe remarked. He was wearing his navy serge suit with a white shirt and a red tie. Good-humouredly he'd cuffed Fergal over the head when his brother had remarked that he looked like part of the street decorations with the red, white and blue.

'You get off, the lot of you. You're all decent enough now. I'll do me hair, see yer da and follow on. I won't be late. Save me a space in the pew and don't go sitting at the back hoping you won't get noticed. Today I want us all to be noticed,' she said firmly, smoothing down the folds of the borrowed dress.

Thankfully the small party left and Brigid dragged out the curling papers in haste and brushed her hair, which immediately fluffed and frizzed up until it looked like a halo.

'Holy Mother, would you look at the cut of it! All that flaming agony like it was a pillow of nails that I had me head rested on all night, and it finishes up looking like a furze bush,' she muttered as she jammed on the grey-and-white wide-brimmed hat, also lent by Tessie Mulhinney, as she couldn't go into the House of God with her head uncovered and to wear her shawl would ruin the effect of the dress that had been bought for the wedding of the eldest of the Mulhinney girls and which she'd promised not to get destroyed.

She went into the front room and smiled sadly at her frail

husband, wishing he could accompany her.

Dessie turned to look at her.

'You . . . look . . . like . . . a . . . real . . . lady . . . with . . . the . . . hat, luv.' He got the words out with great difficulty but she saw love and admiration in his eyes, and for a second before her was the face of the young, handsome Dessie Slattery who'd turned to face his dark-haired, fresh-cheeked colleen of a bride.

'Ah, don't be giving me that owld flannel, Dessie Slattery! Me that's been your wife these twenty years and longer.' She smiled, but her heart was heavy, so very heavy.

'I'm off to Mass now and when I get back it'll be sleeves rolled up and down to work. But once the tables are set out, then our Joe and Fergal will get you outside. Are you sure you'll be able for it? Sitting on just a chair?'

He nodded and she bent and kissed him gently, then rested her cheek against his for a few seconds. In June, on the Feast of Corpus Christi, it would be their jubilee, their silver wedding anniversary, but she knew in her heart that that was one jubilee he'd not see and it was such a heavy cross to bear.

Chapter Seven

There was a holiday feeling in the air. At Mass Father Minehan had spoken at length about the good Christian man who was their sovereign and his virtuous and much-revered wife, Queen Mary. They were fortunate indeed that the hand that guided the tiller of the Ship of State was that of the 'Sailor King'. A good husband and father who ruled over not only a peaceful country but a united and loving family as well.

He'd paused for a minute and everyone knew he was reminding them of old King Edward and his string of mistresses. He'd then gone on with prayers for the King and Queen. Edward, Prince of Wales. Albert, Duke of York, and his Duchess, Elizabeth of Glamis, Mary, the Princess Royal, and the rest of the Royal Family.

Joe and Fergal walked home from church with Jimmy Kelly and Bryan Shea. Both were due to leave school that summer and were starting now to keep their eyes and ears open for an opportunity, a chance of work.

'What's it like working over there?' Jimmy asked, trying to hide his admiration for the Slattery brothers' experience of the world.

'Flaming awful in the winter and you spend all your time running round making cans of tea and trying to keep out of the bosses' way while you're at it,' Fergal replied.

'I know you start like that, but you can get on, like, can't yer, Joe?' Bryan put in.

'If you know someone, a skilled man, like, and get to be mates or get on the right side of the blockerman,' Joe grinned. 'We've got one called "Morphia". He comes up to you and asks if you've nearly finished that job and if you say, "Yes," he'll say, "Good, 'cos I've got more for yer."'

They all laughed and then Joe became serious again.

'If they catch you skiving, smoking or going over the wall – that's being out of the yard in working hours – then you get either the DCM or the OBE.'

Both the younger lads looked at Joe bemused.

'Sounds like a medal or something,' Jimmy said.

'Well, it's flaming well not,' Fergal answered.

"DCM – Don't Come Monday – and OBE – Old Brown Envelope, your wages,' Joe grinned at them again.

'Oh, yer, I see,' Jimmy said, nodding seriously.

'I'm supposed to be working on the *Salmon*, a submarine,' Fergal informed them. 'But all I do is make tea and be the gofer.'

Neither Jimmy nor Bryan needed to have this explained to him.

'And I'm welding on the *Fearless*, that's a destroyer.'

'They're making an awful lot of navy ships,' Jimmy said thoughtfully. The future prospects of a job seemed quite good.

'Only to keep up with the Germans. That Hitler feller is boasting they'll have the biggest fleet in the world soon, an' we can't have that, can we? Come on, let's get a move on. It's a holiday,' Joe reminded them.

When they arrived home the lads took off their ties and jackets and Brigid removed her cumbersome, troublesome hat.

'Isn't it a heart-scald anyway?' she said thankfully as she placed it with care on the overmantel, out of harm's way. 'It was desperate. Wasn't I in fear and dread in case it fell off while I had me head back to receive Communion or got crushed as we came out of church, and now I've a headache coming on. I don't know how the Quality put up with it all, and the size of some of the hats *they* wear would have you destroyed altogether.'

Lizzie and her younger sisters were despatched to get the food out of the press and on to the tables outside while Brigid had a hasty cup of tea and looked in on her husband, who was asleep.

'They'll have the tables covered with that white paper by now but keep them bits of cloth over them plates or everything will be ate by the flies. And Lizzie, try and see what herself next door is putting on their tables,' Brigid instructed.

'Joe, will you go and see Greg Doyle, just in case the pair of you can't manage? We'll be ready to get yer da out in about an hour.'

Joe looked at her with concern. 'Mam, do you think it's wise to take him from his bed and put him in a chair?'

Brigid shook her head sadly. 'No it is not, but isn't he entitled to see the fun for a while? Hasn't he lived in the hope of seeing this day for months now? We'll bring him in as soon as he tires.'

'Fergal and Greg can give me a hand to turn the bed around so he can still see out through the window, though he'll not get much sleep,' Joe replied quietly, the edge of brightness gone from the day with his mam's words.

The Robinsons at the top end of the street had a piano which had been manhandled out on to the pavement. At the bottom end Dermot Brophy had an old fiddle and Maurice 'Morrie' Reilly had a small hand accordion, known as a squeeze-box. Somewhat discordantly, with the fiddle and squeeze-box a few bars ahead, all three instruments started the whole thing off with the National Anthem.

Then everyone sat down to eat and drink and hands were slapped and warnings about 'eating like a pig' and 'making a show of us' came thick and fast but had little effect. For the kids it was heaven. They hardly ever had cake or lemonade. It was worth sitting for hours listening to Father Minehan going on and on about the King.

The noise level, low at first, rose higher and higher as time went on, and Maudie Kemp looked around her smugly. It was all a great success. The decorations were tasteful and plentiful. They had sandwiches, meat pies, fairy and butterfly cakes, jelly and

Victoria sponge cake, tea for the grown-ups, and bottled lemonade and ginger pop for the kids.

At the top end of the Catholic table, she noted, there seemed hardly anything to compare with their tables. And they were covered in sheets of white paper, not proper cloths, and with no decorations on them either. They also had only an old fiddle and squeeze-box, not a piano. Yes, she had every reason to pat herself on the back, but as yet no one had even had the decency to thank her for all her hard work. That was the only fly in the ointment.

The afternoon wore on and when the Kelly, Shea, Doyle and Walsh menfolk returned from the promised 'swift pint' at the Elephant, the barrel of beer was broached. Bottles of cheap sherry and some home-made 'wine' were also produced for the women, and after Brigid had taken one sip, she declared it was as good a drop of poitín as she'd had since her last visit home fifteen years ago and that there'd been no duty paid on it for sure.

Eventually, the tables were taken in and the women gossiped and the men drank and discussed the state of the country, the state of Europe, their football teams and then told jokes.

Dessie was holding up well, Brigid thought. The bit of excitement had bucked him up. He sat swathed in quilts and supported with cushions and his eyes darted everywhere, missing nothing. He'd refused any food but when Gerry Walsh offered him a glass of 'the good stuff' he'd accepted it.

'That'll do yer good, Dessie. Better than that medicine them doctors keep fillin' yer up with. Geerrit down yer, lad.'

'Aye, fill yer boots,' Bernie Doyle added.

A little way away the women were grouped.

'Did you hear on the wireless the goings-on in London?' Tessie Mulhinney asked, knowing full well she was the only one who owned a wireless set.

'We'd have to have the ears of an elephant to do that,' Maggie Walsh answered tartly. Trust Tessie to go showing off.

'Well, the crowds were in the streets by the thousands and their

Majesties rode in an open carriage to Westminster Abbey. The King in a fancy uniform, I can't remember the word they used for it, a marshal but something to do with a field as well, I think.'

'Sounds as though *she* needs the ears of an elephant,' Biddy muttered.

'Maybe she's had too many glasses of sherry,' Mary Kelly added.

Tessie ignored them. 'The Queen, God bless her, was all in white, they said, with a choker of five rows of pearls set with diamonds an' all kinds of jewels. And she had on a white toque. I think them hats are so smart even if the young madams these days say they're old-fashioned. Dignified. Aye, that's how I'd describe them. Classy an' dignified.'

'You should tell that to that Maudie Kemp up the street. The thing she had on her head looked like a pudding basin with the tail feathers of a crow stuck on it,' Maggie Walsh commented acidly.

'And then there was the dog.' Tessie was not to be turned from her few minutes of glory.

'What dog would that be?' Brigid asked.

'Well, it seems there was a mongrel of some sort that got in amongst the soldiers and then got under the royal carriage and couldn't be shifted by anyone. Went the whole way to the Abbey it did, trotting under the royal carriage. The Jubilee Dog they were calling it on the wireless!'

Brigid decided it was time the subject was changed for she could see a coldness developing towards the garrulous Tessie and, after all, she'd been good enough to loan her the outfit.

'Doesn't your one from next door to me look as if she's after going to a posh wedding in that suit?'

'Well so would we, wouldn't we, Brigid, if we was married to a foreman boilermaker?'

'Ah, she's not a bad little woman – for a Protestant. She wouldn't say boo to a goose.'

'I wouldn't be wed to him for a big clock! The stuck-up owld bully. He has the whole family terrified of him.'

'Well, you're not terrified of him, Brigid, are yer, not after the belt you gave him?'

'Ah, now don't be going on about that, it was years ago.' Brigid jerked her head in Dessie's direction as a sign that she didn't want him upset. Lizzie was beside him.

Celia Milton was sitting on their doorstep, which was as close as she'd managed to get to her friend all day. Cautiously, they'd held a very stilted conversation which had come to a halt when Lizzie caught the glimpse of disapproval in Dessie's eye as he asked her to fetch Joe to take him back in. But Dessie was beyond saying anything about their conversation. Despite the drink, the pain was almost unbearable now and he needed more medicine to make him sleep. He was exhausted but it had been a great day and he'd *known* he'd have the strength to enjoy it.

The May evening wore on and the first bright star appeared in the gathering dusk. At the bottom end of the street there was a great singsong and a good deal of jigging going on to the music of the fiddle and squeeze-box, and loud renderings of popular songs and more sedate dancing at the other end.

Richie Kemp had had far too much to drink according to his mother, who had gone in search of her husband to tell him to go and sort out his son. She found Harry leaning on the top of the piano, glass in hand, and in virtually the same state as his son.

'It's a fine flaming example you're setting, Harry Kemp!' she snapped.

He grinned foolishly at her.

'It's a cele . . . cele . . . a great do,' he replied.

'Well, it might be for some!' Maudie's lips snapped together like a steel trap and she stormed off. After all the work she'd put in, she was going to have two drunks on her hands and wouldn't *that* look nice. It would be remembered and remarked on for weeks to come.

Celia had gone in to get a cardigan as it was getting nippy now and on her way out she almost fell over Richie, who was sitting on the step but who got to his feet unsteadily.

She drew back from him as the smell of beer hit her full in the face.

'Richie Kemp, you're drunk! You stink of ale!'

'I'm only a bit tipsy. You should see me when I'm *really* drunk,' he boasted. 'I can hold me ale. Me da can't and Mam's gorra cob on with the pair of us.'

'I don't blame her.'

He leered at her. 'Won't you change your mind and let me take you out, Cee?'

'Don't you mean "court me"? Isn't that what you said to Da? Well, the answer's still the same. No. Now shift yourself out of my way.'

'Only if you give us a quick kiss, Cee. No one will notice.'

'I'd sooner kiss a—' She was about to say 'pig' but he lurched forward, grabbed her and pressed his moist, beery mouth on hers.

She pulled away and gave him a violent shove as anger surged in her. How dare he? How dare he, and in public? She raised her hand and slapped him hard across the face. So hard that those closest to them turned around, including Joe who had just come out of their house after seeing his father settled and comfortable in bed.

'Is he annoying you?' Joe demanded.

'Mind yer own bloody business, you . . . you bloody cogger!' Richie slurred.

It was the other cheek this time that took the full force of Celia's hand and Richie staggered backwards.

'No, he is not annoying me. He will *never* annoy me! I just hate him!' Celia answered vehemently.

Charlie and Maudie were immediately on the scene and Bill Taylor from number five had crossed the street.

Joe turned away. A wave of fury swept over him. That creep. That drunken slimy creep. How dare Richie Kemp lay a finger on her, and yet . . . yet why should it bother him so much? His thoughts returned to his da and Lizzie. He had been on his way to ask her to keep nipping in to check on Da, as he would himself.

The incident was glossed over by Maudie, who apologised profusely for her son, but Charlie was as annoyed as Celia.

'How dare he, the drunkard?' Charlie shouted. 'I've a good mind to teach him a lesson myself.'

Maudie's expression was grim. Oh, she'd make him suffer in the morning, by God she would – and Harry as well. If he'd stayed sober this wouldn't have happened. He would have taken his son by the scruff of the neck, belted him and then made him apologise to the girl, that's what she'd have made him do if he'd been sober.

The sudden and unexpected appearance of the Reverend James Gore caused her to change her expression and she thanked God he hadn't appeared five minutes earlier. He was visiting as many of his parishioners as was possible on this splendid day, he informed them. It was a little too quiet at the Vicarage, he was a confirmed bachelor and his housekeeper, Mrs Henderson, had gone to join her family celebrations.

He was offered a drink but politely refused and Annie secretly thought his presence rather put the damper on things as she watched him moving between the groups of people who immediately stopped laughing and singing and listened respectfully to whatever he was saying to them. But at least now there would be no more arguments to spoil the day.

The noise and the stepdancing and jigging at the other end of the street was still going strong and Lizzie, breathless and pink-cheeked, eventually tore herself away to go to get a drink.

'Here, Lizzie, have some of this, girl,' Biddy called out.

'If I take a drop of that it'd burn the throat off me. No thanks. Plain water will do for me.'

She met Joe coming down the street.

'Da's in bed and I think he'll sleep,' Joe said. 'He's exhausted

– he stuck it out far longer than I thought he would – but will you keep an eye on him?'

'Of course. I've had the feet danced off me. I'm worn out, but Mam's having the time of her life so let's let her have a bit of fun for a change.'

Joe managed a smile that didn't convince his sister.

'What's up with your face?'

'Nothing. I'm just a bit concerned about Da, that's all.'

Lizzie shrugged and went indoors. Something had upset Joe. She sat and drank two cups of water in the kitchen. Then she tidied her hair before going to the privy and letting herself out by the back yard door. She'd just walk slowly up the jigger and back into the street, to get her breath and calm down. She might even catch a glimpse of Celia and maybe get a few words with her. Everyone was pretty well occupied now. She wondered if Cee had been having her toes crushed flat by someone with a pair of size-ten boots like she had.

As she turned the corner and passed the first couple of houses, which were empty, she saw with surprise that the vicar from Celia's church was there. Well, that would put the mockers on things at this end all right, she thought. Just imagine if Father Minehan put in an appearance and old Mr Brophy going hell for leather on the fiddle and Mr Reilly on the squeeze-box. Most of the men were tipsy, to put it mildly, and Biddy Doyle, thanks to the home-made 'wine', with her skirt above her knees, was jigging like a thing possessed to 'The Mason's Apron' as though she were fourteen instead of well turned forty. Then to her amazement Lizzie caught sight of the white clerical collar, the long black soutane, and the dark biretta-covered head of their parish priest. He too was obviously 'doing the rounds' on exactly the same pretext as the vicar.

'I see that feller of yours has turned up. A feller in a frock. Is he a shirt-lifter or what?'

Lizzie turned. It was Richie Kemp and he stank of ale.

'Well, at least he's joining in, not like that old misery of yours!' she retorted, for Father Minehan had a glass in his hand, half-filled with home-made 'wine'.

Richie laughed nastily. 'You lot can do anything you like and then go and confess to him and it's all forgotten. You can do it again and again and again. So, I'll give you something to tell him about.'

His words were slurred and she was about to slap his face when he grabbed her and tried not only to kiss her, but to get his hand down the front of her blouse.

She started to scream and kick, her fingernails raking the side of his face, drawing blood.

'You bitch! You bloody bitch!' he yelled, drawing back and raising his arm threateningly.

The blow didn't come, for as Lizzie, white and trembling with shock, stepped back, Joe caught Richie, swung him round and hit him hard on the chin and then in the solar plexus.

Instantly bedlam ensued. Maudie screamed at Harry to *do* something, demanding if he was going to stand there and let his son be beaten to a pulp by that lout.

Brigid stormed up to Maudie and demanded to know what Maudie's son had done to her daughter and if she wouldn't tell her, then she'd get the same treatment as Brigid had meted out to Charlie Milton all those years ago.

Her words brought a flood of anger to Charlie's face and Celia, heedless of anyone's notice, had her arm around Lizzie and Lizzie was crying and clinging to her friend.

It was the combined efforts of the Reverend James Gore and Father Minehan that parted the protagonists.

Richie was barely able to stand and the vicar held him up, the disgust and anger clear in his expression.

'Father, he molested our Lizzie. He was trying to rip the blouse off her. What else was I supposed to do?' Joe demanded, still furious.

'Calm down, Joe. Calm down, he's drunk.'

'Drunk is it? Seventeen and drunk! And what were *they* doing to let him get like that?' Brigid demanded. 'Jaysus! Beg pardon, Father, but I'm banjaxed with it all. Isn't his old feller just as drunk? Well, shouldn't someone go up for the scuffers?'

'I don't think that will be necessary, madam. Let's not let the situation get out of hand entirely,' James Gore said sharply.

'So, it's all right for him to get blind drunk and force himself on young, helpless Catholic girls, is it?' Joe snapped back.

'Now, Joe, calm down.'

'Like hell I will, Father, and I'm not begging your pardon either.'

'No manners even for that son of Satan who leads you to worship plaster idols. I saw him drinking spirits not two minutes ago,' Charlie Milton sneered. He'd had a few pints himself and after Richie Kemp's attempt to force his attentions on Celia he couldn't care less about the lad being dragged off by the police. It was Joe Slattery and the priest that he violently objected to.

'I'll thank you to remember that the Father here is a man of God, like myself, and as such deserves the respect of everyone here,' Mr Gore said loudly and in a tone that brooked no dissent. 'You are a disgrace to your church, Charles Milton.' The vicar's face was white as he turned to Maudie and Harry Kemp and thrust their son at them. 'As is your son, Mrs Kemp. You, as his parents, have the responsibility to see that at his age he doesn't get into this disgusting state, but I realise now that he gets no example from his father. I don't object to a small amount of drink on a special occasion such as this, although the Law states he must be twenty-one before he can be served liquor. All things in moderation is my motto.'

Maudie wished the floor would open up and swallow her. A public ticking-off of her son, husband and herself by the vicar in front of the whole street *and* a Catholic priest, and all because Harry wasn't strong enough to exert control over their son. She'd never been so humiliated in her entire life.

She shoved Richie bodily into their house and dragged Harry in behind her. 'Get in that house the pair of you!' she screeched and slammed the front door shut.

'Thank you, Reverend. I'm only sorry that this celebration of a good man's twenty-five years on the throne had to end like this,' Father Minehan replied with dignity, although there was an edge of coldness to his voice.

'Brigid, I'd take your daughter in now, she's had a nasty experience,' he advised.

'The whole lot of them is a "nasty experience" that we have to put up with every day, Father,' Biddy Doyle said loudly.

The priest rounded on her. 'I think you should apologise for those words, Mrs Doyle. They are uncalled for and you are in a shameful condition for a Catholic wife and mother. Bernard, take her home,' he thundered in the voice of the pulpit.

Brigid turned in time to see Lizzie, assisted by Celia Milton, going up the steps of the house. The light of battle came again into her eyes. The Jubilee celebrations for Roscommon Street might be over now all through the fault of that Richie Kemp and his parents, but she was having no one from next door in her house.

She pushed her way though the small crowd but before she reached her own doorstep Celia came flying back out.

'Sir! Your Reverence! Father! Come quick! Lizzie said to come quickly! It's Mr Slattery. We think he's . . . dead!'

Brigid froze and clapped a hand over her mouth. The priest gathered up the skirt of his soutane and rushed towards the doorway, followed by Joe and Fergal. The group of stunned and startled people from both ends of the street parted to let them through.

Chapter Eight

Lizzie was inconsolable. She couldn't believe it. She'd been so upset by Richie Kemp's attack on her that as Celia had led her towards the house all she could feel was sickening disgust at the moistness of the mouth, reeking of ale, that had covered hers, and the sense of violation as his sweaty hand had closed roughly over her breast.

Celia had taken her into the kitchen, sat her down and got a cup of water from the scullery. She'd been half aware of the shouting and fighting in the street and had thought immediately of her da. They'd wake him up and it would upset him terribly, for the bed had been turned around to face the open window. Frantically she'd pushed Celia's comforting arms away.

'Da. I've got to see if Da's all right, with all that noise outside,' she'd cried.

She'd been relieved by the seemingly sleeping figure of her father but when she'd taken hold of his hand, hoping it would make her feel better, it had been cold. Stone-cold. Her scream of anguish had sent Celia rushing in and then she pleaded, sobbing, for Celia to get Mam and Father Minehan quickly. The noise outside had stopped and she'd fallen to her knees and held her da's hand to her cheek until the priest had prised her fingers apart and gently raised her up and turned her towards her mother.

All the family – Josie and Bernie holding on to each other and crying; Joe, his face set in lines of anguish, holding Emmet tightly to him; Fergal clutching the bedpost for support – had gathered around the bed as Father Minehan gave Dessie Slattery the sacrament of Extreme Unction, the Last Rites, even though his soul had departed from his body and ascended, as they all believed, to another and better world. Lizzie sobbed in Brigid's arms the whole time.

Brigid herself was white and shaken. The anger at Richie Kemp and Celia Milton had drained away when Celia had come running out of the house. She was totally heedless of what Lizzie's tears were doing to the borrowed dress, she, too, was stunned. Oh, she knew he was dying. She expected it and had tried to prepare herself, telling herself she'd be calm because he'd be out of his pain, but she hadn't expected it to happen like this. It was so sudden. She'd been so pleased and happy at the way he'd held up and enjoyed the day.

'Hush now, alannah, hush,' she whispered over and over like a gramophone record to her heartbroken daughter.

Lizzie looked up. 'Oh, Mam, Mam, I . . . left him. I was going out again to dance and enjoy myself and he died alone, Mam. He died alone and I'll never forgive myself for that.'

Brigid made a huge effort to pull herself together. They were all looking to her now for comfort and guidance.

'Lizzie, child, stop all this nonsense. He wasn't alone. God and all His holy angels were with him. Can't you tell by the look on his face. He was happy, child.'

Joe, who felt as if he had been hit by a block of cement, was trying to remain calm, mainly because of the effect Lizzie's guilt and tears were having on Emmet and his two younger sisters. He *had* to stop it all degenerating into mass hysteria.

'Lizzie, he died in his sleep. He'd had a . . . great day. I'd only just left him.'

'But you asked me to look in on him and I didn't, I *didn't*.'

'Lizzie, stop blaming yourself. There was nothing anyone could have done.'

Father Minehan was also anxious to avoid hysteria. 'Lizzie,

your mother and Joe are right. He wasn't alone, he was happy to go and now he's past all pain. You've nothing to feel guilty about. Why shouldn't a young girl enjoy herself at a national celebration?' He moved quickly on for it hadn't been much of a celebration for the poor girl, he thought angrily. 'It's not for him that we grieve, it's for ourselves, those he left behind, but we must comfort ourselves that we'll all see him again.' He motioned and they all kneeled as he began the Rosary.

When Father Minehan had gone, the routine, mundane matters had to be attended to. Mrs Tiernan from Dorrington Street had been summoned from that street party to lay Dessie out. Between them Brigid and Joe got the younger ones, Fergal included, to bed after giving them a cup of hot sweet tea and half an aspirin each.

After Mrs Tiernan had left, Tessie and Maggie came over with white sheets which they pinned on the walls. Tessie had brought four candles, four brass candlesticks and a brass crucifix. The three women worked in silence until everything was to their satisfaction.

'He looks well now,' Maggie said.

'He'll look even more . . . dignified once Mr Coyne and those fellers of his have been round tomorrow. I'd not let the neighbours in until they've been, Brigid,' Tessie advised. He *would* look more dignified and decent in a coffin.

'Where would I be without you both? Tessie, would you look at the state of your good dress. I'm sorry but . . .' She indicated the stains left by Lizzie's tears.

'For the love of God, Brigid Slattery, don't be worrying about an owld dress at a time like this.'

'Go on in the kitchen now to Joe and Lizzie, it's past one o'clock. We'll say a few decades and pray for a bit, then see ourselves out,' Maggie instructed. Both she and Tessie thought with relief that at least Brigid had enough money to give the poor man a decent burial.

Lizzie was still sobbing quietly and Joe was sitting at the table, his head in his hands. The priest's words were true, he thought.

They were only grieving for themselves, but that didn't make it any easier to bear. As his mother came into the room, he got up.

'Come on, Mam, sit down and have this.' He pulled the teapot and a mug towards him but Brigid shook her head.

She sank wearily down into the armchair by the range. 'No, lad. Aren't I awash with the stuff already? I feel as though I've had gallons of it. I knew. I knew in my heart that it couldn't be much longer and I wouldn't wish him back here for the pain he had in it, but it doesn't make it any easier. Tessie Mulhinney and Maggie Walsh have been saints, so they have, God bless them.'

'Aye, and so would Mrs Doyle had she been her usual self,' Joe added, remembering for the first time in hours the scene that had ended the Jubilee party.

Brigid remembered too. Even in her dazed state she recalled Lizzie, supported by Celia Milton, coming into the house.

'Are you still destroyed at what that . . . that drunken pig did to you, luv?'

Lizzie shook her head, her eyes red and swollen. All thoughts of Richie Kemp had gone from her mind, blanked out by the memory of seeing her father lying so pale and still.

'Merciful God, at least that's something. But what was that bold rossie from next door doing in here?'

Lizzie was so tired of all the pretence, she looked across at Joe, who nodded briefly.

'Mam,' she began tiredly and with a waver in her voice, 'Celia Milton and me have been friends for . . . for ages. Since we were ten. She got me my job. She's nice. She's kind and generous and we made a rule never to talk about religion. That's why I turned to her after . . . what *he* did. That's why she brought me into the house.'

Joe instantly intervened before Brigid could speak. 'Mam, don't go upsetting yourself any further. It's not the girl's fault that she's got an arrogant bully for a da and I've heard you say her mother wasn't a bad little woman. Those were the very words you used.'

'But she's still a Protestant, and haven't we had to put up with him making a mock and a jeer of us all for years?'

'I know, but their vicar gave the whole lot of them a right telling-off, him next door included. If the clergy can at least be civil to one another, why can't our Lizzie and Celia Milton be friends?'

It was all too much for Brigid. She shuddered to think about what would happen if the two girls were seen walking arm in arm up the street, laughing and talking. But Lizzie wouldn't be laughing for a long time. Nor would anyone in this family. She sighed heavily.

'Well, as long as it's kept a secret,' she conceded.

Lizzie looked thankfully at her brother as Brigid got up.

'I'm after going to try to sleep now. Lizzie, come on up with me. Joe, leave all this and get to bed.'

Joe nodded and rose, wondering what was going on next door. Despite all the Slatterys' turmoil, he still couldn't get Celia Milton out of his mind.

Annie was out in the street with a tin tray, collecting the dishes and cutlery that belonged to her, but her hands were trembling so much that the crockery, and especially the glasses, were in grave danger of being dropped and broken. Unconsciously, she was gnawing her bottom lip. She wished she could stay out here for ever amidst the litter and debris of the party.

Charlie was livid. He'd had a few drinks, which always made him more aggressive and insulting, but he certainly hadn't bargained on being spoken to like that by the vicar, and in front of everyone. She'd stood rooted to the spot, a wave of sheer terror followed by nausea washing over her. She shuddered at the memory. And then there was Celia. If she had any sense she'd go straight to bed and hope thereby to escape Charlie's anger, at least until tomorrow.

At least Frederick had behaved himself for once. There had been no fighting or arguing with any of the other lads. Frank and Eddie Kemp had gone around emptying the dregs of the beer and other drinks into one glass. She'd seen them but she hadn't commented. Eddie Kemp had already been sick, but she thanked God that Frederick seemed not to have drunk much of the disgusting slops.

She could delay no longer, she had to go in now for the street was deserted. Flo Taylor from number five had collected Maudie's belongings and placed them on the step. There'd be hell to pay in *that* house too. The situation would be the very reverse of that in her own home. Maudie had a tongue like a viper. She looked at the Slattery house and sighed. She'd seen Mrs Tiernan go in. Poor Mr Slattery, he'd looked so frail and ill, but he'd seemed to be enjoying everything before he'd been taken in again.

She wished she could go and knock and offer Mrs Slattery her condolences. The poor woman must be distraught. For an instant she wished it could have been Charlie who had been laid out in the parlour, then she said a hasty prayer for such wicked thoughts.

Charlie stood with his back to the range in the kitchen, his hands behind his back, and Annie's heart sank. This was his usual stance when there was going to be a row.

Billy was standing behind the chair that Celia was sitting in and they both looked pale and edgy.

Billy gave her a half-smile. He'd had a boring and frustrating day. He hadn't been allowed to go to the Wynnstay as some of the other lads of his age had done, a blind eye having been turned on rules and regulations for the day. Things had gone a bit better in the early evening, except for Nettie Taylor from over the road, who had dogged his steps all damned day. Every time he turned around she was there and he couldn't stand the sight of her.

She was a big, raw-boned girl with buck teeth and straight mousy hair. She had thought that by simpering and fluttering her eyelashes she would make herself look attractive. It only made her look stupid, as had the sickening way she'd kept sidling up to him and giggling. She had some daft idea that he liked her. Nor had he enjoyed Richie Kemp's company much either.

In his opinion, Richie was a loud-mouthed, big-headed dope who thought he was God's gift to women. It was after Richie had made a pass at Cee, and she'd well and truly belted him, that he realised that even though they lived next door and had grown up together, he didn't like Richie at all.

He knew Richie was jealous of him because he had a better job and Richie never missed an opportunity to imply that it had all been because of Da's position. It wasn't, not entirely. He'd worked damned hard himself, going to evening classes while Richie just hung around, read stupid comics or listened to the wireless. Richie did as little as possible while always managing to appear busy. He thought he was fooling Mr Roberts, the blockerman, but Fred Roberts had seen too many like him and had him well taped.

Charlie was stinging with humiliation. It was almost a physical pain. Well, it was the last time they'd go to *that* church. Who did the man think he was, telling decent, upright members of his congregation that they were a disgrace and taking the side of a bloody priest. He wasn't having that.

As his wife entered the room the dishes rattling on the tray annoyed him further.

'Put those bloody dishes down, woman, before you break the bloody lot,' he bawled.

Annie fled to the sanctuary of the scullery where she held on to the edge of the sink, feeling faint with fear. Then slowly, like an automaton, she started to fill the sink and wash up.

'Right, miss, and what have you got to say for yourself? Pandering to that slut next door. Putting your arm around her and comforting her. Setting foot in *that* hell's kitchen of a house.'

Celia was trying to stay calm. She wanted to shout back but shouting would only make things worse. She clenched her hands tightly in her lap, her eyes downcast.

'What was I supposed to do, Da?'

'Let her get on with it. She probably flaunted herself and him drunk. She'd likely been enticing him. She was probably asking for it.'

Celia's cheeks instantly flushed with anger. She wasn't going to let him speak about Lizzie like this.

'Just like I did, Da? I suppose you think I flaunted myself too? As you said, he was drunk and disgusting. She . . . she was so upset and no one was taking any notice of her at all, what with the fight. I *hate* that Richie Kemp. It's all his fault.'

Charlie spluttered with rage.

Billy decided it was time to try to back his sister up.

'She's right, Da. It *was* all Richie's fault and no one was taking any notice of Lizzie.'

Charlie turned on him. 'Oh, so it's "Lizzie" now, is it? Don't tell me that you've been running after that little Papist whore?'

They were both shocked at his words but Celia recovered first. She sprang to her feet, her eyes hard, her fists clenched at her sides.

'Don't you call her a "whore", Da! She's a good girl, I know. I work with her!'

'Not for much longer you won't,' he yelled, his face turning puce, a vein on his forehead beginning to throb.

Celia was incensed and past caring now.

'I'm not leaving my job over this! If I get my hands on Richie Kemp I'll give him such a belt.'

Billy placed a hand on her shoulder. 'Da, that's not fair. It *was* his fault and I'll be belting him too when his mam and Cee have finished with him. He's a creep. A smarmy, idle, lying toe rag.'

Confronted with the first rebellion of both his older children Charlie's rage increased.

'By God, I won't be spoken to like that by either of you!' he thundered, rushing towards Celia. He hit her with such force that both she and Billy fell backwards.

For his age Billy was big but he had always been afraid of his father. Old habits die hard but he could hear his mam crying in the scullery, and his sister had tears in her eyes and was holding the side of her face. He could see a trickle of blood from her mouth seeping though her fingers.

'Do that again, Da, and I'm going for the police, I swear I will.' Inside he was quaking but he held his ground and looked his father squarely in the face.

Charlie glared back and tried to push him aside.

'Get out of my way. I haven't finished with her or started on you yet, and there'll be no police brought in here!'

He lunged again at Celia. Billy tried to hold him back and push him aside but the full force of Charlie's fury prevailed. Celia was sent reeling against the wall and fell, screaming out in pain and terror. Da had never hit her like this before. Oh, he'd given her many a slap across the legs over the years and there'd been punishments like being kept in or sent to her room with no tea, but nothing like this. Her mouth was full of warm salty blood. Her lips were already swelling. Her head and right shoulder were throbbing, as was the right side of her face, and it hurt to open her mouth. She wondered dazedly if he had broken her jaw. Through the haze of pain and terror she realised that her da and Billy were arguing.

Charlie had turned on his son, but for once the lad didn't shrink away from him and in his hand he held the heavy brass poker.

Billy's face was white, even his lips were bloodless. 'Start on Cee again or Mam or me and I'll use this. I swear it.'

Charlie stood and glared at the lad and started to raise his arm, but let it fall as his son, poker in hand, raised his arm too. Charlie muttered an oath and stormed out through the scullery into the yard, brutally knocking his petrified wife out of his way. The glass she'd been holding shattered around her feet and they heard the back yard door slam.

The sound galvanised Annie. Ignoring the mess she ran into the kitchen where Billy was helping Celia to her feet, and Annie cried out loud when she saw the girl's face.

'Mam, get some cold water, quickly. We might be able to do something to stop the swelling. She'll be black and blue tomorrow. How's she going to go to work like that?'

'She won't be going.' Annie looked up at her son. 'Oh, Billy, he'd have killed her but for you, lad. I've never seen him so mad.'

Billy nodded but now it was over he was ashen. Suddenly, nausea claimed him and he dashed into the scullery and vomited into the sink.

When he felt better, and he'd cleaned the sink with bleach, he went back into the kitchen.

'I'm sorry, Mam. I . . . I've cleaned it up.'

Annie gave him a grateful look before turning her attention back to her battered and shaking daughter.

'Oh, Cee, luv, why didn't you just keep quiet? You knew what kind of a mood he'd be in after all that trouble outside?'

'Mam, I wasn't going to let him call Lizzie a whore.' The words were painfully formed and spoken.

'But . . . but to go into the house with her, Cee.'

'Mam, Lizzie is my friend. My best friend.' The words were slurred as her lips had swollen to twice their normal size.

Annie went white with shock and felt faint. Charlie *would* kill her if he found out about that.

Determinedly she pulled herself together. 'I think bed is the best place for all of us,' she said, wishing heartily that Charlie would never come back.

Between them they got Celia upstairs and Annie undressed her and once again placed a face cloth wrung out in cold water against the side of Celia's face, which now felt as though it were on fire.

'Do you think you could be able to swallow a couple of Aspro, luv?'

Celia tried to nod but the movement sent bursts of pain from her jaw to her forehead.

Annie went downstairs, upset, and for the first time in many years, truly angry. It wasn't just Charlie she was furious with. She was angry with herself as well. Why hadn't she stood up to him like Billy had done? Why couldn't she have defended Celia? Even a female animal or bird would attempt to protect its young. She should have fought Charlie like a tigress, but she hadn't. She'd stood petrified in the scullery and now she felt so weak, so useless and so terribly guilty. What use was she at all? What kind of a mother was she? It would be a week before Celia would be able to go to work and even then she'd have to explain the fading bruises with the old and worn-out excuse of walking into a door or falling down the stairs, which no one ever believed. But there was one thing she could do and, grimly, she promised herself, she *would* do it.

When she returned she raised Celia's head and held the glass of water to wash down the tablets. Only a little of the water passed the girl's lips, most dribbled down her chin. Gently, Annie wiped it away and then cradled Celia's head in her arms, her eyes full of tears. It had been a terrible day for many people in Roscommon Street. The Jubilee would be remembered here but for all the wrong reasons.

'Don't try to talk, luv, but if you agree with me, just squeeze my hand. I . . . I'm going to send flowers, a small wreath from us, when they bury poor Mr Slattery. From Annie and Celia Milton, that's what I'll put on the card. I've a bit of money I've managed to scrape together without him noticing. Are you happy with that, luv, because if you're not I'll just put my name on it?' She felt the pressure tighten on her hand and she smiled. If *he* dared to hit either of them, she'd go herself to the police station and have him arrested. The thin shell of hatred, that had started with dislike, hardened around her heart. She had promised long ago to 'love, honour and obey . . . so long as ye both shall live.' She had no option but to obey, but she neither loved nor honoured him now, and she would never do so again.

After she'd slammed the front door of number eight, Maudie stood for a moment, beside herself with rage. Harry was still grinning stupidly and was slumped in the chair into which she'd shoved him, yelling at the same time that it was a pity he didn't fall and break his neck.

'Look at you!' she shouted. 'Look at you! You bloody fool! You've disgraced us. You've made us a laughing stock. I'll never be able to hold my head up again in this street,' she yelled, but to no effect. Already his eyes were closing and he was slipping into a stupor.

She turned her attention to her son, who was half sitting, half lying on the sofa. She was at the end of her tether with him and she stormed into the scullery and snatched up the long strip of thin leather that they both used to strop their open razors before shaving. She began to belt Richie with it repeatedly.

'You! You're fit for nothing! You don't even have a decent job like Billy Milton. You're too flaming lazy. After all I've done for you, this is how you end up. This is the way you repay me. You go and insult Celia in that disgusting way, and it serves you right that she slapped your face in front of everyone.' She thought her head was going to burst with anger. 'Not content with that, then . . . then . . . you try to . . . to molest *that* one! THAT ONE! That bloody common little floozie. Oh, I should have let that lout Joe Slattery beat the living daylights out of you! Do you hear me, Richie Kemp?' She struck the final blow and let the razor strop fall to her side. She had utterly exhausted herself, and for what?

She flung the strop in the general direction of the table and as she did so, Richie baulked and was then sick all over the kitchen floor. It was the final straw for Maudie. She rushed into the scullery, filled a bucket full of cold water and threw it over her son, the floor and her husband before she went upstairs.

The twins, who had been sitting on the landing quaking with fear, fled to their bedroom in case their mother started on them next. Like Foxy Milton they hadn't had a good day. Eddie was still feeling awful but he was thankful that he'd been sick in the jigger and Mam hadn't seen him. Now he didn't understand why anyone actually enjoyed drinking. All it did was make you feel dizzy and ill.

In the bedroom, Maudie was so worked up she couldn't sleep. She tossed and turned, vowing that by God they were both for it in the morning when they'd sobered up, and what's more, Richie could scrub every inch of that floor no matter how hungover he was.

Dessie Slattery's Requiem Mass was on the Friday morning. All Brigid's neighbours had called offering condolences and help. None of them could be called well off. Most just managed to keep their heads above water and pay their way in the world, so she was doubly thankful for every bit of assistance.

Tessie brought over a black dress, stockings, a hat and even shoes. Maggie and Biddy, who had apologised profusely for getting into such a state, said they would chip in with both the cost and the making of the sandwiches for the mourners, who were coming back to the house after the interment in Kirkdale Cemetery.

For Lizzie, each day seemed endless and unreal. She'd gone into work on Wednesday at Brigid's insistence, to take her mind off things, but she'd been like a clockwork doll. She wasn't eating either, which worried Brigid. That night Lizzie had entered the parlour, kneeled beside her da's coffin and sobbed her heart out, and no amount of comforting seemed to help. Joe had even offered to risk the wrath of Charlie Milton and go for Celia, but although her friend was the one person she really wanted with her now, Lizzie refused. She knew Celia would never again be allowed to set foot in this house.

The floral tributes – just sheaves of flowers that had been bought with the coppers collected by Biddy from the neighbours – the Mass and sympathy cards had all arrived early that morning. To keep her mind off the ordeal Brigid was going to have to face, and face with some dignity and fortitude, she stood all the cards along the window ledge in the semi-gloom of the parlour. The curtains had remained closed since Monday night, as had those of all the houses at the end of the street, as a mark of respect for Dessie.

The big brass bed that took up most of the space was empty. She'd shared the single bed in the attic room with Lizzie and each night they'd cried themselves to sleep. The undertakers had removed the coffin to their chapel of rest on Thursday morning at Brigid's request.

The bed now seemed out of place in here, she thought. Yet all her children had been conceived and born in it. She'd never sleep in it again for she couldn't bear the thought of waking up, reaching out and finding herself – alone.

She turned away from it and its memories. The flowers too had been placed in the room and carefully she concentrated on reading the words on the black-edged cards. There was a small wreath of white and yellow carnations and as she took off the card and read it, a huge sob caught in her throat. In small, neat writing the message read, 'With our sympathy and condolences, Annie and Celia Milton.'

Brigid leaned against the fireplace to steady herself. God alone would know what the poor timid little soul would have to suffer from *him* – and her neighbours too come to that – once this was seen and commented on. He'd already beaten his girl, she'd heard, until she wasn't fit to be in work.

Lizzie came to tell her that the hearse had arrived, as had the carriage for the family that was to follow it. The rest of the mourners would walk behind it to the church.

Wordlessly Brigid held the card out to her and Lizzie read it.

'Oh, Mam, I *told* you she was good and generous and kind. I know that she's been belted badly because Mr Henderson said something about her "falling downstairs". Her mam is terrified of him too.'

'Then I don't know how much courage the poor soul must have found in her heart to do this, but I'll never forget her kindness,'

Brigid choked, then recovered herself.

'Do you think we should keep the card back, Lizzie, luv? I mean, well . . . with . . . *him*?'

Lizzie nodded vigorously. 'He . . . he'd half kill them both and no one up that end of the street would speak to them again. Oh, Mam! Why does it all have to be like this? Why can't people stop hating each other for no other reason than the church they go to?'

'Sure, I don't know, Lizzie. It's always been like this here in Liverpool and I suppose it always will be. There's people who say it was even worse years ago. That there were riots. But we'd best be off. Are the others ready?'

Lizzie nodded. With a final long, backward glance at the brass bed Brigid walked out and closed the door behind her. She was a widow now and would remain so for the rest of her life because the love she had for her kind and gentle husband would never die. Death was the biggest thief of all and the only certainty in this life, but she firmly believed she *would* be reunited with him one day.

Chapter Nine

Throughout that summer and autumn, Joe Slattery and Celia Milton met regularly at the Pier Head on Wednesday afternoons, and most Saturday nights Lizzie and Celia met to go to the pictures or to a dance or to the theatre music halls, although the latter seemed to be losing their popularity as the number of cinemas increased.

Celia had returned to work on the Monday after the funeral, a week to the day after the disastrous Jubilee party. Mr Henderson made no remark about her appearance and Celia had tried to arrange her hair so that it partially covered the still yellowish-blueish bruising.

Lizzie wasn't able to speak to her friend properly until lunchtime, when they both went to the stockroom where they ate their sandwiches.

Lizzie threw her arms around Celia and they both burst into tears. When they could speak, they sat down and wiped their eyes.

'Oh, Cee, it's been awful. I wanted you to come in, and our Joe said he'd go for you, but I knew . . . I knew your da had belted you.'

'It's a lot better now, Lizzie, really it is. But it was terrible. I thought he'd broken my jaw. I thought he was going to kill me. Our Billy had the poker . . .'

'Oh God!' Lizzie cried.

'No, he didn't use it. Da slammed out. It was Mam who thought of and paid for the flowers.'

'I know and Mam was so touched, so grateful, but we kept the card, Cee. We didn't want you to get into more trouble.'

Celia nodded. 'The atmosphere at home is awful now. It's so bad our Billy says he's glad to be at work and he goes to his mate Jack Shacklady's house on Kirkdale Road, and Foxy's turned into an angel. But there's a difference in Mam now. I think . . . I think she hates Da. She won't speak to him unless he asks her a question and a couple of times I've caught her looking at him and her eyes have been so cold.'

Lizzie sighed. 'My Mam's different too, Cee. She seems to be bottling everything up inside and she won't go in the parlour except to clean. She sent our Joe and Fergal to that second-hand furniture shop further along Great Homer Street to get another single bed and mattress for the attic. She's been sharing with me. We've all begged her not to be like this but . . .' Lizzie shrugged.

'It's going to be harder for me to get out now, Lizzie. He watches me like a hawk. Fortunately that stupid Nettie Taylor fancies our Billy, so I'll ask her to cover for me. She works in a shop so Wednesday afternoon she's off too. She'll do it. She'll do anything if she thinks it'll please our Billy and he can't *stand* the sight of her.'

Lizzie had managed a smile. She didn't blame Billy Milton one bit. Nettie Taylor was downright ugly, and stupid too.

Since then they'd both drawn strength from their friendship but when Lizzie had told Joe what Charlie Milton had done to Celia his anger was so intense that he'd deliberately finished early on Wednesday, and waited to see her in the jigger between Dorrington Street and Sackville Street. Lizzie had promised they'd both walk up Rose Vale that day and as Joe had stepped forward Lizzie had discreetly and quickly walked on ahead.

Celia was more embarrassed than afraid as they walked a little way up the jigger.

Joe reached out and gently touched the side of her face. 'Is this what he did to you?'

Celia nodded. The touch of his hand had made her go hot then cold.

'Because you comforted our Lizzie and came into our house? It's all right, there's no need to be frightened. I – I could kill him, but I won't. I didn't need to belt Richie Kemp. I heard his mam did that and he's being skitted something awful at work about it. I don't know how it got out. I think your Billy had something to do with it, though.'

Celia nodded. 'He doesn't like Richie Kemp.'

'Who does? He's an idle no mark with a mouth like the new tunnel, he always has been.'

She felt easier in his presence now. 'Eddie told Foxy his mam screamed at him and his da for hours, then Richie was sick and she threw a bucket of water over him and then made him scrub the floor next morning and sent him to work.'

'I heard there were quite a few missing on Tuesday morning. I went in to see Fred Roberts, my blockerman, to explain, and he sent me home. He's a good skin, is Fred, but your Billy's got guts.'

'Yes, he picked up the poker and threatened to hit Da but . . . but he was terrified inside just the same.' She couldn't bring herself to betray her brother's physical sickness. She didn't know Joe Slattery that well.

'Promise me, Celia, that if he ever starts on you again you'll come for me? Between us Billy and I will sort him out.'

She nodded and looked up at him, thinking how terrible she must look with the bruising still visible on the side of her face.

'Everyone calls me Cee.'

Joe smiled down at her. He'd give Charlie Milton a dose of his own medicine if he ever laid a finger on her or her mam. Only bullying cowards hit women.

'Can I see you, Cee? I mean meet you, take you out?' He knew very well what he was facing if she agreed, not only from Brigid but everyone he knew, but he was as sure now that just as day follows night, he loved her.

Celia looked up at him with tears sparkling on her lashes and inside fear fought with joy and joy won.

'I – I'd be killed if anyone saw us.'

'Then we'll have to make sure no one sees us.'

He'd smiled and had taken her hand as they walked down the jigger. Halfway down he'd reluctantly let go, but they had agreed to meet at the Pier Head that Wednesday afternoon.

Joe was quite willing to forfeit his pay, if he could get the time off, but after the first week, with his new qualifications, he was put on the night shift which meant regular twelve-hour shifts and far more money.

There had been a snide comment from Richie Kemp about him being one of the 'Royals' now, the name given to favoured men. Joe had ignored him as had most of the other men in the vicinity. Richie wasn't liked. But Albert Lynch took exception to the remark.

Albert was a huge, bull-necked man, known to all as 'Friggin' Albert' because of his constant use of the word. Joe had smiled grimly, remembering an instance earlier in the year when Albert Lynch had been told to go up the mast with him. No one liked working up masts because if you got a 'flash', a burning sensation in the eye from the welding arc, it could cause you to loosen your grip and maybe fall. It had been known to happen. Albert had refused in his usual manner but Fred Roberts had told him they'd rigged up a bosun's chair for him. The reply had been that Albert wouldn't go up there 'in a friggin' three-piece suite'.

Lynch had grabbed Richie by the throat and told him to keep his friggin' gob shut or he'd do it for him permanently, like.

Joe and Celia both knew the risks they ran but throughout those warm summer months and the golden days of autumn they grew closer and finally admitted to each other their love. On summer afternoons the ferries were always crowded but they made for the same spot in the lee of the funnel. There they were shielded from view by the crowd, apart from the people in their immediate vicinity who took little notice of them.

Here Joe held her for the first time and kissed her, and here they wondered too about their future. But whichever way they looked at it, there seemed to be no escape from the bigotry and bitterness that surrounded them.

'What's to become of us, Joe?' Celia had asked one blustery afternoon in September.

'I wish to God I knew, Cee. If Da had been alive and well and working I could have left, but now I'm the main breadwinner. I can't leave Mam and the kids. Our Emmet can be a holy terror at times; he'd have her demented. It'll be another year before our Josie leaves school. I know that having three wages coming in sounds a lot and I have had a big rise, but it doesn't add up to what your da earns and I won't let Mam go down and half kill herself working for Cunard when their ships come in and need a quick turn-round. She insists on doing her couple of evenings in India Buildings, though. But we haven't got much, Cee. You must have noticed that when you brought our Lizzie in. Mam sold almost everything to pay for that specialist and the medicine. She's trying to get some things around her again, to make us a decent home with some of the comforts we never had before. I couldn't leave, Cee.'

She'd kissed him gently on the cheek. 'I know, and things were so hectic that I never noticed anything and I wouldn't want you to leave, I'd feel so guilty. Oh, Joe, there's no solution, we'll just have to be thankful for these few hours.'

And for as long as they last, Joe thought, because one day someone was bound to see them. They took risks but neither of them cared. Live for today, Brigid was always saying, and that's what they did – all they could do.

With November came the fog. Not just the fog from the sea creeping down from the estuary, and fingering its way up the river, but the double density of it as it spread and mingled with the smoke from hundreds of chimneys, both factory and domestic.

It made life even more difficult for Celia and Joe, for the trams stopped running and the foghorns boomed out over the Mersey. The kids thought it was great and yelled out, 'Oggy on the river! Oggy on the river!' but most of the Mersey shipping was at a standstill or moved slowly, the steam whistles sounding off continuously. The ferries still ran, unless it was just too thick, but at a snail's pace.

It also meant he was out earlier and home later, for although the fog had no affect on the trains that ran under the river, Joe still had to get to James Street and then to the yard in Birkenhead. Often when he arrived it was to find that the crane drivers had been sent home. It was impossible for them to work in fog. It wasn't much better for anyone else, in fact it was downright dangerous, unless you were working inside a confined space in a hull.

Charlie Milton questioned Celia very closely about her reasons for going out into the peasoupers and often she just didn't have a convincing excuse and had to stay home. She knew both Mam and Billy thought it was Lizzie she was going out with. She went cold with fear at the thought of what would happen if they knew it was Joe Slattery.

For such emergencies, Joe had carefully chiselled out the mortar from around a brick in the wall that divided the yard, making it possible for the brick to be slid in and out. Notes were left there if they were unable to meet. Only himself, Lizzie and Celia knew of its existence.

'Mam, that wall is in such a state down there that if one of the kids leans on it it'll fall, probably into next-door's yard,' he'd said when Brigid had questioned his reasons for all the noise and work.

'I'd be glad for it, so I would,' Brigid had muttered.

By the end of a week of being stuck in the house every evening, and on her Wednesday afternoon off too, Lizzie was so fed up that she told Brigid she was going to the Rotunda fog or no fog, even if it took her hours and hours to walk there.

'Well, it's glad I am not to be having you under me feet all day and night, moping and mooning around. But if you get lost, Lizzie Slattery, then it's your own fault,' Brigid replied. She was in the middle of giving the kitchen floor a thorough going-over before the new lino arrived, she hoped on Monday morning, and so far both Emmet and Bernie had trailed across it twice to her acute annoyance.

'Mam, I don't know why you're bothering with that now. Leave it until tomorrow night or you'll wear yourself out trying to keep the kids off it. This flaming fog should have gone by then.'

Brigid got to her feet. 'You're right, Lizzie. It'll be destroyed with them all walking in and out on it. I'll put me feet up for a change.'

'So, you're not mad at me then?'

'Not at all. Go and get lost, if that's what you want. It's desperate out there,' was the cutting reply that came to Lizzie from the scullery.

Brigid was still finding it hard to come to terms with her loss and was often irritable, snappy and sometimes angry. Angry at Dessie and God for leaving her in the heart-scald position of trying to cope with a growing family alone. Then she'd calm down and tell herself she'd more or less coped for years before Dessie had died and apart from Emmet, who often put the heart across her with his antics, the others weren't much trouble.

Josie in her last year at school was working very hard. She didn't want to go to work in a factory or shop. She wanted to be a waitress in a decent café or even a restaurant and had got books from the library on etiquette and silver service.

'What in the name of God does that mean?' Maggie Walsh had asked as she, with Biddy, Tessie and Brigid, shared a cup of tea the previous miserable foggy morning.

'Merciful God, how should I know? Aren't I just thankful she's got ambitions, not like that other young rossie who won't even open a book?'

'They're all the same these days. There's not one of my lot who isn't as thick as the wall. And I don't know what to do with Patsy, she's that flighty.'

'Ah, don't be giving out like that, Biddy, they'll be grand. They'll make their way in the world.'

'Just like my Bernard has, I suppose,' Biddy answered acidly.

Tessie had been thinking hard. 'I think silver service means knowing how to lay a table.'

'And what is there to know about laying a table?'

'Knowing how to put all the knives and forks and spoons in the right order and how things should be served. Not just dolloped on a plate and ate with one knife and fork. Years ago I remember going to one of Dermot's relation's wedding. Some posh cousin four times removed or something like that – God knows why they asked us – and I was on pins the whole of the day in case we made a show of ourselves. There was soup and then roast lamb with vegetables and potatoes and then a pudding and wine and champagne. There were different knives and forks and spoons for everything and glasses too. I didn't know where to start an' when the waitress called me "madam" I didn't know what to say to the girl. Me nerves were shredded, I can tell you. So that's what I think silver service is.'

'Well, your Josie won't be much trouble to you, Brigid, if she gets something like that,' Maggie said. 'Not like them kids of Maudie's, always in trouble and causing a row,' she laughed.

It was common knowledge that the Kemp twins and Richie often got belted to bits by their shrew of a mother, and it gave the party of neighbours great satisfaction, especially Brigid.

'I heard an' all that Harry Kemp wants to keep pigeons but *she* won't let him,' Biddy informed them.

'That feller has a cross to bear with that one.'

'He has so. Even the divil himself would find herself a trouble to him,' Brigid agreed.

Biddy rose. 'Well, I'd better get back. Bernie will be moaning I'm out all day jangling.'

Maggie and Tessie rose too.

'I wish to God this damned fog would lift, there's hardly a feller in the street in work because of it,' Tessie said irritably to her neighbours as they'd left.

Lizzie stood under the arcade in what little light, trapped by the fog in a small sickle shape, filtered out from the shop windows.

Her eyes were red and sore from peering into the gloom and she'd covered her nose and mouth with a scarf but now the scarf was moist and uncomfortable, not to say unsightly, and she was cold from standing in the dripping dampness. She wondered if Celia would come. Her note had said, 'I'll try, but don't wait more than ten minutes.'

Lizzie had no watch so she asked the time of the theatre doorman. The ten minutes were well up. Celia wasn't coming tonight. She'd half expected it. Her own mam thought she was mad so Cee wouldn't stand a cat in hell's chance of getting out. She went through the double glass doors to the glass-fronted ticket office, resigned to the fact that she would see Wee Georgie Wood on her own. In fact, the theatre would only be a quarter full – if that. Only fools like herself would come out in weather like this, she thought, but she couldn't *stand* another night in.

At the interval Lizzie decided that she'd had enough. There was no atmosphere, no feeling of excitement and anticipation with only this bit of an audience. It would take her hours to get home, unless of course a howling gale had blown in from the sea and shifted all the fog.

There had been no gale and if anything the fog was worse. She could hardly see a hand in front of her. She knew she'd taken a wrong turning when she could no longer see even the faint finger of light from a streetlamp. Oh God, I've come down a jigger somewhere, she thought irritably. Well, the only thing to do was to turn around and, keeping one hand on the wall, follow it until it came to an end. That way she would know she was once again on the main road back at the Rotunda.

It was slow progress and she knew Mam would be worried and very probably angry with her for going in the first place.

She hadn't gone very far when she tripped and stumbled, crying out with the pain of scraped shins. Then she began to slide and fall, landing on her back in what looked like a cellar of some kind. Shaken, she sat up. She didn't seem to have broken any bones but as she got to her feet she staggered as a knife-like pain shot through her left foot. It was her ankle. She didn't know if it were broken after all or just sprained, but she did know that she couldn't put any weight on it and that she was trapped down here in the darkness and the cold.

She heard scuffling sounds, and terror at what the dank darkness might hold, and the possibility of being stuck here for God alone knew how long, made her start to scream and shout for help.

At last she was hoarse and had to stop. She was frightened and cold. No one would hear her and her foot was adding to her misery. She thought about Mam: she'd be worried sick. A bright dart of hope flashed through her mind. Maybe Mam would send Joe or Fergal out to look for her. Then her hope died. Even if she did it wouldn't be for ages as they would think she'd stayed until the end of the performance. Then they might search around the main road and the theatre, but would never think of coming down here. Even *she* had no idea at all of where she was.

She sat on the cold, damp flags huddled up, trying to keep herself warm as best she could. Tears began to fall down her cheeks. There were rats down here. That's what the scuffling noise was. She hadn't seen them – yet – but they were there.

What if the fog didn't lift for days? It had lasted a week already. What if no one ever came down this jigger, even on clear days?

She would die of cold and hunger down here and as she got weaker then the rats would swarm over her and eat her. She'd heard of people who'd died like that, too weak and feeble to fend them off. She began to sob loudly. She didn't want to stay here and die. She wanted to go home, that's all.

'Oh, please God, help me?' she said aloud, then she began to gabble the Our Fathers, Hail Marys and Glory Be's, counting them off on her fingers. Her beads were at home on top of the little chest of drawers Mam had bought second-hand last week.

It seemed as though hours had passed when she heard the noise above, outside. A sort of shuffling. It wasn't like the scuttling noises down here that were almost beside her now, even though she'd kept moving around as much as her ankle would allow. Someone was up there! She groaned as she got to her feet, her limbs having become numb with cold, but she began again to shout as loud as she could. There was no reply and she stopped, ears straining, to see if the sound had gone, passed on by without hearing her. Then she heard it again and renewed her efforts.

This time she was rewarded.

'Who's there? Where are you?'

Lizzie thought the male voice sounded vaguely familiar but dismissed the thought. 'I'm down here, in this cellar or something. There's a door or a cover been left open and I fell and I think I've broken my ankle. Oh, please get me out. Please help me.'

'Well, don't move while I think of something.'

'Just hurry, please. I've been stuck for ages and there's rats down here. Me mam will be out of her mind with worry!'

'I got lost myself. Can you reach up and grab my hand?'

A pale disembodied hand appeared in the darkness above, out of reach.

'No, you're too far away.'

'I think you've fallen down a delivery hatch. It'll have a bit of a slope, can you try and crawl up it?'

Relieved to know where she was and that help had arrived,

Lizzie tried on her hands and knees to climb a few feet up the slope, but each time she fell back, crying out with pain.

'I can't! I keep slipping back.' There was a sob in her voice now.

'Look, get hold of my overcoat. I'll take it off and throw it down. Grab a sleeve if you can.'

Dimly she could see the garment and made a wild grab and caught not only the sleeve, but the back as well.

'I've got it.'

'Then hang on while I pull.'

Slowly she was hauled upwards until at last she was out. She felt the edge of the cover that she'd tripped over and her nerves gave way. Sitting on the damp cobbles she broke down in floods of tears, tears of sheer relief.

'Come on, cheer up. You're out now. Where do you live? I'll try and get you home, what with your foot an' all you won't make it on your own.'

'Roscommon Street, in the middle, and thanks, thanks for everything.' She was shaking as she looked up and through her tears and the fog she saw that the hands that had pulled her to safety belonged to Billy Milton.

'Lizzie Slattery! I thought I recognised the voice. What the hell were you doing? How did you get here?'

With tears still pouring down her cheeks and trembling with cold and shock she grabbed at his pullover and clung to him. He wasn't just a stranger, he lived next door.

'I was at the Roundy and wandered down here and then I fell and – and – I've been terrified that no one would come and the fog would go on for days and the rats would eat me.' She broke down completely and sobbed against his chest.

Billy, unsure of what to do, gingerly put his arms around her. She was so small and thin and in such a state that a feeling of protectiveness came over him. The poor kid, he thought, God knows how long she'd been stuck down there. He'd been to his mate Jack

Shacklady's house on Kirkdale Road and got lost the way she had, and if it hadn't been for her cries he'd have probably ended up down there with her as he'd shuffled along.

Lizzie's sobs were subsiding but not her trembling. She must be frozen stiff.

'Here, put my overcoat on, you'll get pneumonia.'

Her own coat was so thin it wasn't much use at all. He helped her struggle into the thick tweed coat which came down to her ankles.

'Now, put your arm around my neck and let's see if you can hop or hobble along.' If she couldn't it was a long way to have to carry her, he thought, although he was sure she would be as light as a feather. She looked as if she could do with a few good meals.

Lizzie did as she was told and found that she could hop on one leg with Billy holding her firmly around the waist, but when they finally reached the arcade, recognisable by the dim lights, she was exhausted. So, there was nothing else left to do but pick her up and carry her.

'You look for the streetlights. We'll follow them, or maybe it will be better if we walk in the road, I can feel the tramlines under my feet then.'

'What happens if a tram comes?' Lizzie asked, a little calmer now. She felt so safe and secure with him.

'If it does we'll get on it, but I don't think there will be any. They stopped running hours ago. Jack's da is a driver and he was home very early. He said it was terrible. He had his conductor out on the road ahead of him with a torch until they got back to the depot, then he had to walk home.'

They rested a bit every now and then. They both sat on the dank wet cobbles and Lizzie, now over her ordeal, began to feel very shy and a bit awkward. She'd never really spoken to him before, not a real conversation, and here he was carrying her in his arms and she with her arms around his neck, clinging to him for dear life.

Hours seemed to pass and she began to feel that they would never get home, but they'd at least been talking to each other and Lizzie thought he was very pleasant and not a bit like his da. She felt much easier, more comfortable with him.

When they finally got to Roscommon Street he'd have to put her down and she'd just have to hang on to him. Mam would be so relieved to see her that Lizzie hoped she wouldn't start on him. He *was* nice – just like Celia – and she wondered idly and with a faint fluttering of her heart whether this nightmare in the fog would be the start of something in the nature of what Celia and Joe now felt for each other, for Celia often poured out her heart to her friend.

As they reached the top of the street he set her down and she took off his overcoat.

'Thanks. I really mean that, Billy.'

'I was glad – well, not glad you got lost or hurt your foot, but . . . well, glad I found you. *You* I mean, not someone else.'

'I was glad too.'

They looked at each other in silence until Billy, shrugging on his overcoat that she had handed him, said hesitantly, 'Lizzie, can I see you, like? We could go somewhere but it would have to be on Saturday nights. Our Celia and your Joe manage it.'

'You're not supposed to know about that, Billy Milton!' she cried.

'I know. But I watched our Cee one night taking the brick out and putting a bit of paper in and then putting the brick back.'

'And you read it?'

He nodded and looked embarrassed. 'I know I shouldn't have, I mean it was private.'

'And you never told anyone?'

'Nobody. Can . . . can we, Lizzie?'

Lizzie was pleased although still unsure.

'What about that Nettie Taylor? I thought she was your girl.'

'I can't stand Nettie Taylor. She's a real pain in the neck!'

Lizzie smiled up at him. 'All right then, but there'll be holy murder if any of us is caught.'

'If our Cee can take the chance then so can I,' he smiled back.

'Leave a note under the brick. I'll tell our Joe and you tell Cee because I won't be going into work for a few days and after tonight Mam is not going to let me wander out on my own again for a while. In fact I'll never hear the end of this.' Lizzie looked down at her swollen foot, then hobbled the few steps to their front door. Before she knocked she turned and through the dimness she smiled and waved to Billy, who stood watching her, a smile on his face.

Chapter Ten

'Well, thanks be to God! You've had the heart across me!' Brigid exclaimed. All evening she had been annoyed with her daughter for being so pig-headed, insisting on going out.

Joe had tried to calm her for there was no work for him tonight. Word had gonc round that thc cranc drivcrs had been sent home again.

'Mam, she'll be all right. There'll be other people there and you know that those going home in the same direction stay together. It's easier. She'll be fine. We're well used to fog by now, we never get through November without having at least one bad lot.'

Brigid had tutted but as the hours passed her temper had turned to anxiety.

Now she scrutinised her daughter. Lizzie was pale, her eyes red-rimmed, and she looked worn out.

'What's the matter with you?' she asked.

'It's my foot. I've hurt my ankle. I left in the interval.'

'In the interval? Then where've you been until now, may I ask?' Brigid demanded.

Joe helped Lizzie off with her coat and scarf, sat her down in the armchair and bent to take off her shoe.

Lizzie groaned loudly.

Joe looked serious. 'This is in a bad way, Mam. It's twice the size it should be.'

'And how did you do it?'

'I fell. I got lost and wandered down some jigger at the back of the Roundy.'

'You should have stayed on and come home with the others in the audience like a sensible person would.'

'I was fed up and anyway there was hardly anyone there. Then I tripped over the cover of a delivery chute and fell into the cellar.'

'Holy Mother of God! How did you get out of there and with that foot and all?'

'I . . . I . . . managed to crawl, slowly, very slowly, up to the top and then I kept one hand on the wall and sort of hopped and hobbled along.'

'And you've walked home with your foot like this?' Joe's eyes were fixed on her questioningly but she dare not say anything about Billy Milton, not yet.

'It was awful! I walked in the road, on the tram lines, but I kept having to sit on the cobbles and rest.' Then the shock, the lies but also the relief had their effect, and Lizzie instantly burst into tears.

'Ah, come on now, Lizzie, luv. You're home. We'll get that foot bandaged and some hot tea down you and you'll feel much better.'

Wiping her eyes Lizzie nodded as her mother went into the scullery to fill the kettle and get a bowl of cold water, which at this time of year would be icy.

'When all this "ministering angel" bit is over, I think Mam should go to bed, she's absolutely worn out with the worry of you. It was damned selfish of you, Lizzie,' Joe said as he tore a clean piece of linen, usually used as a tea towel, into strips for bandages. He raised his hand to quieten her imminent protest. 'I know you were bored and that's why you went out. *Everyone* is bored.'

'Now put your foot in that and Joe put those bits of bandages in too.' Brigid placed the bowl on the floor and passed Lizzie the cup of tea she'd put on the table.

The tea, the cold water which eased the pain and the heat from the fire in the range were all beginning to have their effect and

Lizzie would have given anything to have gone to her bed, but she knew Joe had not been fooled by her fabricated story about her escape from the cellar and walk home. And she wanted to tell him about Billy.

'Come on now, I'll help you to bed.'

'Mam, if you don't mind I'll just sit here a bit longer. It's cold up there and I'm still shaking, look.' She held out her hands, which were indeed shaking.

'All right then, but Joe, don't be letting her fall asleep down here. It's her bed she needs.'

Brigid hauled down a piece of flannel from the overhead rack.

'Mind now while I get this shelf out of the oven. I'll wrap it and put it in your bed, Lizzie.'

'Thanks, Mam. I won't be long. I promise.'

The younger children and Fergal had gone to bed long ago, bored because there was nothing to do and nowhere to go. They had no wireless, no board games, no comics or books. The games they could play, like cherrywobs, grid fishing, kick the can, lally-o and ollies, were for outdoors but you couldn't play in the street in the fog.

Joe got up and drew the end of the wooden bench from under the table towards his sister and sat on it.

'Right! Now I want the truth. Was Celia with you? You couldn't have crawled *up* a delivery chute and you couldn't have come all this way alone and in this fog on that foot.'

'No, Cee couldn't make it, you know what *he's* like. And I did fall into that flaming cellar and I was cold and frightened and there were rats.' She shuddered at the memory.

'So, *who* did get you out and bring you home then?'

'Billy. Billy Milton. He was lost himself. He'd been to his mate's house. He – he had to carry me most of the way and he put his overcoat on me too.' She paused, waiting for some reaction.

'So, is that it?'

She shook her head. 'He – he asked me out next Saturday night.'

Joe looked across at her steadily. 'And what did you say?'

'I – I said I would. He's nice. He's like Cee, and there's no need to look at me like that, Joe Slattery. He's going to tell Cee and I said I'd tell you.'

Joe looked at her with a mixture of pity and anxiety. 'Lizzie, you're mad.'

'I'm no madder than you!' she shot back defiantly.

'I suppose you're right but . . . but it's different for me.'

'Why?'

'Because it was something that just happened . . . gradually. And you seeing him makes the odds of all four of us getting found out much higher.'

'You only see Celia on Wednesday afternoons. I know Mam is suspicious about some of the excuses you give: "going into town", "going to the pictures for the matinée because of night work". I'll only see Billy on Saturday nights and Mam thinks I'm out with Cee then,' she replied stubbornly.

'You don't know him, Lizzie. He might get cold feet and spill the beans. He's afraid of his da.'

'No he won't. He must have thought of that before he asked me out, he had long enough. And anyway you didn't know Cee, either, not properly, when you met her after the Jubilee party. I know I don't *really* know Billy, but he's kind and nice and he helped me, and I might . . . we might . . .' Her voice faltered.

'Well, if you're set on it . . .'

'I am,' she answered emphatically.

Joe shrugged. 'At least there's some hope for you two. You can both leave home and get a place of your own eventually. I can't. I have to keep the family. We've been over and over this time and again, Cee and I. We can't look to the future or make plans. We just have to take each day as it comes.'

He sounded so weary and dejected that she reached out, took his hand and squeezed it.

'We'll *all* find a way, Joe. We will.'

'Aye, and pigs might fly and the Pope might become Grand Master of the Orange Lodge.' He bent down to bandage her foot. 'When I've finished this I'll help you upstairs or she'll be down wanting to know what's keeping you and I'll get the blame.'

A conspiratorial smile passed between them but in Joe's eyes there was sadness.

By Monday the fog had cleared, much to everyone's relief. Lizzie had spent much of Sunday with her foot resting on two orange boxes stacked on top of each other in the vain hope it would be well enough for her to go to work on Monday. She had persuaded Joe to put two notes under the brick in the yard. One telling Celia what had happened. The other folded and with the letter B on it.

'That one's private,' she explained.

'You'll be lucky if Mam lets you out at all next Saturday night. Not after this performance.'

'It'll be better by then. I want to go into work on Friday or I'll lose nearly all my pay,' Lizzie protested.

'If you go into work and stand on that ankle all day Friday and Saturday, it will be as bad as it is now. We don't even know if it's broken or not although I think you'd be screeching with pain if it was.'

'Well, I'm going out on Saturday night no matter what happens and I've told Billy so.'

'You *do* realise what will happen to him if old Milton finds out?'

'He went for his da with a poker the night he belted poor Cee. Anyway, you've been putting Cee in the same position for months now.'

He'd had no answer to that and had taken the pieces of paper down the yard.

Lizzie had said she would meet him under the clock at Lime Street Station at seven thirty and he wasn't to worry if she was a few minutes late because by hook or by crook she'd be there. That thought was still in her mind as her mam started on her tirade of complaint.

'You can't rely on anyone these day at all! Didn't I tell that feller I wanted the new lino down by tea time and here it is four o'clock and no sight nor sign of him at all?'

'Well, you said he wouldn't get paid until he brought it – didn't you have a row with him over that?'

'That's not the point, although I've more sense than to be parting with hard-earned money before I've the goods inside the house and inspected too. Didn't I spend all yesterday moving things out of here and scrubbing that old stuff within an inch of its life? And wasn't I worn out with the whole lot of it?'

'The lads did help, Mam,' Lizzie reminded her.

'Not with the scrubbing they didn't, and our Josie is little better than useless with the scrubbing brush. She sloshes water everywhere and doesn't she think she's the smart one, doing it on purpose so I won't be after asking her again? Well, I'm up to that bold one's tricks.'

Her words were interrupted by a loud hammering on the front door, and wiping her hands on her pinafore Brigid went to open it, a few choice remarks about the lateness of the hour ready on her lips.

Lizzie was moved into the parlour while Brigid stood over the man laying the new lino.

Lizzie didn't feel comfortable in here now, yet there had been a time, most of her life really, she admitted to herself, when she'd always been in here. She looked at the bed standing in the middle of the room in splendid isolation and wondered if anyone would ever sleep in it again.

Joe put his head around the door and broke her melancholy brooding.

'It's down, and to Mam's satisfaction, but I can't say I envy that bloke, not if all his customers are like her. "Pull it over a bit, it's not square. Mind you cut it properly around the hearth or the whole lot will be destroyed,"' he mimicked his mother's voice.

Lizzie laughed. 'I gather he's gone then?'

'Oh, aye, you can say that again. Got his money and beat a hasty retreat before she found something else for him to do. Fergal and I are going to move all the stuff back in – the heavy stuff anyway. Mam, our Josie and Bernie can cope with the lighter things, not that there's much.'

'It *is* better now, Joe. She manages to get something each week, or saves for a few weeks for bigger things. We've even got a clock on the wall now, we never had one of those before.'

He nodded. 'I know, and she deserves a bit of comfort too. She's slaved all her life for us all.' It was true, but it meant that Joe only felt more trapped. Brigid wasn't getting any younger either; how could he leave her – ever?

'I'll take you back in when I've finished.'

'What about your tea? You're off to work soon.'

'Oh, I'll just have a butty or something.'

'To last you all night? You'll need more than that.'

'I've got my carry-out. God, Lizzie, you're getting to sound just like Mam!'

He'd ignored Brigid's protests about having no proper meal to set him up for the bitterly cold night and left for work. Halfway up the street he saw Billy Milton coming towards him on his way home, having finished his shift. They nodded to each other curtly and Joe winked. Billy wasn't a bad bloke. Lizzie was probably right. It made sense that he'd be like Cee in nature and he admired him for his stand against his father. It wasn't an easy thing for a quiet lad to do, and he'd leaked it out at work that Richie Kemp had been belted like a ten-year-old by his mam. He wondered why Billy was alone. Usually, Richie Kemp was in tow, although whenever he'd seen them it had always appeared to be Richie who was doing most of the talking.

When he got to the yard he found out why. Richie was working overtime.

'Bloody hell, that's a change,' Joe remarked to Kenny Hartley.

'Well, it's like this – or so I heard – first off his mam says he's got to grab every bit of ovvies he can and second, Les Baxter, the chippies' blockerman, caught him skiving. Sitting having a smoke in the fo'rad gun tower placing. He was bloody lucky he didn't get the OBE. Baxter's about the softest blockerman in the yard, but meladdo's got to stay on to make up his time – without pay!'

'I'll bet that pleased him and it won't please his mam if there's no extra money in his pay packet. She'll want to know why. That's one I wouldn't like to have to live with.'

Joe found his tools in the space under a pallet of cut timber. It was either cart them home every night or hide them and hope to God no one found them. Tools were always getting pinched. He started walking through the yard, picking his way carefully between miles of lead piping, cables, wood and other obstacles, then climbed up the ladders that connected the staging at the bow end where he was at present working, welding the thick steel armour plating of Job No. 992, the destroyer HMS *Foresight*.

It wasn't a bad night, he reflected. The sky was clear and inky black. There was a full moon with a milky rim around it that foretold frost, but that was better than rain or snow. He was grateful for the moonlight for there was no lighting, save that from the interiors of the huge fitting-out sheds which filtered out on to the bank. He could hear the water of the river lapping against the bottom of the slipway.

The Mersey was black and calm and the moonlight cast a silver pathway across it to the Liverpool landing stage where the lights of a Cunarder, about to depart, made a dazzling show. The sight of a ship lit up like that always made a tingle run down his spine, probably because like most men in the yard, once the keel was laid it became more than a huge lump of steel, it gained a sort of personality of its own.

It wasn't easy standing on the wooden planks of the staging which surrounded the ship like scaffolding, but Joe was used to it by now. He'd had more than a few 'flashes' but when they'd happened he'd just hung on for dear life to whatever he could grab. He'd nearly fallen the first time it had happened, panicking at the sudden blinding pain in his right eye. These days he managed to deal with them.

He was working along with George Cope and Bill Beswick, high up on the bow, and was therefore thankful there was no wind. It wasn't a job for a man without a head for heights. From time to time conversations, jokes and curses were heard clearly on the frosty air and after about an hour, Joe was wiping the sweat from his brow when Fred Roberts arrived beside him, puffing a bit for, as he muttered to himself, he wasn't as young as he used to be.

'I didn't expect to see you here tonight, boss,' Joe remarked pleasantly.

'Neither did I and I'm too bloody old to be climbing up and down bloody staging all night. Ernie Whittaker's gone sick, so I'm stuck with the lot of you for tonight at least. We picked straws, all the day foremen. I got the bloody short one.'

'Will they have you in in the morning too?'

'Like hell they will! There's enough of them on days to cope without me. They can sod off! No doubt that big-headed get Charlie Milton will be chucking his weight around.'

Joe didn't reply. He knew what his boss thought of Milton. In fact nearly all the blockermen had had a run-in with Milton at some time or other.

'Jevons, the foreman plater, has left instructions that the templates for the next section are out by one sixteenth of an inch. There were some caustic remarks about his apprentices and journeymen and the way they should all be back in the bloody classroom instead of marking out and brightening, I can tell you. So, we've to leave them. They'll have to be done from scratch. A fine bloody waste of good steel and time. You're to move on to the next section. That applies to the lot of you. Parker up there in the crane will lower the plates on to the staging. Cope, you're the most experienced, guide them down. I'm off down now. Every damned idiot in the yard seems to be on this shift tonight! I'll be backwards and forwards all flaming night and I'll have to have eyes in the back of me head.'

Joe nodded and looked up at the dark, latticed metalwork of the big gantry crane overhead. There wasn't much point doing anything until the new plates had been lowered, and George Cope was in charge of guiding the load down, not an easy task in the darkness. At least the moonlight helped and Cope had a large white piece of rag attached to a pole, like a flag, which he waved slowly up and down and from left to right, signals that Parker, the most senior and experienced crane driver, followed.

'I see you don't get a bollocking and made to work on, without pay, for standing around skiving. The blockerman's Royal as usual.'

Joe turned around and faced Richie Kemp. He looked past the lad to where Roberts had just reached the tall framework of posts.

Voices carried clearly in the frosty air, despite the clanging of metal and the hissing of the arc welder.

'Well, just for your information I'm not skiving. The bloody platers have cocked things up. We're to work the next section. Anyway, isn't it past your bedtime?' Joe was openly derisive.

Richie's face turned red. He'd always hated Joe Slattery and not just over the incident with their Lizzie. When they were kids he'd never bested Slattery in the many scraps they'd indulged in and now Slattery had a confident, quiet but somehow supercilious air about him. He'd noted the direct and derisive looks he gave him and his answers to any questions that *had* to be asked were always given in a sharp and patronising tone of voice.

George Cope yelled that the load was down and Joe began to turn away.

'You'd better get back to whatever it is you're supposed to be doing, lad, or you'll be here until midnight, and try and explain *that* to your mam. Clear off, I've got work to do.'

The word 'lad' and the reference to Maudie enraged Richie. He was almost the same age as Slattery but by using the word 'lad' Joe Slattery was inferring that he was a kid, ruled by his mam. He was deliberately insulting him. Billy Milton, who had gone home a long time ago to a warm kitchen, a hot meal and the pleasure of listening to the wireless, he envied. Joe Slattery he hated.

Joe Slattery had just started his shift. He had a better job, more money, more prestige *and* he was popular with his workmates and blockermen alike. God, how Richie hated him.

He lunged out at Joe, aiming for his head with a length of six-inch lead flush pipe he was holding, but George Cope yelled a warning and Joe turned quickly, one arm raised to protect his head, the other clenched into a fist with which he lashed out wildly.

He heard Richie yell, the cry seemed to be suspended in space, then it became fainter and fainter. He stood paralysed as George Cope and Bill Beswick yelled warnings and instructions down to the men working below and then bedlam ensued on the moonlit bank. Men were running and shouting and somewhere an alarm bell was clanging.

All Joe remembered was Fred Roberts getting hold of him by the shoulders and guiding him slowly towards the ladder, saying over and over, 'It wasn't your fault, lad. He'd no right to be up here at all. He took a swipe at you first and he'd have killed you with that length of pipe or it would be you who'd have fallen. It wasn't your fault. You were defending yourself, lad.'

The words all kept going round and round in Joe's head, but they didn't seem to make it any better. He'd lashed out and Richie had fallen.

By the time the ambulance arrived Richie Kemp was dead, his back and neck broken in the fall. His sudden lurch forward to strike Joe and the first deadly crystals of ice that had formed on the staging had caused him to slip and lose his balance. Joe's fist hadn't even touched him.

Had he lived he'd have been crippled, probably from the neck down, the driver informed the white-faced workers and foremen who had assembled around the ambulance.

Joe was taken into the office and given tea laced with brandy that Fred Roberts had sent one of the men racing up to the Queen's Arms at Hinterdon Road to buy. The ambulance men had wrapped a heavy blanket around Joe but none of it helped. The sound of that cry would live on in his memory for the rest of his life and would torment his dreams for months.

Chapter Eleven

Maudie was far from pleased when Harry had arrived home and told her that Richie had to work overtime and wouldn't be in until much later, about nine, he'd surmised. Richie had told her specifically that he wouldn't be working tonight. Harry was also very evasive and vague about the reasons for his son's lateness, a habit he'd cultivated over years of experience of having to answer Maudie's shrewish demands.

'Well, that's very nice. His tea will be ruined and I went down to Mooney's Pork Butchers for the sausages and into Costigan's for best New Zealand butter for the potatoes. Margarine just doesn't taste the same, and Annie agrees. They always have butter. Celia served me. The other one thankfully wasn't there. Off with a sprained ankle or something, so Celia had heard from the Manager. She's probably too damned lazy to get out of her bed, more like, the little slut. And didn't that Mulhinney woman from down the street try to push in in front of me as well?

'"There's a queue here, in case you hadn't noticed. That Slattery girl is off," I said to her.

'"Well, it doesn't take long for you to get served, not with the few measly bits you buy, missus," she said.

'The cheek of the woman! Measly, indeed! Well, I wasn't having that. Celia looked very embarrassed so I deliberately bought more than I intended. I had everything measured out to the last ounce. Mr Henderson served her in the end but I bought *two* pounds of best butter. You should have seen her face when I asked Celia for that!'

Harry ate the meal she placed in front of him but refused to meet her eyes as she sat at the other end of the table rambling on. If he looked up she'd start on something or someone else and ruin his meal. He'd been looking forward to it all day. They always had Mooney's home-made pork sausages with mashed potatoes on Mondays. Maudie got up at the crack of dawn to have her washing on the line by lunch time so she had time to shop.

Richie's tea was between two plates, balanced on top of a pan of boiling water. That way it wouldn't dry out so much. As Harry ate he thought he dare not tell her tonight that Richie wouldn't be paid for working late. She'd find that out soon enough on pay day and then there'd be skin and hair flying.

He smiled smugly to himself. His pigeon loft was finished and awaiting removal from Bert Scott's back yard. Bert was a widower and lived in Back Roscommon Street. They'd got friendly one Saturday night in the pub. Bert had told him about his pigeons and Harry had sighed heavily and poured out his ambitions. He hadn't even had to ask Bert for help, he'd volunteered and gone on to tell Harry all about the clubs he belonged to and his prize birds. Harry had been in transports of delight.

Bert had said there would be no problems about nosy interfering mothers, wives or sisters. It would be dead easy to make it in two halves in Bert's yard. Then, when they'd finished assembling it, Harry would, with Bert's help, move it across the narrow entry and into his own yard. Harry, under Bert's guidance, had already picked out a couple of young birds. Maudie went to her Women's Church Group on Monday nights. Tonight she'd come home to find the pigeon loft installed and that would be that. He'd have a hobby and a place to escape to. There were bolts on the inside of the door as well as the outside. She could yell at him all she liked but she couldn't get at him and he'd listened to that voice for so long that now he was able to blank it out – almost.

Maudie had washed up, fiddled with her hair and put on her hat. Then she'd shrugged on her coat, buttoned it up tightly, wrapped a knitted scarf around her neck and pulled on her woollen gloves. Bluntly she instructed Harry that when 'that lad' got in, he was to have his tea, wash his dishes, put them away and not leave her kitchen looking like the wreck of the *Hesperus*. On no account was either of them to set foot in the parlour as she'd spent part of the afternoon dusting and polishing.

Harry had nodded and sighed and said, 'Yes, luv,' and 'No, luv' but once she'd gone and he was certain she'd not come back for some forgotten item, he was out through the yard and across the jigger to Bert Scott's house.

'Right, 'Arry. You take that end and I'll take the other. We'll 'ave ter manoeuvre it round a bit, like, through the back door,' Bert instructed.

With a lot of sweating, cursing and manoeuvring, the sections of the loft were duly carted from Bert's yard to Harry's and by the light from the kitchen window and the lamp he'd had to rig up in the yard (because the Miltons had one) it was assembled.

Harry stood back and viewed it and a grin of pure pleasure spread from ear to ear.

'Well, there it is, Bert lad, there's nothing she can say now, is there? And she can't get at me either. I'll lock meself in. I'm going to get a bit of a seat to read me magazines in peace. A table, a lamp and a paraffin heater too.'

'You'll kill the poor little buggers with the smell if yer get one of those, 'Arry. If yer want a bit of peace and quiet out here, yer'll have ter freeze until spring.' Bert looked thoughtful. 'Yer know she could take a hatchet to it when you're at work.'

Harry's smile faded. 'Oh no, she bloody won't. I've had enough of her. This time I'm having what *I* want.' There was a new note of determination in his voice.

'Isn't that someone hammering on yer front door knocker?'

Harry listened and then nodded.

'Probably Charlie Milton come to complain about all the banging and hammering.'

'Well, good luck with 'im, mate. I can't stand the feller. A bloody stuffed shirt, that's what 'e is!'

Bert let himself out and Harry went reluctantly back inside to see who was hammering the door down. Just when he had a bit of peace and quiet and could admire his much-longed-for loft too.

The sight of a police sergeant on his doorstep was not what he'd expected at all. His first thought had been that it was Maudie home early after she'd had a row with someone, which she frequently did.

'Is it the . . . wife?' he asked tentatively.

'No, sir. You *are* Mr Harold Kemp?'

Harry nodded.

The sergeant took off his cap. He hated this part of the job. 'Look, I think we'd better go inside, sir. Half the curtains in the street are flapping and there's not so much as a breath of wind, so it's not through draughts.'

Harry led him into the parlour. It was the right thing to do. She'd go mad if she found out he'd taken someone as important as a police sergeant into the kitchen but another, more frightening thought was beginning to take hold of him.

'Is it . . . my . . . lad?' He wondered what Richie had done now. God, it must be something terrible to warrant the police coming to the house.

'I'm afraid it is. Look, there's no easy way around this, sir. I'm sorry, I'm very sorry, but there's been an accident at Laird's and . . .'

Harry sat down suddenly on the polished hide sofa. 'Is he badly hurt?' he asked.

The sergeant twisted his cap in his hands. 'I'm afraid he's dead, sir. He fell, I believe, from high up on the staging. They've taken him to Birkenhead General, to the mortuary. He wouldn't have felt much, if it's a comfort. His neck and back were broken.' He looked at the middle-aged, mild-looking man sitting before him on the sofa whose face was now ashen.

'Where is Mrs Kemp?'

'She – she's at the Women's Church Group. St George's,' Harry replied automatically in a toneless voice.

'Do you want me to go for her, sir, or would you rather do it yourself?'

Harry couldn't think properly. 'I – I'll go if you'll come too, please?'

All the shock, horror and pleading were in his eyes and the sergeant nodded. 'I'll come up with you to St George's, then I'll get a car to take us to hospital and bring you both back here. Have you any relations, friends, neighbours you'd like to come in?'

Harry shook his head. There was Maudie's brother who lived in the south end of the city, but they hadn't spoken for over fifteen years. She'd had a row with both his sisters and his brother years ago too, and so they'd been well and truly ignored and had been excluded from all family get-togethers. Sometimes he'd have welcomed a night out with his brother.

'There's . . . there's Charlie Milton from next door,' he replied at last. He was the only person he could think of.

He'd walked up the street, crossed Netherfield Road North and along St George's Hill, accompanied by the sergeant, who now and then gripped his shoulder to steady him. Sometimes Harry felt the flags of the pavement were coming up to meet him and he was cold. Very cold.

He went into the church hall and stood looking vaguely around him at the assembly of women of all ages, who one by one caught sight of him and turned to gaze at him with irritation and curiosity, until finally Maudie caught sight of him too. Instantly the tight-lipped, sour expression spread across her face and she rose, excusing herself as she walked towards him. Now what was the matter? In the name of the Almighty couldn't she have a few hours' enjoyment without him coming and making an utter spectacle of himself, of them both, for she could see that he even had his old cardigan, work jacket and boots on? He could at least have changed.

All these thoughts fled from her mind as she caught sight of the policeman standing discreetly in the shadows of the porch out of sight. Her hand went to her throat.

'Oh, my God! What's wrong? What's happened?'

'It's . . . it's . . .' Harry's voice failed him. Shock took its toll, he stuttered and tears slipped down his weathered cheeks.

Maudie took hold of him by the shoulders and shook him gently.

'Harry. Harry, luv, what's wrong?' she asked in a quiet, softly urging voice that not one woman in the room would have believed she possessed.

Harry could only shake his head.

'I'm sorry, Mrs Kemp. There's been an accident at the shipyard. Your boy, Richie. Well, I'm afraid he's dead.'

Maudie's mouth dropped open and for once in her life she was struck dumb. Richie dead! Not Richie, whose dinner she'd left on the pan to keep warm. Not Richie she'd been annoyed with so often. No, not Richie!

Totally stunned, they were both shepherded into the waiting police car that the sergeant had sent for using the telephone in the blue box at the junction of Netherfield Road North and St George's Hill.

They were first taken to number eight Roscommon Street for Harry to get a coat and cap. The police constable who was driving was sent to fetch Charlie Milton, to explain briefly. Then he drove the Kemps through the new road tunnel to Birkenhead and the hospital.

They were both dazed and bewildered but the staff were very kind and sympathetic. It was another casualty from Laird's, a fatal one, but they were used to it. They also knew it was important not to be blasé about it. Maudie broke down when she saw her son lying on a mortuary slab covered only by a coarse cotton sheet, which somehow made it seem worse. She'd thought he would still have been in his working clothes. Oh, he'd been the bane of her life, he'd disappointed her in so many things but he was her son, or he *had been* her son. She turned to Harry for comfort but he seemed to be in a state of total shock, just staring ahead, white and mute. It was a mortuary attendant who led her out, got her a chair and then a cup of tea.

As she sipped her tea she wrinkled her nose at a strange smell. It wasn't death – she recognised that smell well enough – it was clinical. In a flat tone she asked the attendant what it was.

'It's formaldehyde. We use it to . . . well . . . preserve the . . . em . . . it, until the post mortem.'

Maudie nodded, unable to reply, and sat rigidly upright while the procedure was explained to her. When they were both sufficiently calm they were to be driven back to Roscommon Street. The police were sympathetic but reserved, and she got not a single word out of Harry. She'd always been the domineering one, making all the decisions, but now when she needed him so badly he couldn't summon up the strength to comfort her. He was in a world of his own. One he may never return from, she thought fearfully.

Both Charlie and Annie were waiting when they arrived home. Annie helped Maudie to take off her coat and hat and tried to think of the right things to say, but she'd never really liked the lad or Maudie either. Then she thought of Billy and how she would feel in Maudie's place and she put her arms around the woman as she broke down again. She felt so sorry for poor Harry, who Charlie was trying to talk to, asking stupid, tactless and totally inappropriate questions such as 'How did it happen? Who saw it? Why was he up there in the first place and who was the foreman in charge?'

Harry said nothing. He just stared ahead into space.

Annie left Maudie and went up to see the twins. Both knew something awful had happened because there'd been a policeman at the door and Da had said something about Richie and going for Mam and being good until they got back. They were sitting on their beds, wan-faced and with their unopened homework books around them.

'What's the matter, Mrs Milton?' Frank asked with a tremor in his voice.

'I'm afraid there's been a terrible accident at the shipyard,' Annie began.

'Is it our Richie?' Eddie asked, eyes wide with fear.

Annie nodded. 'He fell. It was an accident. He . . . he's gone to . . . heaven.' She tried to put it as gently as she could.

'You mean he – he's dead?' Frank asked.

She nodded. 'Collect your things together, you're coming to our house with me to sleep. I'll come back up for you.' She left them sitting side by side, clutching each other tightly and trying to hold back the tears.

Charlie knew Maudie kept a small bottle of brandy, for just such occasions, Annie had told him, and he searched the dresser cupboards until he found it. He poured out generous measures for both of them.

It calmed Maudie but not Harry as he'd hoped, so he began to ask Maudie similar questions.

'It's someone's fault, Maudie, even if it's just negligence by the foreman. We should have it investigated more thoroughly.'

'Don't you think they will do that anyway?' Annie asked timidly.

'In their own time they will.'

'But there's nothing we can do now . . . not tonight. I'll take the twins home with me. We'll manage. It'll be better for them to be with Frederick. You ought to get Harry to bed, Maudie, and then go and try to get some sleep yourself.'

Maudie shook her head. 'No. No, we'll be all right but thanks for having the twins. I can't . . . I just can't . . . think about them. I know it's wrong, it's selfish but . . .' She broke down again.

Annie put her arms around her. She understood, or at least she *thought* she did. Grief took people different ways. Charlie nodded his approval. Annie was being very calm and practical and she was right, there was nothing they could do now, but he was going to make damned sure he found out about it all tomorrow and just who was to blame.

Next door, both Celia and Billy were still up, anxiously waiting. All they'd heard was that there had been an accident at the yard and that Mr and Mrs Kemp were going over there and that Mam and Da had gone next door to wait for them to come home and see to the twins.

Their mother took the two young boys upstairs and began to reorganise things.

'Why aren't the pair of you in bed?' Charlie demanded of his son and daughter.

'We couldn't go, Da. We wouldn't have slept,' Billy answered.

'What's the matter, Da? I know it's something awful,' Celia pressed her father.

'Richie Kemp is dead. He fell from the staging, just under the top of the bow. By God, someone will be nailed for this.'

They were both stunned. Neither of them had liked Richie, but DEAD! DEAD! Dead at seventeen. It wasn't conceivable.

The sound of a car pulling up outside made Charlie move the parlour curtain aside. He saw Joe Slattery, looking dazed and bewildered, being helped out by John Tyson, the head foreman. His expression changed. He should have known! Joe Slattery worked permanent nights. He would have been working on the staging, too, and he hated Richie. Charlie remembered the Jubilee party.

'Accident my bloody foot!' he muttered. Slattery had pushed the lad! Well, he was going to make sure that Slattery paid for this. There'd be no bloody priest or vicar to save him this time.

'Da, where are you going?' Celia cried as Charlie stormed from the room and into the lobby.

He didn't answer, and she and Billy followed.

'Da, what is it?' Celia cried.

'It's that bloody Slattery lad from next door. He's just come home in Tyson's car – the head foreman bringing him home. It wasn't an accident. That bloody Papist pushed him. He killed Richie Kemp.'

As the front door slammed Celia turned to her brother, her eyes wide with disbelief and horror.

'No! No! Joe wouldn't do that! He wouldn't!'

'For God's sake, Cee, don't say that to Da! What's going on? What the hell has been going on?'

'Oh, Billy, I don't think Joe would have anything to do with it. I really don't.' Celia was near to tears.

'Neither do I, Cee, but you know how vicious Richie could be.'

'No! No matter how much he was provoked, Joe wouldn't do that.' Without another word she rummaged in the dresser drawer for a piece of paper and a pencil and scribbled a note, then she ran down the yard with it before her mam came back.

Annie was startled to learn that Charlie had gone back to see the Kemps and that he was very angry. She'd managed to settle the boys down and hoped they would sleep. It was an awful shock for everyone and they had been left waiting and wondering for hours, poor mites. She herself felt sickly and had a terrible headache.

'I really should go back, too, and I think the doctor should be called. Harry – Mr Kemp – is in a terrible state.'

'Mam, if they said no then leave it,' Celia advised. Annie sighed and left the room.

As she walked into the Kemps' kitchen she was in time to hear Charlie laying down the law.

'Maudie, I don't think there was any accident at all. I think your poor lad was pushed *and* I know who did it. I've just seen Tyson, the head foreman, dropping that Joe Slattery off and a more sheepish, guilty-looking feller I've yet to see.'

'You – you think he did it?' Annie gasped.

'He'd every reason and every opportunity up there to make it look like an accident.'

Maudie wiped her eyes and got up and started to put on her coat.

'Maudie, where are you going, luv?' Annie asked. She was very distressed. She kept thinking, what if it had been Billy? And the Slatterys weren't as bad as *that*. Say what you would about them, but they were all religious – in their own misguided way, of course, but they wouldn't kill anyone.

Maudie's face was set. 'I'm going to the police station. Now.'

'You can't! Maudie, you can't! Not when he – Richie – isn't . . . cold.' Annie was horrified.

'It's best done now. I'll come with you. Strike while the iron is hot. Someone's going to pay for this,' Charlie stormed, leading Maudie by the arm to the door.

Annie sat down next to Harry, who still hadn't said a word. She was shaking. Oh, what a terrible, terrible night it had been, and it wasn't over yet.

Brigid hadn't heard the car. She was enjoying an evening's peace and quiet as Josie was sitting at the table with her nose stuck in a book. Bernie was over at Biddy Doyle's with her friend Patsy, and Emmet was with Declan Walsh. But as she heard the front door close she frowned.

'Divil a bit of peace we'll get now,' she said to Lizzie but she looked up in astonishment as Joe walked into the kitchen. So did Lizzie, who was sitting with her foot up, her arms stretched wide. Secured around her hands was a skein of grey wool that her mam had been winding into a ball to knit Emmet a pullover for school.

'Joe! What's the matter? Are you ill, lad? You look desperate.'

Lizzie dropped her arms, shook off the wool and got to her feet with a grimace. Her brother looked awful. His face was drawn and haggard.

'Joe, what's happened? There's something gone on at the yard, hasn't there?'

Josie looked up from her book. Mam was right, her brother seemed ill.

Joe looked at the three of them blankly. 'Richie Kemp . . . is . . . dead.'

'Oh, Mary Mother of God, have mercy on us!' Brigid cried, crossing herself. She hadn't liked the lad one bit, but her thoughts were for his mother.

Lizzie took her brother's arm and led him to a chair. 'Joe, what happened? He can't be dead.' She, like Celia and Billy, found it utterly unbelievable.

'He – he was working late, I – I've forgotten why. I – I was up on the staging under the bow with Fred Roberts. Richie . . . he just . . . appeared . . .' His eyes were swimming with tears and Lizzie squeezed his arm. 'He – he started to say things, the usual rubbish. He had a pipe or a stick in his hand and then he sort of . . . lunged at me and I raised my arm to protect my head and lashed out with the other arm and he . . . fell! Oh God! I'll hear that scream for ever and ever! It was terrible!'

Instantly Brigid was at his side. She gathered him to her just as she had done when he'd been a small boy and had hurt himself.

'It wasn't your fault, acushla, it wasn't your fault. He fell. Didn't he go for you first? Wasn't he going to clatter you with that stick thing? Weren't you only defending yourself? If he hadn't been so . . . nasty it wouldn't have happened. That's what I'm saying, Joe.'

'Mam! Mam, I don't remember properly. It all happened so fast. I don't know if I caught him with my fist and he lost his footing. I just don't *know*!'

'Well, how did you get home?' Lizzie asked. She was shocked and in a way sorry for Richie Kemp, but she knew Joe would never do anything like that deliberately.

'Fred Roberts called Mr Tyson, the head foreman, who called Mr Costain, one of the Directors. Every accident has to be reported immediately. Mr Costain drove me home.'

Lizzie thanked God that Joe had actually said the word 'accident'. 'You see, they can't think you did it deliberately. They knew it was an accident otherwise they'd have had the police in and kept you there, wouldn't they?'

Brigid seized on her daughter's reasoning.

'She's right, Joe. Now look, lad, calm yourself. Would it help if I sent Josie here to go for Father Minehan?'

'No, no, not yet, Mam. I – I . . . just . . . want . . .'

Lizzie knew it was Celia he wanted but couldn't have. Oh, life was so rotten! Even though she had hated and despised Richie Kemp, he didn't deserve to die before he'd even had much of a life. She too went and put her arms around her brother, but she was wondering how she was going to get a note to Celia.

Eventually when they'd calmed Joe down a bit, after Josie had been sent to Paddy McRory at the Elephant with a cup and an explanation, and had returned with a 'drop' of Powers, Lizzie went up to the attic room and scribbled a message for her friend. Then on the pretext of going to the privy, she went down the yard. As she removed the brick there was already a note there. She took it out and replaced it with her own. Then she hobbled back to the scullery and scanned the lines. The colour drained from her face and she grabbed the edge of the sink for support. No! No, they couldn't say that Joe had *killed* Richie. He hadn't. It was an accident! But she couldn't tell Mam or indeed anyone, especially not with Joe in the state he was in already. She dreaded to think of his reaction when he was suffering enough already. Anyway, from the sound of it it was self-defence. She screwed up the piece of paper, then bent her head. 'Oh God, don't let this happen, please? You know he wouldn't do anything like that. Please, please help us?' she prayed.

The desk sergeant looked up from the mound of papers and open books on his desk as Maudie and Charlie entered. Respectable-looking anyway, he thought, even though he wasn't particularly pleased at the interruption. He was trying to work out the rest-day rota for the next week. He was already undermanned with Jones and McNeil off sick.

It was a dimly lit place, Charlie thought, and untidy. There were scattered papers on the desk, and the hearth in front of the fire grate was littered with bits of charred paper, cigarette butts and empty cigarette packets.

Charlie didn't beat about the bush.

'I want to report a murder.'

The sergeant looked back in astonishment which gave way to annoyance. He'd heard nothing about a murder. They didn't look like a pair of cranks but you never could tell these days.

He put down his pen.

'Right, sir, if you could explain a bit further. Nothing's been reported to us tonight and there's nothing in the Day Book either.'

Charlie didn't like the man's attitude. It was patronising and he obviously didn't believe them.

'This lady is Mrs Maud Kemp of number eight Roscommon Street. She's my next-door neighbour. Her son, Richard, was killed tonight by a person called Joseph Slattery who lives next door to me on the other side. They both work for Cammell Laird, as I do myself. I'm a foreman boilermaker.' He drew himself up with all the dignity he could muster but the man was still a good head taller and broader and now had a disgruntled look on his face.

'Just hold on there, sir. This happened when and where?'

This annoyed Charlie even more. The man was a fool.

'I said tonight, at about a quarter to nine at Cammell Laird's shipyard. I take it you *have* heard of them?'

The sergeant took the sarcasm as an affront to his position and dignity.

'Oh, indeed I have, sir,' he answered acidly. 'It's on the other side of the river and I have to tell you that as such it does not come within the jurisdiction of the Liverpool City Police. It's a matter for the Birkenhead Borough Police. You'll have to go to them.' He picked up his pen again and glared down at Charlie.

The colour rushed to Charlie's face. 'You mean you're not going to do ANYTHING? ANYTHING at all about a murder?'

'We can't, sir. Report it to Birkenhead Borough and their CID will take over. They've probably already done so. Now, I think it would be best if you took Mrs Kemp here back home. If she's just lost her boy it's a doctor she should be seeing. She's in no fit state to be out at all, never mind being dragged down here by you. Good night to you both and I'm sorry for your loss, Mrs Kemp. Birkenhead Borough will sort it out, they're a good bunch of lads. Watkins!' he shouted, and a young constable appeared.

'Show this lady and gentleman out and shut the damned door firmly. It's damned cold in here.' He glared after Charlie and Maudie's retreating backs. There hadn't been a word or a tear out of her. She'd a face like a hatchet and as for the bloke, foreman boilermaker he might be but it didn't justify him barging in here demanding this and demanding that.

'A right pair, those two. The lad's not even cold. Hard-hearted Hannah and the Avenging Angel just about sums them up. Thank God it's not on our patch,' he said to Constable Watkins, raising his eyes to the ceiling before concentrating again on the rest-day rota.

Chapter Twelve

All the way back to Roscommon Street Charlie fumed. Maudie too was livid, although she remained silent. The visit to the police station on top of everything else that had happened tonight had left her reeling, and Charlie's voice battered against her ears.

'I'm not standing for this. We were treated as cranks, no marks, idiots, and with disbelief and sarcasm too! That Slattery lad is as guilty as hell, Maudie, and I'm not going to let it go. I'll be in touch with the Birkenhead Police first thing in the morning. You've had enough to put up with for one night. That sergeant was downright rude and arrogant, maybe we'll get more civility out of the Birkenhead lot. All I – we – wanted was justice. God in heaven, your poor lad hadn't even started to live.'

Maudie sniffed and wiped her eyes with the edge of her scarf. She agreed with him totally, but she just wished he'd shut up. She had Harry to worry about too now. He was acting very strange indeed and men had been known to have heart attacks and die after hearing such shocking news.

As they walked down the street Annie was waiting on her doorstep.

'What did they say?' she asked fearfully. She'd lost track of the time altogether. The night had been one long succession of terrible events. In fact it was the worst night of her life and it wasn't over yet by any means.

'They were abusive and arrogant and I'm going to write to that feller's superiors. I got his number.'

'But what are they going to do?' she asked timidly.

'Nothing. That's what they're going to do, Annie. They won't even lift a finger, they said it wasn't in their area. We have to go to Birkenhead Borough Police.'

Annie was aghast. 'Now? Tonight?'

Maudie shook her head. 'No! Not tonight. I couldn't face that journey again. Harry . . . well, Harry is . . .'

Annie drew her neighbour towards her as Maudie's expression crumpled and her shoulders sagged with grief, worry and weariness.

'You're shocked and upset. It's all been a terrible ordeal. I'll come in with you and make some tea. Do you think we should call the doctor out to Harry?'

'Hot, sweet tea and warmth for shock,' Charlie fulminated. 'There's no sense in paying out hard-earned money to doctors who will only say the same thing.'

Annie looked up at her husband and felt her heart hardening against him. He was a fine one to call the police arrogant. It was a case of the pot calling the kettle black, and he was callous and overbearing too.

'Would you go to the phone box at the bottom of the street for me,' Maudie asked Annie, 'and call Dr Fraser?' She glared at Charlie; he was so pompous and it wasn't his son who was dead. It wasn't his wife who was feeling so broken and he wasn't sitting at home staring into space, as Harry had been when she left him, a fact she now regretted. The trip to the police station had achieved nothing. In fact it had made her feel worse.

'Of course I will.'

Annie took her by the shoulders to guide her the few steps to her own front door. Maudie's place was at home with her poor husband.

'When I get back from the phone, I'll sit with you until the doctor comes,' she offered, refusing even to look in Charlie's direction.

Maudie allowed herself to be led into her clean and tidy kitchen where her husband was sitting, exactly as she had left him, but she breathed a sigh of relief and thanked God that he wasn't lying on the floor or slumped unconscious in a chair.

Slowly and wearily she took off her coat and hat and from force of habit hung them both up on the row of hooks on the back of the door. Then she went and sat next to Harry and patted his arm.

Annie bustled about, filling the kettle, getting out cups and saucers, and before she'd left to run to the phone box to summon Dr Fraser, she'd placed two cups before her silent neighbours.

Everything seemed so unreal, Maudie thought. It was like a dream. She'd wake up soon and Richie would be there listening to the wireless and Harry would be reading his pigeon magazines and she'd tell him again that she was having no loft in her yard. But she *knew* it wasn't a dream. It was so dreadfully real. She felt as cold as ice even though the kitchen was warm. Her anger had subsided and grief and shock were overtaking her again.

'Harry, luv, drink your tea,' she urged. He seemed not to have even heard her. Not noticed that she or anyone else was or had been in the room. She'd heard that shock could strike you deaf and dumb, even cause you to lose your memory. Oh God, what would she do if Harry were to end up permanently like this? He wouldn't be able to work, and with Richie dead what would she do? She'd be a woman with no money coming in and the twins to bring up. She'd have to go out to work, get a job and she hadn't had a job since before Richie had been born. She'd be like Brigid Slattery and the rest of them. Go out cleaning offices or taking in washing and mending. The tears started again but they weren't just for Richie or even Harry, they were for herself and the predicament she might now face.

Annie hadn't stopped to get her coat from her own home, but she didn't feel the cold at all, even though a layer of hoarfrost was beginning to cover the pavement and the roofs. As she ran past the Slatterys' house she noticed that the door was open and she heard the sound of raised voices. She didn't stop to see what was going on. Harry Kemp needed Dr Fraser, and quickly.

Brigid had been trying to get Joe to sleep, if not in his bed, then on the sofa.

'You need to sleep, Joe. Isn't it the body's way of healing?'

'Mam, it's not my body, it's my mind. Even when I close my eyes I can still hear . . .'

Lizzie took his hand and squeezed it, then she leaned forward and whispered, 'Why don't you go for a walk? I'll get a message to Celia somehow. It's Cee you need, Joe, not me or Mam.' Joe shook his head. As much as he loved Celia and needed her, his tortured mind sought only rest.

Lizzie was worried. She'd never seen him look so gaunt and afraid, and his fear only heightened her own. Shock could affect people in all kinds of ways. She remembered how guilty she'd felt after she'd found Da dead, and now Joe was thinking he was to blame for Richie Kemp's death.

Brigid's rosary beads slipped through her fingers. Only the occasional quiet click of the crucifix against the beads broke the heavy silence in the room. As she prayed she looked at Lizzie and Joe and there was pain in her eyes. She would willingly go through the agony of guilt that her son was suffering. She was strong. She'd taken hard knocks all her life. In fact she thought all women were stronger than men in times of real crisis. Look at herself next door, she thought. The poor little woman was terrified of her bullying husband, yet she'd sent that wreath and card when poor Dessie had died, risking her husband's wrath and a boycott by her neighbours.

They were all startled by a loud knocking on the front door.

'In God's name, who would that be at this time of night?' Brigid said irritably, but Lizzie had instantly got to her feet.

'I'll go, Mam. You sit there. It's probably Mrs Walsh or Mrs Doyle. You know how fast bad news travels around here.'

She was totally taken aback to see Charlie Milton on the doorstep.

'What do *you* want, hammering on the door like that, frightening the life out of my mam?'

He didn't answer and before she could protest or stop him he'd pushed her aside and was barging down the lobby towards the kitchen.

She ran after him as best she could with her hurt ankle, shouting, 'Get out of here! Get out!' but she was too late, he was already in the kitchen.

Startled by Lizzie's shouts and then the appearance of him in the doorway, Brigid got up, her temper rising.

'Get you out of this house, Charlie Milton! You might well have that poor wee thing of a wife terrified of you, but not me. Get out! Get out of my house this minute!'

Charlie pointed a finger at Joe, who had also stood up.

'It's his fault! He pushed Richie Kemp. It was no accident. It was murder, cold-blooded murder, and I'm going to make sure he swings for it!'

Brigid was livid. The light of battle was in her eyes.

'May God blast you to all the fires and torments of hell! That lad fell. Wasn't he after braining my lad with a pole or a pipe or something? Wasn't it his own fault with the murder he had in his own black heart? Wasn't it God's justice? And I hope he's roasting in hell this minute. Sure, he shouldn't even have been up there at all. Mr Roberts said so and Mr Tyson agreed. I'm sorry for herself's loss but what, may I ask, is any of it to do with you? Now get out of my house!'

Charlie didn't move. 'What business is it of mine?' he roared, stinging at the ferocity of her attack. 'The lad's father is struck dumb with the shock, but Mrs Kemp and I went to the police. We reported it as a murder and demanded investigations into this . . . alleged . . . accident.'

There was a brief second of utter silence, then Lizzie grabbed hold of Joe and pushed him back down on to the sofa and held him there forcibly.

'Take no notice, Joe. Take no notice of him, he's mad. He only wants to make you angry enough to belt him and then he'd get you charged with assault because he knows you never laid a finger on Richie Kemp. He thinks he's so clever but it'll take more nous than *he's* got to fool me.'

They were both bloody mad, Charlie Milton thought. Lizzie's scornful words had revealed one of his motives but before he could move or speak Brigid snatched up the big, heavy metal ladle that hung by the side of the range and was used for dishing out scouse or hotpot and belted him hard across the shoulders with it.

He was a big man, but then she was no lightweight and she had the full force of her anger driving her. He tried to shield his head with his arms as she continued to lash out and rain blows on him as he moved all the way down the lobby and into the street. At the same time she called him all the names she could think of and at a volume only a few decibels below the wailing and screeching of a dozen banshees.

Lizzie and Joe both followed her, Lizzie hanging on to Joe's arm.

'Joe, leave it! Leave it! Things are bad enough!' She too was furious at Charlie Milton's accusations, but having Joe belting him too wouldn't help at all. Mam was doing very well on her own. She was right out in the street now and Charlie Milton was still cowering under the ceaseless frenzy of Brigid's attack.

The yelling and cursing brought people to their doors and when they saw what was going on, the Taylors, the Robinsons and the Beswicks came quickly down the street. From the other end came the Walshes, the Doyles, the Mulhinneys, Jimmy Kelly and Bryan Shea, and the whole thing looked as though it might degenerate into a public slanging match.

'Accuse my lad of murder, will you? Well I'll give you murder,

Charlie Milton!' Brigid screamed, still laying about him with the ladle.

'He killed Richie Kemp. He pushed him!' Charlie roared back, while still trying to fend off the blows or grab and wrest the ladle from her.

'The lying swine! The bullying creature that he is. It's him what needs pushing!' Biddy Doyle screeched.

'Your old feller could do with a push, Biddy Doyle. He might get out of bed and get a job!' Bill Taylor yelled back.

It was Dr Fraser, pushing his way through the crowd, who put an end to a quickly escalating war of words and a situation that was on the brink of turning very nasty indeed.

'What, may I ask, is going on here?' he thundered, looking around at them all in turn. 'I was called out to see a man in deep shock having just lost his son and what do I find but a small riot going on. Madam, I suggest you give that instrument to me.'

'Didn't he barge into my house, Doctor, and accuse my son of murdering that Richie Kemp? What was I supposed to do? I've no man like himself to fight *my* battles for me,' Brigid snapped.

'It *was* an accident, sir,' Lizzie added. 'The head foreman brought our Joe home in his car.'

'It's bloody murder he committed. He hated Richie and it would have been easy to just push him off the staging,' Charlie yelled.

Dr Fraser was not entirely happy at being called out in the first place, and to find the street up in arms, abuse and accusations hurled, only added to his indignation.

'That is a matter for the police, not me, you or anyone else here to decide. Now, I suggest you all return to your homes, I've a sick man to attend to.' He then turned on Charlie.

'And just what right have you to take the law into your own hands and force your way into houses and accuse people, Mr Milton? None that I can see.' His voice was so cold and his manner so stern and authoritative that the crowd melted away.

Fergal took hold of his brother's arm and Lizzie took her mam's and they guided the family back to the house.

Charlie had stormed off up the street in the direction of the pub, forgetting it was long past closing time, and Celia, Billy and Annie, who had all stood transfixed on their doorstep throughout the whole episode, glanced fearfully at each other.

Annie was filled with the sickening terror that always claimed her, but both Celia and Billy were filled with anger. Da *was* mad, Celia thought, her eyes seeking and finding Joe's. Their brief glance spoke volumes. For Celia, Joe's grey-green eyes were filled with love and helplessness. For Joe, Celia's blue gaze held concern and love and longing.

As Fergal stood back to let Joe go through the doorway Celia reached out and quickly touched Joe's arm. She longed to put both her arms around him and just hold him, he looked so awful. For two seconds his fingers covered hers before Billy pulled her away.

Once back indoors Celia urged Billy to get some sleep, he had work in the morning.

'So have you,' he replied.

'But I don't have to get up so early or travel so far. I'm going to sit with Mam and try to calm her down.' Suddenly she clenched her fists and her eyes filled with tears of anger and frustration.

'Oh, I *hate* Da, I really do. He thinks he's above God, even. I hate him!'

Billy nodded his agreement before kissing Annie on the cheek and going upstairs where Foxy and the twins were all sleeping in the same room. He didn't mind going up to the attic room just for one night. The further away from his da the better, he thought.

When he'd gone Celia sat next to her mother on the sofa, took both Annie's cold hands in her own and began to chafe them gently. Her poor, poor mam. What a terrible night she'd had. How she hated even the smallest argument and would go to any length to avoid it. But this public screaming match on top of Richie's death had affected Annie badly, even though she'd not moved from the doorstep. Da's behaviour had been terrible and she really *did* wonder if at times he lost control of himself.

'Oh, Mam, you're going to have to either ignore him totally or stand up to him. He's a bully and always has been.'

Annie gazed into the fire in the range, seeing castles and clouds and whirling shapes that changed by the second in a sort of dance. The pictures in the flames were hypnotic and she could feel the tension lessen. Celia was right.

'Oh, Cee, you don't know how much I hate him now, but I can't. I just *can't* stand up to him.'

'Mam, if he ever belts you, you can go to the police.'

'And what can they do, luv? Come round and stand outside the door day and night? Besides, he's never raised a hand to me.'

Not yet, Celia thought grimly, remembering the night he'd beaten her.

'I . . . I . . . admired Mrs Slattery tonight, I really did. Him barging in like that, accusing her son of murder and calling them all dreadful names. That poor lad was shocked, too, and in no fit state to stand up to your da, and Mrs Slattery has no man to protect her. Oh yes, I admired her. I just wish I had her strength. Does that shock you, Cee?'

'No, Mam. I admired her too.' Celia paused, trying to form and gather the words in her mind, and when she did speak it was slowly and hesitatingly.

'Mam, there's something I've got to tell you. You know that Lizzie Slattery and I are friends and we've been friends for five years. Well . . .' Again she paused, then realised she couldn't tell Annie about Joe and herself. That would be too much for her mam to bear. She'd worry herself to death over it. 'I . . . I know Joe Slattery a bit and from what Lizzie says he wouldn't harm a fly, let alone do . . . do something so awful as what Da's accused him of.'

Celia was quite amazed to see a smile lift the corners of her mother's mouth. She'd expected disbelief or recriminations.

'Lizzie's a bright little thing.'

'She is, and she's strong and determined too. She has a temper to go with her hair but I'm . . . sure he – Joe – isn't so quick to flare up.'

This time Annie smiled openly and fully. 'Lizzie takes after her mother then. Yes, I *do* admire them both.'

'Then you'll try to be like them and stand up to Da?'

'No, but I'll not speak to him directly ever again.'

Celia sighed heavily, thinking of the future and the atmosphere there would be in the house.

Suddenly Annie bent forward, clutched her abdomen and groaned. Celia was up in a trice and put her arm around her mother's shoulders.

'Mam, Mam, what's the matter?'

Annie shook her head and then straightened up slowly. 'It's nothing, Cee, luv. Just a stitch I get now and then. The pain's gone now.'

'Mam, you should see Dr Fraser.'

'No, there's no need for that. It's nothing. Women of my age often have things like this – headaches, hot sweats. It's just my age. You know, the "Change".'

Celia didn't look convinced. Mam hadn't been well for months, but she lived on her nerves and she *was* middle aged.

'Well, let's get to bed before Da comes back. It won't be long before he realises it's well past closing time.'

Annie nodded her agreement and got to her feet slowly. She felt far from well. It was true that the pain had been slight and occasional to start with but now it had grown worse. She wouldn't go to the doctor, she was afraid of what he might tell her and she would be very embarrassed if he were to suggest an examination. So she'd almost convinced herself that it really was the Change of Life, even though she still got the curse each month.

Lizzie had managed to calm her mam down. She'd sent Fergal to bed, for he looked terrible and he'd have to be up for work in the morning. She felt desperately sorry for Joe for she knew he was still blaming himself. Guilt was written all over his pale, drawn face and it haunted the look in his eyes.

'I'll speak to Cee tomorrow and we'll fix something up,' she whispered to her elder brother as he got to the kitchen door.

Joe just nodded. He felt worse now after Charlie Milton's accusations. If you flung enough dirt, some of it would stick, he'd heard his mam say. Suppose the police *did* come? Suppose the likes of Charlie Milton convinced them it wasn't an accident?

He was so confused that he'd begun to doubt himself. He'd never be sure in his mind that his fist hadn't caught Richie, causing him to lose his balance. Suppose Celia believed it and never wanted to see him again? Although the look in her eyes and the fleeting touch of her fingers had told him she didn't believe her da. Sleep, he thought in desperation. He'd get precious little of that tonight.

When Lizzie was certain Joe had gone to bed she sat down beside Brigid.

'Mam, what are we going to do? People, people might start to believe there's something in *his* accusations.'

Brigid was still shaking with suppressed anger and she was exhausted, but she wasn't going to let Charlie Milton get away with this.

'I'll tell you what I'm going to do, Lizzie. I'm going over there myself tomorrow and see this blockerman, this Fred Roberts. Wasn't he there? Didn't he see all of it? Joe said he did. I'll find out the truth of it all and then . . . then I'll have another go at that evil, lying pig we have the misfortune to live next door to. That'll put him in his place.'

'Mam, don't you think it better to let things alone? It will all die down in a few days.' She was thinking of both her brother and Billy Milton. What kind of a chance did they have now, any of them? She tried to think of an old adage. Something about the path of true love never being easy. Well, God alone knew how hard theirs was going to be. Oh, she didn't want to think about it at all.

'Die down, is it? It won't, but I'm going to get our Joe's name cleared once and for all this time! I'll stand outside those gates until kingdom come until I get to see who is in charge of the place.'

'Mam, our Joe won't be happy about you going over there,' Lizzie pleaded.

'Well, I'm going and I don't care if the whole flaming street knows about it. I'm not having people even think that my son is a murderer. Shame on you, Lizzie Slattery, acting up like this. Telling me what or what not to do. Have you no pride, no feelings at all? Isn't he your brother and don't we all rely on him since yer da passed away, God rest him?'

Lizzie nodded. Mam had made up her mind and Lizzie knew from experience that there was nothing more she could say to stop her going over the water on the ferry tomorrow. As she went wearily up the stairs she wondered what her brother's reaction would be to a visit to his foreman by his mam.

Chapter Thirteen

The atmosphere next morning was much quieter, more subdued than normal, Lizzie thought.

'Emmet, Bernie, Josie, when you've eaten that bread wash your hands and get over the road to Mrs Walsh's house.'

'Ah, Mam! Do we have to? It's ages yet before we have to go to school,' Bernie protested.

'Yes, you do *have* to go. I'm not having any trick-acting and fighting in here. Not this morning when we're all destroyed.'

'We won't. We'll be dead good, Mam, promise. Cross me heart an' hope to die,' Emmet pleaded. School was bad enough without having to leave so early.

'Hasn't there been enough death and talk of death, Emmet Slattery? I'll give you five minutes and you'll be up to something. I'll hear no more of it,' Brigid replied in a tone of voice that brooked no further argument.

Joe came down the stairs followed by Fergal. Joe looked as though he'd been up all night and Fergal didn't look much better.

'Just a cup of tea, Mam, please,' he said, sitting on the old sofa to put on his boots.

'Will that keep body and soul going? It will not, so you'll get some food inside you.'

'Mam, please don't go giving out about it,' Fergal begged.

'Giving out, is it? Would you look at that window there. There's frost all over it and the pair of you want to go to work with empty bellies.'

Lizzie intervened. 'Mam, leave them.'

Brigid shrugged, more worried than annoyed. She herself was subdued but her mouth was set in a line and determination blazed in her eyes.

After they'd all gone Lizzie tried again.

'Mam, don't go, please? It will only make things worse. It'll upset our Joe and Fergal, it'll embarrass them.'

'You can talk until you're blue in the face, Lizzie, but I'm going and that's my final word,' Brigid replied as she tidied her hair and wrapped her thick, warm shawl over her head, clasping it tightly to her. She'd give the two boys a head start before she left the house.

When she'd gone, Lizzie wrote a note for Celia, explaining that Joe would be in the usual place at the usual time tomorrow afternoon. She'd told her brother nothing at all about this, but she knew just how much Celia longed to comfort Joe. She'd seen the look that had passed between them last night and she'd noted Celia's gesture of sympathy too. She hoped she herself would be able to see Billy at the weekend, probably on Sunday. Her foot should be much better by then.

Father Minehan called half an hour later and Lizzie hobbled to the door to let him in.

He gave the usual blessing: 'God bless all in this house.'

Lizzie replied, 'Amen,' and then sat down on the old sofa, grimacing at the pain in her foot.

'Is your mother not home, Lizzie? I heard there was some trouble here last night.'

'There was, Father. It was terrible. Only for Dr Fraser I think the police might have had to be called in the end.'

The parish priest looked sombre. 'I heard that the Kemp boy was dead. An accident, I believe.'

Lizzie nodded. 'He fell from the staging. His back and neck were broken.'

'God rest his soul,' Father Minehan replied, shaking his head. The loss of a young life was a tragedy, no matter what his creed or colour might be.

'He . . . Richie, made some kind of nasty remark, then tried to belt our Joe with a piece of lead pipe. He slipped and fell. His blockerman saw the whole thing but Mr Milton from next door came round and accused our Joe of murder. Mam was furious, and kept on belting Mr Milton until he was out in the street. Then everyone else came out and it was shaping up for a battle royal until Dr Fraser arrived to see Mr Kemp. He's in a severe state of shock. He can't speak. He's struck dumb with it all.'

Father Minehan crossed himself. 'God have pity on him.'

'It's not my place to say so, Father, but he does need God's help, what with Richie's death and having to live with her – Mrs Kemp.'

'Ah, yes, I remember her well from the Jubilee party.'

'She went to the police with Mr Milton.'

The priest was incredulous. 'And her son barely cold? Has the woman no feelings?'

'I think it was mainly Mr Milton. Anyway, Mam's gone over to the yard this morning to see our Joe's foreman and get the truth. She insists on clearing his name and I think she's right, but whether our Joe will think so is another matter.'

'Her journey won't be wasted, Lizzie. I'm sure the police over there will have already looked into the matter. It's part of their job.'

Lizzie looked worried. 'He never said anything about that, Father.'

'Maybe not. If there was a senior man who witnessed everything they would have spoken to him. I imagine there will be a post mortem and an inquest, but they are just formalities. The inquest will be opened and then adjourned so they can release the lad's body for burial.'

Lizzie felt reassured. Father Minehan would know all about these things.

He got to his feet. 'My prayers are for you all, but especially Joseph. Will you tell him to come and see me – when he's ready, and your mother too?'

'I will, Father.' Lizzie tried to rise.

'No, child, stay where you are. I'll let myself out. Tell your mother I called.'

'I will,' she answered, thinking how different his attitude would be if he knew of her feelings for Billy Milton and Joe's for Celia.

Brigid sat on the hard, slatted wooden seat in the saloon of the ferry that ploughed its way across the choppy grey river, weaving occasionally between larger ships. The waves were white-crested, the spray being thrown upwards by the force of the wind. Her head was held high, her shoulders were squared. She'd have the truth of this matter before the day was over.

When at last they drew alongside the stage at Woodside she got up, walked out on deck and waited, with a couple of hundred other people, for the rattle of chains and the dull thud that was the signal that the gangway was down.

She walked with the crowd up the covered tunnel and out into Chester Street, and caught a tram to New Chester Road, to the entrance of the shipyard whose high wooden gates were open wide. They were painted black with white lettering two foot high. Cammell on one gate and Laird on the other. There was a man sitting in a little booth so she crossed over to him.

'Can I 'elp yer, missus?' he asked with a trace of suspicion in his voice. Probably one of the wives out to cause trouble by demanding to know if her husband actually got paid and, if so, then where had the money gone?

'You might, an' all. I want to see Mr Fred Roberts. I'm Joe Slattery's mam.'

His expression changed to one of sympathy. The news had

shocked everyone who'd arrived for work that morning, himself included.

'I don't think Fred Roberts is still here, missus.'

'Where is he then?' Brigid was not going to give up on her mission easily.

'He was with Mr Tyson and Mr Costain – he's a Director – but I think they've all gone home, 'aving been up all night, what with the police down 'ere and asking all the lads questions and taking statements. There wasn't much work done 'ere last night, I can tell you that, luv.'

'I've been up all night meself and so has our poor Joe and he turned in for work this morning,' Brigid stated firmly.

'I'll phone up and see.' He hadn't the heart to turn her away, yet it was a big decision for a gatekeeper to make. He used the phone only occasionally and then when it was only absolutely necessary, for he distrusted the instrument. He preferred to send one of the young can lads instead. He dialled the number carefully and waited.

'Mr Tyson, sir, I'm sorry to trouble you, but Joe Slattery's mam's here an' would like ter see Mr Roberts, iffen he's still here, of course.'

Brigid watched him closely, trying to judge by his expression and the succession of curt nods what the answer would be.

The gateman replaced the receiver carefully. 'He said Fred Roberts is still with him, and Mr Costain too. Something to do with insurance, but you're to go up to Mr Tyson's office.

'Sykes!' he bawled at a young lad who was in the act of moving some cut timber.

The lad came over to them, his expression wary.

'Show Mrs Slattery here up to the office. I can't leave the gate. Mr Tyson's up there so wipe yer hands and yer snotty nose and don't say a single word to anyone.'

The lad did as he was bid with the sleeve of his jacket. Brigid followed him. When they reached the office a very smartly dressed young woman was sitting at a desk hammering away on a typewriter.

At their appearance she stopped and looked up. Her thinly plucked eyebrows rose in speculation and her expression became one of superiority.

'Are you Mrs Slattery?' she asked Brigid, completely ignoring the boy who turned and left wordlessly.

Brigid nodded.

'Then follow me, if you please,' came the curt instruction.

Brigid was aware of an impression of sparseness and tidiness but nothing specific registered in her mind as she was ushered in.

Fred Roberts looked exhausted. His face was lined and weatherbeaten and his eyes seemed to have sunk and were dark-circled. John Tyson was dressed in a dark office suit, worn and shiny on the sleeves and elbows. He looked tired and concerned, and his crumpled shirt and jacket bore witness to a night without sleep. As she was ushered in he rose.

'Mrs Slattery, please sit down.'

Fred Roberts, without being asked, pulled the chair from the corner of the room and Brigid sat gingerly on its edge.

'I hear Joe has turned in this morning.'

Brigid nodded. 'I thought it best, sir.'

John Tyson nodded slowly although Fred Roberts shook his head. The lad was still in shock. His mind and attention would be dwelling on other things. His co-ordination and reflexes might be affected and there could be a further accident. No, on this point he disagreed with them both.

'I'm led to understand that Mr Kemp is in a bad way,' John Tyson said.

'I wouldn't know about that, sir, but it's Mrs Kemp and Mr Milton I've come about.'

'I don't understand. Mr Milton, you say? Surely he wasn't here last night?' He looked up at his foreman, a frown creasing his forehead, puzzlement in his eyes.

'No, sir, he wasn't here, I can vouch for that, but he's here this morning,' Fred Roberts answered. He was suddenly becoming aware of Brigid Slattery's motive in coming here.

'He – he barged into my house last night, sir, and accused our Joe of . . . murder. He said my lad had pushed Richie Kemp because he'd always hated him. That's the way of it, sir, and may God strike me down dead here and now if it's not what he said and did. And he'd been down to the local police station with Mrs Kemp and told them they should come and arrest our Joe at once.'

'And did they come?' John Tyson's expression was as grim as Fred Roberts'. Neither of them liked Charlie Milton but he was a good workman. This, though, was the act of a madman.

'No, sir, they did not but it wasn't for the want of them two. They were told it was the job of the police here.'

John Tyson rose and walked across to a door that bore the nameplate 'K.J. Costain', knocked and then entered. Fred Roberts and Brigid strained to hear the conversation until John Tyson accompanied by Mr Costain himself came into the office.

Brigid felt very apprehensive. A Director no less. The really big boss, and he looked so smart in his well-tailored suit, white shirt and restrained green and blue tie. He also looked very sombre indeed.

'Would you all come into my office, please.' It wasn't a question, it was a command, Brigid thought as she trod very warily on the carpet and again sat gingerly on the edge of the chair that was indicated by Mr Costain. The two other men stood as Kenneth Costain leaned forward across the desk, tapping the top of it sharply with the pen he'd picked up. He'd been asking and had asked questions half the night. Now the police had statements and were satisfied it had been an accident.

'Now let me get this right. Mr Milton went to the Liverpool City Police and told them that your lad had murdered young Kemp? That he had deliberately pushed him off the staging because of the personal animosity there was between them? Then he forced an entry into your home and accused Joe to his face of murder?' He'd driven the lad home himself and Joe Slattery had looked like death, but he was certain there had been no foul play on Joe's part.

'That's the way of it, sir. Everything you've said is the truth. I – I'm a widow, sir, with young ones to bring up. I've no man to turn to, so I took the big ladle to Charlie Milton and chased him into the street. He'd no right to cross my doorstep or accuse my lad of anything, and poor Joe as white and drawn as if he'd heard the banshee wailing on the yard wall all night.'

'Roberts, do you know where Milton is?'

'I do, sir.'

'Then go and get him and bring him up here – now!' The order was issued in a tone of suppressed anger.

'It'll be a pleasure, sir,' Fred replied grimly before leaving the office.

Mr Costain picked up the telephone on his desk and pushed a button. Then he asked for a cup of tea to be brought in.

Within a few minutes Miss Claybourne appeared with it.

'Would you hand it to Mrs Slattery, please, Miss Claybourne. She's come a fair distance and has endured a great deal of upset and abuse.'

The cup and saucer were handed over by Lucille Claybourne with bad grace and a tight-lipped expression that didn't go unnoticed by either Brigid or Mr Tyson.

Brigid sat and sipped it in silence, her eyes downcast. The china was very delicate. All they'd ever had were white muggen cups. How the rich lived, she thought. China cups at work and carpet on the floor too.

She hadn't expected to be treated so well. All she'd wanted to do was speak to Fred Roberts and clear Joe's name. She had nothing in common with the well-dressed, well-spoken man who sat opposite her across the leather-covered desk with its fancy silver inkstand and pens. It seemed an age before there was a knock on the door and Fred Roberts walked in followed by Charlie Milton.

Charlie was astonished by the presence of his next-door neighbour, seated and drinking tea out of a china cup in the director's office. She shouldn't have been let in the yard, never mind Mr Costain's office, the very inner sanctum. He'd asked Roberts why he'd been sent for but the man had just glared at him and said, 'You'll find out soon enough.'

Kenneth Costain stood up as he felt the situation warranted it.

'Milton, as you can see Mrs Slattery has made a special journey and she is very distressed about your behaviour and the accusations you have made about her son pushing Richard Kemp off the staging last night. You even went to your local police station and demanded they arrest Joe Slattery, I gather.'

Mr Costain's voice was as cutting as a knife. Charlie said nothing. Anger and humiliation consumed him. That bloody woman! That bloody woman with her flaming brood of scruffy, half-educated kids, had had the nerve to come over the water to see Mr Tyson and was being treated like a queen. She didn't even have a coat or hat, just that black shawl, the uniform of her class and as such, beneath his and definitely Tyson and Mr Costain's association.

'You were not here last night but Mr Roberts was and he witnessed the whole thing. Kemp, so I believe, was working unpaid overtime for being caught idling and smoking and had no business to be up on the staging at all. Then he made a detrimental remark to Slattery.' He pulled a piece of paper towards him. '"The blockerman's Royal again," I believe were the exact words. Then he attempted to strike Slattery with a piece of lead piping. Slattery put up one of his arms to protect his head and lashed out with the other to defend himself.

'It was freezing last night and ice had begun to form on the staging. Kemp lost his footing and fell. That's the sworn statement Mr Roberts gave to the police last night and they accepted it, having other testimony as well.' He turned to Fred. 'Is everything I've said correct, Mr Roberts? You would swear to it in any court in the land?'

'It's exactly as you say, sir, and yes, I'd swear to it.'

'Then what in God's name did you think you were doing, man, spreading lies like that? Interfering in something that had nothing at all to do with you in the first place? Forcing an entry into a widow's home and causing more trouble and distress? Mrs Slattery has a very good case if she should decide to sue you for slander and I wouldn't blame her at all. In fact I'd advise it.' He had a son of sixteen and knew what he'd do if he were faced with a similar situation.

He leaned across his desk to press home the severity of his words.

'It's a very, very serious matter and I couldn't keep a man working here who has a reputation for making false accusations and telling downright vicious lies, no matter how good a workman he might be. Do you understand that, Milton? So let's hope that a public apology and some form of monetary remuneration will suffice.' He turned to Brigid for her reaction.

She was sitting with her back like a ramrod and her chin tilted upwards and was the very picture of outraged dignity.

'I don't want any money from him, sir. Sure, it would burn a hole in my purse. I'd throw it in the fire, so I would. But an apology would do. To our Joe here in the yard before his workmates, and to me before *all* my neighbours.'

She was taking great pleasure in watching Charlie Milton squirm in silence. His face was suffused with the blood of anger and a vein at his temple was throbbing.

He was furious though he had no alternative, he could see that, but his pride fought with practicality and would have to be sacrificed. Not only would he get the sack but he'd be publicly sued with all the humiliation that would bring and he'd be a marked man. He'd never get another job. No one would employ a 'troublemaker', not even in the most menial of jobs, which was what he'd be reduced to. His status as a foreman would disappear overnight. He knew he was right but it was obviously impossible to prove it. There were few foremen who got on well with him and Fred Roberts was not one of them. It would be hard, so very, very hard to stand and apologise – twice. The Slattery woman was exacting her pound of flesh all right, but at least she wanted none of his money.

He nodded curtly.

'Right then, I'll call a mass meeting and when you get home you will apologise to Mrs Slattery and her entire family, in public, and I'll send someone over to make sure my instructions are carried out. If they are not then don't set foot in this yard again or I'll have you arrested for trespassing. Now you can go and continue your work.'

Charlie walked slowly from the room, his anger almost a physical pain. She'd beaten him again. She'd already attacked him in the street and made a show of him before Dr Fraser, but the worst was yet to come. He didn't even know if he could do it, but what were the consequences if he didn't comply? They didn't bear thinking about.

Brigid placed the delicate cup and saucer carefully on Mr Costain's desk and then rose to her feet.

'Thank you, sir. I knew I'd have justice from you and I'll always be grateful, and if there's ever anything, any small wee thing at all that me and mine can do for you . . .'

'Quite. Thank you, Mrs Slattery. Thank you, Roberts.'

The interview was over for them both and although all Fred wanted to do was go home to his bed, he'd stay on. He'd take a great delight in seeing Charlie Milton's humiliation. The man was an arrogant fool to even make such damned stupid accusations.

As they reached the door of the head foreman's office and Fred opened it to let Brigid pass through, Tyson called out to him.

God Almighty, he hoped he wasn't going to be asked to see the woman home, Fred thought.

'Fred, get off home. You look like a feller who's been on the batter for a week. I'll sort Milton and young Slattery out.'

Fred Roberts breathed a sigh of pure relief.

Ten minutes later all work was stopped. The hammering, banging, yelling and the hissing of arc welders all ceased as the men, instructed by their foremen, gathered before the office. Joe had been sent for but for what reason he didn't know, as had Charlie Milton, who knew exactly the reason for the summons.

Both Joe and Charlie came out behind Mr Tyson and walked on to the small raised platform. The head foreman's voice didn't carry and it wasn't very clear to those at the back of the crowd but those near the front would relay it later, almost word for word but with their own remarks and embellishments.

'We are all aware of the terrible tragedy that occurred here last night, the death of young Richard Kemp. And some of you will no doubt have heard sinister accusations made by Mr Milton about that fall, that *accident*. Mr Milton, who was *not* on these premises last night at all. Accusations made against Joe Slattery's part in the affair.' He paused for his words to have time to sink in.

Charlie Milton was looking down at his boots and it had begun to dawn on Joe that Milton was going to have to apologise and refute the accusations in public and he wondered how Mr Tyson had heard of it. His heart returned to its normal rate of beating and he felt as if a huge weight had been lifted from him.

He turned his head in time to see Charlie Milton step to the edge of the platform and take out of his pocket a piece of paper on which there were words that had been typed. Then he listened, his eyes downcast, as Charlie read out the formal apology Mr Costain had dictated to Miss Claybourne. He wasn't one to gloat really, but this time Charlie Milton had gone too far, Joe thought. Milton's lies could have resulted in him being arrested, tried and swinging from a hangman's rope in Walton Jail across the Mersey in Liverpool.

Charlie read the words in a clipped, cold tone that had not one ounce of emotion of any kind in it. He was doing it only to secure his job and his position but he'd never forgive the Slatterys, nor would he forget – ever. He'd bide his time. He'd watch and wait.

Chapter Fourteen

At half-past six Charlie Milton got off the train, went up the stairs and into the big lift that took them to ground level into James Street. The streets that ran down to the Pier Head and the river seemed to act like tunnels for the wind, even in summer, he thought.

He turned up the collar of his overcoat as a protection from the icy blasts that now were gaining in strength and severity. As he walked up to the tram stop he looked about him for Billy. More often than not they came home together, but tonight there was no sign of him.

By the time Charlie alighted at Netherfield Road he was already consumed with impotent rage, for he'd seen Joe and Fergal Slattery and Jack Hey, a foreman plater, get on the same tram, and they were the last people he wished to encounter. Luckily, they'd gone upstairs, probably to smoke, a habit he didn't approve of.

He hurried his steps so he would at least get home ahead of them. It had been utterly humiliating to have to read out that apology; his own son had been amongst that crowd. It now annoyed him that the boy hadn't even sought him out to attempt to show some sort of solidarity. He'd got either an earlier or a later train.

Billy had in fact been one of the first out of the yard gates when the hooter sounded and had run up to Green Lane Station. He had been shocked, squirming with shame and embarrassment, as he'd stood with all the other men and boys when his father had read out the apology. All afternoon he'd kept his head down and tried to ignore everything his fellow workmates said. It hadn't been easy for it had been the main topic of conversation in the yard all day and his da was far from popular to start with. He had rushed home desperately to prepare his mam and Celia for the terrible mood Da was bound to be in when he arrived home.

'You're home early, Billy. Are you ill or something?' Annie said mildly, concern in her eyes as she returned the rack of lamb to the oven after basting it.

'Mam, Da will be in soon and he'll be in a terrible temper, worse even than he was at the Jubilee party.'

As her son explained, the colour drained from Annie's face and she felt weak and sick. Last night had been bad, or so she'd thought then, but now her apprehension turned to terror.

Celia glanced at Billy and bit her lip, but before she could speak the front door slammed and her father's heavy footsteps were heard in the lobby.

They all applied themselves industriously to their tasks, seeming totally engrossed so as not to have to speak to him first and so unleash the wrath upon themselves. Billy was in the scullery washing. Celia was setting the table and Annie appeared fully occupied with the meal.

Charlie glared at them as he placed his bowler hat on the dresser. He had no intention of wearing it in public again today. No, that badge of office, that symbol of power, would not be besmirched further. He'd wear the trilby he wore for going to the pub or other casual outings.

'Leave that meat alone, woman. In ten minutes we all have to go out into the street. Jack Hey has come home with Slattery. That bloody woman from next door came to the yard complaining. I've already had to read out a flaming statement to save my job, and me a foreman boilermaker.'

So it was a 'statement' now, Billy thought. There was no mention of the word 'apology'.

Glancing at her mother, who was already white-faced and

shaking, Celia said, 'Why out in the street, Da?' thinking that this sounded remarkably like a public apology and one that he'd obviously been forced to make. Billy was right: Da was in a terrible mood.

'Because I have another bloody statement to make in front of the entire bloody street,' he yelled back at his daughter. 'That feller Hey is even now knocking on everyone's doors.'

Celia's heart felt like a lump of ice.

'Everyone, Da?' she asked timidly.

She was ignored.

Annie began to sniff and turned away, hoping her husband wouldn't notice. Oh, dear God, she thought, life wouldn't be worth living after tonight. Everyone at their end of the street would pity them and those at the other end would gloat and she didn't know which was worse. She felt again the dragging pain in her abdomen but didn't dare cry out.

'And you can stop that bloody snivelling, woman!'

Celia went over and pretended to be helping her mam with the meat. Via the 'post box' in the yard, she'd heard from Lizzie that Mrs Slattery was going over to Laird's and she knew that her da must have had a right rollicking, maybe even threatened with the police, for all she knew. That *must* be it, for her da would never apologise to anyone. A worse night lay ahead of them. Now she really believed her brother.

Joe felt as though he were sleepwalking, and hadn't uttered a word all the way home. Only Jack Hey had remarked on how cold it was, how bitterly the wind was blowing. Fergal had gone ahead to warn his mam and sisters.

'Will you have a cup of tea, sir?' Brigid asked Jack Hey as he came in with Joe. 'You must be perished with the cold. Those trams would have you frozen with the draughts that are in them.'

'Thank you but no, Mrs Slattery. I've a lot of doors to knock on and the sooner we get this all over the better it will be for everyone,' he replied sombrely before Lizzie showed him out.

'Tidy your hair, Mam, and put on your shawl,' she said when she returned to the kitchen. 'You and our Joe will have to be ready when Mr Hey comes back.'

'So, giving the orders, is it now, Lizzie Slattery? I'm well able to have the sense to make myself look presentable, even though I haven't got a coat or a hat.' Brigid took off her soiled apron and replaced it with a clean one.

'You and Fergal can come out with me and our Joe, but the rest of you can stay inside. This performance only concerns me, Lizzie and the lads. You can look through the parlour window if you like.'

The three younger children all scuttled into the front room and jostled for the best view from behind the curtain.

'God, isn't it amazing *him* having to go out and apologise to Mam,' Bernie said, her cheeks flushed with excitement.

'Oh, shut up, Bernie, and grow up!' Josie reprimanded her.

Bernie pulled a face and whispered to her brother, 'Get her! She's just got a cob on because she can't go out too.'

Both Joe and Lizzie wondered whether Foxy, Celia and Billy would be bound by the same restriction. Neither of them could see Charlie Milton allowing his family to be amongst that crowd.

When Jack Hey came back it was to inform them that nearly everyone was assembled under the streetlight outside Maudie Kemp's house and that Charlie Milton was standing on his front step with his family. He didn't say he'd had three doors slammed in his face from the houses opposite Charlie Milton's.

'Right then, Mrs Slattery. Joe, we'll go now. Are all the rest of the kids coming?'

'No they are not. Just Fergal and Lizzie. The other three are in the front room.'

He nodded. It was best not to involve the kids; things were bad enough with their warring parents. He lived in Birkenhead – 'the one-eyed city' as Liverpudlians called it – and personally couldn't see any reason for all the bitterness and hatred across the Mersey in areas of this city. And it was passed from generation to generation too, so there seemed no end to it.

Draped in her shawl, Brigid emerged, her head held high, and, like a queen, accompanied Jack Hey up the street to the lamp outside Maudie's house, with Joe and Lizzie following her. There was no sign of Maudie, Harry or the twins, and clearly Celia and Billy, who were standing with their father, dare not risk even a quick glance, with their da almost shaking with suppressed fury. Annie stood on the top step, as far back into the shadows of the lobby as she could get.

Jack Hey stood with his arms folded across his chest and a grim expression on his face. Charlie took his place beside him, his eyes firmly fixed on the piece of paper the foreman plater had handed him. His words were again read from typed notes and in the same flat, unemotional tone. There were murmurs of 'Aye' and 'Shame' and 'Bloody liar', but Jack Hey silenced them with a steely glance that slowly raked the crowd.

When Charlie had finished he shoved his way roughly through the crowd, back towards his own front door.

The crowd began to disperse and return to their homes, but Biddy Doyle made a point of patting Brigid's arm.

'There's the justice, Brigid. That'll take him down a peg or two, the puffed-up, snooty creature that he is.'

'It will so but I'm sick to death of it all, Biddy,' Brigid replied quietly, guiding Joe, Fergal and Lizzie towards home.

They didn't dare look at Celia or Billy, who lingered as long as they could on the steps, then turned to follow their father.

Brigid ignored them, too, but as she ascended the steps to her front door, she caught sight of Annie Milton in the shadows of her doorway, looking scared to death. God help the poor wee soul, she thought. She'd have a desperate night with himself, that was for sure, and they'd probably hear it all with the walls being so thin. Impulsively she leaned across the doorway.

'God bless you, Mrs Milton. I know that there's not a bit of wickedness in you. Good night and God help you for I think you're in for a bad night altogether.'

Charlie, Billy and Celia had gone in and Annie shut the door quickly, her heart beginning to pound. Oh, she hoped that Charlie hadn't heard anything but when the kitchen door slammed she realised he'd gone straight in, no doubt for his tea. There was bound to be some complaint about the meal for it would surely have suffered during the time they'd been standing on the step. Annie's stomach was churning and yet Brigid's words had encouraged her in her determination never to speak directly to her husband again.

Wednesday afternoon was crisp and clear with weak sunlight that gave only an illusion of warmth, yet everyone was glad of its brightness. The last two days had been so dark, overcast and traumatic. Lizzie had persuaded Joe to go to meet Celia. He hadn't wanted to at first, thinking she'd at best have doubts about him, and at worst that she would reject him. But then he thought of how much she too was suffering in that house. They'd all heard Charlie roaring abuse at his entire family the night before, and so Joe had gone.

As usual they'd travelled by different routes and on different trams and had walked a few feet apart until they got to the landing stage, bought their tickets and boarded the ferry. That had been the really hard part, Celia thought, the pretence. But now they stood together in the lee of the funnel and for the first time in what seemed like years to both of them, Joe took her in his arms.

'Oh, Cee, I've missed you so much. I swear to God I have. I wanted *you* to comfort me, Cee, to tell me I had *nothing* to do with Richie's death. Our Lizzie wanted me to go for a walk and try and get word to you, but I . . . can't even remember now what night it was.'

Celia buried her head against the rough tweed of his jacket.

'Oh, Joe! I wanted to come to see you so much. You looked so awful. I just wanted to hold you.' She gazed up at him, incipient tears in her eyes. 'Joe, what are we going to do? What are we all going to do? Things are even worse now. Mam knows that Lizzie and I are friends and she's not complained or told him. In fact, after all this she has stopped speaking to him. She'll answer his questions but that's all. The atmosphere is terrible.'

She broke down in tears and Joe held her tightly. She was right. Things were as bad as they could get. There seemed to be no answer, no place for their love in this city. If only they could emigrate – go off to America or Australia, get married and start a new life – but he couldn't leave Mam to cope on her own and without his wage.

Joe gently touched Celia's cheek.

'I love you, Cee. I'll always love you, no matter what happens. Will you remember that?'

She nodded slowly and he bent his head and kissed her and she returned his kisses and clung more closely to him. She'd risk everything for him. Everything. She wasn't going to give him up no matter how bad circumstances became. At the back of her mind the germ of an idea was born, an idea that was so radical that she dismissed it completely – for now.

Richie Kemp's funeral was on the Friday, and the people from the top half of Roscommon Street attended the service in St George's church, as did Mr Tyson, representing the shipyard management. He noted there were very few of the foremen or indeed workmates of Richie's who had taken a few hours off without pay to attend. Not even Billy Milton was there, just a pale, thin woman that someone said was Annie Milton and a tall, slim girl with blonde hair who seemed more concerned about her mother than anything else. Even in death the lad had few to mourn him, apart from his sour-faced mother, his shrunken, haggard father, who didn't seem to even know where he was, and two identical lads who clung to each other rather than their parents, which Tyson considered odd.

Earlier that day Biddy Doyle and Maggie Walsh had refused to draw their curtains over, as had Brigid, but Tessie Mulhinney had said they should.

'Why so? Didn't he try to get our Joe blamed?' Brigid demanded heatedly.

'She's right, Tessie,' Biddy agreed.

'And didn't your one from number eight go with that divil from next door to the police?'

'All I'm saying is what Father Minehan said. The whole thing has been terrible but at the end of the day a young life's been lost and we should remember what Our Lord said: "Love they neighbour as thy self."'

The three other women looked grim, and then Maggie Walsh nodded. 'But only because the father has said so, mind.'

'I hear she's got the Co-op and there will be a do afterwards. Not a wake: they don't hold with things like that,' Biddy sniffed.

'Sure, they could have invited the King and Queen and the entire Royal Family and I wouldn't care less,' Brigid snapped.

'Is she keeping them two hooligans off school?'

'Those two should be sent to a reformatory. They're always picking fights with our Declan and your Vinny and your Emmet,' Maggie said with venom.

Brigid hadn't answered, but as the cortege (which fortunately didn't have to come up the road from the Great Homer Street end) left for the church, the curtains at every window were closed over.

On Saturday night Lizzie announced she was going to the pictures.

'And you with the bad foot! I'm tired of telling you, Lizzie Slattery, you won't be fit for work on Monday.'

'Mam, it's all right now. It's fine.' Lizzie ignored Joe's glance in her direction and her mother's silence.

'Well, I'm fed up with being stuck in, and what with the funeral and everything.'

'Sure, the last time you were "fed up" stopping in, didn't you end up in a cellar? Isn't that where you hurt your foot, and now you're off out again.'

Lizzie shrugged. 'Mam, it isn't foggy now.' She hadn't seen Billy for ages, so bad foot or not, she was meeting him tonight.

Brigid cast her eyes to the ceiling and wondered, did mothers back in Cork, her home town, have to deal with such head-strong young rossies as this one of hers?

Billy was waiting for Lizzie and instead of going to the pictures or the music hall, they went for a trip on the ferry. Celia had said it was a good place to go, even though there was always a chance of someone seeing them, but anywhere they went they took that risk.

As they stood on deck and watched the lights of the Liverpool waterfront fade, Billy put his arm around her shoulder and drew her closer.

She looked up at him.

'What's it been like, Billy? Really like, I mean? I haven't been able to talk to Celia.'

'Terrible. Really terrible. Da said Mam and Celia had to go to the funeral but they didn't want to go. The vicar went on and on about a young life snuffed out like a candle and things like that. Cee said the bit around the grave was really awful. It was so cold and miserable and sort of . . . final. We never really liked him or his mam, but Cee said poor Mr Kemp looked bad and was very vague.'

Lizzie sighed. 'Everything is a mess. A flaming mess. Your da will never forgive Mam for what she did and she'll never forgive him either. It's all made things worse.'

Billy looked into her eyes.

'I know. It was bad enough before.' He paused. 'Do you . . . do you really care for me, Lizzie?'

'How can you ask that? Would I risk God knows what to come and meet you, Billy Milton?'

'I mean fond enough to stand all the insults and yelling that we'd get if we were seen together. Seen to be courting?'

She returned his gaze, thinking how much he looked like his mam, not his da. It was a serious question and a very serious situation, one she didn't even like to think about too deeply.

'I – I – don't know.'

'I'm so fed up with all the pretence, Lizzie. I hate it.'

She stood on tiptoe and kissed his cold cheek.

'I know, but even our Joe and your Celia don't seem strong enough to . . . to . . . do that. Half the trouble is that they all think we're just kids, messing around and not knowing our own minds. If we were older . . .'

'Your Joe is eighteen, nearly nineteen.'

'I know but it would break Mam's heart and she's enough to put up with as it is – and besides, he can't just go off and leave. Well, he could, but he won't. I know him.'

They clung to each other, heedless of the cold wind, both feeling so trapped and desperate, but both sure that they did love each other and that that love would only grow. They would never let it be relentlessly ground down and die because of religious bigotry or circumstances.

Maudie looked over at her husband and sighed again. He was no better and she was seriously worried. Worried and frightened. She'd been to see Dr Fraser but all he'd been able to tell her was that shock and grief took time to get over. Everyone took it differently. But how much time? she'd thought frantically. She asked Dr Fraser that question but had received no encouraging reply. It was just 'time'.

She had somehow got through Richie's funeral with the help of her neighbours, Flo Taylor, Hetty Robinson and Sall Beswick. They had all commented that Charlie Milton had done her no favours at all by the carry-on out of him, and now she agreed with them. She'd never really been sure in her heart that Richie's death had anything to do with Joe Slattery. Fred Roberts and John Tyson were not men who would lie about something like that and Fred Roberts had given a sworn statement to the police. No date had been set as yet for the inquest and she was glad. She didn't want it all raked up again so soon.

'Will I put on the wireless, Harry, luv?' she coaxed.

He shook his head slowly, still in an endless dark vacuum from which he didn't seem to be able to break out.

Upstairs the twins were banging around and it was irritating Maudie. She got up and went to the foot of the stairs.

'If you two don't stop that flaming noise, I'll take your da's belt to the pair of you!' she yelled.

Silence instantly ensued and she went back into the kitchen. Harry had been like this for what seemed like an age, so he hadn't been able to go to work. In fact he hadn't been back since the accident almost four weeks ago now.

Suddenly she realised with a jolt that it wasn't long to go to Christmas. It would be a terrible Christmas, not only because of Richie's death but because now money was becoming tight and she'd used nearly all she'd managed to save for a rainy day. Well, the deluge was nearly on them now and she cast desperately about trying to think of something, anything, that would help. Her eye alighted on a new copy of Harry's pigeon magazine that the 'book man' had brought last Friday night, along with the comic she allowed the twins to have. Unlike the comic, the magazine had been left untouched on top of the dresser. She'd always been adamant that she'd not let him keep pigeons but now maybe it was time to think again. Needs must when the devil drives, she thought.

She went and picked up the magazine and sat beside him.

'Look, luv. I found this on the dresser. It's your magazine, the *Pigeon Fancier.* Would you like . . . well, would it help if you had a loft and a few birds? I – I wouldn't mind . . . now.' She'd put up with almost anything to get him even half back to normal.

Slowly Harry picked up the magazine and turned the pages.

'Would you . . . do you mean . . . Maudie?' he stammered slowly.

At last there was a spark of interest in his eyes and hope made her heart leap.

'Yes. Yes, of course, luv. You can have a loft and some birds. Didn't Bert Scott say he'd pick some for you?'

Harry nodded slowly. 'He did. And we – we'd built a loft. I – I don't know where it is now.' He was desperately trying to remember.

Maudie too nodded. She knew that Bert Scott had removed the contraption back into his own yard the night after the accident.

'It's at Bert's, just across the jigger. You can both bring it back.'

'When? When, Maudie?' He was looking at her like a child who had asked for sweets and had, for once, been given them.

'Now, if you like. I'll go and see Bert – or would you rather go yourself, luv?'

Harry seemed to shake himself mentally, then he stood up. 'I'll go over. He'll be wondering what I've been doing, messing him around. I should have paid him for the squabs he's been keeping for me too.' Concern returned to Maudie's eyes. She was so thankful that the depression seemed to have lifted, but he didn't seem to realise or remember that Richie was dead and buried. It was as though that night and the weeks that followed had never existed. At least she knew he'd soon be able to return to work. Catching sight of that flaming magazine had been inspirational, and she'd just have to shut up and not complain about it. It might even give the twins an interest – keep them all occupied and out of the house, which, because of circumstances, was, for the first time ever, in dire need of a thorough clean.

PART TWO

1935

Chapter Fifteen

'It's not going to be a very "Merry" Christmas, Cee, is it?' Lizzie said as they'd walked to work along Great Homer Street.

They'd passed shops full of Christmas fare. Huge bunches of holly and mistletoe hung beside Christmas trees outside greengrocery shops. Butchers had already started to display plucked or unplucked turkeys, geese and capons, and both girls knew how hard and how long they would have to work in the coming week. There had been a run on all the ingredients for Christmas pudding and cake and mince pies, to say nothing of biscuits and the usual things like tea and sugar and jam.

'No. I suppose it's not, with the Kemps coming to us for Christmas dinner, but Mam's right really. She's only gone over Da's head and asked them for the sake of the twins and Foxy. Poor Mr Kemp isn't that much better for all she's let him keep pigeons, and Mam says he's out there with them for hours on end. Shuts himself away, and he's got a bolt on the inside of the door. He has times when he just doesn't seem to see you, or speak to you or answer your questions. It's as if you're not even there. It's frightening, Lizzie, it really is.'

'I bet it is,' Lizzie agreed. 'Is he like that all the time? At home as well?'

'I think so, but she's so awful that I think most of the time he just ignores her anyway.'

'It's not going to be a bundle of laughs in our house either. Mam will be thinking all the time about Da. She's been scraping money together for months, even though she's in Tessie Mulhinney's tontine club. All she can afford to save is a shilling a week.'

Like many other women in the city Tessie Mulhinney ran a savings club. Women gave her a set amount each week, whatever they could afford, and at Christmas they received a lump sum back to help meet the extra cost. Tessie didn't take a percentage as some women did.

'A shilling's not bad.'

'It's not good either. It's only two pounds and twelve shillings and that doesn't go far,' Lizzie had replied.

Celia looked gloomy. 'Everyone's out visiting on Boxing Day so I won't get to see Joe at all.'

'And I won't see Billy either. Oh, it's all such a flaming mess,' Lizzie snapped.

'Don't keep going on about it, Lizzie. For God's sake we all *know* it's a mess.'

'I just wonder what's going to happen to us all, Cee,' Lizzie replied miserably.

As Celia and Lizzie predicted, Christmas passed with little cheer and no merriness whatsoever and things didn't get much better, for in the bitterly cold, dark days of January, the whole nation was plunged into mourning by the death of the King; George V had been popular and Queen Mary was well liked and greatly respected. Everything that could be draped in black crepe was festooned with it and everyone wore mourning or, if proper clothes were beyond their means, black armbands. Brigid, Maggie and Biddy listened to the commentator's sepulchral voice detailing the procession on Tessie Mulhinney's wireless, and after it was over Tessie confided in her neighbours that she didn't like 'the new one much'.

'What's the matter with him? He's young, handsome and dead charming,' Maggie Walsh asked aggressively.

Tessie looked perplexed. 'I know all that, Maggie, but I just can't take to him. There's something about him. He's too handsome and yet he looks sort of . . . weak. He's got a weak chin. He doesn't look strong and capable like his da was, God rest 'im.'

'There's no pleasing some people, is there? Isn't he young and clean-shaven whereas himself that they've just taken on a gun carriage and with horse following, God luv him, had whiskers and was, well . . . mature?' Brigid argued curtly. 'Like him or not we're stuck with him an' his weak chin, though I think that's criticising him too much. Give the poor feller a chance.'

'If he's weak it's because he was terrified of his father, that's what I heard,' Biddy Doyle said nodding sagely.

'And what's so bad about that? Even royal princes probably need a bawling out at times. Left to their own devices they'd probably get up to all kinds of things that would disgrace their mam and dad. Look how his owld grandfather carried on. Shockin', it was. No example at all. It's a wonder King George turned out to be a decent God-fearing man,' Maggie answered tartly, putting an end to the debate.

Finally, it was May and a balmy one too, warm and with soft breezes. The State Funeral and the winter months were behind them now, Celia thought as she and Joe got ready to leave the ferry. She loved this month. Everything looked so fresh and new. There was blossom on the trees in the parks. New leaves stirred against the blue canopy that was the sky, and in their shade the ground was carpeted with bluebells.

The seed of the idea that had formed in her head all those months ago had gained strength and now hurtled around in her mind constantly, to the exclusion of everything else, apart from the hours she spent at work, and even then there were times when she was preoccupied.

She had mentioned it to no one – yet. The whole thing depended so much on Joe and his attitude to what she intended to do. She decided to sound Lizzie out tomorrow.

As they watched the sunlight sparkling over the grey waters of the river, Joe's arm tightened around her waist and he sighed and smiled down at her.

'Well, they've got a fine day for it.'

Celia was puzzled. 'For what?' It was just an ordinary Wednesday afternoon.

'The maiden voyage of the *Queen Mary.* Over 80,000 tons and a floating palace, so they say. I'd have loved to have seen her. I'd have loved to have worked on her. She's the biggest and fastest ship in the world.' Joe looked across to the shipyard where he worked.

'Why couldn't they have built her here?' Celia followed his wistful gaze.

'She's too big. She'd never get out of the river. There's not enough depth under her keel at the bar.'

Celia looked mildly puzzled.

'The water's too shallow; she'd run aground. She'd get stuck, and she's so big it would take half a dozen ocean-going tugs to pull her free and they couldn't go through that performance every time she came in or left the river.'

Celia nodded absently but she'd lost interest, thinking as always that soon they'd reach the Liverpool landing stage and they would have to part. She'd go straight home but Joe would walk to Lord Street or maybe even down to Church Street before he caught a tram. Well, she was fed up with the whole thing. They were going round and round in circles and getting nowhere, and with each week they ran the risk of being found out. Their luck couldn't last for ever.

Joe walked up James Street and into Derby Square with its large statue of Queen Victoria in the centre, and caught a number 30 tram that went out to Aintree. It was the first to come along and it didn't really matter about its final destination. Most of them went the same way – more or less – until they reached the Rotunda.

When he alighted he felt the sun warm on his back as he walked along although he wasn't feeling very happy. The old familiar frustration had returned. He did love Celia and he ached for her. There were times when he'd not been able to control his feelings but she always drew away from him, reluctantly and often with real longing in her eyes, sometimes with tears even. Oh, it would have all been a damned sight easier if Celia had been the same religion but he'd never pressure her on that point.

His mind was filled with all the usual fruitless thoughts and in frustration he kicked a small stone with his boot as he trudged along.

The sound of kids' voices broke through his reverie and then he caught sight of Frank Kemp running towards him at full pelt. The lad's face was scarlet with his exertions and he was panting but when he saw Joe he stopped, panic fighting with indecision.

'What's the matter with you and why aren't you at school?' Joe demanded.

Frank looked around. There were no other adults in sight – he was going to have to trust Joe Slattery.

'Our kid . . . me . . . brother, an' Foxy . . . down by the canal . . . Our kid's all right . . . but . . . but . . .' he gasped.

'But what?' Joe took him by the shoulders and shook him.

'Foxy's stuck, like.'

'Stuck?'

'He's got his leg stuck in something and he's going to drown.' The lad's face crumpled and he burst into tears.

Joe was off like a shot, his legs and arms working like pistons. Frank followed.

When he reached the canal bank he could see Eddie Kemp shouting and thrashing the water with a piece of discarded timber. There was no sign of Foxy. Then a pair of hands appeared, clutching at the empty air. For a brief instant a small pale face broke the surface but disappeared almost at once.

'Is that where he is? Was that him?' Joe demanded.

Tears were streaming down Eddie's cheeks. 'Yes! Yes, he's there.

We never meant this to happen. We were only messing around.'

Joe already had his boots, shirt and jacket off.

'This is getting to be a habit,' he muttered. 'I'm getting fed up with Foxy and his antics,' then he plunged into the chilly water of the canal, water that was so murky he could see nothing. He caught a glimpse of a dim form, just a shadowy outline. He dived deeper and grasped the lad. He heaved and pulled but he couldn't get Foxy free and he felt as though his lungs were about to burst. He struck out upwards, surfaced, took a huge gulp of air and then dived again.

This time he could see that it was weed tangled around a submerged old bike that the boy had his foot caught in. Gripping Foxy around the waist, he gave an almighty wrench and, finally, the lad's leg was free and they were both propelled to the surface by the force of Joe's effort.

The twins helped Joe drag himself and then Foxy on to the bank.

'Is he dead? Is he dead, Joe?' Frank asked, trembling with shock and not realising that he'd called Joe by his Christian name for the first time ever.

Joe had turned Foxy over so he lay on his stomach with his head turned to one side, and was pressing his hands on Foxy's back, trying to force the water from his lungs.

'One of you run up the road, there's a phone box on the corner. You don't need money, just dial 999 and tell them we need an ambulance, and for God's sake be quick.'

Frank disappeared rapidly, his face even more flushed.

Eddie began to cry noisily. 'Me mam will kill us and so will Mr Milton! We were only having a bit of a skive and it was hot and Foxy said we – we'll all go for a swim in the canal.'

'You bloody little fool! Hasn't there been enough accidents and deaths at your end of the street already? You all deserve a good hiding just for skiving off from school, never mind letting this stupid little get talk you into swimming in that filthy water.'

Eddie's sobs got louder and were annoying Joe, who knew if help didn't arrive soon Foxy Milton might die.

'Run up to the road and see if there's any sign of that damned ambulance.'

Thankfully, just as Joe heard the loud clanging bell of the ambulance, Foxy started to come round, coughing and spluttering.

'Thank God for that,' Joe breathed. 'Come on, lad, cough it up. Get it out of your lungs.'

He sat back on his heels and watched the ambulance men work on the boy until he was able to sit up. Then they picked Foxy up, wrapped him in blankets and carried him back to the vehicle.

'You'd better come along too,' one of them shouted over his shoulder to Joe.

Joe shook his head. 'No, mate. Get his mam. His name's Frederick Milton. He lives at number ten Roscommon Street.'

'What about those two?'

'Oh, don't worry about them. I'll take them home.'

'All right, but then get yourself home and into dry clothes,' the ambulance man shouted back.

With his hair still plastered down by canal water, his jacket, boots and socks on but his shirt over his arm, Joe walked the pale-faced pair of trembling lads towards home.

When they reached the top of Roscommon Street he looked down at them.

'Well, what are you going to do? Do you want me to tell your mam or do you want to do it yourselves? You're going to get a good hiding either way, so it's your choice.'

The twins looked at each other, shocked and petrified. They'd skived off school, which was bad enough, but Foxy had nearly died and there'd be hell to pay over that.

Frank finally spoke. 'Will yer . . . will yer . . . ?'

Joe sighed and walked down with them, and hammered on Maudie's door until it was flung open.

The angry words died on Maudie's lips as she caught sight of the trio on the doorstep.

'They decided to have the afternoon off from school, Mrs Kemp. Then they went swimming in the canal, or at least Foxy did. He got his leg caught in some weeds, you know the state that canal's in. I went in after him and he's gone to hospital by ambulance. You'd best go and tell Mrs Milton that the young hooligan is safe and to get up there as soon as she can.'

The expression on Maudie Kemp's face was so grim it looked as though it were carved from granite, and Joe couldn't help but feel sorry for the two lads. Many a time he'd skived off school himself and he'd gone swimming in that canal without a thought for his safety or the filthy water. They'd used their jerseys as bathing trunks, shoving their leg into the sleeves of the garments and knotting them around their waists. Mam had belted him often enough for that too.

'If it hadn't been for this one here, Foxy Milton would have drowned. He went to find help.' Joe inclined his head in Frank Kemp's direction and then walked away.

Maudie was fuming as she hauled the twins into the lobby.

'This time you've gone too far and so has Foxy Milton!'

Eddie was in tears. 'Mam, it wasn't our fault. *He* wanted to go swimming. It was Foxy who wanted to go, not us, and it was him what told us to skive off too. *He* said we wouldn't get caught.'

'And if Foxy Milton told you to put your hand in the flaming fire I suppose you'd do it. Just you wait until I get back from seeing his mam.' She dragged them towards the stairs. 'Get up the dancers to your room this minute and don't move until I get back! You've gone your ninety-nine and three-quarters this time!'

It was Celia who answered Maudie's frantic knocking.

'Mrs Kemp! What's the matter?'

'Is your mam in, Cee?'

'Yes, come in, what's wrong?'

'Those two horrors of mine and your Foxy – that's what's wrong, girl.'

Annie was baking. Her hands, arms and the rolling pin were covered in flour. The kitchen was filled with the smell of bread cooking.

'Maudie, what's wrong?'

'It's your Frederick. Don't get upset, he's all right.'

Annie dropped the rolling pin and began to wipe her hands on her apron. 'Oh God, now what, Maudie?'

'They took it into their heads to have the afternoon off from school and go swimming, in that filthy canal! God knows what you'd catch in *that* water. Foxy – Frederick – got trapped by some weeds. I don't know it all, but that eldest Slattery lad went in after him and dragged him out. They've taken him to Stanley Hospital, but he *is* all right.'

At her words Annie went pale and Celia uttered a cry. She was dying to ask if Joe had got home safely but instead she said, 'Don't worry, Mam, I'll come with you. I'll get our jackets while you wash your hands and take off your pinny.'

Annie turned to Maudie. 'Oh, what possessed them? Frederick knows he'll get a hiding if he plays truant, never mind being half drowned. Hospital or no hospital Charlie will go mad.'

'I can't say I blame him,' Maudie sniffed. 'Of course, it would have to be that Slattery lad who yanked him out. I'm going back now to sort those two fiends of mine out. What the hell is wrong with kids today? They have far more than we ever had when we were their age but that doesn't seem to be enough. Oh, no! They do whatever fancy takes them. Never mind about missing lessons and worrying us long-suffering parents half to death. Well, those two won't only be getting a belt from me, I'm taking them back to school and Mr Longstaffe can give them a good talking-to and a few strokes of the cane as well. Maybe then they'll all learn to behave.' With that she stormed out.

* * *

'In the name of God, what's happened to you? Aren't you soaked to the skin?' Brigid cried as Joe came into the kitchen.

Joe explained.

Brigid was outraged. 'You go risking your life for the likes of him! It's not the first time either and look at all that's happened since. You want to keep clear of that lot down there.'

'What was I supposed to do, Mam, let him drown?'

'All you'll get is dog's abuse from himself next door, and don't expect any thanks from your one at number eight either.'

'Is he really all right?' Lizzie asked.

Joe shrugged. 'I suppose so.'

'Well, no doubt we'll hear it all later on through the walls when Mouth Almighty gets home. Take those wet things off. Wouldn't you know it's your best trousers you had on too. Well, thank God it wasn't your Sunday suit. I'll get you your dinner, you've to be at work in a couple of hours' time.'

Lizzie sighed. They'd hear part of it tonight through the wall as her mam had said, but it would be tomorrow before she'd get the full story from Celia.

There had been a good deal of shouting that evening but, as Lizzie had expected, it was on their way to work next day that she heard the whole story.

'I don't know what gets into that little fiend, I really don't. He has poor Mam demented and Da says he'll finish up on the gallows.'

'That bit we heard,' Lizzie said flatly.

'And Mam was in floods of tears. Upset by the shock of going up to the hospital to bring him home, and of Da's ranting and raving. I got hold of our Foxy myself, after he'd been sent to bed, and he won't be able to sit down for a week. I told him that if he ever, *ever* does anything again to upset Mam, I'll strangle him with my own two hands. Is Joe all right?'

Lizzie nodded. 'Mam went on a bit about risking himself and getting no thanks, but apart from ruining his trousers, he's fine.'

'I thought . . . well, I thought he might have left a note for me.'

'He really didn't have time, Cee.'

'I guessed that,' Celia sighed. 'Can we go out at dinner time? I want to talk to you.'

'What about?'

'Joe and me, and you and our Billy.'

Lizzie shook her head. 'Where will we go? Someone will see us. We're better off stopping in the stockroom, Cee.'

'I suppose you're right,' Celia agreed with yet another sigh.

The morning seemed to drag and they were both absent-minded and duly reprimanded by Mr Henderson, but at last the closed sign was put on the door, the window blind drawn down and Mr Henderson went to his little office and shut the door. Alfie rode down on the delivery bike to Stephenson's on Great Homer Street for chips, and the two girls went into the stockroom to eat their lunch.

'All right, what is it you wanted to talk about that concerns us all?'

'There *is* a way out for us, Lizzie. I thought about it ages ago. At first I just pushed it from my mind it was so . . . unthinkable, so crazy, but things have got so bad lately.'

Lizzie was exasperated. 'What way out? What idea, Cee?'

'It's very simple. We get pregnant. We'd *have* to get married then.'

Lizzie's eyes were round with horror. 'God Almighty, Cee, we can't do that!'

'I know it won't be easy, Lizzie. I know I'll get a good hiding and then be thrown out on the street, but I don't care. I just want to be with Joe.'

'Cee, I *couldn't* do that! It's a terrible mortal sin and think of the shame it would cause our mams. We'd break their hearts and, like you say, we'd all be thrown out after Mam's had the parish priest around. But then what will we all do?'

'Oh, Lizzie, I love Joe so much and I hate Da and the atmosphere at home. I *can't* stand it any more.'

'Have you told our Joe about this "idea"?'

'No, and I'm not going to because if I do he'll never agree to go along with it.'

'You're right there and well, if you do . . . do "it" . . . where will you live? Joe won't leave Mam.'

'Would she take me in, Lizzie?'

'I don't know, Cee. I just don't know. You know what she's like about your da. And where would Billy and me go?'

'You could sort something out. At least you and our Billy can leave, get somewhere of your own. Out of sight, out of mind. You getting married to our Billy would only be a nine-day wonder, then they'd all forget. If – if your mam took me in I'd still have to live in Roscommon Street and the whole street would turn against me. I know that. You can't run with the hare and hunt with the hounds, as they say.'

'What about your poor mam? You know she's not well, Cee.'

'I'd still be able to see her. He'll be at work all day. Will you *think* about it, Lizzie?'

'There's no point at all in me thinking about it, Cee. I *couldn't* do it. I just couldn't do it. Mam would kill me and so would Father Minehan. And having the pair of us pregnant just wouldn't be fair on her, Cee, even if it did happen to both of us together, which it might not.' Lizzie shook her head. She could see no advantage at all to this plan of Celia's. 'But if you're sure, really sure, Cee, then you know I'll stand by you.'

'Thanks, Lizzie.'

Lizzie had no appetite now for her single thick slice of bread and margarine or the apple Celia had given her. Things were bad enough but what Celia had in mind just didn't bear thinking about.

Chapter Sixteen

The following Wednesday afternoon Celia suggested they go for a long walk along Otterspool Riverside Promenade. Its name sounded very grand and conjured up visions of ladies in all their finery accompanied by well-dressed men: in fact it was very run-down.

'What do you want to go there for?' Joe asked, looking at Celia with slight amusement when they met up at the Pier Head.

'I'm fed up with the ferry and it's about time we changed our plans. We've been so lucky so far that I'm terrified that it can't hold for much longer.'

He had no answer to that and so they'd gone. They did walk for a bit. The salty smell of the river was strong but the tide was out and the exposed mud of Devil's Bank and the other sand and mud flats that skirted the Garston Channel gave off noxious odours.

'It stinks to high heaven, Cee.'

'I know, but it won't be so bad when the tide comes in.'

'In about another two hours,' he commented drily.

'Well, let's get away from it.' She indicated the patches of grass and overgrown and straggling shrubs beyond the paved roadway of the promenade that had the very rural and misleading name of Otterspool Gardens.

She sat down on the grass in the shelter of a huge, but poor, straggling rhododendron whose purple flowers looked blown and undernourished. She looked around. Thank God there wasn't another soul in sight, she thought. Virtually no one came here during a weekday afternoon.

Joe sat beside her and took her hand. 'You look as miserable as sin. Has your da been having a go at you? I heard him yelling again last night.'

'No, it was Foxy he was bawling at. He dropped a plate and it smashed. You'd have thought he'd done it on purpose just to annoy him and upset Mam, the way he carried on. I felt like saying why don't we get enamel ones, they won't break, but . . .' she shrugged.

'Then what's up?'

'I – I . . . feel so miserable nearly all the time now, Joe.'

He took her in his arms. 'I know, Cee. There are times even in the middle of all the noise at work that I can't get you out of my mind.'

She looked up at him, her eyes filled with longing. 'Oh, Joe, I want you so much. Some nights I can't sleep just thinking of you . . . and us.'

He bent and kissed her. They'd been over this hundreds of times, but there was no solution.

Celia leaned back, pulling Joe with her. She was nervous, but she *was* going to go through with it. She was determined to do what she had to – and to keep on doing it until she got pregnant.

Their kisses became more and more passionate and then she took his hand and placed it on her breast.

He groaned. 'Oh, God, don't, Cee, or I won't be able to stop myself.' There was such longing in his voice.

'I don't want you to stop, Joe. I *want* you.'

He pulled away and looked down at her.

'I want you, Joe. I mean it. I love you so much and want you so much that I don't care, I just don't care. Can't we give ourselves to each other in the few hours we spend together?'

'Celia, do you know what you're saying?'

'Yes. I love you and I want you.'

'But what if . . .' He was afraid to even say the word 'pregnant'.

'I won't. I just *know* I won't. Believe me. Don't you love me enough?'

'I love you too much, Cee, that's the trouble.'

'Then . . . take . . . me. Love me.'

Before he could reply she'd pulled his head down and had opened the buttons of her blouse. As his fingers touched the soft, rounded breast all his reservations and self-control disappeared. She was *his* and there was no one else in the world.

Next morning, as they met up on Great Homer Street, Celia was quiet. It had been painful at first, even though she knew he was trying to be so gentle with her. But then she'd abandoned her inhibitions and caution and they'd stayed until they heard the voices of children on their way home from school. But now she felt differently.

'What's up, Cee? You've hardly said a word,' Lizzie questioned.

'I . . . we went to Otterspool yesterday.'

Lizzie grabbed her arm and stopped and looked at her friend closely. 'What did you go there for?'

'To . . . to . . . do what I told you I was going to do.'

'You mean you . . . and our Joe?'

Celia nodded.

Lizzie didn't speak for a few minutes. Shock had rendered her temporarily silent until Celia saw the look of curiosity beginning to dawn in her friend's eyes.

'What . . . well, I mean . . . what was . . . ?'

'It was wonderful, Lizzie. Not at the very beginning, but he was so gentle and I love him so much, Lizzie, and we just stayed there for ages.'

Lizzie hadn't thought that Celia really meant it, but now . . . Would it be the same for herself and Billy? She'd never know because she was so afraid. It was the worst thing a young girl could do. And she wouldn't bring such shame down on her mam. It was different for Celia, she hated her home, and as for Joe, well, being a man they never really got the blame. In fact their mates often admired them for it although she knew Joe would never breathe a word, not even to herself.

Men were subject to uncontrollable urges, Mam always said when warning herself and Josie. Mam always stressed they were not to let themselves get into a situation where these 'manly urges' surfaced and took over.

'And you really don't care if . . . if . . . you get pregnant?'

'No. I've told you, Lizzie, I don't care. I want some life with Joe.'

Lizzie sighed deeply and wished they didn't live next door to each other, in the same street, in the same city, never mind this one with all the bitterness and hatred and heartache. She could see nothing but trouble brewing for Celia.

The day seemed endless. There were busy times when half a dozen or more women came in with their lists of groceries and the girls were rushed off their feet, weighing and measuring and filling the dark blue bags with tea and sugar, flour and cocoa, then twisting them at the corners to make sure their contents didn't spill out. Mr Henderson himself sliced bacon and ham on the big machine that had a circular blade rotated by a handle, a blade so sharp that he didn't trust either of the girls to use it. Then there were slack periods when things had to be tidied away, shelves had to be restocked and counters wiped clean. And at the end of it all, when Mr Henderson dismissed them, Lizzie was still troubled by Celia's actions.

To Celia's intense disappointment she got her 'curse' right on time, at the end of the month. She'd always been as regular as clockwork. They went to Otterspool every Wednesday afternoon now although they didn't go on Sundays when there were always too many people about, taking advantage of the fine weather and the sea air – such as it was.

Finally, as the days of summer lengthened and June turned to July, Celia realised she was pregnant. She told Lizzie but swore her to secrecy until she was absolutely sure. She'd tell Joe at the beginning of August when she'd be two months gone.

Although her plan had worked she was afraid – afraid of what lay ahead – and one small doubt nagged in her mind no matter how much she tried to obliterate it. What if he refused to marry her? He'd said he would stand by her no matter what, but what if he changed his mind and said she'd trapped him? What would happen to her then?

Lizzie didn't tell Billy about his sister's pregnancy. She didn't think he could keep the fact secret. Their relationship was more tempestuous than Celia and Joe's, and Lizzie found herself never quite able to confide in him. She had a hard enough time keeping her own mouth shut, particularly to Joe. What she did do, though, when the kids were in bed and there were just herself and her mam left sitting in the kitchen, was to praise Celia's good qualities. She was a such a hard worker, clean and tidy in her appearance, and presumably was just as neat at home, too. She was honest, affectionate and generous.

She went on so much that Brigid had looked at her suspiciously and said, 'Is she after being canonised then? According to you she's got all it takes, but there's a Saint Cecilia already so she'll have to change her name.' After that Lizzie had toned it down.

The first days of August were stifling. There was no breeze and a shimmering heat haze hung over the cobbled streets and the calm water of the Mersey. The rubbish in the back entries and the smell from the ash cans became unbearable, even though Annie poured bleach and Jeyes Fluid over everything in sight with a reckless disregard of the cost.

It was in August that the risk from disease was at its peak, carried by the swarms of flies and bluebottles. She had sticky flypapers, long strips of brown paper covered with glue, hung in every room in the house and two in the privy. She covered all food with muslin before it went into either the larder or food press. The milk was in a large jug which was immersed in a bucket of cold water on the cold-flagged floor and pushed right to the back of the larder.

Celia was beginning to feel sick, and after a day's work was exhausted. She blamed this on the oppressive heat, an excuse Annie accepted. She too felt drained and the pain she suffered didn't help. She also seemed to have a permanent headache and everything was so much of an effort.

Each night Celia took a couple of plain digestive biscuits to bed with her for when she awoke nauseated and faint in the morning. She also had a little pot of Bourjois rouge which she applied to her cheeks before she came downstairs, for quite often she looked like death warmed up.

On the Saturday evening when Billy was getting dressed to go out to see Lizzie, Charlie decided it was so pleasant a night that they'd go and view the Palm House, in Sefton Park. A magnificent glasshouse, it contained all kinds of tropical flowers and shrubs and palm trees and, as Charlie remarked, it was only the price of their tram fare.

Annie said nothing. She didn't even attempt to show any enthusiasm. She didn't want to go. She didn't feel well and although it was slightly cooler now, she had no interest in tropical plants and she'd have to listen to his bombastic comments, his snobby remarks. The heat in the Palm House would be stifling too. But she put on a small white straw hat and picked up her bag and white cotton gloves and told Celia that she wouldn't be late in.

Celia was entrusted with the care of Foxy and the Kemp twins, as Maudie and a very reluctant Harry had agreed to go to the park with them. They were pretty quiet for the moment, Celia thought thankfully, making boats out of paper and pushing them around in the sink in the scullery with pieces of stick, so she decided to go and have a lie-down. She felt so drained after working, being on her feet too and then walking home in this heat. Even Lizzie said it sapped the strength from you and that when she got home she was going to have a good wash-down in the scullery, for her clothes were sticking to her.

She was suddenly wakened from her doze by someone screaming and yelling. She could smell smoke heavy in the air! She jumped off the bed, flung up the window and then went to the door. As she opened it she reeled backwards before the pall of dense, choking black smoke and she heard the crackle of flames. She slammed the door shut. Oh God! Foxy and the twins, she thought desperately. She *had* to get out and go down and find them, but the staircase was already ablaze.

Panic took hold and she began to scream. Then from the open window she heard voices – a lot of voices – and thankfully the frantic clanging of the bells of fire engines.

She tried to take herself in hand and think straight. Foxy and the twins would have got out, they had been downstairs in the scullery and if they'd have come up they would have made enough noise to wake her, and someone had obviously raised the alarm. At that moment wisps of smoke curled under the bedroom door. She could see small tongues of fire licking around the door frame and could smell the paint as it blistered and melted. The heat in the room had become so intense that suddenly the panes of glass in the window exploded and shattered into lethal shards but fell, fortunately, down into the street below.

Now she was fighting for breath. The heat was scorching her lungs and the smoke was suffocating. She crawled to the window, not even noticing the small pieces of glass that had fallen in and which cut her hands and knees. Then jets of water came pouring in and she dragged herself up to the open window.

The night sky was illuminated by the orange glare of the flames. The whole house must be alight, she thought. Below her was a crowd of neighbours, including her own horrified parents, Foxy and the twins and Joe. Joe was shouting something to her but she couldn't hear for the noise. The roaring of the flames was behind her now and her dress was scorched. She was terrified, so utterly petrified that she couldn't move, and any minute now the flames would engulf her but she was shaking with terror.

Below the firemen, helped by Joe, Greg and Bernard Doyle and Gerry Walsh, held out a tarpaulin.

'Celia, jump! Jump, for God's sake!' Joe yelled, beside himself with anguish.

'Come on, luv, you won't get hurt. We'll catch you. Jump! You've got to jump!' one of the firemen yelled.

The heat was more intense now and the smoke was choking, but although Celia had managed to get one leg over the windowsill sheer panic numbed her.

'Jump! Cee, jump!' Joe was nearly in tears but she didn't move and he could see the flames beginning to lick the wood of the window frame. Dragging a ladder from the back of the nearest engine he propped it up against the wall of the house.

''Ere, lad, you can't do that. The whole lot might go and collapse any minute,' the senior fire officer shouted. 'I've seen it happen before.'

'I don't bloody care! She's terrified! I'm going up for her.'

He was up the ladder in a moment.

She looked so terrified and vulnerable, like a rabbit caught in the glare of a lamp. Seeing him so close Celia let go of the windowsill, the tears streaming down her grimy cheeks.

'Come on, Cee. I'm here, I won't let any harm come to you. Give me your hand,' Joe pleaded desperately, for the flames were leaping and roaring only a few feet away now.

'Joe! Oh, Joe! I'm frightened,' she sobbed.

'I know, but trust me, Cee.'

A fireman had followed him up. 'Get out of the way, lad. It's not as easy as that.'

With a few more reassuring words to Celia, Joe let the fireman pass him on the rungs of the ladder. Then he began to descend as the man yanked Celia from the window, threw her across his shoulder and began his descent amidst the jets of water from the fire hoses that were now trained on the upper storey of the house.

As soon as they were down, Joe took her in his arms. She was close to collapsing.

'Cee, luv, are you all right? God, but you gave me a fright. I thought I'd lost you!' Joe rocked her in his arms, watched by all the occupants of Roscommon Street.

Amongst the crowds were Billy and Lizzie, home early because they'd had one of their frequent arguments which was forgotten as soon as they saw the inferno.

'Oh God, that's it now, Billy,' Lizzie said quietly as Charlie Milton pushed his way through the crowd and tried forcefully to yank his daughter from Joe's arms.

'Get over there with your mam, you . . . you . . .' he spluttered with fury. The fact that his home was in smouldering ruins didn't seem to register or upset him as much as the sight of his daughter locked in the arms of Joe Slattery.

Before Celia could move, Joe had released her and grabbed her da by the lapels of his jacket. There was murder in his eyes.

'She's just been nearly roasted alive and where were you? Where were you and your wife when that little sod Foxy managed to set fire to the kitchen curtains, messing about with matches, so I'm told, with the Kemp twins?'

Foxy had readily given this information to the firemen and the neighbours. When they'd got bored with the paper boats the boys had started rolling newspaper very tightly to make spills, lighting them with matches and seeing whose lasted the longest. But it had all got out of hand and when the curtains caught fire, they'd fled.

'That doesn't give you the right to treat her like some kind of . . . floozie!' Charlie yelled. 'Annie, take her inside Maudie's.'

'No!' Celia cried, clinging closer to Joe. 'I'm staying with him. I love him and . . . and . . .' she looked up into Joe's face, 'I'm pregnant.'

Charlie, Annie and Brigid all looked as though they'd been hit with a sledgehammer. Murmurs of shock and disapproval rippled through the crowd, which by now consisted of all the residents in the street. Then all hell broke loose. Charlie dragged his daughter away from Joe and thrust her at her weeping mother, with the instruction to get them all into Maudie's house – this was a private matter.

Brigid glared at her son, then caught sight of Lizzie.

'Get this lot inside that house and up to bed, Lizzie Slattery. I've plenty to say to your brother about all this!'

Lizzie took her shocked sisters and brothers inside without a backward glance, but before Brigid could launch herself into the fray, Charlie Milton fell sprawling on the wet cobbles at her feet. He'd lashed out at Joe, but Joe had ducked and then sent Charlie sprawling with a blow to the jaw that left Joe's knuckles skinned.

The chief fireman took them all in hand. He was used to scenes of mass hysteria, and blame and abuse being hurled.

'Right. The lot of you, get back to your homes. The show's over. And I can't see for the life of me what the pair of you are doing belting hell out of each other. That lad saved your girl and you are all out for half killing him! That's a fine display of gratitude, I must say.'

Grim-faced, Brigid stepped forward. 'Sure, he won't be the only one who's going to give meladdo here a belt. I'm his mam and if what I heard is true, then there's some answers I want from him! Get in that house this minute, Joe Slattery!'

Chapter Seventeen

It hadn't been much of an outing, Maudie had thought on the way home. Twice Annie had nearly fainted in the hot, humid and stifling conditions in the Palm House. Harry had been no help either, he just followed them in complete silence while Charlie Milton, in between reviving his wife, had read out loud from the little plaques attached to the plants, giving the species, the country of origin and other boring and useless information.

In the end Maudie stated very firmly that she'd had enough. Wasn't it damned well hot enough outside without being nearly suffocated in here and couldn't he see his wife was ill? It was as plain as the nose on your face.

Annie had cast her a grateful look, as had Harry, though Maudie knew her husband just wanted to get back to his blasted pigeons. In fact no one, including herself, had wanted to go in the first place. A trip on the ferry to New Brighton would have been better. At least you'd get some sort of breeze, even if it was only that generated by the movement of the ferry itself.

No one had spoken a word on the way home, but Maudie had linked arms with Annie. Her friend looked so ill and exhausted that Maudie was afraid she'd just drop like a fly at her feet. Nothing had prepared them for the sight that met their eyes when they turned the corner into Roscommon Street. Now it looked as though she was going to have to take them in, and while she felt sorry for Annie, Charlie Milton had a damned cheek making free with her hospitality. Although the fire was now out you could feel the heat in the walls of her house and the smell of smoke was pungent and seemed to be filtering right through the bricks themselves.

Charlie was livid. Not only had he lost his home, but the whole street had seen his daughter in the arms of that no mark Slattery. When she'd announced that she was pregnant, in front of the entire street, his temper had snapped. He'd lunged at Slattery but missed. Slattery had fought back and to his mortification he'd been the one who had ended up on the floor.

He was about to slam the door behind him but the fireman had yelled at him to go easy, he wasn't sure what state the adjoining houses were in. His men were still training their hoses on both houses either side of what was now little more than a shell.

'Thank God the roof is still intact,' the fireman announced for the benefit of the crowd that stood around gazing in a sort of malicious trance. 'If it collapsed it would take the other two with it.'

Maudie filled the kettle while both Celia and Annie sat together on the sofa crying and trembling with shock. Maudie told Billy to stop Harry from sliding off to hide himself away from the world in that smelly loft in the yard, and so Harry had sunk into an easy chair. His face was pale, his eyes glazed, and obviously his mind was elsewhere.

Foxy and the twins were upstairs cowering in the twins' room. They were terrified of the retribution they knew would come sooner or later. They might even be sent off to a reform school. The police and the fire bobbies didn't look kindly on kids who attempted to burn down houses and it had been stupid to mess with fire – and the fact that Celia had been nearly killed didn't help either. At first they'd all started to blame each other but gradually fear had taken hold.

'Here, luv, get this down you.' Maudie passed Annie a cup of tea but Annie's hands were shaking so much that Maudie put it on the nearby table. Celia felt as though her throat was raw and her breathing was coming in little shallow gasps. She just didn't seem to be able to take deep breaths. The shock and the fear were now setting in and she clung to her mam tightly. Oh, she hadn't meant to tell anyone about the baby and now the entire street knew. And Joe, what would he think? She'd glimpsed the look on his mam's face as Brigid had shoved him towards their house. Her sobs grew louder.

Maudie passed a cup to Charlie with a very bad grace. 'Get that down you, and then hadn't you better go and see if there's anything to be salvaged in there?' she snapped.

'Later,' he snapped back.

'Well, don't blame me if the vultures in this street get there before you and go picking over your stuff. Maybe you should go, Billy. I told you they're like a swarm of locusts.'

Billy looked uncertainly at his father but it was to his sister he spoke.

'Will I go and see what I can find, Cee?'

Charlie exploded. 'You knew about this, didn't you? You knew she was carrying on like a whore!'

'No, I didn't!' Billy shot back with some spirit. 'And she's not a whore!' He was summoning up all the courage he had, because he wasn't going to let anyone call Celia such a name. She loved Joe Slattery, just as he loved Lizzie.

Charlie rounded on his wife, who was trying to overcome her terror and soothe her daughter. Annie felt so ill herself and had done all evening. Now there were just too many terrible things that had happened at once. Everything was jumbled up in her mind.

'Then you must have known, Annie! Didn't you ever ask where she was going and who with? Doesn't a mother know when something like . . . like . . . this has happened?' His rage increased because Annie made no effort to deny it or even to answer him. She just sat shaking and sobbing.

Finding no outlet for his anger, he turned on Celia and yanked her to her feet.

'You little whore! You dirty little slut! Rolling around, God knows where, with . . . him . . . that ! And now the whole bloody street knows what kind of a tart I've got for a daughter!' He pushed her back and she sank on the sofa, breathless and speechless.

'I blame you for this, Annie! It's *your* fault! She's always confided in you, never me! You *must* have known!'

'Charlie – I . . . didn't! Oh, God help me, I had no idea and that's the truth!'

'Don't lie to me, woman! I'm not a fool and, by God, I'll have the truth!' In one swift movement he pulled his wife to her feet and struck her hard across the face.

Celia screamed and Billy, fury rising in him, stepped between his parents, but it was Maudie who elbowed him aside. Her eyes were blazing and she wagged a bony finger in Charlie's face.

'I'm not having *that* in *my* house, Charlie Milton! My Harry has never raised a finger to me in twenty-five years. You touch her again and you'll be out on the street and I'll put you there myself! Now get out and see if there is anything left at all next door, and don't slam the flaming door or we might have the walls falling down around us. Go with him, Billy. This is no place for you just yet. Your mam's upset and she's got a flaming right to be.'

It was with great reluctance that Billy followed his father.

Maudie went into the scullery and emerged with a small towel she'd wrung out in cold water.

'Here, let me see your face, Annie, luv. The bloody coward. Well, if you're staying with me I'll not have a carry-on like this.' Maudie's lips were set in the familiar thin line as she gently pressed the towel to Annie's cheek.

'Oh, Mam! Mam! I didn't mean you to find out like this!' Celia cried, hugging herself and rocking to and fro with remorse.

'Then just how *did* you expect her to find out? When you had the baby in the flaming privy?' Maudie's voice was full of disgust.

Annie was calmer now. Maudie's presence was a relief. 'Oh, Cee, why? Why did you do it?' she asked despairingly.

'Because . . . because I love him, Mam. I've loved him for over a year and I couldn't give him up.'

'You mean you *wouldn't* give him up,' Maudie snapped. 'Well, we'll soon see how much he loves you now, won't we? Look at the state you've got your mam in, to say nothing of your da, and now they've not a roof over their heads nor even a change of clothes. God knows what's going to happen. Oh, I'll put you up, somewhere, but I'm not having *him* giving me the payout in me own home, so he can shift himself and find you somewhere else – in time, of course.'

Maudie patted Annie's arm.

'Now I'm going up to those three. I've let them stew for long enough up there, and by God they won't put a foot wrong after this because I'm going to threaten them with the police. I'm going to tell them I'm dragging them all down to the police station and having them charged with arson.' Maudie turned and stormed up the stairs. If Charlie Milton had brought that Foxy up with more sense and responsibility then he wouldn't now be standing in the wreckage of his home, she thought angrily to herself. It was always Foxy bloody Milton who dreamed up these things. He was the one who was always leading Frank and Eddie into trouble. Annie was too soft with him; she never told Charlie about his escapades she was so afraid of rows. Well, she'd teach Foxy Milton a lesson tonight, all right, and one he wouldn't forget either.

Downstairs Celia took the cloth gently from Annie and wiped her mother's tear-streaked face.

'Mam, I could kill him for hitting you and I think our Billy feels the same way. I'm glad Joe hit him.' She bit back the tears. 'I do love Joe, Mam. You know I'd never, never do anything like . . . this if I didn't.'

'But what's going to happen to you, Celia? I mean now of all times. When we've nothing, nothing at all.' Annie felt as though everything was happening to someone else, that she was standing on the outside of a window looking in on this nightmare. The home she'd built up over the years by careful management lay in ruins. She'd scrimped and saved a penny here, a sixpence there, occasionally five or even ten shillings when Charlie had been in a good mood. It had enabled her to buy good but second-hand things that she'd washed and polished and cared for. All her precious little collection of treasures, like Celia and Billy's photo's when they'd been babies, all gone now. The teething ring made of ivory with a real silver bell on it that Charlie had bought in a pawnbroker's sale. They'd both cut their teeth on it. Billy's prize for English at school: the epic poem *The Song of Hiawatha*, bound in a nice blue leather calf and with his name printed inside. These were the things that had little monetary value but were, to her, beyond all price and could never be replaced. A lifetime's work and memories gone up in flames in a few minutes and all because of Foxy.

'Oh, Cee, I tried to bring you up decently, all of you,' she sobbed quietly.

'I know, Mam, and I'm not wicked or a slut or . . . what Da called me. I love Joe Slattery, truly I do.'

Annie shook her head. She couldn't bring herself to think of the future. She just couldn't. She drew Celia towards her into the circle of her arms, as if to protect her, but she knew that it was too late for anything like that – for Celia at least. She could do nothing to help her daughter. The last ounce of courage had gone when Charlie had hit her. It was something he'd never done before and now she'd fear him even more because of it.

There was complete silence in the house. Foxy and the twins had gone to bed, suitably chastened after a good talking-to from the police constable who patrolled up and down the street in case there was more trouble or looting. Whilst Foxy was squeezed into the twins' bed Billy would share with Charlie the bed Maudie and Harry slept in. Maudie herself would sleep up in the attic room and Harry on the sofa, if she could ever get him out of that damned contraption in the yard, which was where he'd retreated after the fire. Annie and Celia would have Richie's room. It had only a single bed, but they'd manage for tonight.

Annie was helping Maudie get the rooms sorted out and Celia lay curled in a corner of the sofa, her aching head resting on her folded arms.

Billy came in first, carrying a big bundle and looking like a chimney sweep.

'There's not much, Cee. Some blankets that were in that old sea chest – you remember how thick it was – and some clothes which all need washing, they're so black with smoke. Where's Mam?'

'Helping upstairs. Mam and me are to have Richie's room and you're to share with Da.'

It was the first opportunity Billy had had to speak to his sister alone and after he'd put down the bundle, he sat next to her.

'Are you really . . . expecting, Cee?' he whispered.

She nodded. 'Joe didn't know until tonight. Only Lizzie knew.'

'Lizzie knew!'

'Yes, but I swore her to secrecy. I – I told her what I was going to do. I said that she and you should . . . do the same.'

'What for?'

'So they'd have to let us get married.'

Billy paled beneath the soot. 'God, Cee, does Da know about Lizzie and me? We – we've never done . . . anything.'

'No, and no one's going to tell him. I hate him! I really hate him!'

'If he goes for Mam again I'll kill him, Cee. I will. I swear to God.'

'You won't have to. You heard Maudie and it *is* her house and he should be grateful that someone took us in.'

Billy sat looking down at his hands. They were black and he reeked of smoke. Next door he'd worked in angry silence beside his da. They'd only been able to search through the things downstairs because the staircase had gone and two of the ceilings had collapsed. He didn't want Mam to see the black and twisted objects that had been her pride and joy. His da hadn't spoken either as he kicked and shoved blackened furniture that disintegrated on impact. The smell had been awful too, and water had dripped down the walls and squelched underfoot. Da had muttered that the fire brigade had done more damage than the fire itself.

'You'd better get to bed, Billy. You've work in the morning.'

He rose, nodding his head slowly. All he had were the clothes he stood up in and they were a mess. They were his best clothes too. It was the worst night in his life, what with losing his home, Cee nearly being killed then flinging herself into Joe's arms, then Da hitting Mam. When would he ever get to see Lizzie again? he wondered.

Charlie's return came within a few minutes of Billy going upstairs. He too was filthy, his face streaked with sweat and soot. He bore an armful of assorted clothing, all soaked and reeking of smoke. Seeing his daughter curled up on the sofa he dumped his burden on the floor. All the fury and humiliation of the night seethed through him again. Roughly he pulled her to her feet and she screamed in fright, bringing Annie, Maudie and Billy rapidly down the stairs.

'You little bitch! Sitting there as comfortable and as contented as a bloody cat! With the bloody morals of an alley cat too. Letting other people run after you and wait on you. Don't think this will all blow over because it won't,' he roared. 'No, by God it won't! You're not fit to live under any decent person's roof!' He dragged her towards the kitchen door.

'No, Charlie! Please!' Annie begged, tears coming down her cheeks. 'Oh God! How much more can I stand, Charlie?'

'Well, she's made her bed and now she can lie on it the way she's done with *him*. Let's see if he wants her now!' he jeered. 'Soiled goods, that's what you are. He's just used you, you stupid, dirty little whore! Get out of my sight! Get out!' he bellowed.

As he dragged an hysterical Celia down the lobby, Maudie

gripped Annie's arm tightly. She wouldn't interfere between Celia and her father but her eyes narrowed and her feelings for Charlie Milton were written all over her face.

Charlie opened the front door and thrust Celia on to the step. She tried to brush her hair and her tears from her face with hands cut and burned and with fingernails broken and bleeding.

'Da! Da! Please, don't throw me out! You've nowhere to stay, so what will happen to me?' she sobbed.

'You can go and live with *them* or, better still, you can go to hell! You should have been left to burn in that bedroom. You and your bastard! You should have burned because you'll burn in hell.' He pushed her hard and she staggered on the bottom step and fell on to the pavement.

Charlie shut the door and turned round.

Both his son and Maudie were looking at him with such hatred that he could almost feel it reach out and claw at him, but his wife was lying on the floor in a dead faint.

Celia sprawled on the flags of the pavement, the flagstones Maudie scrubbed each day. She was hysterical, sobbing convulsively and crying out, unaware of what she was doing or where she was.

Eventually she pulled herself to her feet. The pain of her emotions was far worse than the physical pain. She'd scraped her knee and her arm as she'd fallen and her hands were cut and now smarting where the flesh had been burned as she'd clung to the red-hot wood of the bedroom window frame. There were also cuts on her hands and knees from the broken glass. Her head was pounding but it was nothing, nothing at all compared to the pain that was tearing at her heart. She'd known at some point there'd be a scene like this, but not on top of all the trauma she'd lived through today.

Her dress was torn, dirty and wet and her hair straggled untidily over eyes red and swollen with crying. She caught hold of the nearest lamppost and leaned against it. The street was empty and silent now. The sky was dark and so heavy that she felt it was pressing down on her. Again she fought for breath. Poor Mam. Oh, her poor timid little mam, but Maudie wouldn't stand for Da hitting her again and for that Celia was thankful. Annie could do nothing for her now. No one could. No one would even want to help her, except Joe.

Wiping her face with the hem of her dress she walked slowly, dragging each foot as though her shoes were made of lead, past the house that had been her home, even though at times she'd hated it. The light from the streetlamp blurred and faded and threw the building mercifully into shadow. They'd all lost so much in that fire, but she'd lost everything. Now her only hope was that her gamble would pay off and, as her da had said, to go to Joe. To beg and plead with his mam if she had to, but if Brigid Slattery wouldn't take her in then God alone knew where she could go. She didn't.

Chapter Eighteen

Brigid had fumed silently, her face set with barely concealed anger and shock as she followed her eldest son into the house and closed the door behind her on the mainly stunned crowd out in the street. Lizzie and the younger ones were waiting in the lobby, Lizzie with eyes like saucers with fright . . .

'Didn't I tell you to get this lot to bed, Lizzie Slattery? Is it deaf you are as well as being daft?' Brigid snapped.

Lizzie shoved her siblings up the stairs. 'Get up there and don't any of you dare to come down,' she hissed at them.

Brigid pointed to the kitchen door. 'You, meladdo, in that kitchen now. And it's the rounds of the kitchen you'll be after getting by the time I've finished with you.'

As Joe did as he was told, Lizzie's footsteps could be heard as she ran quickly downstairs and followed him.

Brigid lowered herself into the armchair where Dessie had sat so often and thought, as she did in times of crisis, of just how much she needed him. But this was the worst crisis yet. How she longed for Dessie's support, his quick grasp of the situation and the knack he had of sorting things out far more rationally than herself. But this would have been beyond him even. This was the worst disaster she had had to cope with since his death and she must cope with it alone. And cope she would, she told herself determinedly.

'Right, the pair of you, sit down on that sofa and you, Joseph Slattery, can tell me why your one from next door threw herself into your arms and then announced to the whole street that she's . . . got herself in trouble. And there's yourself holding on to her like that. Holy Mother of God! Aren't I persecuted enough? Don't I rely on you, Joe, to set an example? Tell me it's lying she is. That you've nothing to do with the matter at all.'

Joe looked his mother squarely in the face. He was full of remorse for the heartache he knew he was causing her, for her loss of dignity and respectability. The events of the whole evening had been so dramatic, so devastating, that he'd hardly known what he was saying or doing.

He'd been frantic and distraught as he'd watched Celia clinging to that windowsill with the sight and the sound of the flames behind her. When she was safe he'd been so relieved that he hadn't even thought about the people who had come out into the street. Then when she'd told him about the baby, he just hadn't known what to think, it had all been so confusing, but he hadn't even had time to gather his scattered wits before her da had dragged her away and then tried to belt him. God alone knew what she would be going through now. A surge of anger rose and then died. If he went up to the Kemps' he'd never get a foot over the doorstep and the door would be shut in his face. There was no chance of seeing her tonight.

'Well?' Brigid demanded.

'No, Mam, she's not lying. She wouldn't lie about a thing like that.'

Brigid just seemed to slump back in the chair, exhausted by the last couple of hours, drained of all emotion. 'Oh Holy Mother, have pity on me.' It was a prayer, a true supplication.

'Mam, we've been seeing each other now for a year. I love her and tonight I nearly lost her and . . . the baby.' He looked down at his blackened hands because he couldn't look into his mother's face and see the heartbreak in it. He knew how much he'd betrayed her.

Lizzie started to cry softly. She knew Celia must be in a terrible state of shock and half crazed by nearly being burned alive. She'd seen the terror in her friend's eyes. Celia must have been demented to have blurted out she was pregnant. Poor Cee, Lizzie knew she would have told Joe soon, when they were alone so they could work out a plan, but now . . .

'So what do you think of your fine friend now, Lizzie Slattery? Not quite such a saint now, is she?'

'Mam, she – she didn't mean to tell the whole street. She was going to tell Joe soon, but with the fire . . .' Lizzie's sobs became uncontrollably louder, and as her mother's eyes narrowed speculatively Lizzie realised what she'd done.

'You knew, didn't you? You knew all the time, Lizzie Slattery! And not a word nor a hint out of you!' Brigid's anger was growing by the minute.

'I'm sorry, Mam. I – I . . . didn't want to upset anyone,' Lizzie answered. Her own heart was heavy. In God's name how would she ever get to see Billy again? She felt she was watching the destruction of her own love and future happiness. They both knew, she and Billy, that one day they'd have to run away. They had no future in this city, but there were also shipyards on the Clyde and the Tyne.

'Upset is it? Upset! Haven't I the right to be more than just "upset"?' Brigid cried.

'Mam, I'll marry her,' Joe said quietly.

Brigid turned on him. 'You *can't* marry her, you eejit!'

Joe's expression changed. 'I will, even if it's only in the registry office.'

'And be damned—' Brigid's reply was cut short by a loud knocking on the front door.

'Go and tell whoever it is that our Joe has me destroyed altogether, I can't see anyone.' Brigid groaned inwardly thinking now she would never be able to hold her head up in this street for the very shame Joe had heaped on her.

As Lizzie, still with tears running down her cheeks, opened the door, an utterly distraught Celia fell into her arms, her face streaked with tears, her blonde hair damp and falling untidily across her face.

'Lizzie! Oh, thank God it's you, Lizzie,' she sobbed.

Pushing aside her own distress Lizzie was appalled. 'Cee, what's happened? You're shaking like a leaf and you're cut and bruised and burned. What's he done to you?'

Celia clung to Lizzie tightly, her face buried against Lizzie's shoulder. 'He – he belted poor Mam and . . . and he's thrown me out. Oh, Lizzie, the house has gone . . . and Maudie won't have me, Da will see to that. I've nowhere to go.' Celia gave herself up to deep, racking sobs which increased the tremors that already held her in their grip.

Before Lizzie could reply Brigid came into the lobby followed by Joe.

'Get *that* one out of this house! Sure, hasn't she caused enough trouble already?'

Lizzie's eyes were pleading. 'Mam, look at her. After all she's been through tonight she's destroyed and he belted her poor mam and has thrown Cee out in the street.'

'Well she's not stopping here!' Brigid fulminated.

Celia lifted her head from Lizzie's shoulder and pulled away from her friend's comforting embrace.

'Oh, Mrs Slattery, for the love of God help me. Please. What can I do? I've nowhere now. Please don't turn me out.'

Instantly Joe pushed past his mother and took Celia in his arms. 'Mam, if you turn her out on the street, then I'll go with her.'

'And so will I,' Lizzie added without pausing to consider the consequences. 'Mam, she's expecting,' she pleaded.

'And isn't that the cause of all this? What kind of a girl is she to carry on like . . . that?' Brigid was still so outraged that her anger had not abated.

'She's a decent, hard-working, loving, quiet girl,' Joe said.

'Decent and quiet, is it now?'

'Mam, it's my baby. It's your grandson or -daughter,' Joe pleaded.

'Would you want it to have to go into an orphanage, Mam?' Lizzie added.

Some of Brigid's wrath was fading, for the state the poor girl was in was enough to touch the coldest heart.

She looked at the trio, her hands on her hips. There was something in Joe's eyes she'd never seen before: determination mingled with love. He meant it. He would go. She felt so frustrated and impotent in the face of such resolve. His arms were around the girl, who was near to collapse, and Lizzie, her eyes full of tears for her friend's plight, had her chin up, a sure sign of doggedness. Well, she'd been shamed before her neighbours and friends already so what would it matter now if she took the girl in – for the night anyway? No one who called themselves a Christian could turn her out on to the streets after the terrors of the night, her home burned out and herself almost killed. She, Brigid Slattery, wasn't like that Charlie Milton.

'Ah, get the girl inside then. Sure she's half dead with the terror of it all.'

The expression in Joe's eyes softened and he breathed easier while Lizzie hugged her mother.

'Oh, thanks, Mam!' she cried. 'She *is* a good girl, she really is, you wait and see.'

'Well, we'll see about that. Aren't I the disgrace of the neighbourhood already? Didn't she tell the whole street the state she's in?'

'But *you've* not slammed the door in her face, Mam. *He* has and what's more he's belted her poor mam.'

Brigid's features softened. 'God help that poor little woman being married to that bully and having her home burned down and her girl near to being killed, without *him* belting her. She'll be in the same state as this one here but I'd bet my life on the fact that herself at number eight won't stand for any more of *that*. She's taken them in, after all, and she can show him the door if he belts the poor wee soul again, and she *will* so.' She never thought she'd live to see the day but for once Brigid was glad Maudie Kemp was the woman she was.

Celia was given hot strong tea and Lizzie wrapped her up in a blanket she'd taken from her own bed. The night was still warm so she didn't need it, she said emphatically. In silence Brigid had bathed all the cuts and with a needle had gently removed the small pieces of glass that had been embedded in Celia's hands and knees as she'd crawled to the window.

'Lizzie, shift yourself and bring in that bottle of TCP that's in the scullery. These cuts will be after turning septic otherwise,' She covered Celia's burns with dripping, which everyone used for burns and scalds.

'She can have my bed, Mam. I'll sleep on the sofa,' Lizzie offered, as she tidied their rudimentary first-aid items away.

'No, I'll sleep on the sofa,' Joe offered, thankful that Celia was calming down now. As was his mam.

'And how can you do that, Joe Slattery? Wouldn't she have to share with Fergal? No, I'll . . . I'll sleep in the bed in the front room. She can have my bed upstairs in the attic with Lizzie.' The girl could have slept on the sofa, but she was still in a state and Brigid felt that Celia Milton would relax and sleep in the same room as Lizzie. The last thing she wanted now was a miscarriage to contend with.

Both Joe and Lizzie said nothing but Mam had not slept in that bed since Da had died and they appreciated the decision Brigid had made, knowing that the events of the night were more than enough for her without having to bear all the bitter-sweet memories that bed would evoke.

'Go on now, the pair of you, go up and get some sleep. You've Mass in the morning, Lizzie, don't forget.'

As Lizzie helped Celia to her feet and helped her upstairs, Brigid poured herself another cup of tea. It was so stewed you could stand a spoon up in it, she thought, but she was too exhausted to wet a fresh pot.

'Thanks for everything, Mam,' Joe said humbly.

'I haven't said I'll have her for ever so don't go thinking I will.'

'I know, but like I said, we'll get married and find a room somewhere else. I don't want to leave you, Mam, but I will if I have to.'

Brigid felt she'd been put through a wringer, and she had a blinding headache with the strain of everything. 'Thank God we still have a decent roof over us. That fire bobby said we were lucky it hasn't damaged the structure or something like that and now . . . all this.' She passed a hand wearily over her forehead and looked up at her son. 'There's no need for you to go, lad. She can stay for a while as long as she stays inside, except for going to work, that is. I can't make the money stretch to feed another mouth, you know that.'

Joe nodded. 'She'll be happy with that, Mam.'

'And if himself comes down here, ranting and laying down the law, he'll get no change out of me, the great bullying amadame that he is! He threw her out so she's no longer his responsibility.'

'If he comes down here at all I'll lay him out cold, Mam, I swear it,' Joe said grimly.

'You will not. Hasn't there been enough trouble already, Joe? I'm worn out with it all.'

'I'm still going to marry her, Mam. I love her and I won't have my child branded a bastard and all that goes with that.'

Brigid sighed heavily. 'I'm going to early Mass. I don't want to have to face Maggie, Tessie and Biddy just yet and I want to ask some advice. But get yourself to bed now, lad. I've our Emmet's jacket to mend. Hasn't the little bowsie ripped it on a nail? But still that's the least of my worries. Thank God he isn't after burning the house down – yet.'

Joe bent and kissed her before he went up the stairs. How he longed just to hold Celia in his arms all night, to soothe her, calm her doubts, to tell her he loved her and was going to marry her come hell or high water, but Mam wouldn't stand for that.

Brigid sewed the triangular tear in the sleeve of her youngest son's best jacket while thinking about her oldest and what she would say to the parish priest in the morning. Even when she'd finished the mending she sat for a long time staring into the empty fire grate, thinking of Celia and Annie Milton. Girls of that age were eejits about lads, but it was to their mams that they usually turned in times of trouble. Her heart was heavy as she thought of the poor frail woman who'd lost everything, including her daughter.

Brigid saw no one from the street at Mass. Most people went to the later services for Sunday was the only day in the week when they could have a few hours' extra rest in bed. She waited until everyone had gone before she approached Father Minehan.

'Up bright and early this lovely morning, Brigid,' he remarked cheerfully.

'The morning may be lovely but I'm so destroyed I've not the heart to enjoy it, Father.'

The priest's expression changed to one of concern.

'What's gone wrong, Brigid?'

'Everything. Everything is as desperate as it can be. Can I talk . . . in private, Father?'

'Go on up to the house while I take off these vestments – Father Healy is taking the eight o'clock Mass. Miss Whelan will show you into the parlour and tell her I said to give you a cup of tea. You must be famished.'

Brigid nodded her thanks but she knew she'd get no cup of tea out of Miss Kathleen Whelan. In fact she wouldn't even repeat the priest's instruction.

Kathleen Whelan, who'd been at the presbytery for as long as anyone could remember and terrified all the kids and some of the grown-ups as well, greeted her with a face full of suspicion and annoyance at the fact that anyone should interfere with His Reverence's breakfast at this early hour.

Brigid sat uneasily in the sparsely furnished but clean parlour that smelled of beeswax, twisting her hands in her lap, full of anxiety. Her eyes roamed around the holy pictures on the wall and the statue of Our Lady of Lourdes standing on a shining table, its surface covered with a starched white cloth. A little night light burned in a blue glass bowl at the statue's feet.

True to his word it wasn't long before the priest joined her.

'No tea?' He turned towards the door but Brigid stopped him.

'Ah, I wouldn't be up to it yet, Father, thank you.'

He sat opposite her in a worn winged leather Queen Anne-style chair, his hands on his knees.

'What is so terribly wrong, Brigid?' he asked, leaning towards her.

Haltingly and in anguished tones she told of the events of the previous night and when she'd finished the expression on his face had changed. Gone was the smile and the concern in his eyes.

'Father, what am I to do? As a Christian woman I couldn't turn her out the state she was in, and he insists he'll marry her. God help us, my poor Dessie must be turning in his grave but what was I supposed to do?'

'She announced her . . . condition . . . in front of the entire street, did you say?'

'I did so. There was no help for it. She just flung herself at him and said – well . . .'

'I see.'

'God knows how I'd manage without his wage. Our Josie is starting in the kitchens of the Stork Hotel next week and our Lizzie is working and I do a bit myself, but if he marries her at the registry office . . . well, it's no marriage, is it, Father? And I *won't* be having them living in sin under my roof!' she finished emphatically.

Father Minehan was deep in thought. He'd known the family for years. He'd christened Joe Slattery and his sisters and brothers.

He'd heard their First Confession. He'd given them their First Communion and he'd seen the Archbishop confirm them all. He'd anointed Dessie Slattery the night he'd died and prayed over his grave. They were a good, decent family and as Brigid had said, what else could a Christian woman do? Pass by, like those in the parable of the Good Samaritan? And even Mary Magdalene had found forgiveness.

It was a radical idea of solving the problem and one he didn't really approve of, although other priests – younger priests – were not like-minded.

'Brigid, go home now and try and have a rest. I'll make some enquiries.'

She was startled. 'Enquiries about what, Father?'

'Well, it will need the Archbishop's dispensation, but it might be possible – I'm only saying *might* – for Joseph and this . . . Celia to be married in the vestry of the church. We'd need a registrar to come out, of course, as they do in the normal way of things, but . . .' he shrugged.

Brigid's eyes were suddenly filled with tears of thankfulness and relief. It was something she had never heard of, even he'd hinted he didn't approve of it and they would be bound by the decision of the Archbishop, but there was a hope. That's what he was telling her. A small flicker of hope that her son could marry the girl in church. It wouldn't matter that it wasn't at the foot of the altar steps, that there would be no Nuptial Mass, just an exchange of vows and rings. But it would be legal and binding in the eyes of the Church and the Laws of the Land. They could then have the bed in the front room and another baby would be born in it. Herself and Dessie's grandchild.

'Thank you, Father, and God bless you!' The tears were wiped away.

'Get off home now and rest, but don't say a word to anyone until I have some news for you.'

'Will I not tell our Joe then?'

'Not yet. It's no use them building up their hopes.'

Brigid again thanked him and called upon all the saints to bless him before she walked back home with her lighter heart. If they could be married in church then at least her neighbours wouldn't be able to make too many derisory remarks.

Things had been strained that day with Josie, Bernie and Fergal all giving Celia surreptitious but curious glances. All they'd been told was that because of the fire Celia would be staying with them for a while, but Brigid knew it would only be a matter of time before they heard the truth.

Celia was still shaken and Brigid made her stay in bed until dinner time. Lizzie and Joe took it in turns to sit beside her, Joe stroking her forehead tenderly and telling her things would work out, while fuming at the way she'd been treated. At the other side of her Lizzie gently held her friend's hand and told her over and over again that things would be all right now, Mam and Joe would see to it all.

'But what about you and our Billy, Lizzie?' Celia had asked once.

Lizzie had shrugged miserably. 'We – we won't be able to see each other for a while, but things will blow over . . . in time. This will be a nine-day wonder and then, well, we'll see.' She tried to sound reassuring and even cheerful, but failed miserably. It would be at least a month now before they dared to meet.

On the Monday when the kids had gone to school and Fergal and Lizzie had left for work, Celia came downstairs. She was still bruised and grazed but was calmer now. Joe made her sit in the easy chair by the range while Brigid folded up the dirty washing which she would take to the bag wash later on. She hadn't the energy to go through all the rigmarole at home.

'I – I should be going to work. Mr Henderson will wonder.'

'He will not, for I've sent a note in with our Lizzie saying you're after being too shocked and upset with the fire. But you'll go in later in the week.'

Celia felt gauche and uncomfortable. 'I – I don't know what to say to you, Mrs Slattery, except that I'm so sorry and so grateful and I'll give you all my wages.'

Brigid nodded curtly. 'And what about your own poor mam? I hear he belted her.'

Celia nodded. 'He did. It was awful but Mrs Kemp told him she'd put him out if he carried on like that again.'

'Ah, that one has a tongue that would cut the horns off a cow when she gets going. Will you go on up there to see your mam, let her see you're safe? She must be destroyed with the worry of it all.'

Again Celia nodded. 'Only Mrs Kemp should be in, everyone else will be out.' She was trying hard to keep the tears at bay. 'Oh, poor, poor Mam. She's had a terrible life with him. We all have. And now she hasn't even a roof over her head and all her things have gone, and she's not well either.'

'That brother of yours would have the Pope himself demented. He should be sent to a reformatory. Haven't you saved him twice already, Joe?' Brigid carried on with her tasks.

Joe looked at Celia before he spoke 'Mam, I've been thinking. Maybe at the end of next week we'll go off to Brougham Terrace. There's no other way.'

Brigid stared at him in consternation. Now what was she to do? What if she said nothing and they went off to the registry office? Could she tell them about her conversation after Mass yesterday? She decided to risk it.

'I had a chat with Father Minehan yesterday. I'm not supposed to tell you and he doesn't approve of it himself, but he's trying to get permission from the Archbishop for you to be married in the vestry. It's some sort of new way of going on favoured by the younger element of the clergy, so he said. I take it you'll not find fault with that, Celia? The baby will have to be baptised and brought up in the Catholic faith, of course.'

For the first time in days Celia smiled. There was hope of a church wedding which she knew both Joe and his mother cared deeply about. She didn't mind where she was married as long as she had Joe beside her, and Brigid had called her Celia for the first time since she'd taken her in.

'Then you can have the front room.' Brigid tried to sound matter of fact.

'Mam, did he really say that?' Joe asked.

'Yes, but he also said not to expect it to go ahead smoothly. But I couldn't let you go to that desperate place with not an ounce of sanctity in it.'

Celia got up and put her arms around Brigid's ample shoulders. 'I won't disgrace you, Mrs Slattery. I'll work too, after I've had it.'

'Well, we'll sort all that out when the time comes.' Despite herself Brigid couldn't help but like the girl.

Joe too hugged his mother. 'Won't you feel great, Mam, being a granny?'

'Will you stop all this way of going on? Isn't her own mam just up the road? She'll be a granny too. But not a word to her about the church.' She knew it was going to be hard to keep quiet in front of Maggie, Tessie and Biddy but she'd just have to get on with lifc. Thcy all would.

Chapter Nineteen

After lunch when Brigid went to the bag wash and Joe went early to work to see if there was a chance of some extra hours, Celia decided to try to see her mother. There was no 'post office' in the wall now for the yard was full of debris. She had to avert her eyes as she passed her old home for the sight of it weighed heavily on an already laden heart.

She was glad that the street was empty, save for some very young children who were playing in the gutter and sitting on the kerb. Like her mam everyone did the weekly wash on Mondays but she knew Annie would be out of her mind with worry for she had no idea where Celia had gone and what sort of a state she'd been in.

She knocked on Maudie's door, full of trepidation, not knowing what her da had instructed Maudie to do should she come back. The wait, standing on the very steps she'd been flung down only a couple of days ago, seemed interminable. At last the door opened slowly and to Celia's relief it was Annie who stood there.

She threw herself into her mother's arms and they both dissolved in tears and clung to each other.

Maudie appeared, wiping her hands on her apron.

'For God's sake, get in here, the pair of you, before everyone's out on their doorsteps gawping!' she instructed. The sharp but practical tone calmed Celia as Maudie closed the front door behind them.

Annie led Celia into Maudie's kitchen, now a shadow of its usually pristine self.

'I'm in the middle of the washing and I've no wish to hear what either of you has to say. Then no one can accuse me of "aiding and abetting" so to speak.' Maudie was referring to Charlie and they all knew it.

'When I've finished out there in about half an hour, I don't want to see you still here, Celia.' Maudie turned away and went back into the scullery.

Annie had spent the whole weekend in a state of near collapse and Maudie was already getting fed up with having them all living under her roof. Her once neat and spotless home was beginning to resemble a dosshouse. Her regime had gone completely to the dogs and she fully intended to ask Charlie Milton when he got in from work to go and see the landlord about finding them another house. She'd never really liked him and having him take over what was *her* domain infuriated her.

When the scullery door closed behind Maudie, Celia gently touched the side of her mother's face. It was so bruised that one eye was half closed.

'Oh, Mam, I'm so sorry. I could kill him, I really could.'

Annie took her hands. 'Never mind all that now. Oh, I've been so worried about you. Are you all right? Where've you been, Cee?' For an instant anger filled her eyes and her grip on Celia's hands tightened. 'What kind of a father is he to throw you out like that? He's mad. He's a monster!'

Celia's eyes began to fill with tears, not for herself but for her mam. 'I know all that, Mam, but how are you managing? Oh, all your lovely things, gone. I can't even look at next door.' She brushed away her tears.

'I – I – went to Mrs Slattery's house and begged her to take me in, and she did. That's where I've been. Oh, it's not as tidy or quiet or even as clean as our house used to be, but she's been very good to me, Mam. I love Joe and we're going to get married so I won't be disgracing you more by being an unmarried mother. Mrs Slattery says we can live with her, have the front room. She's even been to see their priest. They've got some new rules or something so we can get married in the vestry of the church.'

Annie looked horrified. 'Oh, Cee no! Not in his Church. You know you'll be looked down on, cursed and even spat at by some. You're not one of them.'

'Mam, I don't care! I don't bloody care! I just want Joe and my baby. I thought you'd be happy for me to be married in a church rather than Brougham Terrace.'

'Oh, Celia, he'll kill you! He'd sooner see you dead than be married in their Church.'

Celia shook her head, refusing to be intimidated. 'Mam, you don't understand. Joe won't let him near me and neither will his mam. You know what a temper she's got and she's not afraid of him. Remember how she belted him and drove him out into the street?'

'But, Celia, you'll need his consent and he won't give it.'

Celia's blue eyes became cold. 'Then I'm not going to tell him and, Mam, please, please don't tell him. Promise me you won't tell him? I *won't* have my baby born illegitimate. I *won't*.'

Reluctantly Annie nodded. She'd spent the past two days in a dream-like trance and she felt that she, like Charlie, was beginning to lose all touch with reality. Even to do the smallest, meanest chore exhausted her, and no matter how much she tried she couldn't summon up any enthusiasm or concentrate on buying new clothes for them all. Maudie had had to go to town with her and what she'd bought was mainly what Maudie had picked out. She had to admit that Maudie was being very kind to her and Billy, but there had been a few rows between Charlie and Maudie, which both she and Harry had listened to in a dull, dazed silence.

'Mam, she's kind – Mrs Slattery, I mean. They're so overcrowded but at least she'll have another pair of hands to help with the work and another wage packet coming in.'

Annie nodded. 'I know she's kind and I'll always be grateful to her for giving you a home and I'll never, never forgive him for throwing you out on to the street like that, after all you'd been through.' She picked Celia's hands up again and looked at the cuts and the burns that were already beginning to heal.

'She bathed them and put fat on the burns.'

Annie nodded. 'She's a kind woman, and will you tell her that, Celia? At least I know where you are and that he . . . Joe . . . is going to marry you.'

Celia hugged her mother. 'Mam, I'm only a few doors away, I can come and see you on my half-day off.'

Annie bit her lip, her eyes full of anxiety. 'Someone is bound to see you and tell him.'

'So what? He can't touch me now, Mam.'

'I know but he can . . . he can . . .' Annie's voice faltered.

Maudie stood in the doorway. 'He can take it out on you, Annie? Not in *my* house he won't. Now I think you'd better go, Celia, and if you're going to come visiting then come down the jigger and use the back door. And don't come too often, I'm sick to death of fighting with your da! You'd need the patience of a saint to put up with him.'

Celia got to her feet, as did Annie, who embraced her daughter.

Celia smiled. 'I just had to come and see you, Mam. And after all, you're going to be a grandma.'

'Yes, well the least said about that the better!' Maudie interrupted and Celia knew it was time to go. She hugged and kissed her mam and thanked Maudie for letting her in, then walked down the lobby, opened the front door and went down the steps that Maudie hadn't had time to scrub yet.

She looked across the street to where Nettie Taylor lived and as she stood there the front curtain moved. She drew in her breath. Oh God! She'd been seen. Flo Taylor would be over like a shot to know what was going on and she'd make sure Da would hear about her visit and then she'd not be able to see her mam at all.

Her steps were as heavy as they'd been on the way to Maudie's house.

She'd tried to see her mam again later in the week but Maudie wouldn't let her in.

'Don't think I'm taking any notice of *him*, I'm not. I won't be dictated to in my own house. No, Flo Taylor came sticking her nose in. She collared your da on his way home on Monday night.'

'I saw her curtains move when I left,' Celia answered miserably.

'Your mam told me, in secret of course, that you're going to marry *him* and in *that* Church.' Seeing the look of trepidation on the girl's face she carried on, 'I won't tell anyone – I swore to your mam I wouldn't – but I don't approve at all, not one little bit, and how you can live in that house with all those scruffy kids after the home you were used to, I don't know.'

Celia pointed to the yard next door. 'Look at it now, Mrs Kemp. Just a pile of black bricks. It's not *anyone's* home now and I'm grateful that Mrs Slattery took me in. I love Joe and we're going to get married and at least Mam will know where I am and that I'm safe.' And with that she'd walked away.

'So, herself wouldn't let you in then? Sure, it's only what I expected,' Brigid remarked on Celia's return.

'It's not because Da's told her I'm not to go. She said she won't be dictated to by him in her house. She doesn't approve of me getting married in church.'

'Ah, I thought she'd be giving out to him. I'll say that for the creature, she'll not have him ruling the roost, and as for approving, well *my* friends and neighbours don't approve either, but they can like it or lump it.'

The following day Celia went back to work with Lizzie. Lizzie desperately wanted to see Billy and had begged Joe to give him a message from her at work.

'How the hell can I do that? I know we're both working on the same ship, this new design submarine, the *Thetis*, but I work nights, he works days.'

'Well, can't you go a bit early one night and see him before he clocks off?'

Joe raised his eyes to the ceiling. 'God in heaven, Lizzie, there's thirteen thousand men work there and when that whistle blows there's an almighty crush to get out of the gates. I'll never see him.'

'Well, can't you go in very early and see him, make some excuse?' Lizzie pleaded.

Joe frowned at her and shoved his hands deeper into the pockets of his trousers.

'It's not flaming much to ask, is it, Joe Slattery? It's all right for you – you're going to marry Celia – but how can I get to even see Billy now?'

'Lizzie, I know how you feel about him, but this isn't the time to see him. If you two get caught there'll be bloody murder in the street. We'd have to move out.'

'Well, I don't care! I hate this street! I hate this city!' she cried.

'But at least the pair of you can up stakes and go. Both Celia and I know that we're always going to live with Mam.' His expression softened. 'I'll try to see him. I'll ask Fred Roberts if he can square it with Billy's blockerman for Billy to just nip out of the gate for a few minutes. What do you want me to say?'

Lizzie's eyes were shining. 'The ferry. Tell him . . . tell him I'll see him at the usual time in the usual place on Saturday.'

Joe nodded. 'For God's sake, Lizzie, just don't get caught. Or get yourself into trouble.'

Lizzie was scornful. 'Oh, that's dead rich coming from you, isn't it? You can get Cee pregnant but Billy's not to lay a finger on me.'

'I didn't mean it to sound like that, you know I didn't, Lizzie. Just think of Mam and Celia and Billy's mam.'

Lizzie sighed and nodded.

* * *

She'd bought her ticket for the ferry and stood on the landing stage watching the New Brighton ferry draw ever closer. The other ferries were ploughing their way to and from Woodside and Seacombe.

Occasionally she looked back and glanced up at the clock on the tower of the Liver Building that faced the river. The eighteen-foot-high Liver Bird was etched against a slowly darkening sky, the last rays of the sun turning its wings gold and orange. Oh, she hoped he was going to come. She prayed that nothing awful had happened. Joe had had a few words with Billy as promised and he'd said he would be here, but Joe had also said it was too soon for them to meet. It was just tempting fate.

She began to walk up and down the stage. The ferry was very close now, and it being a pleasant evening there were plenty of other people waiting to board for a bit of a sail and some enjoyment in New Brighton. At last she saw him, running along the stage towards her, his face flushed, his hair ruffled by the river breeze.

'Oh, I never thought I'd get here, Lizzie, I'm sorry,' he panted.

'Never mind, you're here now. What kept you?'

'The trolley came off the wires and the tram was just stuck there, right at the junction of Whitechapel, Lord Street, Church Street and Paradise Street. It was blocking the entire junction. There was chaos. All the traffic was snarled up and people were yelling and shouting, so I got off and started to run.'

She reached out and took his hand. 'Come on, let's join the crowd. Thank God there is such a crush. We won't be noticed.'

They leaned on the rail and watched the greyish foaming wake of the ferry. Billy put his arm around her and she looked up at him.

'Has it been very bad? I know you've only been living with Maudie a week.'

'God, it's awful. She snaps everyone's heads off if they leave anything lying around and it's just so cramped. The kids have their tea first, then we have ours. We can't fit eight around a small table, and the kids have everyone mithered to death. You know what our

Foxy's like with the twins. They've all been belted already for poking about in what's left of our house.' He sighed. 'I suppose it's because we always had a room each at home,' he finished gloomily.

'Celia went to see your mam.'

'I know, and that bloody Flo Taylor saw her and told Da and there was a big row. Poor Mam got the height of abuse from him again, but he didn't hit her, he didn't dare. I'll say that for Maudie, she's only small but she can't half keep Da under control. Mam and Mr Kemp seem to spend hours just staring into space.'

'At least Mr Kemp's got his pigeon loft.'

Billy nodded. 'Yes, but Mam's not well, Lizzie.'

'With all she's had to put up with, losing her home, him belting her, having him throw poor Cee out like that, it's no wonder. Her nerves must be shredded to pieces. Did you know that our Joe and Cee are going to get married and live with us?'

'No.'

'I thought your mam might have told you. Cee told her, the other day, and there's a possibility they could get married in church, in the vestry.'

'God, does Mam know that?'

Lizzie nodded. 'Yes, Cee told her. It's something new but they've got to get permission from the Archbishop.'

Billy looked at her with dread. 'Oh God, Lizzie, Da will kill her.'

'He'll have to kill our Joe and me mam first.'

Billy looked down at her with helplessness in his eyes. 'Everything is such a mess now. A right flaming mess.'

'Don't you dare tell anyone, Billy, because she's supposed to have your da's permission because she's not twenty-one.'

'I won't, but where does all this leave us, Lizzie?'

'Ten times worse off than we were before.' She leaned her head on his shoulder. She couldn't do what her friend had done. It would break her mam's heart. It was different for Celia, she'd be just a daughter-in-law, but Lizzie was very close to her mam and had been ever since Da had died, and another rushed wedding in the family would be just too much.

'When all this has died down, will we get engaged, Lizzie? Then when we've saved up enough we could run off somewhere.'

Lizzie was confused. It was so sudden and it was such a big step to take. She loved him, of course, but . . .

'I'd like to get engaged, Billy, but I can't think about us running away, not yet. Not for a long time.'

'I didn't say we'd run away soon. We'll have to save up and if we're engaged, well, it's halfway to getting married, isn't it?'

'Yes, but I couldn't wear a ring. Mam would want to know where it came from and there'd be more trouble.'

'Well, what about something else, a locket? You could hide that under your blouse or jumper and we can go and have our photos taken so you can put them in it.'

She reached up and kissed him on the cheek. 'I'd love that, Billy.' She loved him every bit as much as Celia loved Joe, but a locket would be tangible proof for her at least. Something she could touch and it would remind her all the time that Billy loved her and that one day they'd be together, like Celia and Joe.

Brigid decided on the Sunday that she'd have to face her neighbours. In the past week she'd seen virtually nothing of them at all. That fact alone told her that they had heard she'd taken Celia Milton in. Emmet and Bernie would have told their friends. She decided to tackle Maggie Walsh first.

When Maggie opened the door and before she could utter a word, Brigid took the plunge.

'Are you up to your eyes with the dinner, Maggie? If you are I'll come back later.'

'No, we're not having it until later today – *his* ma is coming round – so you'd better come in.' Maggie's tone was far from hospitable and her expression was decidedly frosty.

'Morning, Gerry,' Brigid said to Maggie's husband, who was reading the *Catholic Herald* without much enthusiasm. Maggie had bought it after Mass so her mother-in-law couldn't accuse him of becoming 'a lapsed Catholic' and go blaming her for it.

'Gerald, you can read that in the front room but don't make a mess in there. She's coming this afternoon. There's things here to be discussed and sorted out. Declan, go and tell Biddy Doyle and Tessie Mulhinney to come in here for a few minutes.'

Gerry Walsh sighed heavily but got up out of the chair. Declan was not as amenable.

'Ah, Mam, do I have to go?'

Maggie rounded on him. 'Yes, you flaming well do! And don't be all day about it either.'

When he'd gone Maggie put the kettle on.

Brigid thought she could have cut the silence with a knife.

By the time the tea was made and poured out, Biddy and Tessie had arrived, both with expressions of severe disapproval on their faces.

'Sit down, the pair of you,' Maggie instructed as she handed round the cups of tea.

'I've only to look at the three of you to see you're after being full of disapproval.'

'Well, what did you expect?' Maggie asked sharply.

Brigid settled herself into the chair Gerry had recently vacated. 'Our Joe is going to marry her.'

'Oh, Jesus, Mary and Joseph!' Biddy crossed herself.

'Sure, she's not the divil himself, Biddy Doyle, and I didn't see your Bernard or Gregory at Mass this morning.'

Biddy sniffed. She had a set-to every Sunday morning to get the pair of them to go to Mass and quite often she lost the battle, as she'd done today.

'I suppose it'll be registry office and that's not being wed at all, not so far as the Church is concerned.'

Brigid didn't reply but looked to Tessie for some glimmer of encouragement and support.

'What was I supposed to do, tell me that? The poor girl was half crazed with the night that was in it. Her home gone and then thrown out into the street. Into the flaming street. He pushed her so hard didn't she finish up in the road itself, and herself already cut and burned and bruised? Our Joe loves her and he's going to marry her,' she stated firmly.

'One day that feller will roast in hell,' Tessie said, her voice much less disapproving in tone.

Brigid was encouraged. 'She's a decent, quiet, hard-working girl. I know she's been brought up a Protestant, but that's not her fault. Your man is supposed to be a Christian but what kind of a Christian is it who carries on like Charlie Milton? Didn't he belt his poor little wife and she terrified out of her wits of him?'

'It's still not right, Brigid,' Maggie persisted.

'Am I saying it is? Sure, our Joe's felt the lash of my tongue, so he has, but she's not a bold strap like your Patsy, Biddy.'

'I've given our Patsy the rounds of the kitchen, I can tell you. "You'll finish up like Celia Milton," I told her. Well, that wiped the smirk off her face!' Biddy was only too aware of her daughter's shortcomings.

By the time Tessie had finished her tea she'd come to a decision. 'Well, when is it to be, then?'

Brigid breathed easier. 'They've not set a date yet, but it'll be soon. I'll tell you all. Haven't I been destroyed thinking I was being treated as if I had leprosy by the lot of you? Haven't we been friends all these years? Haven't we all helped each other out? Now I'm after asking for your help and your support.'

'Well, you've got it. Now we know he's going to marry her we can stop all the tongues wagging. It happens, Brigid, luv, from time to time. We'll all stand by you,' Maggie said firmly.

Brigid got to her feet. 'Wasn't I banking on that all along? Never once did I think you'd cut me dead. Now I'd better get back or the dinner will be destroyed altogether. God help the man who gets our Josie. She's little better than useless!'

As she crossed the street Brigid felt so much better. She was relieved and thankful. They *had* all helped each other over the years and she *did* consider them friends, which was why she'd been so anxious. Things might just come right, after all.

It was three weeks later that the dispensation came through and Father Minehan imparted the news to Brigid, after he'd sent one of the altar boys down to say he wanted to see her urgently.

'There won't be a do afterwards. It's not called for or expected, and I haven't the money to be wasting on a hooley,' Brigid informed Joe, Celia and Lizzie.

Joe was so relieved. 'We don't care about that, Mam. All I care about is Celia and you.'

'Joe's right, Mrs Slattery. I . . . we disgraced you but I'm happier now that you'll have some dignity again. You've been so good to me.'

'Hadn't you better try and get word to your mam? I know your one from number eight won't be after having you over the doorstep that she scrubs so hard it's worn away with it all, but can you write a note? Send it through the post. Your mam could burn it before himself comes in from work.'

All three of them knew they could get a message to Annie via Billy, but they dare not say so.

'I'll do that. It's a good idea. Thanks, Mrs Slattery.'

Brigid looked at the girl with affection, an affection that had grown over the past weeks. She was a good girl. She was neat and clean and she and Lizzie had cleaned the whole house for her last weekend, even though they'd been on their feet in the shop all day. They'd started on Saturday night and finished on Sunday night, worn out, but the place looked like a little palace. It was so tidy and every bit of furniture she owned had been polished to within an inch of its life. Everywhere was shining. Left to herself, Lizzie would never even have thought of doing such a thing.

'Well, now that you're to be part of the family, Celia, will you give over with all this "Mrs Slattery"?'

'I – I was being polite. Was that the wrong thing?'

'It was not.'

'Then what am I to call you?'

'Well, certainly not "Mother-in-law". Dessie's mam was a holy terror, so she was, and God forgive me for speaking ill of the dead, but I couldn't stand her. Oh, she was desperate. She'd eyes like a hawk and I hated her coming round. If there was a speck of dust or a bit of dirt anywhere, sure to God she'd find it.'

'Brigid?' Lizzie suggested.

Brigid cast a withering glance at her daughter.

Celia looked at Brigid with horror. 'Lizzie, I couldn't do that. It's so disrespectful; she's your mam.'

'And that's what you can call me, Celia. Your own mam will always come first in your affections, don't I know that for a certainty, but Mam or even Ma will do nicely.'

'Would you mind if I called you Ma?' Celia asked timidly. Brigid had touched a tender spot. She loved her mam dearly and she couldn't call Joe's mother 'mam' too. She didn't like the title 'Ma' but she'd just have to learn to like it. Anyway, it wasn't just the title, Brigid had been good to her.

'Not at all, Celia. Now while this great amadan here can make himself useful by going out and getting me some coal the pair of you can decide on what you're going to wear. I'll go over and ask Tessie if she'll lend me that frock and hat again, the one I wore for the Jubilee.' For a few seconds Brigid stared at the dying embers in the fire, which had to be kept going summer and winter for cooking. The Jubilee now seemed years and years ago. Dessie had died that night and only eight months ago the King himself had died.

When they were alone Lizzie turned to her friend, who was soon to become her sister-in-law. 'What will you wear, Cee?'

'I don't know, Lizzie. I've not much money. I had to buy clothes after the fire.'

'I thought I might go down to Middleton's. Quite often they have some nice second-hand things in. Once when I went in they had two wedding dresses.'

Celia looked at her with interest. Middleton's sold only quality second-hand clothes. In fact the words over the door read 'Middleton's Superior Ensembles'. Ever since she'd been a little girl she'd dreamed of what she would wear for her wedding, but circumstances had changed so much now that those ideas had been banished. But if she could get a second-hand dress from Middleton's it would be great.

'Will we go down there on Wednesday afternoon? I know Mam will let us keep our wages for one week, and our Josie and Bernie can go along to the flower ladies in Clayton Square late on Friday afternoon and get what flowers are left, cheap. We'll make a couple of posies. It'll be great, Cee, just you wait and see.'

The morning of the wedding resembled the chaos that had ensued on the morning of the Jubilee, Lizzie thought as she helped Celia dress in the cramped attic room they shared and from which everyone had been barred. Mam was wearing the grey frock belonging to Tessie and had put on the hat in case she forgot all about it with trying to see to everyone else. Josie, Bernie, Fergal and Emmet wore their Sunday clothes but Joe had a new suit and shirt, and a carnation pinned to his lapel.

Josie and Bernie were both sulking because they'd been for the flowers and had even helped Lizzie to make them up into posies using paper doilies and silver foil, but weren't allowed to have posies themselves.

'We're guests, too,' Josie had complained.

'You're family. Anything left over will do for buttonholes for Mrs Mulhinney, Mrs Doyle and Mrs Walsh. Stop flaming well moaning,' Lizzie had replied sharply.

'Well, Mam's got a flower.'

'That's because she's *Mam* and she's sort of doubling up for Celia's mam, you eejit!'

When Lizzie had finally finished she stood back and looked at her friend. 'Oh, Cee, you look lovely, really lovely!' she exclaimed.

They'd been in luck. Mr Middleton had just had the wedding dress brought in and it wasn't too dirty around the bottom so they'd just washed the hem and Brigid had ironed it until it was dry.

It was very plain, with a simple high neckline and long tight sleeves, but it was made of a heavy embossed satin which made it look very elegant and expensive. There was a short veil and a circlet of white wax flowers, too, and they'd got the entire outfit for four guineas. Lizzie had given Celia five shillings towards it as her own dress was cheaper than she'd thought she'd have to pay.

It was a pale lilac crepe de Chine with puffed sleeves and a deeper lilac satin trim. She'd borrowed a white straw hat from Tessie.

'Our Joe'll be made up with you, Cee. Thank God he's paying for a taxi. I didn't feel like having to traipse all that way, we'd have been worn out.'

'Do I really look . . . well . . . ?' Celia was very nervous. It had been great having Joe around her all the time. She'd already begun to feel part of this family who, although they had little in the way of material things, were far happier than her own had ever been. She just wished her mam could have seen her today. Not necessarily have come to the wedding, but just seen her in her bridal finery.

'I said you look great and I mean it,' Lizzie replied emphatically, secretly wishing it was her own wedding.'Now we'd better get downstairs. Our Joe and Greg Doyle have already gone, then when it comes back Mam, Josie, Bernie and our Emmet will go, then you, me and our Fergal.'

Celia nodded. Even though Fergal was only sixteen he was to give her away. There wasn't another man or boy in the street who would do it. In normal circumstances Fergal would have been Joe's best man, but the circumstances of this wedding were far from normal.

It was all very discreet. Maggie Walsh, Biddy Doyle and Tessie Mulhinney, with their husbands and a few of their offspring, were seated in the church but when Brigid arrived they all moved into the vestry.

It smelled of incense, musty cloth and candle wax, Brigid thought. Her heart was heavy with disappointment. Oh, Celia Milton looked really lovely in that dress and veil, and Lizzie, too, looked grand, although her hair still resembled a furze bush, but it wasn't the full Nuptial Mass she'd wanted for her eldest son.

Everyone crowded into the small room where the surplices of the altar boys hung on pegs on one wall and a mound of sheet music belonging to the organist leaned precariously against another. The different coloured vestments hung in a big wardrobe and the cut-glass cruets for wine and water and the silver altar bell were placed on a shelf. There was no altar, no music and no flowers. Still, it was better than a dingy room in Brougham Terrace and the important thing was that it *was* in church. Or at least part of it.

Joe looked at Celia with love shining from his eyes. She looked radiant and happy and he felt so lucky. She'd given up everything for him and he was going to make sure she never had a miserable moment in her life ever again.

As Celia repeated the words after the priest Lizzie's hand went to the locket that Billy had given her, a small gold heart-shaped locket on a fine gold chain. His own pledge of love to her. By the time her friend Celia Milton had become Celia Slattery, her sister-in-law, the tears were glistening on Lizzie's lashes and Brigid was dabbing her eyes with a bit of a handkerchief Tessie had given her.

PART THREE

December 1936

Chapter Twenty

Annie looked around at her sparsely furnished kitchen and felt only longing and despair. In her old home, now boarded up while the landlord decided what to do with it, her kitchen had been warm and homely.

In her mind she'd always thought of it as 'her' room. She'd had all her things around her that she'd collected over the years. The blue delftware on the dresser that she'd polished so lovingly each week. The pair of Staffordshire dogs, one at either end of the mantel, they'd belonged to her own mam. The pair of matching brass candlesticks and little copper jugs. The dull gleam of her black-leaded range, usually with some appetising smell coming from its oven or hob. Oh how she missed everything. Each item had had a story to it.

She supposed she should be grateful that the MacDonalds had decided to emigrate to Canada and number 2 Roscommon Street had become available to rent. It was clean and had been well looked after too, but it wasn't 'home' and she doubted she'd ever look on it as such.

They'd been with Maudie for four months and the tensions had grown with each week. The high-pitched whine in Maudie's voice grated on her nerves, nerves that were raw from the constant worry and the illness she knew she was suffering from. She couldn't sleep at night thinking of Celia, just a few houses down the street and yet so far, far away from her.

She knew though she should be thankful to Maudie for the way she stood up to Charlie. The rows were fierce and frequent but Maudie had a tongue like a viper and Charlie was at a disadvantage and he knew it. He'd lost all his worldly possessions and his independence and to a certain extent his pride. He fumed silently most of the time until a word from Billy or herself would cause an eruption of temper.

She had at least developed a degree of immunity to the frequent rows. Because they usually didn't involve her, she was now beginning to get used to them. The terror she had of them had diminished, but she often wished she could have gone and sat in the small and smelly pigeon loft like poor Harry did most nights. It would have been restful listening to the soft cooing of the birds.

Many of the arguments were started by the behaviour of her son and Maudie's twins. Maudie complained that it was always Foxy who had got them into trouble and when Charlie was in he'd demand the whole story from each of the boys in turn, but he always seemed to take his son's side. She herself knew the truth: Foxy lived up to his nickname, but she seldom intervened. She just didn't care any more.

But now she stood alone in this alien, shadowy room.

Maudie and Flo Taylor had helped her scrub it and move in the few pieces of furniture they'd bought. They'd helped her to hang curtains and make up beds.

'Well, there's one good thing about not having much in the way of ornaments, Annie, your Foxy can't go breaking them,' Maudie had commented cheerfully, relieved that at long last she would have her house to herself again. Get back into her old, well-ordered routine and knock some sense into the twins.

Celia was never mentioned, at least not in her hearing. It wasn't as if she worried about Celia. She knew that in her own way Brigid Slattery was looking after the girl and she knew instinctively that Celia was happy or as happy as she could be.

Before Celia had started to show and therefore had to leave

Costigan's, Annie had gone in to buy some small amount of food, just to be able to see and speak to her daughter, and Celia had told her how happy she was. How different it was living at the Slatterys'. There were always small arguments going on but there was no malice in them. It was more like constant bickering and if things reached a certain pitch then her mother-in-law would slap everyone within reach and start 'giving out', as Lizzie called it. But there was no fear, no feeling of nagging anxiety in the Slatterys' house.

Annie sat down on a plain wooden chair at the scrubbed deal table and sighed. She had no tablecloths now, just a piece of gingham oilcloth that could be wiped clean. It was easier but she'd liked shaking out a clean, crisp cloth over her table ready to be set for the meal.

She hadn't the heart nor the will to rebuild another home. She felt so ill. Indeed she looked so ill that Maudie had insisted on taking her to see Dr Fraser. He'd asked her a few questions and then prescribed a tonic, saying she'd be more settled, less anxious when she had a house to call her own again. But it wasn't just the weariness or the headaches. The pains in her abdomen were worse than ever, though she hadn't mentioned them to the doctor. She didn't want to be looked on as a 'moaner' with a new ailment each week.

When they were very bad, so as not to cause any upset, she'd say quietly to Maudie that she'd go up and have a lie down. She'd explained to Maudie that it was just 'the Change' and the woman had agreed that 'the Change' could be sheer murder at times.

At least now she had beds and bedding and a couple of chests of drawers and a small wardrobe upstairs. New lino and rag rugs that she'd made in the evenings when she'd felt well enough.

There was a runner of carpet down the hall and up the stairs, but there was nothing in the parlour – yet. She had a table, chairs, dresser, all second-hand, and all the usual pans and utensils for cooking here in the kitchen, and the cleaning stuff was out in the scullery, but it wasn't 'home'.

She remembered Maudie's words about Foxy and ornaments. There were none, neither were there any trinkets. There were no pictures on the walls, just a plain square mirror on the wall that faced the window. A plain buckram lampshade covered the naked electric light bulb. No, this wasn't her 'home' and never would be.

She suddenly felt so depressed that she laid her head on her arms, which were resting on the table, and began to cry for all she had lost, but most of all for Celia and the baby she carried. Her grandchild, a child who she would never be allowed to love, to cuddle or spoil.

Eventually she wiped her eyes and went into the scullery to bathe them. Charlie and Billy would be home shortly and she'd better have a meal on the table as she'd done in the old days. But now she didn't care whether he liked or disliked the food she put in front of him. Charlie Milton was nothing to her.

'Is it great now?' Lizzie asked Billy as they settled themselves in the lee of the funnel on the ferry. The wild December wind was biting so no one else was on deck.

'I dunno.'

'You must know!'

'Well, it's better having more room and some privacy.'

'It's *got* to be better than having to listen to *her* all day, and having her giving out to your da.' Lizzie snuggled closer to Billy, who put both arms around her to shield her a bit from the wind.

'It is, but well, it's not the same as number ten.'

'Of course it's not – you were born there – but it will be in time and Christmas is only a couple of weeks away now. You can get holly and paper chains and tinsel, that should brighten things up.'

Billy nodded although he doubted that any festive chains and greenery could make that house more cheerful. His mam was making no effort and he knew she wasn't well. In happier days she'd spent weeks baking the cake, the mince pies, the plum pudding, the shortcake biscuits. Jelly and blancmange would be in the larder and the house would be decorated with a festive air to it all.

'I'm supposed to be saving up, remember?'

Lizzie hugged him. 'I know and so am I, but we've got to spend a bit on Christmas presents.'

'Nothing I ever get for Da is right. There's always something wrong with it.'

'God, Billy, you really are a misery tonight.'

'I'm sorry, Lizzie, I wish . . . I just wish . . .'

She sighed heavily. 'Oh I know. Do you think we'll ever have enough to go?'

Billy didn't answer her for a while. He was thinking of his mam.

'Did you hear me?' Lizzie pressed.

'Of course.'

'It's taking ages and ages to save and we both seem to have to given up almost everything. How much have we got now?'

'Five pounds and two shillings, but we won't get very far on that. There'll be the train fare, rent on a furnished room, money to tide us over until we get jobs.'

Three months ago they'd decided the only chance they had was to get away from Liverpool and both their families, although Lizzie would miss everyone and Billy would miss his mam. They were going to Scotland, to Gretna Green first to get married, and then on to the shipyards on the Clyde. Billy had heard that John Browne's was a good place to work. They built really big ships there like the *Queen Mary*.

'Will we have enough to go by spring, do you think, if we don't go mad over Christmas? Last year Mr Henderson gave us five shillings extra and as much of the "perishables", as he called them, as we wanted to take home as they'd only be thrown out.'

Billy did some mental arithmetic. 'I think so. We should have about twelve pounds then.'

Lizzie hugged him again and raised her face to be kissed. 'Oh, roll on spring! Well, aren't you going to kiss me, Billy Milton?'

He grinned down at her sparkling eyes and then kissed her. He did love her but he knew she was the driving force in their relationship. She was only small and slight but she'd tackle anyone or anything. He knew that left to his own devices they would have gone on like this for years, secretly engaged. But next spring they'd get the train from Lime Street Station to start a new life – together.

When the ferry docked again at the Liverpool landing stage they walked slowly up to the Pier Head. A man with a bundle of newspapers under his arm was walking up and down and shouting.

'What's that feller yelling about?' Lizzie asked.

'Something about a late edition, a special notice about the King, I think.'

'Do you know what I heard two of the customers jangling about yesterday, even though Mr Henderson said I was to take no notice of people casting aspersions on the monarchy – whatever that means? Well, these two were saying that he's in love with some American woman and all the world knows about it, except us, apparently. And this woman is divorced! Divorced, of all the daft things to say! How can he be in love with someone like that? Kings are meant to marry princesses.'

Billy shrugged. He wasn't particularly interested in King Edward VIII or the rumours that he'd heard going round the shipyard.

'Come on, Lizzie, there's a tram just about to go. Grab my hand and we'll make a dash for it, there's hardly anyone out tonight. It's only the likes of daft ha'p'orths like us who go for ferry rides in a howling December gale.'

They parted company at the end of Fox Street. Billy got off to walk the rest of the way while Lizzie stayed on until Great Homer Street.

'I'm home and I'm frozen,' she called as she walked down the lobby. The kitchen would be lovely and warm. Cee would be sitting knitting, as would her mam. She grinned to herself. They were both fast workers, the needles just seemed to fly and at the end of the night a pair of bootees or a bonnet would be finished. This baby would have the biggest wardrobe of any other baby in the entire neighbourhood if those two carried on the way they were going.

When she opened the door to her surprise she found only Emmet and Bernie.

'Where's me mam and Celia and our Fergal and Josie?' she demanded.

'Mam, Josie and Cee have gone over to Mrs Mulhinney's. There's some really important news coming on the wireless. Our Fergal's gone up to the Young Men's Club at St Francis Xavier's.'

Lizzie pulled her woollen hat back on and wondered what was so bad that everyone had gone over the road to hear it.

She found Tessie's door open and her parlour crowded with half the men, women and girls in the street. Celia was sitting in an armchair with a cushion behind her back. Lizzie made her way towards her sister-in-law.

'God, aren't you the jammy one? A cushion, an' all, and our Josie and Patsy Doyle sitting on the floor. What's going on?'

'The King is going to make a speech to us all, over the wireless,' Tessie answered for the benefit of those she thought might not understand.

'We know that, Tessie. Isn't that why we're all sitting here cluttering up your best parlour?' Brigid answered, moving a little to one side on the sofa she was sharing with Maggie, Biddy, Tessie and Mary Kelly to let Lizzie squeeze in. Greg Doyle and Jimmy Kelly were perched on the arms.

'What about?' Lizzie questioned. 'We . . . I mean I heard some feller shouting about it.' She was relieved that her mother was too intent on other matters and had failed to notice the slip she'd made. She looked at Celia who winked at her.

'About that American hussy he's got himself caught up with. That Simpson woman,' Maggie Walsh answered.

'What's wrong with her being an American?' Brigid asked.

'Didn't one of my own sisters go there years ago and hasn't she had the grand life, and all? Never short of a penny and she was always sending money home to the mammy in Cork until she died, God rest her.'

'It's not that she's American, I've nothing against *them*. Didn't they help us out in the Great War, after all? No, the brazen, hard-faced madam is divorced. Not once but twice. TWICE!' Tessie informed them.

'Well, in that case she *is* a hussy, like you said, Tessie,' Brigid agreed.

Tessie nodded smugly. 'A crafty one, and all. She thinks she's going to be Queen and him Head of the Church of England and Defender of the Faith!' Tessie's tone was scathing.

'Oh, there's been a lot going on that we know nothing about. There's been rumours going round for weeks. Didn't I tell you he was weak-looking?' Biddy finished with some satisfaction.

Brigid was scandalised.

'Sure to God he isn't going to marry *her*, is he? Divorced, and twice you say, Tessie?'

'Tessie, what time will it be on? Me leg's got pins an' needles in it from balancing on this here fender,' Maureen O'Shea said.

Tessie got up and fiddled with the knobs on the wireless set and Dermot Mulhinney, Gerry Walsh and Bernard Doyle pushed their way into the room and stood with their backs to the wall.

Silence descended. You could have heard even a mouse creeping along the skirting board, Lizzie thought as she looked around at the grim, worried faces, all with uncertainty and concern in their eyes. Edward VIII was King and Emperor; it was a very serious matter.

Then as the cultured, quiet voice of the King came over the wireless, the women crossed themselves and the men looked respectful. Wallis Simpson had been the main topic in the pub earlier that night and the men's views mirrored those of their wives and mothers.

'At long last, I am able to say a few words of my own . . . I want you to understand that in making up my mind I did not forget the country or the Empire which as Prince of Wales and lately as King, I have for twenty-five years tried to serve. But you must believe me when I tell you that I have found it impossible to carry the heavy burden of responsibility and to discharge my duties as King as I would wish to do without the help and support of the woman I love.'

There was a pause and everyone looked at each other in disbelief.

'God bless you all. God save the King!'

The stunned silence that followed the end of the broadcast was broken by Maggie Walsh.

'Well, that's very nice, isn't it? He prefers HER to his country, to us. A nice way of carrying on for a king.'

'Hasn't the man just said how much it hurt him to step down?' Brigid put in.

Tessie was as stunned as everyone else but she did try to be dignified. After all, it was her house. 'He shouldn't have had to abdicate in the first place. The old Queen, God luv her and protect her, should have had *that one* flung out on her ear and given him a good talking-to about his duty to serve, as his father did before him. God rest his soul.'

Maggie Walsh wasn't as philosophical. 'And he's going to *marry* her! *Marry her!* How long before she divorces him when she finds her nose has been put out of joint and that there's no crown of diamonds for her head?'

'Well, there's no use saving for the Coronation now, Tessie, and we've been at it since March,' Mary Kelly remarked.

'What will happen now?' Celia asked quietly. She was accepted now. Her age and upbringing ignored because she was a married woman and pregnant.

'You heard him, Celia. "God save the King." His brother, Prince Albert the Duke of York, will be King and his duchess will be Queen,' Tessie Mulhinney answered.

'Holy God, what a burden to put on anyone's shoulders and he looks so quiet and shy and she's lovely. A lovely, decent young woman. A *real* lady, fit to be a queen, and with those two little girls, it's a family they are. A family not a gold-digging godless woman. Oh, he knew the country wouldn't stand for *her*.'

'At least he's done the decent thing,' Bernard Doyle said firmly.

Biddy rounded on him. 'Decent! Decent, is it? For months on end you never open your mouth and then when you do, don't you come out with something like "decent". He had no choice. It was the Crown or her. Well, I think he made the right choice. She's getting no bargain, that's for sure. Like Maggie said, she'll be fed up with him before long. It wasn't him she wanted, it was a crown on her head and everyone bowing and scraping to her. Serves her flaming well right. I hope she never gets a penny.'

'She'll get a title though,' Dermot Mulhinney said.

'And I could think up a few good titles for that one!' his wife answered acidly.

Christmas that year had something missing, Lizzie thought. Oh, they'd had a bit more money and therefore more food and Christmas luxuries.

Emmet and his mates had gone all the way out to Fazakerley Terminus by tram and then walked to Kirkby and cut huge bunches of holly and brought it home.

Celia, who couldn't do much now, had showed them how to make chains and streamers with crepe paper. The one thing that marred the holiday most for Celia was the fact that she couldn't share it with her mam and Billy. Maudie had put a note through the door saying Celia was not to go near her mam's house as it would cause a row and spoil everyone's Christmas. Celia had said nothing but there had been tears in her eyes as Joe had ripped the note into pieces and thrown them in the fire. Then he'd kissed his wife and patted her hand.

As she'd sat and plaited the red and green crepe paper Lizzie had thought that this Christmas would be the last she'd spend in this house. Next year, if all went well, she and Billy would be married and might have a small house of their own to decorate.

She'd looked across at her mam and suddenly tears had sprung into her eyes, but they'd soon vanished as Emmet and his mates, who had been out carol singing, arrived singing,

'Hark the Herald Angels sing,
Mrs Simpson's pinched our King.'

They hadn't got any further, for Brigid had taken the poker and chased them out into the yard, declaring she would 'be after giving you all a clattering for the cheek and impidince of disrespectful young eejits', and everyone had laughed.

On St Valentine's Day, Celia awoke in the grip of pain, a pain she had never experienced before. She got out of bed slowly, lit the candle on the little table beside the bed as the light switch was on the wall by the door, and looked at the big metal alarm clock that was placed in the middle of the mantelpiece. It was far too early for Joe to be home yet and no one else was up, so she'd make herself a cup of tea.

She didn't want to wake anyone so she didn't put the light on in the lobby, but as she reached the kitchen door another spasm gripped her and she couldn't stop herself from crying out.

Almost immediately the landing light went on and Josie's sleepy but alarmed face appeared over the banister.

'What's up, Cee?'

Celia gasped, dropped the candle which went out, and doubled over. 'Get – get Ma, will you, Josie?' She clung to the doorjamb for support until she heard the sound of movement upstairs and then Brigid's heavy tread on the stairs.

Her mother-in-law wore an old dressing gown and her hair was loose and hung down her back.

'Dear God, are the pains after starting already?'

Celia nodded.

'Josie, get some clothes on you and run round for Ma Tiernan.'

'Will I go for Dr Fraser instead, Mam?'

'You will not,' Brigid snapped, seeing the fear in Celia's eyes. 'There's no need for that. Hasn't Ma Tiernan delivered hundreds of babies? Celia, get back in that bed. Lean on me.'

Celia did as she was bid, then she heard the front door slam as Josie left. Brigid left her lying on her bed and after a few minutes returned dressed and with her hair in its neat bun, followed by a pale and sheepish-looking Lizzie.

'Cee, are you all right?'

'Don't be after asking stupid things like that, Lizzie Slattery. Make yourself useful before you go off to your work. Collect all the newspapers you can find and get that pile of old sheets I've cut up and get the kettle on.' Lizzie fled as Celia screamed out loud with pain.

Brigid tied a long piece of cloth to the end of the bed.

'Here now, when the pain comes pull on this and you can screech like a dozen banshees. It's better for you than trying to keep it all inside.'

Already the sweat was standing out on Celia's forehead and wisps of hair were sticking to it. Brigid wiped her face with a piece of cloth dampened with cold water.

Celia grabbed the cloth tightly and pulled. Oh, she'd never dreamed that it would be like this. The pain was worse than she could have imagined, and how long would it go on for? She was afraid. She was terrified of what lay ahead of her. What if the pain didn't stop – ever? She started to sob, and grasped Brigid's hand as another wave of excruciating pain washed over her.

Lizzie opened the door to her sister who was puffing and panting.

'Where's Ma Tiernan?'

'She . . . she's coming. She told me to run on ahead,' Josie gasped.

'Well, get in the kitchen and start getting ready for work. I'll have to sort everyone out and get our Joe's breakfast when he comes in. God knows when I'll get to work.'

'Lizzie, is that our Josie back?' Brigid yelled.

'Yes, Mam. Ma Tiernan is on her way. Will I come in and help?'

'You will not. This is no place for an unmarried girl. You see to the others and keep that water boiling and when our Joe comes in, he's not to set foot in this room, do you hear me, Lizzie?'

'Yes, Mam.' Lizzie's voice was full of relief. Even though she'd been in the house when her sisters and brother had been born, somehow this was different. Celia sounded as though she was being murdered.

Ma Tiernan duly arrived and took off her shawl and the battered, old-fashioned blue bonnet she always wore.

'Right, I'll just wash me hands. Is everything ready, Brigid?'

'It is so and the pains are coming fast now, so you've not to face hours of work.'

'Thanks be to God for that. With a first you can never tell.'

They all sat at the table while Lizzie sawed chunks of bread which she spread with margarine and handed out. When Celia screamed they all looked down at their plates and both Lizzie and Josie's hands were shaking. Bernie and Emmet had little idea what was going on and Fergal, much to Lizzie's relief, took them over to Maggie Walsh's house before he himself went to work. He would be very early but it was better to be out of the house. He'd never heard anyone scream like Celia. What she was going through must be terrible.

When Joe arrived home after his night shift, it was to find Lizzie getting ready for work herself.

'Where is everyone?'

'Out,' Lizzie grinned. 'Oh, and you're a dad. Cee's had a little boy. Go and knock and see if Mam and Ma Tiernan will let you in.'

Joe's face went from scarlet to white in a matter of seconds and all signs of tiredness vanished.

'Is Cee all right?'

'Of course she is, you eejit! Go on!' Lizzie pushed him into the lobby.

Joe knocked timidly on the bedroom door.

'If that's you, Joe, you can come in and see these two,' Brigid called out.

He pushed the door open gingerly and then a huge smile spread across his face. Celia was sitting up and she looked grand. Tired, of course, but she had on a clean nightdress and Brigid had combed her hair and wiped her face. His mother and Ma Tiernan were tidying up the room. Then his eyes went to the small bundle wrapped up in a shawl that Celia held in her arms.

'Oh, Joe, look! Look at him. He's beautiful.' Celia held out the baby and Joe took him and held him at arm's length.

'God Almighty, would you look at the fist he's making of it? He won't break, Joe. Hold him properly, like this.' Brigid demonstrated and Joe looked down into the tiny, screwed-up face and at the hands curled into little fists and felt a great surge of love and pride. This was his son. *His son.*

'Oh, Cee, isn't he . . . isn't he . . . ?'

'Just gorgeous.' Celia smiled up at him.

'Give him back now to his mammy, he's hungry. They're always hungry,' Brigid instructed.

Joe did as he was told but with reluctance.

'And what are yer going to call him?' Ma Tiernan asked.

'Michael Joseph,' Celia answered. They'd chosen names already. If it had been a girl it would have been Brigid Annie.

'Right, Joe, you get upstairs to bed now. It's Fergal's bed for the next couple of days. She needs her sleep and plenty of rest.' Brigid adjusted the bedclothes and then patted them down to her satisfaction as she spoke, but she was filled with happiness.

Joe bent and kissed Celia's forehead and she caught hold of his hand and held it against her cheek.

'Oh, Joe, I love you so much. We're a family now.'

'We are, Cee, and it'll be a *happy* family he'll have. There'll be no fighting and arguing.'

'There will if you don't shift yourself, Joe Slattery,' Brigid cut in, her tone sharp but her eyes shining with joy.

When Michael Joseph Slattery had been baptised three days later, Celia begged Brigid to let her go to see Annie and show her her grandson.

'You're not able for it, Celia. You've to be in that bed for another week yet.'

'Oh, please. It's only a few steps up the street, Ma, and I won't stay long. She should know. She should see him and be able to hold him too.'

The girl was right, Brigid thought to herself.

'Well, I'll go up there with you, just in case you feel a faint coming on, and you're to wrap up warm. It's bitter out.'

Celia dressed her baby with care for his visit to his other grandmother. She put on the soft little woollen vest, then the flannel one and a white towelling nappy, a smocked dress and finally a shawl, bootees and bonnet that Brigid had knitted.

She did feel a bit shaky as she went down the steps and was glad of Brigid's arm to lean on.

They had both passed Celia's old home so often that now neither of them gave it a glance although some work had been done on it so its appearance had changed.

Brigid reached up and rapped smartly on the door of the house, noting how the brass knocker and key hole shone.

At last the door opened but to Celia's horror it was her father who stood there, and the reason for his presence was obvious: he had a terrible streaming cold.

'Da, I . . . we . . . I want to see Mam.'

Charlie looked at his daughter for the first time since he'd thrown her out, and then at her mother-in-law, a woman he detested. Finally he looked at the baby in Celia's arms.

'You'll not set foot in this house.'

'Da, don't you want to see your grandson? He *is* your grandson, you can't deny that,' Celia begged.

'I want nothing to do with any child of yours and *his* and neither does your mother.'

He made to shut the door but Brigid was quicker. She stuck her foot between the door and the doorpost.

'Aren't you a fine example of a God-fearing, Christian man, Charlie Milton. You're a lying hypocrite! Didn't I see you with me own two eyes all trailing to church on Christmas Day to celebrate the birth of a baby? But you won't even look at this innocent little thing nor let your poor wife see her grandson. You've driven your daughter out and now you won't even let her see her mam.'

Charlie's face reddened. 'Her mother wants nothing to do with her. *We* want nothing to do with any of you. Get your foot out of my door or I'll push the pair of you down the steps.'

Brigid glared at him. 'You've got a short memory. How many times is it now that I've belted you, Charlie Milton?'

Humiliation was added to Charlie's anger.

'I want to see my mam. I've got every right to see her and show her her grandson,' Celia pleaded.

'You lost all rights, as you call them, when you married *him*. Go to hell, the pair of you.'

He pulled the door back to give more impetus to the weight he put behind it but Brigid removed her foot before he could break it. The slam of the door echoed down the street.

Brigid put her arm around Celia, who was in tears.

'Ah, take no notice of that owld get. Next time we'll go round the back way, down the jigger. No one will see us.' But she looked perturbed. 'Well, maybe we'll leave it a few days until he's able for work and the house isn't full of that cold he has on him. But don't worry, you'll get to see your mam. I'm determined on it.'

Joe had been livid but Brigid told him it would do no good at all going up there and having a row with Charlie Milton, so it was the following week that Brigid accompanied Celia and the baby up the narrow jigger that ran between the houses. Neither of them was aware that Charlie had told Maudie and Flo Taylor to keep a close watch on the comings and goings at his home because he didn't trust Brigid Slattery one bit.

'I'll wait out here for you,' Brigid said, pulling her shawl around her tightly. It was freezing cold.

'I won't be long.'

'Ah, take all the time in the world. She's your mam, God help her, and the back of me hand to him! I hope he gets the bronchials from that cold.'

Celia let herself in through the scullery door, noting how tidy the yard was compared to that at number twelve. As she went quietly into the scullery and then the kitchen she could see no sign of her mother. Then she realised that Annie was lying on the sofa in front of the fire.

'Mam. Mam, it's me,' Celia whispered in case someone else was in the house.

Annie opened her eyes and struggled to sit up. 'Oh, Celia! Celia!'

Celia was horrified at the change in her mother. She seemed to have lost even more weight, her skin was a yellowish colour and her eyes were sunk in their sockets and circled by dark rings.

'I . . . I . . . brought Michael to see you. I came last week but *he* wouldn't let us in.'

'I know, he told me. He . . . he's so awful now, Celia. Sometimes I think he's losing control of his mind.'

'He's not hit you again, has he, Mam?'

'No. No, our Billy's sworn to kill him if he does and he will. He's changed a lot, Cee, lately.'

Celia knew he had. Lizzie had told her.

'Here, Mam, this is your grandson. We called him Michael Joseph.' She didn't tell her mother that he'd been baptised already. They seemed to do things much quicker in the Catholic Church. It was in case the baby died, Brigid had explained. And so many of them did.

The tears came to Annie's eyes as she took the baby in her arms. Oh, how she missed Celia and now she knew she would miss this tiny scrap of humanity, too, for Charlie would never let her see him. She'd miss everything. She wouldn't see him smile, cut his first tooth. Watch him take his first tottering steps and be able to push him out in the pram with Celia as most grandmothers did. She rocked him gently while Celia watched her, a slow dread growing in her heart. Mam was ill, really ill.

She stayed for a quarter of an hour, making Annie a cup of tea while she nursed Michael, and all the time she was thinking of Brigid standing out in the cold, but she dare not ask her in. It was with great reluctance that she kissed Annie on the cheek, hugged her and said she'd try and see her at least once a week.

'No, no, you can't, Cee. He's told Maudie and Flo to snoop and then tell him if you come near.'

Celia could hardly believe her ears. 'Mam, he's wicked! He's downright wicked!'

Annie didn't answer. She was too tired now to argue.

When they got back Brigid immediately ordered Celia to bed but she refused.

'I'm fine. I'll just sit here by the fire and nurse Michael.'

Joe took his son in his arms, noticing how pale Celia was, while she took off her coat. Celia held out her arms but Joe shook his head.

'No, luv, let me nurse him. You just sit there and rest.'

Brigid tutted as she put on the kettle and began to prepare the tea. 'Will you make her get back into that bed? She'll make herself ill and then he'll get the colic and then won't we all know about it? Sure, he'll scream the place down with the pain of it, the poor wee soul.'

'Oh, leave her, Mam. It's lonely being stuck in that room and I don't get much chance to nurse him or play with him. Either he's sleeping or I am.'

Brigid was scandalised. 'Isn't he only two weeks old? Play with him, is it? He's not a toy, Joe Slattery. Give him back to his mammy and make yourself useful. Get some knives and forks on that table and don't be giving me that look, meladdo. Don't I know that for most of their lives men get waited on hand and foot, so get off that high horse and shift yourself.'

Joe grinned at her and handed his son back to Celia, who closed her eyes as she nursed him.

Bernie and Emmet were in first, followed by Josie, Fergal and then Lizzie, and as soon as Celia set eyes on her friend she started to cry.

'Oh, why didn't he tell me, Lizzie? Why didn't our Billy tell you that Mam's so ill? I'm so afraid for her and I can't go near her, he's got the neighbours spying on her. Oh, Lizzie, why didn't either of you tell me? Why?' she cried.

Lizzie looked from Celia to Joe and then her heart sank. Celia was so upset that she'd well and truly let the cat out of the bag.

Brigid turned around and glared at her. 'Why should Billy Milton be telling you anything at all, Lizzie Slattery? Just tell me that, you bold rossie?' she demanded.

Lizzie took off her coat and then drew the locket from beneath her work dress. 'Mam, I'm sorry, I really am, but . . . but Billy and me are engaged.' Ignoring the look on her mother's face she plunged on. 'I couldn't wear a ring, so he bought me this instead. I love him, Mam, and I'm going to marry him too, one day.' She bowed her head, waiting for the tirade of wrath to descend upon it.

It never came. Brigid just sank down on a wooden chair and

covered her face with her hands. 'Oh, Holy Mary Mother of God, not you as well, Lizzie?' Her family seemed to be inextricably entangled with the Miltons and she couldn't see or understand why. In a city where there were hundreds of single lads and girls of all religions, why did her two eldest fall for Protestants and all the problems that came with mixed marriages?

Lizzie rushed to throw her arms around her mother.

'Oh, Mam, I'm sorry, I really am, but I can't help it if I love him any more than Cee could help loving our Joe.'

Brigid looked up. 'Don't put the heart across me by telling me that you're . . . you're in the same condition?'

'No, Mam, there's nothing like that! Billy is, well . . . I couldn't . . .' Her voice trailed off as Brigid crossed herself with relief.

'No one else knows?'

'No one, Mam.'

'Then there's to be no mention made of it by anyone in this house, do you hear me, Emmet, Bernie, Josie, Fergal and you, Joe? Not a single word to anyone. You'll all swear to God now, on your poor da's grave, that this will be kept secret?'

They all swore solemnly.

'Then get on with your chores or there'll be no tea tonight. Joe, now will you make your wife go back to her bed. She's upset, I'm upset, and she shouldn't even have been up, never mind out.'

Joe gently took Celia and the baby and half led, half lifted her to the front room and got her into bed.

'Oh, Joe! She looked so . . . awful. She needs a doctor, she really does. How am I going to lie here and not think and worry about her?'

'Look, Cee, I'll have a word with Billy, I promise, as soon as I can, but you know what your da's like. I know Billy is stronger . . . harder, more determined now, but he's still no match for your da.'

Celia clung to him. 'Please, Joe. Try and find *something* out for me from Billy or I'll go out of my mind with worry.'

'Hush now, luv. I'll wait behind in the morning and see him then. Will that do?'

Celia nodded and then sank back on the pillows, exhausted.

Chapter Twenty-One

True to his word Joe had stayed behind to wait for Billy.

'What's up with you? Haven't you got a home to go to? I don't understand you lads today, a lovely young wife and a baby son waiting for you?' Fred Roberts joked.

Joe smiled. 'Oh, this is a bit of family trouble.'

'Isn't it always with you?' the foreman said drily.

'It's Billy Milton I want to see but I don't want his da frog-marching him away.'

'Milton again. I don't know of one single feller in this yard who has a good word for him, all the other foremen included. Well, if it's any help I'll go and see his foreman and old Bowker on the gate. I'll leave a message with Bowker saying Billy is to go and see his blockerman straight away, but don't be hanging around here half the morning and I want no fighting and arguing, understand?'

'Thanks, and there won't be any carrying-on like that. It's just a message from the wife I've to pass on.'

Fred Roberts nodded. 'I suppose you'll be bringing her to the launch of the *Ark Royal* in April?'

'Just try and keep her and Mam away. In fact we'll have the whole lot of them here.'

Joe looked across to where the huge grey armour-plated hull of the aircraft carrier rose from the staging. They were all working hard on her and there were orders on the books for more warships and submarines.

'Do you think we'll have her ready on time, boss?'

'We'll bloody well have to or the Admiralty won't be very pleased and neither will the Board of Directors. I'll go and see Bowker for you now.'

'I really appreciate it, boss,' Joe said sincerely. It would make the whole thing far easier than having to stand at the gate searching for Billy among the faces of the men coming in on the day shift, and what's more his bloody father would know nothing about it.

He walked outside and lit a cigarette while he waited.

Billy was puzzled as he went towards the foremen's wooden shack, laughingly known as an 'office'. He didn't go in; he didn't have to for Joe was waiting for him.

'What's up? Is Lizzie all right?'

'She's OK, but I'm afraid Celia let the cat out of the bag about you and our Lizzie, last night.'

'Oh God!'

'No, it's all right really. Mam didn't explode and go up to your house on the bounce, but she is upset. She's sworn everyone to secrecy, even our Emmet. Still, I haven't stayed behind to tell you just that. Celia went to see your mam yesterday and she's worried sick about her. She says she looks very ill and your da won't call the doctor out to see her.'

'He won't. He won't even admit that she's ill, and you know Mam: she's always been afraid of him.'

'What's the matter with you, for God's sake? Why don't you go to see the bloody doctor?'

'She's that terrified of him she won't let me. She made me swear I wouldn't. Things were better for us when we were at Maudie's. At least better for her. Maudie wouldn't let him bully her and Mam often went for a lie-down and there wasn't as much housework or washing to do. They shared it between them. She doesn't like the house and she hasn't the energy to make an effort, like. In the old days she'd have been made up to have her own place again and she'd be polishing and everything,' Billy said glumly. 'I didn't like to tell Lizzie what Mam had made me promise. I knew she'd only tell Celia, who had enough to think about, what with the baby and everything. And anyway, it wasn't a promise I was happy to keep,' he added, looking shame-faced.

'Well, for Cee's sake will you tell our Lizzie how she is? If she gets better or worse. Cee's going mad with worry and she can't get out of bed for another week. Mam's said she'll hide all her clothes, so if she wants to go out again it will have to be in her nightdress.'

Billy nodded. 'Did Lizzie tell you we were going to go away in the spring and get married, in Scotland? We've been saving for months now and I'm certain to get a job in one of the yards up there.' He paused. 'But how can I leave Mam? Our Foxy's like Da. He doesn't care for anyone except himself and he'll have Mam demented, and she's enough on her plate already.'

Joe hadn't known about the proposed elopement and he was annoyed by Billy's disclosure.

'You can't go and leave your mam, and our Lizzie running off up there with you would break my mam's heart altogether. She's had nothing but trouble to contend with lately.'

'Lizzie's not going to like not going, Joe. Her heart's set on it.'

'You just leave our Lizzie to me,' Joe said firmly.

Billy nodded and glanced around at the men now streaming into the yard and Joe knew that the time was up.

'You'd better get going and I'm going to my bed. I can hardly keep my eyes open.'

'Thanks, Joe. I'll get word to our Celia.'

'How? We can't keep doing this.'

Billy frowned. 'Do you think we could get the "post office" going again?'

'I'd have to chisel out a brick on the jigger wall this time and you'll have to walk down with the notes.'

'Will you do that? I swear I'll leave a note every day.'

Joe nodded. 'Your da's got a lot to answer for, Billy.'

'And don't I know it? But his day will come,' Billy replied bitterly.

When Joe got home he relayed the conversation to both Celia and his mam before he went to bed.

Celia looked stricken but Brigid patted her arm.

'Don't you go worrying now. If she gets very bad then *I'll* call Dr Fraser out. Wasn't he the one she saw last time and he gave her a bottle of tonic?'

Celia nodded.

'Well, it's not done her much good, has it? But never mind, you can rely on me.'

Celia looked at her with heartfelt thanks. Brigid met all the misfortunes and troubles head-on and dealt with them as she saw fit. She was very, very grateful for the strength of character her mother-in-law possessed.

There was never much privacy with the house so crowded most of the time, so after tea Joe told Lizzie that Celia wanted to see her.

Lizzie sat on the side of the bed at the bottom end and Joe sat in the nursing chair by the fire.

It was such a cosy room, Lizzie thought. Even though there wasn't much in it. She and Billy would love a room like this.

'What did you want to say, Cee? Did you want me to get you something?'

Celia shook her head. Joe had told her about Lizzie and Billy's plans and she felt awful. She'd married the man she loved and she'd paid a heavy price, but she knew that Lizzie would have to pay a higher one if she were to go. She'd miss all her family and she'd be riddled with guilt.

'No, it was me who wanted to see you,' said Joe.

'What for? You saw Billy this morning and he's promised to let Cee know how her mam is.'

'Yes he did, but he also told me that you're planning to run off, elope, and get married in Scotland in the spring.'

Lizzie flushed and she twisted her hands nervously in her lap.

'You can't go, Lizzie.'

'Why not?' she demanded. 'You and Cee got married, why shouldn't Billy and me get married too? It's not as though I'd want to upset Mam by living here.'

'It's got nothing to do with Mam really. It's because of *Billy's* mam. She's very ill. She won't have a doctor near her because *he* won't even admit that she's ill at all and as for Foxy, well he's too taken up with his own mischief to worry about Annie.'

'It's not fair, Joe!' Lizzie cried.

'I know it's not, Lizzie.'

Celia reached out and took Lizzie's hand. 'If anyone deserves to be happy it's you and our Billy, but . . . but . . . I think I'd go mad, completely mad, if I didn't have Billy to tell me what's going on up there. I know it's selfish of me, Lizzie – really selfish, after all you've done for me.'

Lizzie was desperately searching for some solution to the problem.

'Well, what can we do? Someone *must* be able to get her to a doctor.'

Joe thought that in reality Annie Milton herself didn't want to see a doctor. She was too afraid of what he might tell her. 'If she gets worse then Mam is going to get the doctor out to her, then he can't blame Billy or Cee.'

'So we'll have to wait,' Lizzie said miserably.

Oh, it wasn't fair at all. They had it all planned and it was going to have been really great. Why hadn't he told her about his mam? Maybe he'd intended to or maybe he just hadn't noticed she was getting worse. If you lived with someone, saw them every day, then you often didn't realise these things. It was only when someone like Cee, who hadn't seen her mother on a regular basis, noted it and pointed it out.

'I'm afraid so,' Joe answered. ' I'm really sorry, Lizzie. And what about Mam, Lizzie? You said you wouldn't want to upset her but she'd be really upset at you not telling her beforehand.'

'Yes, but . . .' Lizzie's voice trailed off. Put into words it sounded awful. That she was prepared to go without a backward glance, leaving her mam yet again bowed down with worry and misery.

'Treat yourself, Lizzie. Buy a special outfit for when we all go to the launch of the big aircraft carrier in April,' Cee said gently, still holding Lizzie's hand. 'I know it's no substitute but you could use it as your wedding outfit later.'

Lizzie didn't want to think about later. Things were bad enough now.

The thirteenth of April dawned with a clear azure-blue sky and bright sunlight, but with a blustery wind, too. Charlie Milton looked out of his bedroom window with relief. Rain would have spoiled the whole day and this was the biggest launch since that of HMS *Rodney* in 1927. It even eclipsed the launch of the *Clement*.

His best suit was ready and hung in the small wardrobe. A clean shirt, crisp with starch, was on a hanger on the hook on the back of the door. His boots were gleaming for he'd spent hours polishing them and he'd bought a brand-new bowler hat for the occasion.

He turned and looked at his wife curled up in the bed. She'd shown no interest or enthusiasm for the launch of the world's biggest battleship and that annoyed him. Both his sons had made an effort. Although Billy would still be in his work clothes the lad had gone and bought a brown coat-type overall to cover his dirty overalls and would be wearing his best cap.

Annie was awake but she pretended not to be. She couldn't face today. She couldn't cope with all the standing around and being crushed and jostled by the enormous crowd that was expected to turn out, to say nothing of the journey to the shipyard. Every tram, bus, train, ferry and the carriages of the overhead railway would be packed.

Each day she seemed to get weaker and the agonising pain was constant now. These days she just managed to keep up with the housework, with frequent breaks to rest and get her breath. Shopping was a nightmare and often she'd asked Mr Henderson to send the order with the young delivery lad.

Each afternoon she lay on the sofa and each night she crawled to bed at eight o'clock. Billy was worried, she could see that, he helped her as much as he could. He was always asking her how she was too. In fact he did it every day and every day she replied that she was much the same. That it would all pass and she was managing. There was no need to say anything to Charlie or even mention the word 'doctor'.

'Annie, you'd better get out of that bed now, or you won't be ready in time. Just make sure that Frederick is well turned out and behaves. We want no repetition of the day the *Clement* was launched. This is going to be a much grander affair, hundreds of thousands of people will be there and everything that floats will be on the river.'

She opened her eyes but she couldn't look at him.

'Charlie, I can't go. I just *can't*. I feel so ill. I don't think I can even get out of bed.'

He was incensed. Today of all days she had to carry on with this play-acting. Pretending she was ill.

'There's nothing wrong with you, woman. It's all in your mind. Dr Fraser said you'd be much better in your own home and now you've got your own home, so pull yourself together and get out of that bed and wear that good herringbone tweed costume I bought you.'

'Charlie, I can't go!' she pleaded. 'I haven't got the strength to stand and the pain . . .'

With a quick tug he pulled the bedclothes from over her. 'Stop all this nonsense, woman, for God's sake.'

She sat up and then swung her legs slowly out of the bed but as she tried to stand she fell, groaning as she caught her head on the edge of the chest of drawers. The room began to revolve slowly and then a creeping darkness enveloped her.

When she came round, her head was resting in Billy's lap and there was no sign of Charlie. She struggled to rise.

'Lie there for a bit, Mam, until you feel better,' Billy instructed. He'd heard his father shouting at her and then he'd heard the thud as she'd fallen, and had rushed in. His da's face was like thunder and he'd not spoken. He'd just walked out of the room.

'Where . . . where's your da?'

'Gone. Gone to work, Mam.'

'But you should have gone too.'

'No, it's far too early, Mam. It's time Dr Fraser came, it really is.'

'No! No, Billy, please. Your da's furious with me as it is. If he came home and found me in bed and learned that the doctor . . .' She gritted her teeth against another surge of pain.

'Let me get you back to bed then. Have a good rest today, to hell with the house and him. I'll take our Foxy down to Maudie's, he can go with them. Do you want me to get someone? Mrs Taylor or Mrs Robinson?'

'No. He . . . he's got them all snooping and spying on me.'

Billy knew it would have been the perfect day for Celia to come and stay nearly the whole day with Mam – everyone would be out – but Celia and Michael, Brigid, Lizzie and all the rest of them were going to the launch. He felt so helpless and guilty as he pulled the bedclothes around her. He went downstairs and got a glass and a jug. He filled the jug with water and took it up to her.

She managed a smile. 'You're a good lad, Billy.'

He bent and kissed her forehead, determined now that as soon as he saw Celia he'd tell her how bad Mam really was.

The Slattery household was in its usual state of chaos. Bernie couldn't find her best shoes. Emmet was complaining that he'd only one decent sock, there was an argument between Josie and Lizzie about whose turn it was to use the mirror. Brigid as usual had got to the stage where slaps were being dealt out liberally.

'Go up those stairs, Bernadette Slattery, and look under that bed of yours. Didn't you kick off those shoes up there after Mass last Sunday? And you, Emmet, aren't I worn out darning your socks? Here.' She reached up to the rack and dragged down a pair of grey woollen socks. 'Now get those on and stop moaning. And less of the fighting in that scullery or I'll be in there and take down that mirror for good and then the pair of you will be looking a fright.'

It was at this stage that Celia emerged, neatly dressed in a dark blue costume and hat that she'd got from Middleton's, and carrying her son, who was well wrapped up in the fanciest of his many shawls.

Brigid looked at her with admiration.

'Aren't I worn out with the lot of them? Why can't you all get yourselves nicely turned out with no fuss like Celia, and she's got Michael to see to as well? You're desperate, the lot of you. That's just what you are, a desperate tribe of hooligans!'

'Here, Ma, sit yourself down and nurse him. I'll get you a cup of tea and Lizzie and I will sort things out,' Celia said. Brigid had no sense of organisation at all.

The kettle was put on the hob and Brigid sat down thankfully, her grandson in her arms. Lizzie had given up on the mirror and between her and Celia order was restored.

'Sure, you'd have no trouble being an army general, Cee, and it's what this lot need. Organisation and discipline.'

Lizzie had her sisters and Emmet ready and sitting on the sofa and had threatened that if anyone moved she'd kill them stone-dead. At least Fergal had already gone to work.

'Right, Mam, give him to me and you go and get yourself ready. We've plenty of time and our Joe and Fergal will get a good spec for us although half of Liverpool and the whole of Birkenhead will be there.'

Brigid gave her grandson to Lizzie. 'Tell me again what herself's name is? Your one who is going to smash the bottle of wine and launch the thing?'

'Lady Maude Hoare. She's married to the First Lord of the Admiralty,' Celia replied.

'Wouldn't you think they'd have someone grander than that – a duchess or countess?'

'Mam, our Joe's explained it to you. It's because it's a battleship belonging to the Navy and not a passenger ship like the *Clement*.'

'Well, it was a *lady* who launched that one, and didn't Queen Mary herself launch that big one up in Scotland? So, wouldn't you think they'd come up with someone higher up than Lady Maude whatever?'

Lizzie gave up. 'Are we all ready now?'

Brigid was securing her hat against the wind with a huge and dangerous-looking hatpin. Suddenly there was an almighty series of explosions and everything in the room shook and rattled.

'Oh, Holy Mother of God! What was that?' Brigid cried, while everyone else looked stricken.

'It's all right, Ma. It's the salute from the other warships. That's how much noise nineteen guns make,' Celia explained calmly.

'Well, I'd sooner not know that, and haven't they any sense at all? Sounding off like that, it put the heart across me. It could give a person a heart attack, so it could.'

Lizzie grinned at her. 'Oh, come on, Mam, let's get going or we'll never get there.'

In the yard there was great activity. All the usual clearing-up of the paraphernalia left lying around, the greasing of the slipway and positioning of the drag chains was almost complete. The 22,000-ton ship that was to carry sixty aircraft was secured to the gigantic gantry cranes by means of wire hawsers which would be wound in as the launch time approached. On the next slipway the keel of the battleship HMS *Prince of Wales*, which was to be 35,000 tons, was rising on the keel plates. Every single thing that could float was on the river and was crowded with people.

Joe watched the growing crowd with some alarm. He had work still to do and if the family didn't get there soon, he couldn't keep a place for them. He'd seen Charlie Milton once, all done up like a dog's dinner and with a new blocker. The man had glared at him but Joe had only smiled sardonically back, which seemed to infuriate Charlie even more.

The launch platform was a very high one, the ship being so large. Mr Johnson, head of the Board of Directors, the Mayor of Birkenhead and a host of other civic and naval dignitaries would go up there, but they wouldn't have as good a view of the whole proceedings as those who had taken their lives in their hands and had climbed to the top of the Birkenhead Town Hall clock tower.

At last Joe spotted his family, Brigid elbowing her way through the crowd as usual.

'It's a good job you got here. In about half an hour you won't be able to move. What kept you?'

Brigid was incensed. 'What kept us? Haven't I had the divil's own job getting this tribe ready, and without Cee we'd still be back there, and then to top it all didn't they go and set off all those blasted guns and frighten the wits out of me?'

Celia looked worried. 'You will be able to stand with us, won't you? I'm worried about Michael. I don't want him crushed.'

'Of course I will. Everything's just about finished now.'

'And you should have seen the crush at the Pier Head and the landing stage – well, you could hardly move. If I hadn't yelled, "Mother and baby coming through" we'd never have got a place on the ferry at all,' said Brigid.

'Have you seen our Billy and Mam and Foxy?' Celia asked.

'I saw your da earlier on – new bowler hat and all, by the look of it. I know Billy's here somewhere but I haven't seen him. Can you see your mam over there with the others?'

They both scanned the good-natured, jostling line of foremen and their families but could see neither Charlie, Annie, Billy or Foxy.

'You'd have the eyes worn out of your head looking for anyone in this crowd. Missus, if you don't mind, me daughter-in-law's got her baby here, so will you stop that shoving. Do you want the girl to fall?' This last was to a small but very stocky woman who was beside Brigid.

There was excitement in the air and a buzz went around the yard as Lady Maude Hoare, DBE, ascended the platform, surrounded by a large entourage, most of whom were in uniform of some kind.

'Well, thank the Lord for that,' Brigid said.

Mr Johnson handed her ladyship a bottle of Empire Wine all done up with red, white and blue ribbons and the crowd fell silent, all straining to hear her speech but they only caught the last bit as the wind was strong and carried her words away.

'I name this ship *Ark Royal*. May God guide her, and guard and keep all who sail in her.'

The bottle was swung out with some force, hit the hull and stayed intact.

'Oh God, it's going to be a repeat of the *Rodney*. Three times they chucked the bottle at that one before it broke,' Joe said.

Her ladyship tried again and with the same result.

'Ah go on, wellie it, yer ladyship!' someone in the crowd shouted.

Lady Maude virtually exhausted herself heaving the bottle but again it didn't break. Everyone was silent, wondering if the bottle would ever shatter or would they give it up as a bad job or indeed send for another bottle. Finally on the fourth attempt the bottle smashed.

The beginnings of a resounding cheer faded and everyone held their breath. The ship wasn't moving an inch.

'What's up with it? Is it stuck fast with all that grease?' Brigid asked.

'Mam, it's not stuck! For God's sake don't go saying things like that aloud.'

Brigid tutted and glared at the woman beside her who had uttered a short sarcastic laugh.

Then Emmet yelled, 'Look! Look, Joe, she's moving!'

His cry was taken up by thousands of voices, and as the huge ship began to gather speed the band struck up 'Rule Britannia'.

The noise of the cheering was deafening, and Joe and all his fellow workmates looked with pride at the huge ship that they'd built with their own hands, and with blood, sweat and tears too. They'd created a living thing with a personality all its own. She wasn't just a great lump of steel.

The tugs that had been standing out in the river waiting moved forward. Then with a noise almost as deafening as the cheering and the sirens of the ships on the river, the anchor chain was dropped.

Everyone was laughing and cheering, but in the midst of the turmoil Celia was silent. Search as she might, she couldn't see her mam. Joe spotted Billy and yelled to him and Billy pushed his way through the gradually dispersing crowd.

'Wasn't that great! Did you see it all, Cee?'

'Yes, but where's Mam and our Foxy?'

Billy's expression changed. 'Foxy's with Mrs Kemp and Mam's not here.'

'Why?' There was a note of panic in Celia's voice.

'She was too ill, Cee. He made her get up and she fainted and he . . . he just left her there on the floor. He walked out and left her.'

'God damn and blast him, the creature!' Brigid cursed.

'Mam, please,' Lizzie begged. She would have liked Billy to have been beside her for the launch the way Joe had been with Celia.

'I got her back into bed and took her some water up in a jug and told her not to get out of that bed all day.'

Celia turned to Joe. 'That's it, Joe. Will you go ahead and get the doctor? As soon as we get in, I'll go and sit with her until he comes.'

Joe nodded grimly. He agreed with Celia.

'Haven't I said all along that you shouldn't have taken any notice of *him*? You should have ignored him and her, Billy,' Lizzie said.

'Right then, we'd better all get back as soon as we can but it won't be easy with this crowd,' Brigid said grimly as she began determinedly to push her way back to the ferry.

It wasn't easy and all the way home Celia had the awful nagging fear that it might be too late for Dr Fraser. When they reached Roscommon Street, Celia handed Michael to his grandmother and went out the back way, up the jigger.

Joe was sitting in Annie's kitchen but he got up when he saw his wife.

'She's not good, Cee. I went up to see her to tell her that the doctor was on his way but that he might be delayed because of the crowds. She looks awful, luv.'

Celia dashed down the lobby and up the stairs but when she saw her mother she dropped to her knees beside the bed and took Annie's skeletal hand.

'Oh, Mam! Mam! We should have ignored everyone! Oh, I'll kill our Billy for not telling me the truth!'

'Hush, it's not his fault.' Annie's voice was low-pitched and unsteady, the tone unlike her usual quiet but precise way of speech.

Hearing voices on the stairs, Celia got up and opened the door, and she breathed a sigh of relief as Dr Fraser entered.

His face was full of anger and concern as he examined Annie and Celia was shocked to see how thin her mam was. She was like a skeleton barely covered with skin.

'Why wasn't I called out sooner than this?' the man demanded.

'She wouldn't let us . . . My brother was supposed to let me know how she was and he didn't. He just used to write "No change" or something like that on the notes.'

'Notes! What notes?' He glared at Celia. 'Don't tell me this ridiculous feud is still going on?'

Celia nodded. 'He . . . Da had the neighbours spying on her. That's why I couldn't even come and see her for myself, and only five houses between us – six if we count our old one – and Da was in every evening so I couldn't come then.'

'She should have been in hospital months ago. Where's your father?'

'At work. They launched the *Ark Royal* today. Billy said he made her get up this morning and she fell, banged her head and then fainted and he . . . he just left her there!' Celia broke down.

The doctor's expression was grim. 'All right now, Celia. I'm going to give her some medicine for the pain. It will make her sleep. I want to see your father when he gets in. Tell him if he won't come I'll send the police for him because his cruel neglect and intolerance in my book is tantamount to manslaughter! I . . . I'm afraid she's dying. I'm so sorry, child. I really am.'

When the doctor had left Joe came upstairs. Celia was sitting on the bed holding Annie's hand and the tears were streaming down her cheeks.

'He's killed her! Oh, Joe, she's dying.'

'Is that what he said?'

'Yes, he said she should have been in hospital ages ago and that he considers what Da's done to be manslaughter. He walked out this morning and left her to die, Joe! All these months she's been . . .' Celia couldn't speak and she clung to Joe sobbing until a movement from Annie caught Joe's eye. If he could have got his hands on Charlie Milton that minute he'd have murdered him.

'Look, luv, she's trying to say something.'

They both bent down over the frail figure.

'Joe . . . get . . . your . . . mam, please?'

He was astounded. 'My mam?'

'Yes . . . Get . . . Brigid.' Without another word Joe left. Celia heard his footsteps in the yard, the slam of the back door and she tried to pull herself together. It seemed ages before Joe came back, although she knew it was only a matter of minutes.

'Oh, God save us! Would you look at her? Oh, the pity of it. The sheer pity of it! Celia, move over while I listen to what she has to say.' Brigid could see that Annie was agitated, she also knew without being told that the poor woman was dying.

'What is it I can do for you, Mrs Milton?'

Annie managed a weak smile. 'Promise me . . . you'll look . . . after them.'

'Don't I do that already? You've no worry about that.'

'No . . . Billy . . . Foxy . . .' Her eyes were beginning to close, the drug was taking effect.

'I will so, I'll have them all. God knows how we'll manage, but we will. You have my word on that.'

Annie nodded slowly. 'Thank . . . you . . . Brigid.'

Brigid took her hand. 'We finally crossed the barrier, Annie. Sure, we should have done it years ago and we could have been such good neighbours.' Brigid swallowed hard. 'Don't be worrying now. Is there anyone you want? Your vicar? Her at number eight?'

'No. No, I want no one . . .' The words died away and Brigid got up.

'She's sleeping now.'

'I can't just leave her!' Celia cried.

'I'll wait,' Joe offered.

'You will not for you'll be taking the carving knife to him as soon as he sets foot in the door – not that he doesn't deserve it. No, we'll take it in turns. Joe, you go and get some sleep, you've been up all night and half the day and you've work tonight. Celia, Michael needs feeding and changing. Send our Lizzie in until you're ready to come back, and don't go rushing or he'll bring it all back up and you'll have to start again and that won't do *anyone* any good. I'll stay until our Lizzie comes.'

Chapter Twenty-Two

It hadn't been a great day for Charlie Milton. He'd stood there alone amongst the other foremen, who all had at least one member of their family with them. Some even had cousins and nephews and nieces, which he didn't consider to be fair at all. Such lesser family members should have been in the main body of the crowd.

He'd looked for Billy in vain and Frederick had been with the Kemps. He'd even had his new bowler knocked off by a young idiot of an apprentice who was throwing a rope to his mate to tie around the blocks and had missed. He'd roared at the boy and had then wiped the dust and dirt carefully off with his handkerchief, which meant that now he had no pristine piece of white linen to use, should he need to.

The performance with Annie that morning had infuriated him. She'd do nothing, absolutely nothing to help herself. This supposed illness from which she suffered was all in her mind, he was certain of it, and this morning she just simply hadn't wanted to come with him and he'd paid good money for a new costume and hat for her.

At lunch time he hadn't gone to the Royal Hotel with all the others. He felt humiliated and so he'd drunk in the public bar of the Manor House pub in morose silence, ignoring all the merriment that was going on around him. And he'd drunk more than he usually did, which hadn't helped his temper during the afternoon as it had caused him to have a thumping headache. Again he'd gone looking for Billy but with no success.

'Have you seen anything of my lad?' he'd finally asked Fred

Roberts, a man he heartily disliked after that affair over young Richie Kemp.

Roberts had looked him up and down and the corners of his mouth lifted in derision as he'd smelled the beer on his breath.

'No. Try the Raglan and if he's in there, then you'll have the pleasure of giving your own son the DCM, won't you? Not that I'd blame the lad for stopping out of your way. He could have gone home – no one knows where anyone is this afternoon. Well, at least I've got work to do. I've no time to be chasing around looking for my relations. They all went home on the bus from the Woodside terminal two hours ago.'

The man had turned away and Charlie had glared at his retreating back.

Charlie walked slowly up the street, having got off at the Great Homer Street end. He looked with disgust and derision at the houses he passed and the dirty, scruffy kids playing on the pavement. They ran away at his approach. ''Ere, come away from 'im, me mam says 'e's a loony,' he'd heard one cry as they all disappeared into doorways.

Well, he'd go and collect Frederick and see if Harry was up to going to the Wynnstay with him later on. It would take Harry's mind off those blasted birds that Maudie hated so much.

'He's here with my two,' Maudie informed him, although he could see by her expression that she wasn't pleased.

'Have you been over to see Annie?'

'No, haven't I enough on my plate today with those *three*, and I nearly lost them in the crowd? All the trams and buses were full. It took hours to get home and now, if you'll mind out of my way, I'll get on with making the tea. Harry's been in for half an hour. What took you so long to get home?'

He didn't answer and she disappeared into the kitchen and left him standing on the step. Well, he wasn't going to ask her if Harry could go for a pint later on. It was demeaning. It was like asking could a child come out to play.

'Wasn't it great, Da? They're going to have sixty planes on that bit that sticks out,' said Foxy when he emerged.

'It's called a flight deck,' Charlie snapped.

Foxy ignored him. 'Five squadrons of Blackburn Skias and Fairey Swordfishes. We could win *any* war with them. We could beat *any* country in the world!'

'Will you shut up, there's not going to be any war, no matter what the papers say about that feller Hitler and the other one, the Italian fool who dresses up like a toy soldier, festooned with gold braid and strutting around the place like a bantam cock. I fought in the last year of the Great War, the war to end all wars. Do you know why it was called that?'

Foxy looked down at his boots. Here comes another boring history lesson, he thought.

'No, Da,' he replied. It was easier to admit ignorance; he could just switch his mind off then. If he said otherwise he'd be asked hundreds of questions. It was like a flaming inquisition. Anyway, he was too old now to be treated like a six-year-old who knew nothing.

As his father lectured him on the suffering he'd gone through to secure his future, Foxy waited for him to find the door key, kicking the toe of his boot against the bottom step. He hoped Mam had something good to eat, he was starving. You never got much of a meal in Maudie's house, she was too mean.

He shut the door and followed his father down the lobby. The house was very quiet and then his father bellowed like a wounded bull and Foxy caught a quick glimpse of Mrs Slattery in the kitchen.

But before he could say a word, Brigid was on her feet. 'Oh, so it's after coming home now,' she said, ignoring his roar of anger.

'You, lad, don't be taking your coat off, get down to Dr Fraser's house now and tell him your father's home. He wants to see him.'

'Don't you dare give orders in my house. Frederick, you'll stay where you are,' Charlie bellowed.

'Well, if you don't go, lad, the police will be here later on. Get going!' Brigid yelled back.

The light of battle was in her eyes. Her rage had been growing all afternoon as she'd sat and thought of the cruel and loveless life poor Annie Milton had had. She'd had more of the material things and he'd a good steady wage coming in, but he was careful with it and anyway what did all that amount to in the end? Oh, if only the poor soul had had the courage to come to her, instead of that sour-faced Maudie who'd spied on her, she'd have put Charlie Milton in his place, so she would.

'Get out of my house before I throw you out, or call the police to do it.' He was livid.

'I'll go when I'm ready, Charlie Milton, and you'll hear me out because I don't intend to be after crossing your doorstep again!'

Foxy ran. This was something more than just an amusement. This was going to be a terrible row. The police had been mentioned.

'Right, you'll listen to me now, so you will. Your poor little wife, that you've bullied all her life, is up those stairs in her bed dying! That's what I said. Dying! And what do you do? You walk out of the room and she in a dead faint on the floor. She's all skin and bone and you've driven her without mercy all her life. Well, I hope you're satisfied now. At least the poor soul has had her daughter and grandson with her all afternoon while you were over the water prancing around, thinking what a fine great bucko you are.'

Charlie spluttered but she didn't give him the chance to get a word out.

'And having the neighbours spying on her and them calling themselves "friends". I'd sooner have a bunch of wild savages living next door to me than that lot! Oh, fine friends they were. I've never forgotten how you and your one from number eight tried to get my lad put in jail over Richie Kemp, nor all the other things you've done against me and mine.

'Now, we'll have to see what kind of good neighbours that lot turn out to be when she's dead and buried. You'll not find them rushing to help out because most of them hate you but are too afraid or hypocritical to say so. Go on up those stairs and look at her. Look at what you've done to her! You've killed her! And wasn't it me she asked to look after your two lads? I'll tell you now that I'll have Billy but not your one that's run out. He's like you and I won't have him in my home. Yes, home. This . . . this isn't a home, it's a flaming prison. Go on up and see her.'

Brigid took a step closer to him and he backed slightly away.

'By God and all his holy saints, you'll burn in hell, Charlie Milton. You'll burn and it's no use you getting on your knees to your vicar or minister or whatever you call him, because he can't help you. There's a greater power up there who sees everything. He can look deep in your wicked black murdering heart. You think about that!' And quivering with rage she pushed past him, walked down the lobby and out into the street. She stood there for a few minutes, her hands on her hips, and her gaze sweeping defiantly over the neighbouring houses, knowing she was being watched.

Charlie was shaken. Not just by the force of her anger or finding her in his home and giving orders, but by the accusations she'd made. At first he'd thought she'd gone completely mad or was drunk but he knew she was neither.

He took a glass from the dresser and then bent and drew out a small bottle of whisky from the cupboard and poured himself a stiff drink. It couldn't be true. Annie was no more dying than he was. It was all her fault, carrying on the way she had done this morning. She just enjoyed being a martyr, that was all. He wondered why Billy was so late. The lad should have been home by now. Maybe he'd come in and Brigid Slattery had chased him out. Billy wouldn't have been a match for that one; he'd hardly got a word in himself.

He took another large gulp, the fiery warmth steadying him. And all that rubbish about him burning in hell and the vicar not being able to help him. Superstitious rubbish, that's what it was. The Irish were known for it, with their beads and candles, their pictures and plaster images.

He was in the act of finishing his drink before going upstairs to see his supposedly dying wife when Foxy arrived back in Dr Fraser's car.

'I see you're consoling yourself already, or is it for Dutch courage? Have you been to see your wife yet?'

Charlie glared at him but he said nothing. The man was a doctor after all.

'No, I've only just got home from work,' he replied grimly.

'Really? Is that what you call it? How many pubs did you visit on the way?'

'I'd be obliged to you, Doctor, to keep a civil tongue in your head. I didn't call you out this afternoon, it was my daughter, who had no right at all to do such a thing. She'd no right to be here in the first place.'

Dr Fraser's colour mounted and his eyes were cold.

'She had no *right*? No *right* to call a doctor to her dying mother? She had every right. You are an arrogant, cruel and vicious man, hellbent on continuing a stupid feud no matter what circumstances arise or people are hurt.'

'It's a matter of principle. It's not a feud.'

'Your wife is dying and you won't even believe it. Did you hear me? She's DYING! DYING! She has a day, maybe less, and you've let her struggle along in sheer agony for months. I should bring a case of Criminal Neglect leading to Manslaughter by Default against you, Mr Milton.' Dr Fraser knew full well that what he had just said was nonsense. There was no such charge, but by the look on his face he could see that Milton believed there was.

'Oh, I well remember you when that young Kemp lad died. You were quick enough to accuse and go to the police then. Well maybe we'll see how much you enjoy their hospitality tonight.'

Charlie couldn't speak. He couldn't move. He had a vision of himself being marched into that same police station, being questioned by that same supercilious sergeant and locked in one of their disgusting cells with common thieves, drunks and pimps, the very dregs of society.

'Well, if you won't go to see her, I will.' Dr Fraser turned to a petrified Foxy. 'You, lad, where's your brother? Is there anyone you can stay with or go to for a few hours?'

'Our Billy – me brother – should be in now or I could go over to Mrs Kemp.'

The doctor nodded. 'Then go to that lady's house until your brother comes in. Go on now. I'm here to see to your mother.'

Foxy was confused and frightened. Da was acting strange and the doctor had yelled at him and said Mam was dying and that Da could go to jail. It didn't take him long before he fled from the bleak house down to Maudie's, which, however unwelcoming, did offer some kind of normality.

Billy came slowly up the street. He'd wandered around the neighbourhood aimlessly. He hadn't wanted to go home and yet he hadn't wanted to go to see Lizzie. It had been a peculiar day. All that fuss and ceremony this morning, asking Joe to get the doctor to Mam, a few pints with his mates at lunchtime in the Raglan just to be sociable, then back to work. All afternoon he'd been busy trying to keep out of his da's way and he was worried sick about his mam now. Yet when the whistle had gone and everyone joyfully streamed out of the gates, he'd hung back.

Fred Roberts, Joe's blockerman, had seen him.

'What's up with you, lad? You've a face like a wet week. Too much ale at lunch time? Well, you're not the first and you won't be the last. I saw your father earlier on, he was looking for you and he didn't seem very pleased.' Roberts winked conspiratorially. 'I'd take your time getting home, he might be in a better mood by then, though I doubt it,' he'd advised.

The front door stood wide open and Billy recognised the doctor's car. His heart felt like a lump of lead as he walked into the hall in time to see Dr Fraser coming down the stairs.

'So, you finally showed up. By God, that poor woman deserved more of a family than she had.'

The words 'deserved' and 'had' stuck in Billy's confused mind. 'She's . . . she's not . . . ?'

Dr Fraser took pity on him. He supposed he wasn't a bad son. Quiet and unassuming like the woman whose eyes he had just closed in death. She'd died with not a single member of her family or friend being there, although she'd not have noticed. The high dosage of morphine had done its work well. He sighed heavily.

'Your mother is dead. I'm sorry, but if someone had come to me sooner . . . well,' he shrugged helplessly. There was no cure for what she'd had, but her last months could have been made more comfortable, the pain eased.

'You'd better go in and see your father – that's if you want to. Myself I'd let him stew. What he did was little better than criminal.'

The words hadn't really sunk in. 'Where . . . where's our Foxy?'

'The young lad? He's gone to Mrs Kemp's house, or so I advised. Perhaps you'd better go there too. Arrangements will have to be made.'

Billy stared at him in horror. The last place he wanted to be was at Maudie's and *he* couldn't make these 'arrangements'. He *couldn't*. He watched the doctor leave, cross to his car and drive away. Then he fled from the house, down the street to Lizzie's house.

They were in the middle of a meal, apart from Joe who had already left for work.

'Celia, luv, you'll have to eat for Michael's sake,' Brigid urged. 'Didn't I see the doctor arrive with my own two eyes and Billy and himself will be home now – not that that devil will be any use to anyone. Billy will come down later, I'm sure, but if he doesn't then I'll send Fergal up, just to ask.'

'Ah, Mam, why do I have to go?' Fergal complained. He was afraid of Charlie Milton.

'Because you're the eldest boy and I say so, that's why. But let's not be after looking on the dark side.'

Fergal nodded glumly and finished his tea, wondering if he could manage to slip out to Jimmy Kelly's or Bryan O'Shea's.

Lizzie and Josie cleared the table while Bernie and Emmet were told to get out the homework books. Hadn't they had a whole day off? Now they could get something done at least to take in in the morning and it was no use them carrying on for she wasn't able for it. One word and she'd clatter the pair of them, Brigid warned.

Celia had fed and bathed Michael and had walked up and down the small front room singing softly to him an old Irish lullaby Brigid often sang, while worrying about her mam. Oh, she hoped the doctor had given Da a real good telling-off. First thing in the morning she'd go to her mam and enter in the front way too. She no longer had any fear of her father. What could he do to her now? What was he, anyway? Just a pompous, puffed-up nobody full of his own pride and importance. Just let Maudie or any of the others speak to her, she'd give them a tongue-lashing. Fine friends they'd been to Mam.

Being in the front room she was the first to hear the pounding, running footsteps that stopped abruptly, and were followed by the sound of the door knocker that echoed down the lobby, waking Michael, who began to cry.

Lizzie beat her to the door and Billy half fell, half staggered into the lobby.

'Oh, Cee. Cee, she . . . she's dead!' Billy started to cry and Lizzie put her arms round him.

Celia buried her face in the shawl that her son was wrapped in and the bitter, salt tears fell on his soft, downy little cheek. Mam was dead! Only hours ago she'd been sitting beside the bed, holding her hand. Only hours ago her mam had asked Brigid to look after them all. The pain in her chest grew and grew until she felt she couldn't breathe.

Brigid took them all in hand.

'Lizzie, take the baby from Celia and go into the warm kitchen with him. Leave these two alone, for a while.' She took the baby from Celia and gave him to Lizzie, then she took both their hands and propelled them to the privacy of the front room. As they clung to each other, sobbing, she closed the door and crossed herself.

'I'll look after them, alannah. I swore to you I would but forgive me for I can't and won't take the youngest. I know you'll understand?' she said softly.

Billy at last made a move to go home at midnight. Both he and Celia were worn out with grief and shock. Lizzie had done her best to comfort Billy and at one stage Brigid had thought of sending for Joe but Celia had said no, and she hadn't argued.

She had asked Billy where his brother was and had been told he was with Maudie or at least Billy thought he was. Well, let the woman keep him, Brigid thought. She didn't like the lad, he wasn't like Billy or Celia, he was like *him*. Then she had a fit of remorse, telling herself that she had promised Annie she would look after them all, but maybe that inhuman savage above at number two would insist on having the lad himself. She hoped he would.

'Celia, will you go to your bed now? You're exhausted. In the morning, when everyone's feeling more able for it, we'll get things sorted out.'

Celia had nodded, kissed and hugged her brother and then went into the front room, sank down on to the bed and fell into the deep sleep of physical and mental exhaustion.

At the front door, as Lizzie clung to Billy, over his shoulder she saw a plain black car draw up outside the Miltons' house. She knew it was the undertakers. So, he wouldn't even let her be washed and prepared at home. He wouldn't even let her lie in her coffin in the parlour so her family could be with her and her friends and neighbours could call to pay their respects. No, he'd killed her and now he wanted shut of her. She knew she would have to divert Billy's attention or make him stay here, sleep on the sofa.

'Billy, luv, I know how tired you are. You'll . . . you'll not get much sleep up there with him. Stay here, please? You can sleep on the sofa, Mam won't mind. She said you could if you wanted to and I . . . I think you should. Just for tonight.'

He looked at her with eyes swollen and red, and thanked God he had her love. He thanked God he'd been so well cared for and comforted in this house and hadn't Mrs Slattery said she'd promised Mam she'd take care of them?

'All right, Lizzie. Just for tonight. I – I . . . can't face . . . him.'

Lizzie led him back to the kitchen where her mother was sitting staring into the fire.

'Mam, Billy's decided to stay for tonight. He can sleep on the sofa, can't he?'

Brigid looked puzzled. Only a few minutes ago he'd insisted on going back. Then she saw the anger in Lizzie's eyes. 'Of course he can. Run up the stairs. Take a blanket off my bed and the quilt off yours and I'll find something to roll up for a pillow. Sit down, lad, and take off your boots.'

She followed Lizzie into the lobby.

'In the name of God, now what's the matter?'

'Go and look, Mam. He's got the undertakers to come and . . . take her.'

'Not tonight? Sure she's hardly cold!'

'I know. I saw them arrive, that's why I made Billy change his mind and stay. Oh, Mam, is there nothing he won't do? He would have let poor Billy walk into . . . that.'

'There's not a single sin nor piece of wickedness that that man wouldn't do. Go on and get those things, then in the morning I'll tell him what that fiend has done.'

Lizzie nodded wearily. She too was utterly exhausted but she felt better now that she knew Billy wasn't in *that* house.

The following morning, very early, Billy listened to Brigid's soft voice as she explained to him that his mam had been taken to the funeral parlour, to lie in their chapel of rest. When she'd said those words her tone had been cutting. Such insensitivity, such coldness she couldn't comprehend but as the lad had said nothing nor broken down with grief again, she wondered if this was the normal way of going on for them. Sure she hadn't expected the poor woman to be waked, but surely there must be an opportunity for people to pay their respects.

'I'll go . . . go and see her, then I . . . I'll go to work. I won't have time to think at work.'

'They won't mind you taking the day off.'

'No, but I'll have to take another one off for the . . . the funeral.' He choked and Lizzie squeezed his hand.

Joe was in the front room with Celia, trying to comfort her, and was annoyed that someone hadn't sent for him to come home.

'Well, if you're up for it . . .'

Billy nodded. 'I'll go home tonight and see about . . . things. There's a ring . . . I – she – would have liked it to go to you, Mrs Slattery.'

Brigid shook her head firmly. 'No. It should go to our Lizzie. Aren't you engaged already?'

Billy could only nod as Brigid handed him the sandwiches she'd made for him to take with him.

When he'd gone Lizzie turned to Brigid. 'Oh, Mam, I wish he wouldn't go.'

'Ah, maybe it's for the best, Lizzie. He'll not have time to brood. I wonder will your one go to his work today or will he stay at home?'

'Oh, he'll go to work. He won't let little things like his poor wife's death keep him away, the puffed-up no mark!'

'Even though I agree, it's not right for you to speak like that.

He's still Billy's da and it's poor Billy who will have to live with him.'

'I thought you said you were going to look after him?'

'Do you think himself will allow that? Don't be an eejit, Lizzie. All I'll be able for is to keep my eye on him.'

'We could get married, Mam, and find somewhere else to live.'

'And how can you do that with the lad in mourning and under the age of consent and will be for another two years. And that fiend will stick it out until the very last day. He'd make Billy's life purgatory, so he would, if he thought he was going to marry you. You know what he thinks of us, the creature!'

There was no more time to argue, Lizzie thought, she'd be late herself if she didn't get a move on.

Billy came down later that evening to see both his sister and Lizzie. He looked to have more of the run of himself, Brigid thought. He was pale and tired-looking but wasn't that only to be expected? Joe had taken the night off. He'd got in touch with Fred Roberts and explained, and had been told to stay with his wife.

'He's a good bloke. Some foremen would have you in or threaten you with the OBE,' Joe had said.

'And don't we know one who would do just that?' Brigid had replied tartly.

'Sit down, lad. Will I get our Joe to go round to the Elephant and get Paddy McRory to give us a couple of bottles of beer?'

'No, no thanks. I just came to say that the funeral is at ten o'clock on Friday morning, at St George's, and then she's . . . to be buried in the churchyard.'

Brigid nodded. She'd already made up her mind that Annie Milton would have the best wreath she could afford. She knew the whole family would chip in. In a small way it would pay back some of the kindness and courage Annie had shown to her when Dessie had died.

'What time will the carriages be here then?' Celia asked.

'A quarter to ten and it's cars not carriages, and only one for him, Foxy and . . . me.' Billy swallowed hard. He'd fought his first real battle with his da over this, but as usual he'd been shouted down. He'd left the house shaking with anger and frustration.

Celia's eyes widened with horror as the meaning of his words sank in. 'No! No! He can't do this to me, Billy!'

'I tried, Cee. I begged, I shouted, I swore but . . . he said if you . . . go, he'll publicly order you to leave.'

'And there was me thinking he'd sunk to the bottom of the pit of wickedness. Isn't he the lowest of the low? Jesus, Mary and Joseph, he's the devil himself to do this.'

'I'm going up there,' Joe announced as Celia sobbed on Brigid's shoulder. 'I'm going to kill him for this.'

'You are not, Joe Slattery. You will not lower yourself to speak to that creature. Can't you see that's what he wants? Have some pride and let your poor wife here have her dignity. Ah, what will it be anyway? That lot from up there all with faces like soured milk and telling each other what a good little woman she was. What a wonderful wife, what a wonderful housewife. Them that were all spying on her not a week ago. Ah, it's only her poor body they'll be burying, Celia, sure her soul is in heaven now and she's free. Free of pain and misery and free of *him*. Always remember that she'll be looking down and watching over you.'

Celia wiped her eyes and straightened her shoulders. 'I'm all right now, Joe. Ma's right. We'll hang on to our pride and I *know* she's in heaven and that she'll be watching over us.' She caught Joe's hand and held it against her face.

'You promised that Michael would have a happy life and he will. He has us, all of us and a grandma who loves him.'

'And an uncle who loves him too,' Lizzie said, stroking Billy's arm.

Celia smiled at her. 'Then he's got everything he needs.'

PART FOUR

1939

Chapter Twenty-Three

Brigid threw the pan she was scouring back into the sink. She already had a headache and the sound of her daughters' voices didn't help. Michael was going through a fractious stage and both she and Celia had had a very wearying day with him. He, too, was worn out, she thought. But she had a drop of 'Paddy' to put into his bedtime drink, so that should ensure he'd get some sleep tonight. She wiped her hands on her apron and went into the kitchen.

'Right, that's enough out of the pair of you! Give me that mirror now, this very minute. Take it down off that wall, Josie!'

'Mam, I won't be ready to go out. I'll look a fright,' Josie wailed.

'You look a fright anyway and it's *my* turn!' Bernie cried, glaring at her sister.

'In the name of God, will you stop all this? Every time you two are going out we have the same performance. Well, I'm putting the finish to it. Give me the mirror.'

Neither of the two girls moved, but stood glaring at each other.

Josie was seventeen and had gradually been trained and then promoted from the kitchen to the restaurant at the Stork. She was now a qualified waitress and the title 'Silver Service' that she'd long coveted was finally hers. She'd also been courting Davie Dalton from Dorrington Street for a year and, thankfully, it was a match Brigid approved of. Not only was Davie the same religion but he had a decent job, working in Ogden's tobacco factory.

Bernie, at fifteen, was what her mother called a 'bold strap' and her sisters, Lizzie and Josie, had told her she was 'flighty' and a disgrace to the family and further more, no decent lad would look at her with serious intentions if she carried on with all this flirting and making herself cheap.

It was Lizzie who quickly darted in between them and removed the mirror from the wall and handed it to her mother.

'You'd think there was only one mirror in the house! There's the one in our room and one in Cee's room and one in the hall. How many mirrors do you need, for God's sake?'

'That's just it. They're all in someone else's room and it's dark in the lobby.'

Lizzie sighed. 'Then I'll buy you one for your bedroom, then maybe we'll have a bit of peace and quiet on the nights you decide to go out. Personally I think the pair of you are fools, going out when you've work in the morning.'

'You go out and you don't have to be in at ten o'clock,' Josie complained.

'But I usually am on a weekday evening and besides, I'm older and I'm engaged, in case you'd forgotten.'

'Now that's enough! Sure they'll fight over anything, the pair of contrary rossies.'

'Well, at least they won't have the whole house up, Mam, and be waking Michael,' Lizzie replied.

Celia nodded her agreement. Michael was two and was into everything. You'd need eyes in the back of your head for him, Brigid often said.

Celia and Joe were having a rare treat, they were going to the pictures, to the Gaumont at the top of London Road.

Lizzie herself was waiting for Billy to come and collect her for their night out, still a ferry ride to New Brighton. They were saving up as hard as they could, for Billy would be twenty-one in August and Charlie Milton could do nothing at all to prevent them getting married then, and now they had a sizeable amount in their Post Office Savings Bank. Enough to rent a whole house, and there'd be some left for furniture and carpets too.

'What time is Billy coming for you?' Brigid asked.

'Oh, in about half an hour. You know what it's like up there, Mam. There's a row nearly every night.'

Brigid nodded. Ever since Annie had died Billy hated living in that house. He would much sooner have moved in with them but there just wasn't the room and besides, his da was always making it quite clear that he could go nowhere, or do nothing without his permission. Often the rows were furious but Billy was always shouted down and it always ended with 'You'll do as you're told until you're twenty-one!'

Now Emmet too was ready to go out and he too was going to the pictures, with his mates. He felt very grown up having three shillings in his pocket, money he'd earned working as a telegraph boy at the main sorting office in Victoria Street. The rest of his wages he gave to his mother.

It didn't bother him at all that Foxy Milton, who had quietened down a bit, was still at school and would be until he was sixteen, in two years' time. He'd get a Leaving Certificate, then he'd start as an apprentice at Laird's, just as Billy had done.

From the front room there came a fretful wail.

'See now what the pair of you have done! You've woken him up, and his mammy all ready to go out to enjoy herself for a change. You're fiends, the pair of you, and you can both go out looking streelish and it will serve you right!'

Brigid went into Joe and Celia's room and came back into the kitchen with the fair-haired, sleepy toddler that everyone said was the spit of his mother. His cheeks were rosy with sleep.

'Right, Emmet and you two, go out now this minute. Lizzie, I'm sure Celia won't mind if you wait in their room for Billy.'

Lizzie looked annoyed. 'Oh, Mam, you know how I hate it, him coming in the front way and them all glaring and slamming their doors as he walks past.'

'I promised his mam I'd look after him and if they all disapprove that's their business. He'll come to this house the way every other respectable person does, through the front door.'

Brigid then turned to Celia: 'I think you'd better be going off too. It's a lovely evening. You can stroll to the tram stop and if you're here Michael'll start wanting you to nurse him and you'll not get out at all.'

Joe agreed. 'Come on, Cee, Mam's right. We'll stroll down. It's still warm.'

Celia put on her pale blue jacket that looked very smart with her navy skirt and white blouse.

Billy arrived at the time Joe and Celia were halfway down the lobby, so they walked together down the street, which Lizzie didn't mind at all.

Brigid sat in the armchair with her grandson in her arms and began to rock him and hum the lullabies of her childhood. Soon the long blond lashes were closing over his blue eyes. 'Oh, you look so angelic. Sure, your granny in heaven would be proud of you,' Brigid said softly.

Both Celia and Billy had grieved for their mother, but with his father, Billy was almost silent except when there were words between them, usually angry, bitter words on Billy's part.

Brigid remembered how Celia had wept on that beautiful May morning the year before last when Prince Albert, Duke of York, had been crowned King George VI. She'd wept that her mam hadn't been here to see it.

There had been the usual street party, like there had been four years ago for the old King's Jubilee. But this time the Miltons, with the exception of Foxy and his father, had all been down at this end of the street.

They'd listened to all the details on Tessie's wireless, Brigid mused, her mind wandering back.

'In a gold coach, you say, Tessie?' Maggie had asked. They were all darting into the kitchen to make sandwiches and then back out again with them. Only Tessie herself remained stationary and relayed the details. It *was* her wireless, after all.

'Pure gold, the feller said. And drawn by eight grey horses and all them grooms and footmen all in fancy gear.'

'Sure, you'd not be able to get a decent view of them at all if you were in the crowd, not with all those fellers in the way,' Brigid had remarked, en route to the kitchen.

'And the King's robes are in bright red velvet with white ermine.'

'What's "ermine" when it's out?' Biddy Doyle asked.

'Fur. White fur and very expensive. Don't you know anything, Biddy? And the Queen, God bless her, has a gown of ivory satin embroidered all over with real gold thread.'

'Holy God, that must have cost a fortune. What else has she on, Tessie?' Maggie called as she made the return trip.

'An eighteen-foot-long purple velvet train, carried by eight ladies-in-waiting. Imagine: eighteen feet long! Oh, and the little princesses have trains too, fastened by gold tassels. They've white frocks with bows on them and gold crowns on their heads, too, and there's millions out on the streets!' Tessie had finished. Then time had run out. Their own celebrations had been about to start.

Next morning the newspapers had been full of it and had remarked on the presence in the Abbey of Queen Mary.

'Well, fancy that. Her going, the old Queen, the Queen Dowager,' Tessie had called her, for she prided herself on keeping up with these things. 'Breaking with tradition and attending the Coronation, it says here.'

'Well, that's unusual to say the least,' Maggie had remarked.

'And I suppose you remember what Queen Alexandra did last time there was a coronation?' Biddy commented sarcastically.

'Well, hardly anyone had a wireless in those days,' Tessie had retorted. 'Anyway Queen Mary curtsied as he passed her. *Curtsied* to her own son. I think she did that to show everyone how much she approved of him,' Tessie had said sanctimoniously.

'And of how much she doesn't care for the carry-on out of the other two. What's that saying that Simpson woman has, Tessie?' Brigid had asked.

'You can never be too rich or too thin,' Tessie supplied with a sniff of displeasure.

'She's a bag of bones and she'll be all through his money the way she's going on with all the jewellery he buys her, and very tasteless some of it is too.'

'Ah, Mam, it's not! It's modern and dead gorgeous,' Josie had remarked, and had been told that no one was interested in her opinions about *that* woman's jewellery.

Brigid didn't take much notice of what was going on outside her own family and neighbourhood, but now everyone was saying that there was bound to be a war, never mind Mr Chamberlain going over to see that Mr Hitler and coming back with a piece of paper and giving out about 'Peace in our time'. Joe had said everyone knew it was only a matter of time, and that worried her. She'd lost a brother who'd up and joined the Dublin Fusiliers in the last war. His name was amongst those on the Fusiliers Arch that led into St Stephen's Green at the Grafton Street corner.

Joe said Laird's order book was full of ships for the Navy. Fergal was working on the new T-class submarine, HMS *Trident*, and alongside it HMS *Taku* was rising rapidly from her keel blocks. Billy, Joe and Charlie Milton had all been working on the completed HMS *Thetis*, whose sea trials would begin tomorrow, the first of June.

Financially they were all far better off now, Brigid reflected. She had five wages coming in and Joe had made her give up her two evenings a week cleaning in India Building. The house was far tidier, there were far more comforts and she and Celia between them had the place like a palace most of the time. She was a great organiser, was Celia, Brigid thought as she nursed Michael. She'd slowly got everyone to put things belonging to them away. Either in their bedrooms or in the downstairs cupboards.

She looked around, remembering how this kitchen had looked when poor Dessie had been alive. He wouldn't recognise it now.

There was a crisp white curtain over the window and dark-green draw curtains which kept out the draught in winter. Joe had distempered the room, which had caused great upheavals at the time, but the result was worth it. There was a nice shade over the light bulb, new lino and a rug in front of the range that these days gleamed with black lead. The old sofa and easy chair had been replaced by four armchairs, which didn't take up as much space and could be easily moved around. She had a new table and proper chairs with green cushions on their seats, tied on with tapes.

There was carpet on the lobby and up the stairs. She had a dresser on which was displayed blue delftware, similar to that in Annie's house. Celia had begged Joe to buy the same design for she knew that until the day he died her father would never give her a single thing with which to remember her mother by.

Celia insisted that Lizzie wore the small diamond and garnet ring that had been Annie's engagement ring. Celia and Joe's room was always so clean and tidy and Michael slept in a cot beside their bed. Her children hadn't been as fortunate. When they'd been very young they'd slept in an old drawer and then in with Dessie and herself and then finally upstairs with their sisters and brothers.

Brigid looked down at the child and smiled. He was fast asleep. Ah, well, let him sleep in her arms for once, instead of putting him in his cot in that front room.

Joe and Celia walked companionably with Lizzie and Billy.

'Oh, thank God to be out. Sometimes it's like a raving lunatic asylum in there, and our Bernie's getting too hard-faced by far. Mam's going to have trouble with that little madam before long,' Lizzie said grimly.

'No she won't, because I'm going to have a talk with her, put the fear of God into her. Mam's had enough to contend with and now she's got a bit of financial security, I want her to take things easy. So our Bernie can toe the line.'

'Well, at least Josie's not much trouble. Ma likes Davie and she's done great at work,' Celia said.

'Even our Emmet's getting better now he's working and in two months' time we'll have a place of our own. I've got everyone to keep their ears open – Tessie Mulhinney, Maggie Walsh, Biddy Doyle, Mary Kelly. So I won't be a burden to Mam for much longer and there'll be more room for everyone.'

'You're hardly taking up the space of three people, Lizzie,' Billy laughed, looking down at his slight, slim fiancée. He, too, couldn't wait to get a place of his own. He hated Da and he had nothing at all in common with his younger brother, who was turning out to be a really bright lad. Foxy would make a good skilled man, probably a foreman even. He was sharp enough anyway.

'It's just nice to be able to have a night off,' Joe remarked.

Celia looked up at him. 'Do you think there *is* going to be a war, Joe?'

'It's shaping up that way. We're not killing ourselves turning out battleships, flotilla leaders and submarines for the fun of it. There's hardly a yard in the country that's building merchant ships now. I was going to tell you later, but I might as well tell you now. Fred Roberts has put me forward, with himself, to be on the *Thetis* for the sea trials. We go tomorrow morning, that's why I'm off tonight.'

Celia looked taken aback. 'Why you?'

'Because there are only twenty-six of us going to check things, see everything is all right before the Navy officially accepts delivery of her. It's a great chance, Cee. A great honour, I suppose you'd call it.'

'What about you?' Lizzie asked Billy.

'Well, I was going to tell you later, but now Joe's let the cat out of the bag . . . I'm going too.'

'What if your da goes as well, Billy?' Lizzie asked, looking at Joe.

'As far as I know he isn't going. I think Mr Tyson thinks he'll start throwing his weight around, and the brass from the Navy on board wouldn't wear it,' Joe answered.

'Have you two actually set a date yet?' Celia changed the subject.

'Yes, the twenty-sixth of August. The first Saturday after Billy's birthday. Father Minehan has already written to the Archbishop but he said it might be more difficult for me. It might be seen as "opening the floodgates", that's the expression he used.'

'Oh, you'll get it, Lizzie, you will. Are you having the full works?' Celia asked, while Joe and Billy raised their eyes skywards.

'I'm having a white dress and veil and flowers and a bit of a do afterwards, but we don't want to spend too much. We'll need it for furniture. And I won't let Mam pay for anything. All her life she's spent the money she had on us, so I told her she could spend what she wanted to give us on a new outfit. Something of her own for a change and not borrowed from Tessie.'

'What about Josie and Bernie?'

'What about them?'

'You're not having them as bridesmaids?'

'No. They'd do nothing but argue and bicker.'

'You'll have to have someone to stand for you, Lizzie.'

'I know and I'll have you. I stood for you.'

'Lizzie, there'll be murder, you know there will. They'll have Ma demented and there'll be more rows.'

'Oh, all right, I'll have the pair of them, but only if they pay for their own dresses and not fight all the time. Will you say something to them, Joe, about behaving? They take notice of you. Well, our Bernie does. Josie's not too bad. Tell her that if there's any messing about then when she and Davie finally get to the church I'll refuse to be matron of honour and the whole parish will want to know why. Including his ma, who she says is a holy terror and she's glad they won't have to live with her. Her mind's set on a place of their own.'

Celia looked up at Joe and smiled. They both knew they'd not have a place of their own until the girls and Emmet married and Brigid died. That was the way of things and they'd accepted it.

* * *

Later that night, when Billy let himself into the house, Charlie was still up reading the newspaper, and Billy broached the subject of his not being chosen to be aboard the *Thetis* for her sea trials. The answer he got shocked and infuriated him.

'I know you asked Ernie Whittaker – he told me – and I saw your name on the list Mr Tyson had for selection. I pointed out to Mr Tyson that you weren't experienced enough and that I should go instead. It was preposterous you going. I know you're skilled, but I've more experience and I'm a foreman.'

Billy was furious. 'You did what?'

'I asked Mr Tyson to take your name off and add mine.'

'And has he?' Billy could hardly contain himself.

'Yes, he saw the sense in it. Did no one tell you?'

'You know bloody well they didn't. Joe Slattery's going, and Harry Kemp. You had no right, no bloody right, Da, to do that! To even go over Mr Whittaker's head.'

'You're under age.'

'Only for another two months, thank God! I just can't believe you. You knew how much I wanted to go.'

'You never said to me you wanted to go.'

'Do I have to ask for every bloody thing?'

'Stop that swearing.'

'Ah, to hell with you, you pompous get!'

Charlie raised his hand, his face puce. Things had deteriorated lately but Billy had never sworn much. It was the lad's association with the Slatterys.

'Go on, Da, belt me and just see where it gets you. Joe Slattery laid you out after the fire and Mrs Slattery has belted you on a few occasions, so don't think I'm scared of you now because I'm bloody not! It'll be me who lays you out this time.'

Charlie dropped his arm as Billy snatched up his jacket and cap.

'Where the hell do you think you're going?'

'Out. Away. Away from you. I'm sick of you. I'm sick of the way you treated Mam and Celia. The way you've terrified me and our Foxy for most of our lives, and now you've started interfering with my job. Well, I've had enough.'

'So where are you running to then? To your so-called fiancée? That little red-haired tart?'

Billy glared at him. 'In two months I'll be rid of you. I'll never forget everything you've done as long as I live. I hate you. I really hate you.' Billy opened the door.

'Oh, go to hell!' Charlie yelled after him but all he got in reply was the loud slamming of the door.

Filled with rage and disappointment Billy forgot about everything. He just walked and walked and at length found himself outside the Astoria picture house at the bottom of Royal Street. An empty tram was approaching the stop and he glanced up at the destination board: Fazakerley, the furthest suburb of the city. That would do. He just wanted to get as far away from his da and Lizzie and Joe as possible because humiliation was added to his other seething emotions.

He paid his fare and sat brooding in silence. Looking back over his entire life, he could see now just how his father had ruled and manipulated him. His poor mam had been too timid and too terrified to try to save both himself and Celia from the beatings and the cruelty.

They'd both been sent to bed with their legs stinging from the slaps, and nothing to eat was ever brought up to them. They'd have to go all night until breakfast next morning. Once he'd been shut in the small, dark, cobweb-festooned coal place, just off the scullery. He'd been terrified of the dark and of the spiders he knew were lurking in the corners. He'd screamed and screamed, begged and pleaded, but to no avail. Even to this day he couldn't remember how long he'd been in there, but he'd had nightmares for months afterwards.

Then there was Lizzie. He was sick of all the bigotry, he just wanted to be with Lizzie, somewhere on their own, and then for the first time in his life he'd be really happy. But now that the end was nearly in sight his da had cruelly triumphed again by having his name removed from the list of men who were to be aboard the sea trials of this new class of submarine on which he'd worked so hard.

Billy didn't notice the houses getting further and further apart. They'd passed Walton Hospital, gone under the railway bridge at Rice Lane, taken the right-hand fork of the road at the Black Bull pub at the end of Walton Vale. They'd passed the cemetery, and Fazakerley Sanatorium and the next thing he knew was the conductor shaking him.

'We've arrived at the terminus, lad. We don't go no further an' this is the last trip, the last tram until morning.'

Billy got up, thanked him and got off. The night air was warm so he took off his jacket and slung it over his shoulder. Ahead of him there was just darkness with the lights from a house or a pub dotted here and there in the distance. He could make out a lane so he followed it. Perhaps he could get to a house or a pub where he could stay.

Why had Da done it? He was sure it wasn't anything to do with being a foreman and therefore more experienced. All Da ever did all day was chase around after other people to make sure they were doing their job and were not skiving off to smoke or brew up. These days he never really did much work himself. It was just spite, pure spite and jealousy and hatred of Lizzie, her mam and the entire family, including his own grandson. His da didn't want him to appear successful. He supposed that in his da's mind it was somehow taking away something of his own position. Stealing his thunder, so to speak.

He sat down on a patch of grass at the side of the lane and lit a cigarette. Something else Da didn't approve of. He could hear the sounds of the countryside at night. The rustling in the hedgerow, the scuttling of tiny feet, the bark of what he assumed was a fox and then birdsong. A nightingale it must be, they were the only ones he'd heard of that sang at night.

It wasn't fair. It just wasn't bloody fair. Joe was going and Harry Kemp. He knew Fergal had wanted to go but he stood no chance, he was only a labourer.

He got up and walked on, seeing ahead of him the dim tower of a church against the dusky sky.

Before he reached the church the lane veered off and led to a row of stone cottages, and Billy searched around in his pocket to see what money he had. Thirty shillings. He'd see if he could buy something to eat and drink and a place to sleep, even if it was only a barn. It was a warm night.

He wiped his face with his handkerchief, replaced his jacket and cap and knocked on the door of the first cottage. A woman opened it, eventually. She was older than Celia and Lizzie and held a bowl and a tea towel in her hands.

'I'm sorry to bother you so late, but I'm sort of lost and I was wondering if you could tell me where I could buy something to eat and drink and maybe a place to sleep?'

She smiled at him. 'You'll not get anything around here, lad, at this time of night. The inn's shut.'

'Oh. Then I wonder if . . . if you could give me a glass of water. I don't mind paying you for your trouble.'

'There's no need to pay me for that. Go round to the back, there's a pump there. You can give your face a swill and I'll bring something out for you.'

He thanked her and went in the direction she pointed. The yard at the back was obviously a communal one. On three sides there were outbuildings and somewhere nearby was a henhouse; he could hear the muted clucking.

He threw his jacket and cap over a stone gatepost, rolled up his shirt sleeves and began to move the handle up and down until the cold water came splashing down into the stone trough. Oh, it was great, he thought. The cool, clear water was so refreshing. Careless of his stiff collar he put his head under the flow, then tried vigorously to shake most of the water from his hair.

'It'll take hours to dry like that, lad. Here, use this. I saw you from the kitchen window.'

The young woman held out a towel and he thanked her and then towelled his hair. She then passed him a large glass of water which he gulped down.

'You're from Liverpool, I can tell by your accent.'

'Where am I? What's this place?' he asked. Her accent was a country one.

'Kirkby, part of the estate of the Earl of Derby. He owns everything around here, but he's a good landlord. What's your name?'

'Billy Milton.'

'So, Billy Milton, what are you doing out here in a strange place and in the pitch-dark?'

'I – I had an argument with my da, a really bad one. My mam's dead so I just walked out. I walked the streets for a bit, then I got a tram and then I just walked again.'

She studied him in silence for a few seconds until she made up her mind.

'You can come in and I'll find something for supper and you can stay with us. There's me and my husband, John, and his old grandfather. He's ninety but as spry as they come. He's just a bit deaf, that's all. He swears that was the fault of the war. Not the Great War, the Boer War, out in South Africa. It was the noise of the big guns at Ladysmith. He was an old fool my ma-in-law used to say to him, going off like that at his age. He were fifty then. For the Lord's sake don't start him off on his old tales or we'll be up all night.'

Gratefully Billy followed her into a neat but very plain kitchen where the table was set for breakfast. By the open range a wizened old man sat smoking a clay pipe. A younger man was sitting at the table pouring ale out of a big white enamel jug.

'This here's John Wilson, my husband. We're tenants. We grow corn, wheat and some barley and we've a few hens and cattle. This lad's come all the way out here from Liverpool. Had a row with his father, he has. I said he could stay with us and I'll find him some supper.

'"If we turn away strangers in trouble from our door then we ourselves may be turned away from the gates of heaven,"' she quoted. 'Wasn't that what the vicar said in his sermon last Sunday, John?'

Her husband nodded as Billy took the large, work-roughened hand that was extended to him.

'Sit down there, lad. Pop will be going to bed soon. If you want to talk to him you'll have to shout a bit.'

'Yes, your wife told me. Look, you're being very kind. I must pay for all this.'

'You'll not pay for food in this house, not when there's plenty, and you can stay as long as you like. I'll drive you to the tram in the wagon.'

'No, honestly, I'll have to go back in the morning. I . . . I've work to go to.'

'Well, we'll see,' John Wilson said, pouring out another glass of ale and offering it to Billy. 'What work is it you do then?'

Billy started to explain.

He hadn't walked back for the tram and neither had John driven him to Fazakerley in the morning. After the scratch meal of bread and cheese and a few more glasses of home-brewed ale, he'd got talking to John and told him about his job, his father, his mam and Lizzie. John Wilson was a silent and sympathetic listener and somehow it was easy to talk to a complete stranger. There were things he could divulge to this man that he would never have dreamed of telling Celia or Lizzie or Joe even.

He'd felt just a bit dizzy when he got up and John Wilson had helped him up the stairs where a mattress had been put on the floor beside the bed the old man was by then asleep in.

He'd forgotten his da and the fact that he was supposed to be in work the following morning, the morning the *Thetis* was to start her sea trials.

Chapter Twenty-Four

Next morning, Celia, with Michael in her arms, went to the front door to see Joe off.

'What time will you be back?'

'I've no idea, luv. It could be tonight or even tomorrow.' Joe stroked the chubby cheek of his son, who made a grab for his cap and said, 'Da-da.' Joe laughed.

'Will they give you something to eat? You've only your carry-out for lunch today.'

'Oh, they'll feed us. There's two fellers from the City Catering Ltd on board.'

'Won't that be for the men from the Admiralty?'

'Yes, but we'll get something too. Stop worrying, Cee. I'll be fine. I'm really looking forward to it. I helped to build her and it's not often that the likes of me have a chance to actually sail in a ship I've helped build. It's the chance of a lifetime. That's why we're going: to see that everything works and it will. It's a great thing getting orders from the Navy. It keeps us in work and we've had to take on more people too.'

She reached up and kissed him. 'Take care.'

'I will, and don't let meladdo here run you ragged with his antics.'

Celia laughed and then stood on the step watching as he walked down the street that was bathed in the early morning June sunlight.

Harry Kemp passed her, acknowledging her with a nod of his head, still in a world of his own. He'd never really got over the shock of Richie's death, Celia thought sadly.

She looked up the street and saw Maudie standing on her step too. She made no attempt to speak or even recognise the woman's presence by a gesture of any kind.

Maudie Kemp had been no real friend to her mam. She'd always been jealous of Annie. She was always willing to make mischief and cause rows. Oh, she'd let them stay in her house after the fire but Celia knew her da had paid well for the accommodation and board. She'd never forgive Maudie for spying on her mam before Annie had died. When she saw her Da come out she turned abruptly away and closed the door. There was nothing she wanted to say to him.

'Have they all gone?' Lizzie asked, coming down the stairs.

'Yes.'

'Was Billy with them?'

'I don't know, Lizzie. I didn't wait to see. As soon as I saw Da I came in and shut the door.

Lizzie sighed. 'He's probably already gone. He was full of it. How great it would be rubbing shoulders with all the brass from the Admiralty. Feeling he was actually part of something really important. He was made up, especially as our Joe's gone, too.' She glanced at her watch. 'Well, I'd better start and make an effort or I'll be late myself.'

On his way to the yard by tram and train Joe looked for Billy but could see no sign of him. That wasn't unusual, for unless you stuck together all the time you easily got separated. All forms of transport were crowded at this time in the morning.

He reported to his foreman as soon as he arrived.

'All set, lad? We'll be off in fifteen minutes.'

'I am. Have you seen anything of Billy Milton, boss? He was saying last night that he'd had his name put forward.'

'He's not going,' Fred Roberts stated grimly.

Joe was surprised. 'Why?'

'Because his bloody father told Tyson to take his name off the list and persuaded Tyson to let him go instead. Ernie Whittaker was fuming. Milton had gone over his head and Ernie didn't mince his words either, I can tell you.'

'He'll do anything to upset Billy. Anything. Soon he'll be twenty-one and then he'll have his freedom. Still, we'll have to put up with him.'

'I wouldn't blame the lad if he belted the old get for this. He's a nasty piece of work, is Milton, and everyone knows it. I can't understand Tyson, not after that performance over young Kemp's accident.'

'Ours not to reason why, boss.'

'Ours just to do as we're bloody well told.'

They both left to join the group that had assembled outside the head foreman's office.

'How many of them are there? The brass, I mean?'

'There's Lieutenant-Commander Bolus, Lieutenant Woods – he's the Torpedo Officer – and fifty-three others including a couple of stokers.'

'What do they want a stoker for? She's not coal-fired; hardly any ship is coal-fired these days.'

'Beats me. You'd have to be a bloody genius to work out what's going on in their minds.'

They waited, chatting to the other Laird's men that were going until the naval party, plus the other dignitaries and observers emerged, and they followed.

The tug *Grebecock* was to be their escort.

When Celia had gone back indoors the usual chaos reigned and she sighed. It would be so much easier if they all got ready for work in their rooms and then came down to an orderly breakfast, but there was no bathroom, no other sink of any kind except the one in the scullery, which was fought over each morning and often in the evenings as well.

She'd even tried to get them to use a bowl and pitcher as she did, filling the pitcher with water from the kettle, but they'd refused and Brigid had sided with them.

'Ah, won't it be double the work, Celia? All that running around with water, up and down the stairs and they'd still be fighting and someone is bound to get scalded.'

Brigid was now yelling instructions and dragging things down from the rack and throwing them at their owners.

'God in heaven! Aren't I heart-scalded every day with this carry-on?'

Celia smiled. 'Here, Ma, you nurse him while I get this lot sorted out.' She passed her son over to his grandmother.

Brigid sank gratefully into an armchair and tried to keep the struggling toddler on her lap.

Celia got down to business.

'Right, Emmet, you're ready so off you go. I've left sixpence on the dresser, you can buy your lunch today.'

'I told you, Celia, it's a waste of good money. He'll spend it on some cheap rubbish and then buy a couple of loosies and a match.' She glared at her youngest son. 'Don't I know full well that you smoke, Emmet Slattery? You reek of it and at your age it's a disgrace. If your da were here . . .'

Emmet snatched up the money and his uniform cap and fled.

'Josie, I've ironed your apron, cuffs and cap and they've been starched.'

'Oh, thanks, Cee. I didn't have time last night. Sometimes you can borrow someone else's, but not often.'

'You would have had the time if you hadn't gone gallivanting,' her mother reminded her.

'Bernie, your carry-out is on the table and your jacket's over the chair.'

'Why can't I have money for my lunch too?' Bernie demanded, her tone disgruntled. She worked in Woolworth's in Church Street.

'Because you'd not buy anything to eat at all. You'd spend it on make-up, cheap scent and cigarettes, that's why. Oh, I'm up with you and your way of going on, Bernadette Slattery, and you only fifteen. You'd spend the lot in that place you work in if you got half a chance,' Brigid fulminated.

Bernie stormed out, slamming the door behind her.

'That one has the heart across me.'

'Take no notice, Ma. Joe's going to give her a good talking-to.'

'It's the back of his hand that one needs. She gets away with murder, so she does, and she'll be the death of me with her antics.'

'She won't, Ma. She's just a bit rebellious.'

'Well, the other two weren't rebellious.'

'Everyone's different,' Celia smiled as Lizzie came dashing down the stairs.

'Oh, look at the flaming time! I'll have to run all the way and I'll look as though I've been pulled through a hedge.'

'A furze hedge with the state of that hair,' Brigid remarked.

'He'll have a right cob on if I'm late.'

Celia grinned at her. 'He's not changed then?'

Lizzie rolled her eyes to the ceiling as she crammed a piece of toast into her mouth and left.

'Now she'll have the indigestion all day, rushing her food like that.'

'I'll put the kettle on and we'll have a cuppa before we start.'

Brigid sighed. 'You know I don't know what I'd do without you, Cee, I really don't. I'm getting too old for all this. Haven't you them all organised, or as organised as they'll ever be? I'll give himself here his breakfast first. He's like a bag of eels and the temper on him too.'

'Well, he doesn't get that from me, Ma.'

Brigid smiled. 'Ah no, he wouldn't. It's the Irish blood in him.'

The weather was good so there was not much pitching and rolling as the *Thetis* headed out for Liverpool Bay. Inside, too, things were going smoothly. Mr Johnson and Mr Costain watched as the

Laird's men, instructed by their Royal Navy counterparts, got to grips with all the gauges and valves and levers.

It was hot. Joe wiped his forehead with his handkerchief. The heat was something he hadn't even thought of. It was also very cramped. He had to bow his head most of the time or he'd strike it on a bulkhead, and there were pipes and cables and wires everywhere. Somehow he'd thought they would have been boxed in and that there would have been more room when she'd been finished. It was an illusion that had quickly been dispelled.

'I'm sorry I flaming well offered now. Christ, I don't know how they all stick it. You can't move and you're falling over bloody pipes and cables. It didn't seem this small or this crowded when she was on the slipway,' Fred Roberts grumbled.

'No, it's odd, isn't it? I mean she *did* look much bigger. I thought she *was* actually bigger, being a new class of sub,' Joe replied.

'New or old they can bloody well keep her. It'd give a feller claustrophobia.'

'What's that?'

'Fear of being shut into small spaces,' Fred replied.

'I'm used to that then. Our kitchen's a small space with everyone in it all talking and shouting. Now that's what *I'd* call claustrophobia. I wonder what it will feel like when we dive. Sailing under and not across the bay?'

'Well, whatever it's like I hope Charlie Milton hates it, the miserable bastard. Billy should have come, not him. The lad's only just starting his career; Milton's is bloody near finished.'

Joe nodded. Billy would be devastated.

Billy was more than devastated. He woke with a hangover of monumental proportions in the small stone room where he'd spent the night. Sunlight was streaming in through the curtains and there was no sign of the old man.

He groaned as he tried to get up, levering himself on to one elbow. His head felt as though it were about to blow apart and he was very queasy. What the hell had been in that ale? Was it even ale at all, or was it some illegal brew they made themselves? He couldn't bear the sunlight, so holding his head, he went slowly, very slowly downstairs.

'Oh God, you look terrible, lad.' Kate Wilson was baking. The scrubbed table was covered in flour and she was up to her elbows in it. The old man was sitting by the fire and the room was stifling hot.

'I feel terrible. What was in that stuff, Kate?'

'Only good hops, but you're not used to drinking real ale. It's not like the stuff they serve you in pubs in Liverpool. Get back upstairs and I'll bring you something up. It's a cure, my own mam's recipe, and it's never been known to fail.'

Thankfully Billy crawled back to the bedroom and flung open the window but kept the cheap cotton curtains closed. He eased himself down on the mattress and closed his eyes.

In five minutes Kate was beside him with a glass in her hand.

Billy opened one eye and looked at it.

'What's in it?'

She laughed. 'If I were to tell you, you'd think I was trying to poison you. Drink it down now all in one gulp.'

Billy looked at it with suspicion, then did as she'd bidden him. It tasted awful and he gagged but managed to keep it down.

'Now lie down. You'll sleep again and then later, when you've got some food in your stomach, John'll take you for the tram.'

Billy groaned again. 'Oh God, I'd forgotten about work.'

'Will they sack you for having the day off?'

'I don't think so, but you never know.'

'Oh, you'll soon get another job, a fine lad like you.'

Billy closed his eyes. He'd never felt as bad as this in his entire life.

The tests on the *Thetis* were progressing well. There seemed to be nothing amiss anywhere. The dignitaries looked at their watches and Lieutenant-Commander Bolus gave the order to dive. It was two o'clock.

'What's up, sir?' Fred Roberts asked Lieutenant Woods, who seemed unhappy about something.

'Not a great deal. It's not unusual to be trimmed light on a first dive. No cause for anxiety.' He turned away, having decided to check the interiors of all six torpedo tubes.

'Are you feeling OK, boss?' Joe asked Fred, who looked slightly green.

'I'm fine, lad. Get back over there before someone decides to put us on a charge or something.'

'We're not Royal Navy.'

'I know but that won't make any difference to them. If they start chucking their weight around we could all lose our jobs.'

'How long will we be down?'

'God knows. I hope it won't be long and I hope they don't start on any antics like they do with aeroplanes. Rolling over, flying upside down. Oh, I've seen them. Mad they are. Stark raving mad. So I hope these fellers haven't got any ideas like that.'

It didn't bother Joe but it was obviously bothering his foreman a great deal.

It was bothering Lieutenant Woods, too. All the tubes were empty, except number six, which was half full. He cursed. Now he'd have to inspect the bow cap indicators that were situated between the two banks of tubes.

'Leading Seaman Hambrook, check all the bow cap levers. Make sure they're set to "Shut".'

'All correct, sir,' Hambrook, a senior torpedo rating, yelled back.

'Right, open the tubes, one at a time.'

The man did as he was bid. 'Sir, the lever to number five is stiff.'

'Push it harder then.'

'Jesus! There's water spraying out, sir! The bloody tube is full!'

The next instant both Hambrook and the door were flung aside and water flooded into the space.

'Sir, number five tube is open,' Woods shouted to Bolus.

'Blow the main ballast and take her to the surface, Lieutenant-Commander Bolus ordered.

Woods, Hambrook and the torpedo party fought to close the one water-tight door in the bulkhead that wasn't clipped shut.

'The turn buckle's jammed, sir!' Hambrook cried. It didn't help that there were eighteen of the bloody things even though the rest were shut.

'Everyone back into the accommodation area!' Woods bellowed, praying that the second water-tight bulkhead door, which had a fast turning wheel to close it, would stop the flood.

The submarine hit the bottom of the seabed and everyone was flung down to the bow end. Fred Roberts clutched Joe's arm.

'Oh, Jesus Christ! There's something gone wrong! We're being flooded.'

A Royal Navy stoker looked at him hard. 'Don't you bloody well start to panic or it'll spread. The Commander wasn't born yesterday. He'll get it sorted out.'

'Aye, well there's twice the number of people in here than she was built to carry. I know. I helped to bloody build her.'

'You stick to your trade and we'll stick to ours. The Commander will have us up in no time.'

Joe wanted to believe him yet he couldn't stop thinking of Celia and Michael. The only consolation was that Charlie Milton looked terrified out of his wits.

When Billy awoke again it was early evening. Dusk was falling but he felt completely better. Whatever it was Kate Wilson had given him had worked, but he'd been asleep nearly all day. He'd better get back or Lizzie would be worried. He doubted his da had given him a second thought.

'I see you're fit and well again, Billy,' Kate smiled at him.

'I don't know what was in your mam's recipe but it worked.'

'It always does.'

'I'll have to get back. Lizzie, my girl, will be worried sick about me.'

'Ah, you told us all about her last night. She sounds a grand lass.'

'Did I?'

Kate nodded.

'I can't remember half of what I said last night. You must think I'm a right fool.'

'No, we were interested. John's around the back. I'll go and fetch him.'

'Thanks.' When she'd gone he placed ten shillings on the mantel over the range. They'd been so good to him that he just couldn't go without leaving something and he knew they'd refuse if he tried to press it on them.

He looked at the large clock mounted on the wall. Unbelievably it was a quarter to six. Lizzie would be finishing work in fifteen minutes.

The old man was fiddling with the knobs on the wireless that was emitting a variety of strange noises at maximum volume, then suddenly a voice boomed out stating that HMS *Thetis* was in trouble. Apparently she'd not surfaced after her first dive. Billy's face drained of all colour. Oh God! Joe! Joe was aboard!

He ran from the room to look for John Wilson. He had to get home as quickly as possible. He'd pay the man to take him all the way.

Chapter Twenty-Five

John Wilson had driven Billy to the junction of Netherfield Road North and St George's Hill, a busy junction at the best of times.

'It'll be all right from here. I can run the rest of the way, it'll be quicker.'

'I'd say that's your best plan, lad, what with all this traffic.'

Billy shook his hand. 'I'll never forget how good you've been to me, John, I swear to God I won't.'

He stuffed a pound note, the last of his money, into the man's hand, jumped down and ran before there could be an argument over it.

He had to get home now, he just had to. He had to find out just how things stood, what exactly had happened and whether Joe was safe. If Celia didn't know she'd be demented.

He didn't see the lorry until it was too late. The driver tried to swerve but there wasn't room, there was too much traffic in the way. All Billy saw was the slatted metal grille of the radiator, then he felt as though he'd had the breath knocked out of him, and then darkness.

When he came to, John Wilson and a policeman were bending over him and a small crowd had gathered. One man looked ashen and Billy knew he must be the driver of the lorry.

'What . . . happened?'

'Lie still. You ran straight into the path of a lorry,' the police constable informed him.

He tried to get up. 'I can't lie still. I just can't lie here, I've got to get home. It's only down the road. I've got to get home!'

'The only place you're going now, Billy, is hospital.'

'No! John, you know what happened. Kate heard it. You know why I can't go to hospital.'

'Aye, but you'll be no use to your lass or anyone else if you suddenly drop dead. You hit your head on the cobbles, lad.'

Billy was shaking and he felt dizzy and sick as the two men helped him to his feet.

'I'll drive him there. I'll take it easy.'

The constable looked perturbed. 'I've to report all accidents.'

'Well, report it after the lad's in safer hands than ours.'

The constable explained the situation to the sister on duty, a large woman who, with her winged and pleated cap, looked like the figurehead of a ship under sail. Her manner was stern and intimidating and John muttered to himself that she'd be a terror to work for. She called two nurses, one of whom she ordered away to fetch a doctor, the other one she directed to help John to get Billy into a cubicle to wait to see the doctor. Then she pulled the curtain around it.

Both men waited outside, or at least the policeman did to start with.

'You'll both have to wait in the waiting room, if you please,' Sister informed them in a very brusque manner.

'I can't do that, Sister. He's been in a road accident. I saw it and I'll have to remain here until someone relieves me so that I can write out a report.'

The woman pursed her lips and glared at him. 'I'll phone your station. This is most irregular indeed.' She walked away down the corridor, her starched apron crackling.

After half an hour John decided he'd had enough of this waiting about. He got up and went through to where Billy was lying. He'd seen another policeman arrive and the original one leave.

'How is he?' John asked the newcomer whom he'd seen talking with the sister.

'I don't know. The female dragon back there wouldn't let me near him.'

'Well, she won't get me out so easily. Is the doctor in there with him?' John asked.

'I think so,' was the slightly off-hand reply.

'God help us all if that's the attitude of the modern constabulary,' John muttered before pulling aside the curtain.

The doctor who had been examining Billy looked up.

'Who are you?' he asked sharply.

'A friend. I drove him to St George's Hill.'

'It's a pity you didn't drive him home, then this would never have happened. There's far too much traffic on the roads these days.'

John ignored the man and the outraged sister. Billy didn't look well.

'Will you tell him I've got to get home?' he said. 'For God's sake make them understand, John. I keep saying it's important but they keep trying to shut me up.'

'You, young man, are going nowhere tonight. You hit your head and you blacked out. We'll have to keep you in for observation. We don't know what damage that fall could have caused. At best you may be concussed.'

Billy sat up. 'I'm *not* staying here. I *can't* stay here all night! I've *got* to get home!'

'Sister! This patient is becoming very agitated and it's not at all good for him. We'll keep him overnight but I think a sedative is called for.'

The sister nodded and turned to John with a face like thunder.

'Just what do you think you're doing in here? I said you were to wait outside in the waiting room, or better still, take yourself off home.'

John glared at her then went back to wait but a nurse told him he was wasting his time.

She smiled at him. 'They've given him something to make him

sleep. It'll be tomorrow before you can see him.'

'I'll wait.'

'There's no point. He'll be out cold until tomorrow morning. Are you a relative?'

'No, just an acquaintance.'

'Look, why don't you go home? The constable there will give you a phone number to call in the morning.'

Reluctantly John agreed. He couldn't sit here all night. Kate would be worried and he couldn't leave the horse, who by now would need watering. It was a long way home.

Tessie dropped the plate she was drying and it smashed to pieces on the kitchen floor. She ignored it and, dragging off her apron, went as fast as she could across the road to number twelve.

Brigid opened the door.

'Oh God, Brigid, have you heard?'

'And just what is it I'm supposed to have heard, Tessie?'

'Get in that kitchen and sit down. Where's Celia and Lizzie?'

'Both in the kitchen. What's the matter now?'

Both girls were sitting at the table and Tessie thought sadly that those smiles on those happy faces would last only a few moments longer.

'I . . . I heard on the wireless that the *Thetis* is in trouble. She dived and didn't come up.'

'Oh, Mother of God! Is that all it said, Tessie?' Brigid questioned.

'Yes.'

Brigid looked at the two girls and her heart turned over, but she had to be practical. 'Get your things, we're going over there. There's bound to be someone there who knows what's going on.'

A cold fear gripped all their hearts. Brigid was worried for her son, Celia for her husband and Lizzie for Billy. She'd called at their house on the way home, something she never did, and had got no answer at all so she assumed Billy had gone and that Foxy was with the Kemp twins. She'd been so glad that Billy had gone. She'd been so proud to think that he too had been chosen. He'd have been so disappointed otherwise.

None of them spoke all the way over to the yard but Brigid noted that there were far more women of all ages on the tram and train than there usually were. At this time of night they'd be putting their menfolk's meal on the table in front of them. Oh, God help me! she prayed silently, because she knew if anything awful happened, she'd be the one both the girls would turn to.

They weren't surprised when they reached the yard gates to find them closed. A crowd of women and men stood waiting outside, all with worried faces. There were women like herself, with sons out there. Women like Celia with babies in their arms and crying, bewildered toddlers clinging to their skirts. Girls like Lizzie, obviously waiting for news of a sweetheart or brother, and they all had something in common: they were all afraid and they all had anguish in their eyes.

'Has there been anything? Anything at all?' Brigid asked the person nearest to her, a woman of her own age.

'Nothing. Not a flaming word. I've been here since four o'clock and they let the day shift out early and closed the gates half an hour ago. It's going to be a long wait because I'm going to stop here all night if I have to. My husband's on it.'

'I'm staying too,' Celia announced, holding Michael tightly to her. Oh dear Lord, if anything happened to Joe what would she do? Everything they'd overcome, all the barriers they'd broken down and crossed, would have been in vain. All the heartache she'd suffered losing her mam would have been for nothing.

Lizzie kept silent. She looked pale and drawn, and her hand went instinctively to the gold locket Billy had given her, before he gave her his mam's ring. She was staying too.

They waited and waited. The June evening descended in a warm dusk and the North Star was clearly visible. They talked in lowered voices, trying to find reasons and explanations, all trying to bolster each other up. Other women arrived carrying sandwiches and pies, and the men turning up for the night shift waited too, or most of them did.

Brigid turned to Celia. 'Cee, you'll have to go home, mavourneen. You'll have to take Michael home. Sure, he can't keep his little eyes open and he must be hungry and thirsty.'

'No, Ma, I'm not going. I *can't*. How can I when Joe and Billy are out there?'

'Celia, you'll *have* to go. We could be here all night.' Brigid's tone was sharp. 'Go home and get our Josie to look after him, or Maggie or Biddy, and then bring some food back with you. We'll be here if any news does come in.'

Very reluctantly Celia agreed.

Both the train and tram journeys seemed interminably slow and she spoke to everyone, but no one had heard anything more. No one knew what had happened to the *Thetis* out there in Liverpool Bay.

It was a physical effort to keep the tears from her eyes, to control the panic that gripped her. It *couldn't* happen. She *couldn't* lose her husband and her brother. It was too awful to think about but she had to be strong. Having hysterics would help no one.

It was to Tessie's that she went first.

'Mrs Mulhinney, has there been any more news?' she pleaded, her eyes bright with tears.

Tessie's heart went out to the girl. With the fear in her eyes and clutching her baby tightly to her, she reminded Tessie horribly of a painting she'd once seen, entitled *A Sailor's Widow and Orphan.* 'No, luv, but I've got the wireless on and as soon as there's anything – anything at all – I'll come over for you.'

'I'm going back. I only came to bring Michael home and take some food back. Oh, it's awful. It's terrible to see, all the women standing at the gates, just waiting. Not knowing anything . . . anything at all.'

Tessie patted her shoulder. 'Trust in God, Cee. Joe'll be all right. They'll have some sort of rescue underway by now. No one is going to let a brand-new submarine just lie there on the bottom. It's cost thousands to build so the fellers at the Admiralty will be doing *something*. You just look at it like that, luv.'

Sheer willpower kept her from breaking down as she nodded a mute goodbye to Tessie. She'd take Michael to Maggie Walsh – Josie wasn't capable of looking after him, she told herself, trying to keep a grip on reality, to think about what she was doing. Josie was too young and had no experience. He knew Maggie, he knew all of them, but she trusted Maggie the most. Biddy was very slapdash and Tessie was very houseproud and he'd be sure to go and break something. He was a little devil at times and more so when he was overtired. 'Yes,' she said aloud, trying to hold herself together, 'I'll ask Maggie.'

Maggie was very sympathetic. 'I'll look after him, queen, don't worry about him. You've enough on your plate.'

Then Celia went home and faced the questions of Josie, Bernie and Emmet with a calmness she didn't feel and a voice she was trying hard to keep from cracking with emotion. Josie quickly made some sandwiches and put some fruit into a bag, while Celia took two of Brigid's shawls off the hook and put on a warm coat.

'Take that little folding stool with you, Cee. Mam can't be standing up all night. None of you can, so take it in turns. Emmet, get out into the yard and find it and don't be all night about it,' Josie instructed.

With fear still churning her stomach Celia put the straw shopping bag and the shawls over one arm and carried the little stool under the other one.

At the tram stop she saw Maudie with the twins and her brother and decided that this was no time for old grudges and arguments. She'd seen Mr Kemp follow Joe down the street this morning.

'Couldn't you leave them at home, with Mrs Robinson or Mrs Taylor?' she asked, trying to be helpful.

'They all had some kind of excuse ready and anyway this lot would only start messing around and getting into trouble,' Maudie sniffed.

Celia frowned. 'I know they're still at school but they're fourteen. They're not kids any more. They know how . . . how things are.' Because her brother had stayed on at school, Maudie had somehow found the money to keep the twins there too.

She glanced across at Foxy and for the first time in years saw real fear in his eyes.

'What's going to happen to our Billy, Cee? He'd made his bed an' everything before he left this morning,' he said in a quiet voice.

'I don't know, Foxy. I just don't know.'

'God help me, Celia, what'll I do if Harry . . . if anything happens to him?' Maudie swayed worryingly, then seemed to right herself.

'Mrs Mulhinney said the Admiralty will have started some kind of rescue, there's too much money gone into building her so they won't just leave her.'

Maudie was quickly back to her usual angry self. 'No, they won't leave the bloody ship, but they won't give a damn for those on board,' she retorted bitterly.

'They will. It's full of big noises, important people.' Celia was trying to bolster up her own spirits; she certainly didn't need Maudie to think and announce her fear of the worst.

Maudie gave Foxy a slight push. 'Well, you can take him with you. He's not my responsibility.'

Celia was taken aback but then she looked at Maudie, the pity she'd felt for her a moment ago gone. She'd never met such a hard-hearted woman in her life. Of course Foxy wasn't Maudie's responsibility but there was no need to say so in such a callous way, nor to push the lad.

'Come here to me, Foxy. You can carry this stool and these shawls.' She managed a weak smile as she placed an arm around her brother and realised he was trembling. She drew him closer. He, too, was confused and frightened and what kind of a life had he had anyway? She thought of the beating he'd got after the launch of the *Clement*. Oh, he was crafty and inclined to arrogance, just like Da, but he *was* her brother and in the right place and with the right people that could soon be knocked out of him.

'It'll be all right, you'll see,' she comforted as the tram rattled along towards them.

As she squeezed her way into the packed car, the air thick with talk of the *Thetis*, she had to fight back her tears and clasp her hands tightly together in her lap to stop them trembling, for her brother's sake.

Conditions aboard the *Thetis* were bad. Four men in turn had tried to enter the torpedo stowage compartment, passing through the escape chamber, to try to close the door in the water-tight bulkhead between the tube space and the torpedo stowage compartment. They'd all failed. Their eardrums had nearly burst with the pressure and the pain had been excruciating.

'All we can do, sir, is to try to pump out the water and oil. We're tilted to a forty-degree angle. The stern's above the water,' Lieutenant Woods informed Commander Bolus.

Fred Roberts heard him. 'It doesn't take much of a brain to work that out. We're all packed like sardines in here and you can't even stand up. Thank God we've still got lights.'

Joe paled, thinking it would be the ultimate horror if there were no lights.

'Where the hell is the *Grebecock*?' Fred complained. 'That's what the bloody tug was for, to "escort" us, and not a bloody sound out of them.'

'Keep the talking down to a minimum. Save your breath, the air's getting bad,' Lieutenant Woods ordered.

All night they struggled to pump out the water and oil, and gradually the stern rose but the effects of carbon dioxide were being felt by everyone. Then they all heard the unmistakable boom of exploding depth charges.

'They know what's happened. *Grebecock* must have got word ashore. There's another ship up there now,' RN Stoker Arnold pointed out.

'Thank God for that,' Fred said, voicing the sentiments of the entire crew.

'It'll be one of ours, sir, not a merchant ship,' Woods said quietly to his commander.

Bolus nodded. He'd had to be sure help was at hand before he could order any escapes.

'Yourself and Captain Oram will go first. You're familiar with the Davis Escape Safety Apparatus?'

'I am, sir.'

'Then get some notes to take with you from the engineering officer and for God's sake tell them to keep watching for men in the water. I'm hoping to get everyone out before the CO_2 kills us all.'

Woods nodded his agreement. The air quality was getting worse.

'Trust the bloody officers to go first,' Fred muttered to Joe.

'At least there *is* a way out and I suppose they'll be better able to help from the surface.' Joe felt less panicky now, although he was trying not to fall asleep for he knew he'd never wake up.

All through the night the women waited at the gates. It had grown colder and both Brigid and Lizzie were grateful for the heavy shawls.

Just before closing time, the landlord of the Raglan sent a couple of bottles of whisky and a few glasses over.

'Just a tot to keep out the cold and steady the nerves,' Fergal announced as he oversaw the distribution, and many were the blessings that were voiced for the landlord. Brigid, Celia and Lizzie took it in turns to sit on the stool. Brigid hadn't been very happy when Celia had appeared with her young brother.

'What did you bring him for?'

'I didn't. Maudie Kemp did. She was too worried about having her home wrecked by them if she left them that she brought them with her.'

'Holy God, has that woman no sense or feelings?'

'No, she hasn't. She told me he's my responsibility, he *is* my brother.'

'He is so. Well, you'll have to wait here with us, meladdo.'

Foxy sat on the dusty cobbles at Celia's feet, put his head in her lap and burst into tears.

She bent down and put her arms around him. He was only a kid.

'Fergal, can you spare a drop of that?' she called and Fergal handed her a glass.

'Come on, Foxy, drink this, thing might get better soon.' It was all that she could offer him in the way of comfort.

The hours dragged on and women, young and old, stood, leaned against the gates and the wall or sat on the cobbles. Those that had no coats, jackets or shawls were shivering with cold and fear. From time to time a woman would share her coat or shawl with another less fortunate. If they spoke at all it was in tense, quiet voices, though some were sobbing, having broken down under the strain.

It was only Brigid's determination and outward composure that kept Lizzie and Celia fairly calm. Mercifully Foxy was asleep, his head resting on Celia's knee.

Next to Celia, Lizzie was gnawing her lip. Billy meant everything to her. He was her world. What would she do? How would she cope if . . . if he didn't come back? Oh, they'd planned everything and their future looked so bright, but now . . . She just wanted to throw herself into her mam's arms and cry, but she couldn't. Mam too was suffering and she'd had so much worry and pain in her life already that it just wasn't fair to add to the burden.

Celia too was looking ahead into a world without Joe, down long, empty, lonely years, imagining herself and Michael deprived of Joe's love and strength. She gently pushed a lock of Foxy's hair back from his forehead. Would Foxy become part of her future? She didn't think so. Da wouldn't stand for it. Oh, Joe, don't leave us! she prayed silently.

She looked across at Lizzie and the same emotions were clear in both their eyes. At least she'd married Joe and they'd loved and lain in each other's arms and she had Michael, the proof of that love. Poor Lizzie didn't even have that to console her. Then she thought of Brigid. Oh dear God, how could she stand losing a husband and now maybe a son? She leaned towards her mother-in-law.

'This is what it must be like for the miners' wives when there's a pit disaster. We all felt sorry for them but we just didn't know at all how they suffered. It's just this: waiting, waiting, and not knowing, and feeling so helpless.'

'Don't go looking at things like that, Celia,' Brigid rebuked her but silently she had to agree with Celia. God in Heaven, she should be used to this sort of thing, she thought. Hadn't she watched and waited over many long years until Dessie, who she'd loved so much, had died? Now it was her son, the father of her grandson, who was missing, Joe, who'd taken over Dessie's role. How could she bear his loss? And poor Lizzie. How would she take it, all her dreams shattered? But the best thing she could do, she told herself, was to stay calm for all their sakes.

When dawn came, shedding its soft golden light over the dark and dismal buildings and the framework of the huge cranes, now immobile, Brigid got up stiffly. Her mind was made up.

'Mam, where are you going?' Lizzie asked.

Brigid drew her shawl tightly to her and straightened her shoulders.

'I'm going to the gates. To see what in the name of heaven is going on. Sure, they must know something by now. We've been here since half-past six yesterday and not a word out of anyone. Aren't we destroyed with the worry of it all?'

Many of the older women nodded their agreement, their faces etched with lines of worry, many of them supporting their daughters and daughters-in-law. Over the years they'd all learned to be stoical in the face of adversity and poverty. Brigid spoke for them all. They parted to let her through. When she reached the high, closed gates she took off her shoe and hammered hard against them with the heel until at last one gate was opened a fraction.

A ripple ran through the crowd, of hope and fear combined.

Brigid's voice, clear and firm, rose in the hushed air.

'Mr Tyson, sir, do you remember me? I'm Mrs Slattery. Sir, we've been here all night and we're all heart-scalded with the worry. There's young girls out here with their babies in their arms and nearly hysterical. For the love of God, sir, you *must* have some news. Even if it's only bad news, just tell us *something*, please?'

The gate opened a crack more. Tyson did remember her from the day after Richie Kemp died. She was a sensible, dignified woman. But he didn't know much himself, the bloody Navy had seen to that. He too had been up all night but he'd give them the little news he had gleaned.

'Mrs Slattery,' he said sadly, 'I'm sorry you are all having to wait. I don't know what's going on but I *do* know that there's twenty ships out there now. The stern of the *Thetis* is above water and two men, officers from the Navy, have escaped. That's all I know. I swear.' He retreated and the gate was shut again.

The crowd had grown considerably as the day shift arrived and the waiting wives and mothers, hanging on her every word, clustered around Brigid as she relayed the news. When she'd finished speaking she went back to Lizzie and Celia, aware of the grateful glances cast in her direction.

'Mam, if two have escaped there'll be others,' Lizzie said, her eyes full of hope.

'Ah, but they'll be all the Admiralty lot. We'd better settle ourselves again.'

She looked around at the groups of women. 'I don't know what religion you all are, but if you believe in God, you'll pray that the two officers will be the first of many.'

Celia looked with admiration at her mother-in-law. Brigid was the epitome of a patient, dignified, working-class mother and she'd never loved nor respected her more.

Conditions were getting steadily worse inside the *Thetis* as the air became thicker with the gas. Again Commander Bolus decided to use the escape hatch.

Royal Navy Stoker Walter Arnold, Laird's engine fitter Frank Shaw and one other man were to go next.

Fred Roberts spoke directly to Commander Bolus. 'This lad should go, sir. He's a skilled man with a wife, baby and widowed mother to support. And he's young and fit and stands a good chance of making it out.'

Before the Commander could open his mouth Charlie Milton's voice, tremulous and weak with fear, was heard.

'No, let me go, sir. I'm a foreman boilermaker. I've got years of experience. I'm a widower with a young son,' he pleaded.

'You bloody coward, Milton! What he's not saying, sir, is that this lad is his son-in-law and he hates him.'

'That'll do! I don't want to know about domestic feuds at a time like this. The lad goes.'

Joe caught Roberts by the arm and held it tightly. It might be the last time he'd see his foreman, who had always taken his part, supported him and been so good to him.

'Thanks, boss. I – I'll never forget you.'

'I hope you remember that the next time you turn up late at the yard, Slattery.' Fred Roberts made a feeble joke of it. He was almost certain now that his chances of escape were virtually nil. They were carrying twice the number the sub was built for.

They made their way slowly to the escape hatch where Arnold shut the water-tight door after them and pulled down the circular twill trunk.

They'd all donned the Davis Escape Safety Apparatus that consisted of a pair of goggles, a nose clip and a mouthpiece that was connected to a small bottle of oxygen by a flexible tube. The oxygen bottle was secured in front, just below a rubber life belt attached to the chest by shoulder straps.

'What's this?' Joe asked. It all looked so complicated and neither he nor Shaw had been trained in its use.

'It's a rubber apron,' explained Walter Arnold. 'When you're going up you hold it out in front of you to slow you down. If you go up too fast you get oxygen in your blood and believe me that's not good.'

Joe still looked confused and apprehensive.

'When the pressures have equalled, open the valve on your oxygen bottle. That'll fill the rubber lung, that bit.' Arnold pointed to Joe's chest. 'But make sure you turn the valve wheel in the closed position or it won't work, understand? The lung will burst.'

Both Joe and Frank Shaw nodded.

'Then you dive down, under the twill trunk and up to the escape hatch. I'll loosen the hatch clips and remove them and I'll also open a vent valve to let the compressed air out. Then the pressure inside will be the same as that outside. I'll push the hatch open, but for God's sake remember to use your oxygen and hold the apron out. When you surface close the valve at the bottom of the lung, the lung will act as a life belt and turn you on your back.'

Joe thought he'd understood most of it but was glad Arnold was going first.

Suddenly, as the water began to rise in the chamber, Shaw started to panic, which startled and unnerved Joe until Arnold smacked Shaw in the face.

'There's no time for hysterics or panic, do you both understand? Panic and you'll die.'

Joe thought about Fred Roberts and his claustrophobia. He didn't blame Shaw. He felt the same feelings of panic as Shaw did.

Arnold went first, followed by Shaw and then Joe, trying to stay calm and remember all the instructions. It was all over in a matter of minutes. One minute he was inside the trunk, the next he was out, rising towards the surface. He was so thankful he didn't notice how cold the water was. When his head broke the surface he saw a boat, a ship's lifeboat with the name *Brazen* on the side. He struck out towards it, giving silent thanks to his Maker that he'd been saved. All he could think of now was Celia, Michael and his mam.

The air was very bad now, Fred Roberts thought dimly as he fought for breath. There was very little oxygen left. Some of the men had already succumbed to the poisonous gas and the water was rising. Someone had forgotten to turn off the flooding valve after the last escape attempt.

He moved with great effort nearer to Charlie Milton. He himself had already said the Lord's Prayer and asked for forgiveness for what he was about to say.

'You're going to die, Milton. We all are and very soon.' Every word required a huge effort and was dragged out slowly and painfully. 'You shouldn't have stopped your lad or you'd not be here now.' He paused, fighting against the gas. 'Your pride and your spite have killed you and I wouldn't like to be you, Milton. It's . . . it's . . . time for . . . the . . . reckoning. Any . . . moment . . . now you'll . . . you'll face . . . Him . . .'

The voice petered out as Fred Roberts closed his eyes and died.

Blinding terror descended on Charlie.

'By God and all His Holy Saints you'll burn in hell, Charlie Milton!' The words pierced the fog in his brain. It was Brigid Slattery's curse. He frantically tried to gulp in air but his eyes rolled back in his head and he slid beneath the water, already dead.

As the sun rose higher the crowd increased. They had been told nothing. Nothing at all. For some it was too much. They clung together, sobbing in despair. The men smoked cigarettes and looked grim, thinking of their mates trapped down there. They'd been submerged since yesterday afternoon and now it was past noon. Brigid and some other women had again hammered on the gate but to no avail. Celia and Lizzie clung together, just about able to fend off hysteria and exhaustion. Foxy sat on the cobbles, his knees drawn up to his chin, his face between them, his hands over the top of his head as if shielding it. He didn't know what to do or think.

An older woman, her face deeply lined and her eyes full of fear, touched Celia's shoulder.

'Hang on, girl, they've got two out, like they said.'

'That was ages ago,' Celia replied, anguish and torment in her voice. She *wouldn't* believe he was dead. She just *wouldn't*, but she knew she was just holding on to hope by a thread.

A rumour ran around that more men had got out and that now the men on the *Vigilant* had got a wire hawser under the stern and were going to pull *Thetis* up, stern first, and that Wreckmaster Brock was going to climb on the stern and cut a hole in it. There was still time. There was still hope.

'Foxy, do you want to go home, luv?' she asked gently. The lad looked awful.

'No, Cee. It's . . . it's not been the same without you and Mam.'

Celia sighed, her heart heavy with the trouble her family had suffered over the last years. 'No, she said quietly, 'I don't suppose it is.'

Minutes later the hope died when it was rumoured that the steel hawser had snapped as the salvage vessel hadn't been able to hold her position due to the tide.

Lizzie clung to her mother. 'Oh, Mam! Mam! I just wish I *knew*!'

Brigid forced herself to be calm once more. Glancing quickly around, she noticed many women and girls were at the end of their tether. She had to be seen to be in control of herself.

'Lizzie, will you stop this,' she said briskly. 'Cee's got more to ... well, she's got more to worry about and she's not after breaking down.' But Brigid could see that her daughter-in-law was fighting hard against despair. They were all exhausted by fear, anxiety and sleeplessness.

None of them knew that at ten past three the *Thetis* had sunk back beneath the waves, off the coast of Anglesey, her remaining crew all dead.

An hour later a police car drove up slowly and stopped on the edge of the crowd.

'It's the men who got out!' someone said, and the whole crowd surged forward *en masse*.

A Black Maria had drawn up behind the car and a dozen policemen got out and held back the crowd.

Brigid pushed her daughter-in-law through the crush. 'Can you see anything, Celia? Anything at all?' Brigid's heart was in her mouth.

'No. No. Oh, wait a minute! Oh, Ma! Lizzie! It's Joe! He's out! He's alive!' Celia fought her way through, followed by Brigid, Lizzie and Foxy. When Brigid saw her son take his wife in his arms, the tears streamed down her cheeks. All the prayers she had said through that long, long night had been answered.

'Oh, Joe! Joe! I thought I'd lost you. We've been here for hours and hours.' Celia clung to him sobbing with relief and he buried his face in her hair.

'I've thought of nothing else but you and Michael, Cee. But . . . but your da's dead.'

The words didn't register in her mind.

Lizzie grabbed his arm. 'Where's Billy? Did he get out too, Joe? For God's sake tell me the truth, please?' The state of fear she'd been in all through the long hours didn't matter now. Joe would *know*. Joe would *tell* her, even if it wasn't what she wanted to hear. She couldn't speak: her heart felt as though it had leaped into her mouth, but she gazed pleadingly up at her brother.

Joe looked puzzled and shook his head slowly, wondering if she had totally lost her wits.

'Billy wasn't aboard, Lizzie. I swear to God he *wasn't* aboard *Thetis*.'

Her eyes widened and she looked stunned. Had she heard him rightly? Did she long for Billy so much that her mind and her ears were playing tricks?

'Then where is he?'

Joe looked up, scanned the crowd and then pointed. 'There. He's over there.'

It was a couple of disbelieving seconds before her incredulous gaze followed Joe's outstretched arm and she turned and caught sight of Billy on the fringe of the crowd. She clasped her hands over her mouth, her heart began to race and then she was pushing through the crowd towards him.

'Billy!' she cried. 'Oh, Billy! Over here!'

She flung herself at him. 'Where've you been? I . . . we thought you were with Joe.' Tears of relief were falling unchecked down her cheeks.

'No, Da took my name off the list. He told me the night before. I was so mad I just walked out.'

Lizzie reached up and held his face between her hands. It *was* him. He was *here*. He wasn't *dead*.

'Why didn't you come and tell me?'

'I just didn't think, Lizzie, I was so mad. Oh, Lizzie, luv, I'm sorry.'

'It doesn't matter now.' Lizzie was laughing and crying at the same time.

'I ended up in Kirkby with some lovely people. I was coming here but I got knocked over. They took me to the hospital and they gave me something, an injection to make me sleep, but as soon as I awoke I left. It's taken me ages to get here.'

Her eyes were sparkling with tears, but tears of joy and relief.

'Oh never mind that. You're here and I just want to hold you for ever.' She hugged him tightly.

Billy looked down at her.

'You will, Lizzie. "To have and to hold from this day forth", aren't they the words?'

Lizzie buried her face against his shoulder. Celia and Joe were still locked together but Celia's sobs had subsided.

Brigid, with her arm around Foxy's shoulder, heard Billy's words and looked upwards at the clear blue sky and the bright, dazzling afternoon sun.

'Now I *know* you're happy, Annie. I *know* it. From this day forth all our children can be happy. You can rest in peace now, Alannah, you can rest in peace.'

POSTSCRIPT

Factually only four men escaped from the *Thetis*, but I hope my readers will forgive me for using a little creative licence in adding one more man. *Thetis* was raised and salvaged to Moelfre Bay on Anglesey seven weeks later. The bodies of the men were buried in Holyhead. *Thetis* was taken back to Cammell Laird's and refitted as HMS *Thunderbolt* but was destroyed by depth charges in 1943 off Sicily with the loss of sixty-two men.

Lyn Andrews, Southport, 1997

Headline hopes you have enjoyed reading FROM THIS DAY FORTH and invites you to sample the beginning of Lyn Andrew's compelling new saga, WHEN TOMORROW DAWNS, now out in Headline hardback . . .

Chapter One

1945

'Well, there it is, luv, what's flaming well left of it.'

The stocky woman standing next to Mary, her cheap, well-worn brown coat buttoned up tightly and a scarf tied firmly under her chin, seemed oblivious to the fine August morning as she pointed to the Liverpool waterfront.

Mary looked puzzled. The three magnificent buildings looked to be intact. They stood out sharply in the early morning sunlight, ingrained with soot after half a century of standing in air that was heavily laden with grime. Above them the sky was a clear bright blue with a few wisps of cloud like white satin ribbons twisting and trailing across it. The reflection of the sky turned the waters of the Mersey to a pale shimmering blue. They had come down the river past the lighthouse on Perch Rock and then the fort at New Brighton. They'd passed the *Franconia* which seemed enormous in comparison with the ferry. She was on her way to New York and as she passed the three deep blasts of her whistle made Mary jump.

The river was calm and the few ships that were moving left a silvery wash trailing behind them. The foamy white bow wave of the *Leinster*, the British and Irish Steamship Company's regular overnight Ferry from Dublin, drew closer. At the landing stage ready to leave were the Isle of Man ferry *Lady of Man* and the gleaming white-hulled *Empress of France.*

They were nearly there, Mary thought. This was the city where she would make a new and different future. Whilst saving for her fare she'd dreamed about Liverpool: she had big plans but no money to implement them – yet. Oh, she knew things were hard in the city and she missed Colin so much, but life had to go on and Liverpool would become her new home.

Her grip on her little son's hand tightened as the boat drew closer to the landing stage and the *Lady of Man* drew away. Now she could see at first hand the devastation and it horrified her. She was too young to remember the similar destruction of the buildings on the Quays and O'Connell Street in Dublin by the Army and the gunboat in the Liffey after the Easter Rising – the 'Troubles' as her mam and everyone else called those awful days, days that had led to the Irish Free State. But their new status as a separate country had had little impact on the inhabitants of the Liberties. The overcrowding and poverty there hadn't changed.

She raised her hand to shield her eyes and peered ahead in the sunlight. St Nicholas's church was just a pile of rubble, though the blackened spire remained standing. She could see the heaps of rubble and the shells of burnt-out buildings in what had been Derby Square. Only the statue of Queen Victoria seemed untouched.

She was appalled and thought aloud in her soft voice without even realising she was doing it: 'Sure to God, is this what I left Dublin for?'

The woman beside her drew herself up and bristled with indignation.

'Well, we got no help from youse lot. "The Emergency" youse lot called it! The flaming Emergency! Six years with one half of the world killing the other half and it's not finished yet with those little yeller heathens. Holy God, the number of ships and men that sailed from here on them convoys and hardly any came back. Them U-boats was just waiting for them. That's why I've not seen me sister for years. It wasn't bloody safe . . . Oh, *they* said it was and people did go, but I remember the *Lusitania*. It was fortunate that the *Munster* wasn't full of passengers when it was sunk in the dock.

'Some Emergency! You weren't here when night after night them Jerry planes came and half flattened the city. I was. I've 'ad murder with me sister in Ardee Street about it. I tell you, girl, it'll be a long time before I go to see *that one* again, even if she has given me some bits of food. Her son sitting in safety stuffing himself with food we 'aven't seen the like of for years while his cousin, his first cousin mind, is buried in a war cemetery in France.' She sniffed indignantly.

Mary's younger sister Breda Nolan cast her eyes upwards to the blue sky. Everyone was always going on and on about wars, emergencies and troubles. Why keep going over and over it?

She wasn't in the least upset about going amongst strangers, as her mam described it. No, she was looking forward to it. She didn't care what state the city was in; it had to be better than the Coombe. There'd be a rake of things to do, but best of all she would be away from the mammy and the neighbours who'd be spying on you all the time and then go carrying tales.

Even though Breda at seventeen was not as tall as her sister, they were very alike. Both had that black hair, deep-blue eyes and pale skin which alone proclaimed their ancestry. But that's as far as the similarity went. Breda knew she was pretty and she used her looks to further her own ends, which included flirting shamelessly. Where was the harm in that? she often asked indignantly. Wasn't it just a bit of fun?

A bold strap of a girl, was what the mammy called her, and if the Father caught you even just laughing with a lad after Mass there was holy bloody murder and you were marched back home and then the mammy would belt you to bits. No, there wasn't much in the way of fun in Dublin.

Mary thought back over the past six years. She'd argued and pleaded with Col when he'd come back from seeing a recruitment film. *Step Together*, it had been called. There had been recruiting posters in bookshops and in places like Boland's Bakery, Blackrock Hosiery and Bradmola for a long time, but it was really the rally in

College Green when Mr de Valera and Mr Cosgrove stood together and explained Ireland's precarious position that had been the final push Col had needed. After that the numbers in the Local Defence Force had risen to 130,000 with the new members and the British Army had over 20,000 new recruits.

'I'm going to help protect *us*, Mary, and to earn more money. Aren't we a new country? The Treaty was only signed in 1922. That's just over twenty years ago. Sure, how can we stand up to the Germans when Britain is fighting for existence and with the help of its Empire? Hitler could invade us and we could do nothing, *nothing*, Mary. Wouldn't it be worse to have our freedom snatched away again after so short a time and crushed under a jackboot?'

She'd had no answer and had clung to him, weeping.

Gripping Kevin tightly now, she turned on the small woman, an expression of anger on her face. There was sadness in her eyes, but her back was straight and her head held high.

'Let me tell you, missus, that I'm a widow. Yes, a widow at twenty-four and with himself here to bring up, so I won't be having strangers making a mock and a jeer out of us. Aren't you a fright to say things like that? I begged and pleaded with my husband not to go, but no, it was to help protect Ireland from invasion, and we *did* have rationing and a blackout and Dublin was bombed a few times, too. No, my poor Col was dead set on it and dead is what he is. He's buried somewhere in a desert in Africa. I don't even have a grave to tend. If I only knew I could go and see it . . . him . . . it would be a comfort to me.' The tears sparkled in her eyes as she turned away.

The woman patted her arm contritely. 'I'm sorry, girl, I didn't know. There were a lot of Irish lads who joined up looking for a bit of excitement, more money and, like your feller, to feel he was protecting you. A lot of them never came back and it wasn't even their war.'

She crossed herself. 'It wasn't as bad in some ways as the Great War, even though London was bombed then. Jesus, Mary and

Joseph, the slaughter, the sheer slaughter of those lads and they were only lads, some were only sixteen and seventeen! There was 'ardly an 'ouse or a family in our street that 'ad no one killed or wounded. People got embarrassed if their lads came back unhurt.' She decided to change the subject.

'Have you anywhere to go, like, when we get ashore? The housing's shocking. We was overcrowded before the flaming war, now there's people who 'ave been bombed out two and three times, God 'elp them. And all these fellers coming over for work will have to find lodgings as well.' She jerked her head towards the crowd now assembling near where the gangway would be let down.

Mary hadn't really noticed that the ferry was mainly full of men, young and old, who were hoping to get jobs clearing the rubble and starting to help rebuild a port and city that lay in ruins.

Breda had noticed though. She'd spent the first minutes of the trip fluttering her eyelashes, hoping she looked seductive, at one or two she thought looked handsome and well set-up.

'Breda, will you behave and not be making cows' eyes at that lot, showing us all up. Try and get some sleep,' Mary had said sharply.

'Sleep, is it? With the noise out of them all and these wooden seats?'

Mary's patience had snapped.

'Oh, shut up, Breda for God's sake! Haven't I enough to be worrying about? We at least *got* a seat, people are having to sleep on the floor. I wish I could have afforded a cabin for us.'

'Aren't the cabins reserved for the gentry?' Breda asked.

'Not if you've got the money, but we haven't,' Mary had stated flatly.

She had been awake and worrying all night with her six-year-old son tucked in against her side and her sister leaning against her on the other side. The noise level had abated as people tried to sleep on the hard deck but the saloon stank of beer and tobacco. She thanked God it was a calm night. The worried thoughts went round and round in her head. What if things didn't turn out well? She didn't have much money after paying for the one-way-only tickets. There was only a little left of her tiny hoard at all.

She'd sold or pawned everything including her silver cross and chain and her precious wedding ring. She'd cried all the way home the day she left it with Mr Brennen, knowing she'd never have the money to redeem it. It had been so special. A last link with Col. When she was feeling really miserable and lonely she'd used to twist it round and round on her finger to conjure up the look on his face the day they were married at St Catherine's, or the look on his face as she stood and waved him off to join the British Army. That was before the ferry the *Munster* had been sunk. She certainly didn't blame the woman next to her for not crossing the water.

It had been a hard decision for her to make, to leave Ireland, and not only had she her son to look after, but Breda as well. Her mother hadn't wanted the girl to go.

'Won't you have enough finding work and taking care of him?' Kathleen Nolan had argued.

'Mam, it won't be *that* bad. I'll make some kind of fist of it. There's more jobs over there. There always has been. Sure, don't half the country take the emigrant ship?'

'You'll need your wits about you, Mary, in a huge place like that,' Kathleen had said earnestly.

'Mammy, for God's sake, isn't half the population of Dublin living and working in Liverpool?'

'Well, that's as may be, but you'll have to mind that bold strap, she has the heart across me.'

Breda had begged and pleaded and Mary had championed her sister's cause.

'Mammy, you know what she's like and left here without me she'll just run riot and have you destroyed altogether with the worry of it. And now you should have some peace and quiet. You've worked hard all your life for us.' Mary had glanced around the sparsely furnished room that had been her home for years. Things had been acquired over the years and both she and Breda would send money home, like every other boy and girl who emigrated.

So Kathleen had capitulated. It was a tearful Mary and Kevin and an impatient and highly excited Breda that Kathleen Nolan had watched go up the gangway of the ship that would take them all to a new life as so many had done before them.

The thump of the ship's side against the huge rubber tyres that acted as fenders and the shouts of the shorehands as they secured the hawsers drove all thoughts from Mary's mind.

'Kevin, hold on tightly now to Mammy's skirt while I carry the case and the parcel.'

'God, we'll be crushed to bits!' Breda complained, clutching a large bundle to her chest with both hands.

'Then go and flutter your eyelashes at one of those grand looking navvies, maybe they'll help.' There was a note of sarcasm in Mary's voice. It was a terrible crush and she was terrified of Kevin falling and being trampled on. He was so pale and thin for the want of good food. It made no difference that the new Free State had rationing, too. All they could afford was bread and tea, a bit of brisket, ox hearts or rashers of bacon with cabbage, or just scraps that Mammy used in a stew.

In the crush she lost sight of the woman in the brown coat. It was everyone for themselves, although a couple of the lads made room for them, making coarse innuendoes that she ignored but Breda did not.

'Breda, for God's sake stop encouraging them,' she snapped. Now she was beginning to regret that she'd saddled herself with such a responsibility – in a city like Liverpool there was plenty of trouble that bold strap could get into – but she'd done it for her mam.

One of the deckhands caught her eye and she shouted across to him.

He elbowed his way through to her. 'What's up, queen?'

'When we get off how will I get to Hornby Street, please?'

'Catch the number 20 or 30 tram. It's not far, ask the conductor feller to put you off where Scottie Road joins Hornby Street. I think most of the houses are still standing – or maybe they've been pulled down as being unsafe. I don't know, luv, the whole of that area took a hammering. They were aiming to put the Port out of action but their aim and their eyesight was bloody awful. Oh, they got the docks all right, but they also got Anfield, Everton, Kirkdale, Bootle and out the other way Garston and Allerton, too. Still, we got our turn. Berlin, Hamburg, Munich, Dresden. It was a shame about Dresden though. A feller I know 'ad been there once before the war. Full of buildings that had stood for hundreds of years he said it was, all gone now though.'

'Well, they should 'ave thought about that before startin' a flamin' war,' the woman in the brown coat said acidly, hanging on to the deckhand's thick navy sweater with the letters 'B & I' on the front, having elbowed her way through the crush.

'It's all behind us now, missus. Come on then, let's get yer all off.'

Mary felt happier in one way and very apprehensive in another. Happy that he had taken the case and parcel from her, leaving her free to look after her son properly. Apprehensive, though: what if the O'Shea's house had been blasted to bits? What would she do then? After all, they were only first cousins, she'd met them once but she couldn't recall what they looked like. Apparently they'd come over for her mam's wedding and then to wake her poor da, but that was all. No communication whatsoever since then.

Eventually, they disembarked but there was no time to stand and look around. People were pushing past them, so she guided Kevin and Breda towards the row of green-and-cream painted trams that were lined up at the Pier Head. She found a number 30 tram and pushed her little brood aboard.

'Sir, could you put us off on the corner of Hornby Street, please?' she asked the conductor.

He grinned at her. 'Yer can tell yer not from round 'ere. I've never been called "Sir" in me life before. I'm just a working feller, luv. I've a girl your age. 'Ave yer just come off the boat? 'Ere, I'll see to meladdo, you just find a seat. Yer look wore out.'

Mary smiled at his kindness as she ushered her son and her sister to a double seat. She put the case on the floor and gave the parcel to Breda. She'd sit Kevin on her lap, the tram was filling up.

When the conductor came for the fares, he shook his head at the proffered money in her hand.

'I know it's company policy, luv, I'm supposed to charge for meladdo as well. It's usually half-price but what the 'ell. The bloody Corporation can afford to lose a few coppers now and then. Grasping owld windbags the lot of 'em.'

As the tram trundled down Chapel Street and Tithebarn Street, the trolley giving out sparks as it crossed the junctions, Mary couldn't believe her eyes as she twisted from side to side. Oh, they'd heard on the wireless and read in the newspapers of the bombardment by the Luftwaffe on the cities over here. But seeing it with her own eyes she was horrified. Whole streets of houses, churches, shops and pubs were in ruins. It must have been terrifying, yet the people had gone on, day after day, week after week, month after month for six long years, trying to carry on as normal whilst encircled by chaos, loss, ruin and worry.

What kind of job would she get here? How could she make her dream come true? She held her little boy tightly. Oh, Col, why did you have to go? she said silently as the tears pricked her eyes. He'd not had a bad job as a coal-heaver with Murphy's and they'd got a two-pair front in one of the houses in Balfour Square. Once, the Georgian house had been beautiful, when the gentry had lived in them with a rake of servants to see to their every need. But that was many long years ago and the houses were now dilapidated, crumbling and overcrowded.

She'd furnished their rooms with second-hand stuff, painting or varnishing tables and chairs. She'd scrubbed floors and woodwork. When Kevin had been a baby she'd got a deep drawer from an old chest Mr Brannigan had in his yard. She'd lined it with canvas, then calico and then muslin. To cover the wood she'd made a deep frill with cheap gingham and Mrs Dunne, who lived upstairs, had said it was like one of those fancy cribs that you'd pay an arm and a leg for in Grafton Street.

She'd made curtains, cushions, quilts and all her own and Kevin's clothes. Oh, they'd not been doing too badly at all and now she didn't even know if these relations she scarcely knew even had a roof over their heads or might not welcome her one little bit.

When she'd alighted, with some assistance from the conductor who wished her good luck, she looked down Hornby Street and her heart sank. There *were* houses but there were also huge gaps and mounds of rubble, too.

The sun was warm on her back now and people had started to go about their business. A horse and cart passed slowly; the iron-shod hooves of the heavy shire horse seemed very loud as they struck the cobbles and echoed along the street. The cart was decorated with crudely painted daisies and was full of milk churns. It was followed by another proclaiming it contained the wares of 'Blackledge's. Bakers and Confectioners'. Mary ignored them, struck dumb by the sight of the dereliction that surrounded her.

'There's nothing left! It's a wild-goose chase we've come on.' Breda was sure she'd not had a wink of sleep although Mary had said she'd slept all the way. She also had a headache. It was probably the half-pint of porter (which had tasted horrible) that a young navvie had bought her when she'd managed to escape her sister's eagle eye for half an hour. She'd used the pretext that she couldn't stand the smell and needed some fresh air; now it seemed as though they'd come to a place that was little better than the slum they'd left.

Mary glared at her but began to walk down the street, noting the condition of the houses that were still standing. Known as

'Landing Houses' they were three storeys high and had been built in 1900 to replace older slum houses. She could have shouted with joy and relief when she found the block that contained number 18 was miraculously still standing and obviously occupied.

She put down her belongings while Breda leaned against the wall of the next house. Mary knocked loudly and after what seemed an age the door was opened by a large, rather blowsy-looking woman with greying hair and deep lines of worry on her face. She was Mam's age, Mary surmised.

'Mrs O'Shea?'

'Who wants ter know?' Maggie O'Shea's gaze swept over the little group on her doorstep: the obviously bored but beautiful young girl – *that one* was trouble if ever she saw it; the whey-faced little lad dressed in cut-downs that had been skilfully done; and the haggard-looking young woman whose wide blue eyes were full of anxiety.

'I'm Mary O'Malley. Didn't the mammy write to you about us?' Mary paused. 'Mam . . . you remember her? Your sister-in-law, Kathleen Nolan?'

Maggie relaxed, her face transformed by a broad smile. 'I've gorra a head like a sieve these days, it's all ter do with the war. Me nerves are strung like piano wires. Come on in the lot of youse, yer Mam did write, I remember now.'

She led them down a dark narrow lobby that was devoid of carpet, rag rugs or lino.

'It's going ter be a terrible crush, like, with the six of us an' you three, but we'll manage. We're dead good at "managing" after six bloody years. As yer can see, we were dead lucky. We've still got a roof over our heads. Not much of a one but there was a poor soul with a husband away in the Navy and a gang of kids living where next door used to be. She'd been already bombed out three times and when that lot went, she up and took them all off ter Kirkby. They took 'undreds of people out to the country places of a night ter sleep, things were that bad. The Yanks took them in lorries and brought them back in the morning.'

Mary wondered just how they would all manage with nine people crammed into this two up two down house. At home there was terrible overcrowding too but at least the rooms were bigger and if you had a two-pair back or a two-pair front and decent clean neighbours, it wasn't bad at all. Here they'd be all on top of each other. Still, she should thank God that the building was still standing.

She was taken into a small kitchen that served as a dining room as well. Over the range, the mantel was overloaded with bric-à-brac. The lino on the floor had definitely seen better days and there were stained newspapers covering the table in place of a cloth. That was all she could take in of her surroundings for Maggie was busy introducing the family to her.

First her husband Jim who was her Mam's eldest brother and had come to Liverpool looking for work when he was just fifteen. He'd only been able to send money home until he'd married, but it had helped. He was known as Big Jim for he was indeed a big man with a barrel chest and heavily muscled arms. He had sailed on the notorious Arctic convoys to Russia and counted himself lucky to be alive. He was jovial but very much in charge of his family.

'So, you've come ter see us at last, Mary O'Malley? You were just a twinkle in yer mam's eye the first time we were over. The second time was for yer da, God rest him.' He shot a look at his wife. 'And there'll be no bitter words in this house about Ireland being neutral. I'll not stand for it. Col O'Malley did his bit for us and of his own free will too. He fought and died for *our* freedom and now it's *our* duty to look after these girls and the little lad too.'

'I wasn't going to make any such remark, Jim O'Shea,' came the spirited reply.

Mary learned that their eldest son Davie had been killed on D-Day in one of the first companies to go ashore. He hadn't even made it to the beach. The weather had been atrocious for June and every man in the landing craft had been sick. Their uniforms were sodden, their packs so heavy and the swell so strong that he and many others had stumbled, fallen and drowned, a fact Maggie had never forgiven the Army for.

Bryan, who was twenty-two, had come through unscathed but tended to go on and on about his experiences so Big Jim told him it was all over now and everyone wanted to forget and build new lives and besides he sounded like a broken gramophone record. They were all cheesed off listening to him.

Unlike his brother, Maurice O'Shea was a quiet gangly lad of sixteen. He hated his name because his mates called him 'Maury' and he was introduced as such which prompted him to complain.

'I 'ate being called that, it's like being called after the *Mauretania*. Me name's Maurice.'

Maggie glared at her son. 'Well, isn't that a nice way to speak to anyone?' Her words were heavy with sarcasm.

Two young girls in grubby nightdresses stared at the newcomers in silence. The smaller of the two had a mop of gold curly hair and had her thumb in her mouth. The other one was older and bolder and had untidy dark-brown hair and eyes.

'I'm Patsy an' I'm eight,' she announced confidently.

'An' the other one's our youngest, she's six. Lily O'Shea, get that thumb out of yer mouth. I've told yer time an' again, yer mouth'll be out of shape an' when yer grown up yer won't speak proper,' her mother instructed.

'An' then yer'll never gerra feller,' Patsy jibed.

Maggie rounded on her. 'And since when 'ave you been thinking of fellers and the like, Patsy O'Shea? Did yer hear that, Jim? Eight years old and as bold as brass. Any more of that and yer da will take his belt to yer, yer 'ardfaced little madam, an' then I'll take you up to Father Hayes an' tell him about yer sinful goings on.'

Breda's spirits began to droop. Maggie O'Shea sounded just like her mam and at the look on Jim's face she inwardly cringed. Growing up without a da had meant she was subject to just her mam's giving out and chastisement. Now it looked as if she, like Patsy and Lily, would have to obey Jim's rules, like them or not.

Despite the sinking feeling in her stomach, Mary managed a smile. It was like a circus in here, she thought. Were they all like this all the time? But after six years of terror and grief and making do, who could blame them? She'd probably be the same herself.

Liverpool Songbird

Lyn Andrews

Alice O'Connor's family is the poorest of the poor in Benledi Street, the heart of Liverpool's toughest slum. Her bullying father drinks away what little he earns, whilst Nelly, her careworn mother, works when she can and begs when she can't. Since she was five young Alice has also begged in the streets around the docks but she has managed to hold on to the hope of something better, a stubborn optimism that keeps her head held high even in her lowest moments.

For Alice knows she has a gift that allows her to rise above the fate that made her life so bitterly hard. Alice O'Connor can sing like an angel . . .

It is a gift that will take her far, though it is to Liverpool she will always return. But is it enough to bring her the success she needs – and the love and happiness she so desperately craves?

'Spellbinding . . . the Catherine Cookson of Liverpool' *Northern Echo*; 'Enormously popular' *Liverpool Echo*; 'A compelling read' *Woman's Realm*

0 7472 5174 6

HEADLINE

Liverpool Lamplight

Lyn Andrews

Since they were kids fighting in the backstreets, brother and sister Katie and Georgie Deegan have battled like cat and dog. Now Katie is in her twenties and, like her brother, has a full-time factory job. But unlike Georgie, who puts his feet up when he comes home, she does her turn behind the counter in their mother Molly's fish and game shop after a day on the factory floor. Yet when their father dies suddenly Georgie assumes the shop is his – and that his chance has come to rule the Deegan roost at last.

Katie has other ideas, as does her strong-minded mother who is all too aware of her son's devious ways. But, as the shadow of World War II creeps closer and Georgie's illegal money-making schemes gain momentum, neither Katie nor her mother has any idea what troubles lie in store for the women whose lives the ruthless Georgie Deegan is determined to control – at any cost . . .

'A convincing tale, full of strong emotions' *Liverpool Echo*

0 7472 5175 4

HEADLINE

A selection of bestsellers from Headline

LIVERPOOL LAMPLIGHT	Lyn Andrews	£5.99	☐
A MERSEY DUET	Anne Baker	£5.99	☐
THE SATURDAY GIRL	Tessa Barclay	£5.99	☐
DOWN MILLDYKE WAY	Harry Bowling	£5.99	☐
PORTHELLIS	Gloria Cook	£5.99	☐
A TIME FOR US	Josephine Cox	£5.99	☐
YESTERDAY'S FRIENDS	Pamela Evans	£5.99	☐
RETURN TO MOONDANCE	Anne Goring	£5.99	☐
SWEET ROSIE O'GRADY	Joan Jonker	£5.99	☐
THE SILENT WAR	Victor Pemberton	£5.99	☐
KITTY RAINBOW	Wendy Robertson	£5.99	☐
ELLIE OF ELMLEIGH SQUARE	Dee Williams	£5.99	☐

Headline books are available at your local bookshop or newsagent. Alternatively, books can be ordered direct from the publisher. Just tick the titles you want and fill in the form below. Prices and availability subject to change without notice.

Buy four books from the selection above and get free postage and packaging and delivery within 48 hours. Just send a cheque or postal order made payable to Bookpoint Ltd to the value of the total cover price of the four books. Alternatively, if you wish to buy fewer than four books the following postage and packaging applies:

UK and BFPO £4.30 for one book; £6.30 for two books; £8.30 for three books.

Overseas and Eire: £4.80 for one book; £7.10 for 2 or 3 books (surface mail)

Please enclose a cheque or postal order made payable to *Bookpoint Limited*, and send to: Headline Publishing Ltd, 39 Milton Park, Abingdon, OXON OX14 4TD, UK.
Email Address: orders@bookpoint.co.uk

If you would prefer to pay by credit card, our call team would be delighted to take your order by telephone. Our direct line 01235 400 414 (lines open 9.00 am–6.00 pm Monday to Saturday 24 hour message answering service). Alternatively you can send a fax on 01235 400 454.

Name ....
Address ....
....
....

If you would prefer to pay by credit card, please complete:
Please debit my Visa/Access/Diner's Card/American Express (delete as applicable) card number:

Signature .... Expiry Date ....